美国 第 二版

THE LOGOHARP

By Arielle Emmett

艾
素
珊

LEAPING TIGER

PRESS

Alexandria, VA & Hendersonville, NC

This is a work of fiction interlaced with brief references to historical figures, places and events. The names, organizations, locales and events describing the primary characters in this novel are the sole products of the author's imagination or are used fictitiously. Any resemblance between these characters and actual persons, living or dead, is entirely coincidental.

For my family

&

The journalists of the future

NEWS

新华快讯

30 March, 2121: *Western Chinese cities of Urumqi, Kashgar, Turpan, Hotan and Aksu in Xinjiang province were leveled yesterday by a 9.1 magnitude earthquake, the most destructive in recent history. Thanks to mass evacuations organized by the People's Liberation Army (PLA), Urumqi, the industrial center of Xinjiang, miraculously recorded fewer than two dozen casualties. Officials believe a "Futures" narrowcast predicting a geomagnetic pole reversal inadvertently saved millions of lives. Directorate scientists have yet to explain a twenty-two second loss in Coordinated Universal Time (CUT) during the quake, or why atomic clocks controlling Harmonious Recycling in Western China suddenly failed at the quake's epicenter in Tashkent.*

1

JANUARY 2110

THE MANDARIN

高
官

My lover Marco Hsu Yang luxuriates in our sleeping pod. He leans over, kisses me twice *staccato* on my cheeks, my lips, exclaiming, "Your country is China's *whore.*"

My country, as he describes it, is "a spread-eagled bender over gifted with auburn hair and rouged lips. She's covered coast to coast in white, her wedding dress antiqued with yellow snow and sprigs of spruce and gossamer."

"Repeat that, please?"

"A spread-eagled bender over—"

"This is your country, too, Hsu Yang."

"No, never. My parents dragged me here."

Marco is literary, all right. Dark and puerile when he wants to be. His voice silky, then razor sharp, cutting into my bones, my throat, making me bleed with wanting.

For years I've craved his perfection, or at least my teenage notion of it: a doctor-to-be, cynic, exotically Chinese, someone drawn to my prosthetic, half-human allure.

My parents call me "prescient" (I foresee my father's death). As though a shadow has fallen (Marco's hand reaching for my shoulder, and then a blinding light), I foresee my lover's rise to fame. His propensity for solving puzzles and beating every AI opponent in 3D chess games will propel him to algorithmic leadership in China's Harmonious Revolution.

As for me, my future is unknown, blurry. I've had transplants, a nanofiber-ceramic hand, portals installed in throat and brain, my medical aspirations rendered gloomy. When *The Laws of Ice* came down from China's Directorate in the form of tablets written in skywriting, my parents recognized my life would end on a surgical table where machines alter my insides or replace me entirely. I'll work in underground cubicles, chatbots directing my every move. Marco, on the other hand, lives in the afterglow of Mother Country's victory. He recognizes a new form of global shock therapy, both economic and psychological, imposed on us by talking heads, nightly ear drones we can never turn off and messages absorbed subliminally in movies, advertisements and holo-screens on our roads. All these inputs play to our fears of another war, another Ameriguan insurrection, convincing us that Mother Country has the better way.

*

I'm looking back on Marco now. Backward and forward. Time jerks forward, then stands still. Sometimes I resent his superior attitudes. Makes me feel worried, this resentment, maybe hate, recognizing he's untouchable, *hua qiao* (华侨) overseas Chinese, superior by birth.

Marco says all the time he loves me, that I'm "exceptional" in my harlot country. But I think part of it is sexual passion, and maybe the red and gold highlights of my hair. Opposites attract. I'm taken by him, at least his gambler and alien Chinese parts. When he calls my name, Naomi, I just want to sink my bones inside of his, there's such an ache.

Six months ago we married secretly inside a pauper's chapel beneath the crimson and white sandstone cliffs of Zion *Guojia* (国家) Refuge. The roof above was caved in. My retinal screens captured clouds at sunset moving fast into night—violet swirls, grays and sparks of orange, yellows and whites, a *Starry Night* knock-off, then a clear blue shaft dropping down from the sky right in front of us. A sword, maybe. A carpet to Elysium. God knows I didn't understand what it meant.

Shivering at the altar since the snow was icy against my feet and no one was there to marry us, not even a drone, I wondered why my wedding scene seemed like a stage set, hardly real. I guess he wanted to keep any serious thoughts of me from his parents. We exchanged jade rings purchased in Hualien, the Taiwanese marble city. Our vows consisted of silent, furtive looks, eyes toggling back and forth worriedly between the clouds and each other.

"This country has become *Ameriguo*, a pretty nation, a *guo* (国)," he wrote in his economics thesis just before our wedding date. "Ameriguo is a little winter paradise, primitive and greedy. Securitized now as a Chinese trading protectorate, addicted to pleasure. Mother Country floods our continent with cast-off consumer goods, contaminated food and transportation materials that disintegrate on contact. *Ameriguans* are grateful for the crumbs."

Etcetera.

He likes to lecture me. "Evidence of *Ameriguan* weakness is in the teeth, Naomi," he says, examining a batch of X-rays I've kept of my extra tooth pulled when I was a child. He squeezes my upper lip, then takes a pen light to my pallet, pretending he's already a doctor, as though to see a hole left by the extraction. "A white supernumerary tooth grows abnormally long in 2.5 per cent of Ameriguans' soft palettes," he says. "This represents the cast-off wisdom of her ancestors."

I nod, recognizing bullshit. When he speaks like this, he slinks up against me like a cat.

Marco likes to mix stupid messages with nuggets of Chinese wisdom. His accent is perfect and I archive and emulate every tone: *"Wuyuan jianmian bu xiang shi, you yuan qianli lai xiang huì"* (无缘 见面 不 相识， 有缘千里来相会.) This nugget basically means *"If Fate isn't choosing you, you can bump into someone and never connect. But if Fate rules, a thousand* li *cannot keep you apart."* So romantic, I reflect back to him. Except he adds, "I doubt we're really *yuanfen* (缘分)"—i.e., fated to be partners. "More like airships passing in the night, perhaps we meet only at this point, and then go separate ways."

*

Friends knew us as Naomi and Marco when we lived together in a walk-up flat on Thompson Street in the Arbors, though we maintained separate quarters on campus to satisfy our parents. On occasion I called him Marco, when we were close; Marco Hsu Yang or just Hsu Yang when we were not. Periodically we'd fly to Zion Refuge in the Ameriguan West, and sometimes to Taiwan and, once, to Mother Country's Lijiang old city in Yunnan province, a golden land of tigers and pagoda-shaped mountains of snow. Vacations were the good times. But recently he's been in a dark, woe-is-me mood; I try to remind him that the Chinese paramilitary supports his elite education.

"Why are you so pissed off? You'll come out of medical school as a doctor without debt," I say, smoothing his sweaty brow. "Isn't that good?"

"Yeah, no!" he says, ever contrary, covering his mouth with his delicate Mandarin hand.

We both know he'll have to give four years of medical service in the military, just what his father wanted him to do, but his real desire is to play Blackjack in Las Vegas or even Macao to beat the system. Any system. It's pointless to argue about it because his heart is set.

On Sunday winter nights, after long hours cramming for lectures and exams, he leads me out the door. Taking our cross-country skis, leaving the dorms and slipsliding down the hills to backcountry, we look for steep bowls and globes of snow.

"We're a snowflake globe that China shakes," he laughs, guiding me through the dark pines he calls *Songshu* (松树), a lovely seductive sound, "*Song,*" as though the pines actually sing a song. We head toward the lights of North Campus. Passing a sign saying Climax Molybdenum Corporation posted on a laboratory no longer in use, we stop a moment, shivering, making clouds with our breath.

"The Mandarins drink mojitos through a fire hose," Marco opines, pouting as usual, his habit of appearing distant, regal. "Then they toss our globes in the fireplace, fucking us up the ass."

"Stop talking shit!" I slap him. At least I do it with words, realizing I can't stop his mouth no matter how hard I try. I push off, skiing away downhill. It's impossible not to hear what he says.

Marco is the anomaly. I can't figure out which country he hates or loves the most, or whether he confuses "nation" with my body. He's fond of conquering my "nation" every chance he gets. He has slightly crooked teeth and a disarming way of rubbing his cheeks against mine, making fun of brightness and dullards alike, anyone aspiring to a tangible goal, even mine, ambiguous as it is. His resentments are barely disguised, but I sense they come from being surrounded by medical superiors who not so secretly resent China's recalibration of our liberties. Do I feel sorry for him? A little. He's a foreigner, neither here nor there. I can see he feels uncomfortable with all the Mandarins on the ski slopes, even though he's one himself. His way of *"talking story, jiang gushi"* (讲故事) in Chinese is embarrassed, his lips pursed or screwed forward, as though sucking on a sour candy, his voice pitched low and humble.

"Time was," he said, "China and Japan were slaves to the concessions of Europe and America. Now it's the other way around. Even though China 'owns' us, the Directorate in Beijing doesn't care about our local shenanigans. China just wants our markets—raw materials, cheap labor, technical expertise."

"They don't need our expertise," I tell him.

"How would you know that?"

"I just do."

He recognizes I suck up information with anything I read, but I also have these Aeolian vibes telling a story. It's just as though my ears extend like antennae to his secret thoughts. I seem to hear harmonies in wind, waves, rotating cloud banks, street vendors arguing with customers in multiple languages 10 miles away. It's music to my ears (literally), this extra sensory hearing born into me. Marco says I'm absorbing too much Greek tragedy from my parents (formerly actors) since I project their tragic thoughts. He says these thoughts still *control* me. Yet I detect *his thoughts*, feel his grief and joy as my own. Perhaps it's my father who drives me toward Hsu Yang. A dying father envisioning immortality: his daughter, a brain surgeon. But every day I go to the university language labs and read and listen to everything I can about Mother China, too. I want to go there, maybe permanently, to be embraced in a Harmonious Society and warm bosom. This is something Marco and my parents might understand. Or not.

*

In our childhood, Mother Country began saturating us with patriotic messages about loyalty and personal sacrifice. There were arrests of dissidents in Detroit and Washington, D.C., on the intranets, but no one had an accurate count. Our cities transformed quickly into military fortresses *de facto*, most of them subjected to helicopters patrolling above and perimeters of razor wire to keep out gangs. Most skyscrapers had turned into blackened spires from arson or careless wiring, I'm not sure which, and smaller enclaves and even our water reservoirs turned muddy black from coal ash and leaks from molten salt reactors.

Our architects were clever, though. Designing breathing domes covering the cities—at least the big ones left—they created membranes which were practically invisible and gooey in texture. Membranes floated above the cities like egg whites before beating. Blocking ultraviolet and cosmic rays from above, the membranes absorbed and channeled spew from factories worldwide, so that the worst particulates escaped to the outer atmosphere. Before the domes, black spew from Asia traveled in the westerlies, and white ash clouds from the fires of Northern Laurentia painted the sky in sulfur dioxide, arsenic, carbon monoxide and coal dust.

We called this exchange the "Air Trade." China gave us new-style coal scrubbers, thorium reactors and high-through-put skymills whipping the upper atmosphere currents to produce our energy. Laurentia to the North gave us lumber and oil from tar sands. Ameriguo gave everybody movie stars, molten salt reactors breeding fissile uranium-233 and snow, the latter a highly valued commodity.

*

The night I met Marco Hsu Yang was a rare display of polar vortex in our Lake Erie community. Residents joked about the weather: "Ten months of winter. Two months of rough sledding," although mostly we had rain and black ice. But that particular night, it was frigid. His brother Tommy invited me to a birthday party. I heard footsteps above his basement ceiling and suddenly a boy/man came bouncing down the stairs, blowing his nose with a handkerchief, his mop of straight black hair so long that he kept throwing his head back to tame it.

Immediately I noticed his buoyancy. He bounced as though his hips were spring loaded. He had inviting brown eyes, one round like a chestnut, the other almond shaped, more "Chinese." He seemed drawn to my cascade of gold hair held back by a white silk bandanna I wore wrapped around my head, much like a 1960s hippie. He focused on my blue and emerald irises flecked with shards of red rust depending on the light, a retinal display embedded behind the cornea to provide "cloud vision," a sharper 4D focus for storm events and fast-moving predators. Marco talked to me about his acceptance at medical school, describing a certain gynecology professor who labeled vaginas "beavers" in a preparatory class.

"Personally, I find this label disgusting, sexist, incredible, given how far we're supposed to have advanced," I retorted. His neck snapped back, mouth quivering a little, as though no blonde teen had ever talked to him that way.

"Chinese girls aren't that blunt," he went on, cocking his head, as though trying to weigh his confusion. "If they don't like something, they snivel or toss their heads back and walk away."

I shrugged. Surmising he was trying to account for failed hookups, mostly girls turned off by his dirty talk, I switched conversation to our life chances. I told him about wanting to be a physician or researcher or linguist. At one point when brother Tommy and the others piled into coats and rolled outside to throw snowballs, I excused myself and joined them. The boys tackled the girls in heaps and the girls took revenge by throwing icy hard pellets at the boys' cackling mouths. We were red-faced, giggling and panting like dogs. Hsu Yang had a bad cold; he choked, excusing himself, but said he'd wait for me because Tommy mentioned that I had had a heart transplant and he had never met one.

"Half a transplant," I corrected, returning inside to him within 15 minutes. I rubbed my hands and blew on them. "Just some valves and a leaky septum between ventricles, nothing that exciting. I'll be full of replacement parts by the time I reach maturity."

His mouth curled down.

"That's too bad," he said. He took my real hand. "But everyone gets replacement parts these days." I wondered if Marco had any himself. "No," he said, "of course not." But someday, thanks to his reading of a familial genetic map citing his Dad's intractable glaucoma, Marco believed he too would become blind.

*

At the time (and I didn't reveal it), I had a port at the base of my brain, and another in my throat, the two housing all the wiring and firmware for the eventual installation of a *Logos-harp* (shortened to *Logoharp* for branding purposes). The harp's workings are known only to a few medical elites and the Chinese and Ameriguan *Singing Directorate* masters (The Singing Directorate is the name of our highest government body in charge of harmonizing communication to the masses, both in China and Ameriguo).

Think of the harp as an instrument amplifying Aeolian music. On the earthly, practical level, the *Logoharp* conveys explicit, reasoned messages that the Directorate wishes to convey to the public. At the same time, the harp is believed to receive higher-order harmonies conveying both wisdom and warning from unidentified sources in Nature and the Divine. What these signals mean or how they're identified I'm not sure. But I do know the harp enables universal translation of all human languages and, presumably, the extraterrestrial ones that will crop up, enabling the harp's recipient to act as an Intermediary, a public communicator, also known as a *Reverse Journalist* (RJ), meaning a "journalist of future prospects." As such, anyone who receives the *Logoharp* is blessed with great responsibilities on behalf of the State. Once installed, the *Logoharp* can't be removed or shut down. You belong to the State.

Time and timing are elements of the State's instructions to the *Logoharp.* So are surveys of crowd reactions. The Bureaus of Statistics quantify these reactions and report the incidence of mass demonstrations, birth and death rates, buying and spending, industrial production, trade, health and disease. The State, aka Singing Directorate, cleverly named for its attempts at lightness and musical entertainment for the masses, maintains a *Life Clock* to determine the "age deadline" after which individual contributions to our overpopulated society are considered unimportant. The clock spins like a roulette wheel while a pretty announcer reads out the latest numbers, after which elders prepare for a lottery knowing the current age ceiling. Right now, most workers (save for Party Elites) are persuasively retired at age 50. A few last to age 55. Our publics recognize that as natural resources diminish, youth must have its ambitions and jobs. The Directorate is responsible for our "balance."

*

I have no idea why I was chosen as a candidate for the harp. Perhaps my early testing in middle school showed I excelled at Asian languages and music. In my application for candidacy, I wrote that I wanted to convey the truths of "China through

Blue Eyes." I guess someone in the Singing Directorate liked the phrase.

Without telling Hsu Yang (but I did tell my parents, who had to give permission), I elected at age 19 to have portal wiring installed with plans that one day I might work on behalf of the Chinese State. The literature I received (in English and Chinese) described how the harp integrates three ancient elements: *Logos, Ethos, Pathos.* It's all Greek, of course, Aristotelian in origin, not Chinese at all. But the descriptions appealed to me given my background in Greek drama.

The object of the *Logoharp* is to communicate the Word (*Logos)* and the fluctuating meanings of our universe to great leaders who guide publics to a hopeful future. *Logos* rouses public spirit and trust in the Singing Directorate's moral authority (*Ethos*). Lovely harmonies and translations reaching our billions evoke *Pathos* (emotional awakening). Though I'm not sure about this, I'm told that the harp can detect not only the thoughts of our political leaders, but also the explosion of stars and the heartbeats of life forms fearing the death of their planets. *Everything* is in the harp's capture and filtering of signals, conversations, music. I still don't know how it all works.

*

I did reveal to Marco the first night that I have a surgically implanted carbon-nanotube-fiberglass right hand, a replacement for my deformed hand without fingers from birth. The synthetic model has nanocarbon filaments and thin force sensors affording full haptic pleasure which I experienced just touching his sleeve.

"I had an amputation at birth," I said finally. "My heart was rebuilt and then my hand—"

He stared, incredulous. "What's this?"

I laughed, holding up my prosthesis in front of his eyes so he could examine all the circuitry within. The prosthesis can be transparent or flesh toned at the push of a tiny button, but it's too much of a story to explain, so I stood mute, as though to affirm the perfection I couldn't feel inside.

Then I noticed it: His skin was much darker, richer than mine. I stared down at his chapped knuckles, the antiseptically clean fingernails, much straighter and better formed than mine. We clasped hands and it was weird, as though I couldn't do anything but marvel at the contrast in skin color. The softness of his lips came to me a second later, in Aeolian sensation; I wanted, then and there, to place my ear against his belly and listen to every gurgle and pulse. Imagining him pulling me toward him, telling me, very gently, that I would be a success in whatever I tried, but maybe plans for medical school weren't enough?

It was time to go. I reminded myself that I was worthy of this dizzy feeling, that I'm classified as fully human, though

identifying as *human female prosthetic.* We bid each other goodbye. I had brought my air-sleigh and mounted it on the tarmac
outside the garage, revving home on black ice. When I returned
to university a few days later, Marco's face—his holo-texts,
repeated calls—were waiting for me. I slipped on the tiles of
our dormitory hallway trying to find my communicator inside
a heap of luggage and coats. Girly titters swelled in my ears
as I fell.

2

FEBRUARY 2111

TRUE NORTH

真
北

"Naomi's love affair with Marco blossoms in the trash of left-over Michigania, our trashed society." That's how I recorded it in my nanoblog.

Most of the forests southeast of the Arbors and Detroit had been bulldozed for new construction that never happened. There were plans for nuclear waste depots and additional vertical takeoff and landing (VTOL) strips at local shopping malls abandoned for lack of customer traffic. Yet even in the absence of "progress," Marco and I felt lightning strikes as we held hands, skimming in his decrepit NOVA VTOL along the unpoliced air channels leading north. This back country, free and open, is dotted with rotting fences, abandoned barns. Marco loves to retract his sunroof even in bitter cold here, cackling as we freeze our asses off, ice whipping our flesh at unexpected turns.

*

These days Ameriguo still attracts millions of Asian tourists who cross the Pacific in sky tunnels just to see our white peaks, our karst sinkholes and crystal-blue skies. We try to avoid tourists, but they always seem to find us. Loyal local denizens volunteer to preserve what's left of the natural beauties and atmosphere. Since manufacturing and energy consumption have trailed off along with reductions in our population, Ameriguo's emissions are now lower than China's, the Afro-Latin South or Baltica (formerly known as Europe). However, the air spew from abroad is still not safe enough for the millions each year who die from contaminants or viral ailments, most of them *zoonotic* and jumpy, transmitted to humans from sheep, cows and laboratory bats.

Marco and I mostly stay in the Michiganian upper interior where the Mandarins don't come. We call our retreats *True North*, referring to the crossroads between Lake Superior's upper shoreline and the Laurentian hinterland, formerly known as Algoma country. The woods of Algoma remain dense with white aspen, spruce, red pine and white cedar. Practically no one ventures there. But back in the Arbors, where we live as students, miserable half the time cramming under arc lights, we recollect our pleasures in Algoma while we squeeze into our dorm pods. In Marco's pod, a four-paned window of leaded glass, an antique thing, lies frosted above us, its crystals throwing shadows on our skin. My crystals are colored straw and honey; his are whiskey and a cabernet stain just above the tailbone. In this light we barely speak; we drink wine, eat chocolate chip cookies, and what passes between is whispering, prayer and hopes for brighter days.

Early on I realized Marco was scheduled to marry a full-blooded Chinese girl. His grandmother was adamant about keeping the purity of the line. Still, he seems addicted to my body, even my protests, the stonewalling I display when he trots out his Chinese "looking down" attitude. I remind him, or claim (since I'm not completely sure) I have part-Mongolian ancestry, most likely derived from Genghis Khan's thirteenth-century pogroms and rapes of Polish and Austrian women. Unfortunately, I have no hard evidence of Asian ancestry except for my prominent cheekbones and strange upturned eyes. Though I've made noises about proving my lineage with a DNA test, Marco waves me away.

"I don't give a flying fuck about your ancestry," he says, though of course that's not true. But right now we're too busy draining our cups, filling and emptying, filling and emptying again, sometimes five bloody orgasms in one night. Afterward, after the many afterwards, we'll dress and run out of the locked dormitory doors to escape "prison." Biting wind, ice daggers against our cheeks, ski jackets half opened, we cross country up and down hillocks of sand and swamp, clearing bearberry, sand cherry, creeping juniper, brambles everywhere, with torn gloves. "Thank Mother Chy-na," he gloats, shouting at me through the wind. "No one but us would want to ski in this God-forsaken place."

He means Michigania. Michigan the leftover place. When we find our way back to the dormitories, only ski tracks and breadcrumbs of light guiding us, it's violet-dark. We return to our pods or lecture halls to study frantically again, falling asleep sitting upright in our chairs until Monday's first bells ring.

I have premonitions. One of them keeps me awake well before dawn. I see a spinning stage in a roundabout theatre, something like a giant roulette wheel. Round and around, each section of the stage produces a different version of reality. One shows two-dimensional cut outs of Marco Hsu Yang and Naomi hugging their adorable Chinese mixed-blood toddlers. Another: a rocket igniting into space, Naomi grown impossibly tall as she commands from the pilot's seat, gnomes turning dials at her prompts, her skin covered in snake-scales of midnight blue. Another: Hsu Yang explaining his mathematical calculations to a group of Beijing elite, their mouths agape in wonder. When the revolving stage stops, I see an empty corridor. My lover seems to float past me, only his head and upper torso visible, a shrug in his shoulders, until there is nothing I can see but sleeves of his leather jacket. Vaguely I'm aware of bloody bodies: a war of Central Asian mercenaries led by Subutai, Genghis Khan's general, who invades Baltica to the west, then Uzbekistan and Aleutia to the east. All our lives measured, beginning to end, with Cesium atomic clocks.

*

Marco has entered medical school, but seems miserable, more cynical even than before.

It's nearly summer. We take off after our exams, speeding north in his VTOL. Rowing one afternoon on an Algoma district lake, its white-bark aspen and swathes of red pine meeting the shore line in perfect strata, he asks me, "Why aren't all females slaves?" He asks with a grumble and deep frown, as though he has the answer already.

I stumble, resorting to some fractured explanation about women's rights drawn from an antiquated sociology screed. Though I acknowledge that many women were *de facto* slaves once, as servants, prostitutes and concubines in ancient China, he frowns again. "No, you don't get it. Women *are* slaves," he said, enunciating each word as though to a kindergartner. I try not to roll my eyes.

His mother, Fang Wen Jing, who calls herself Wendy, is her husband's slave, Marco says, especially when he slaps her around during his tantrums at dinner. The *fapiqi* (发脾气) happens after spending a full workday relating to his psychiatric patients in a calm, supportive manner.

One night, perturbed about Hsu Yang's open dislike of medical school, and his wife's stoic silence, Dr. Wesley Hsu clutched the narrow end of a soy sauce bottle and bashed the blunt end against Wendy Fang's forehead. The blow knocked her out, leaving a great bloody gash that Marco was forced to staunch with his white T-shirt. Yang then piled his mother into his VTOL, speeding off to the hospital for stitches while his father watched streaming re-runs of CCP's *Chen Chen, Dragon Club* and Zhang Yimou's *Raise the Red Lantern.*

"My mother won't leave him," he said, chewing his lip. "She's a wife, always a wife." He turned to me and smooched my cheek. "But you're my concubine, Br'er Baby. You will never be my slave, even if you wanted to be."

We were fishing as he related this story. The wind felt cold. I was uncomfortable with Marco's tone, his labeling me as a concubine, as though he had already married someone else. Though we sat side by side, Hsu Yang turned away from me, hunched over his fishing line and worms, his hair flapping in the wind. I stood up and jostled the boat.

"We're engaged to be *married*," I exclaimed. Marco stood up and tried to grab me from behind but I butted him with my ass and elbows, knocking him into the water. Pretending to sink, then rising up, he spat out the water. When he swam back to the dock, trailing me as I rowed, he pulled himself up on the ladder, shaking himself off like a dog. Sprinting past me, dripping wet, he cackled and locked himself inside our cabin.

"Open the door!" I shouted. "Hey open up."

"No way!"

I cajoled and pleaded for about 15 minutes until the door flew open. Marco strode right past me, still wet, underwear showing beneath his soaked chinos. Keys in hand, he jumped into his blue turbo and revved away. The vehicle lifted 30 meters into the air and made a rough circuit around the lake, then dipped down, cutting a giant wave of mist as though he were piloting a jet ski. Then he gunned the throttle, leaving a boa of exhaust behind him, disappearing along the service channel into the clouds southwest.

For awhile I sat outside our cabin, feeling a vise pressing down on my brain, as though my portal had absorbed some kind of ammoniated liquid. I started to gag. My face broke out in hives. Watching the afterglow of sunset, then navy twilight, then the darkening outlines of the forests beside the lake, I brought out my chemistry modules and tried to read them on screen in the dark. At midnight I turned in, but didn't sleep.

Around 3 a.m., a jet ski landed on the beach and it took me minutes to realize someone was banging on the door.

"It was a joke! A joke, don't you get it? Concubine! Slave! Who cares? I told you that you'd never be my slave! What's wrong with that?"

I started to scream, then howl. I think it was the first time I ever did, as though I'd been struck by lightning. As he approached me, his arms reaching for my mouth or throat or shoulders as though to jostle me, smother me, I scrambled out of bed, drew back. Perhaps I had seen too many films. I'd learned about the techniques of pushing hands, of thrusting fingers with vital energy, *qi* (气), into throats and hearts. It was semi-conscious, unthinking as I readied to strike. But I did. The middle and index fingers of my right prosthetic hand curved like the neck of a viper. I thrust hard, synthetic nails jabbing his windpipe, but retracting just enough to avoid a fatal fracture. Surely enough to hurt him.

"You're a *flat leaver*, Hsu Yang, as in leaving me flat!" I shouted.

"Christ fuck!" he strangulated.

"Don't you ever—"

"What are you, some fucking robot?"

He gave me an idea.

Days later I felt a twinge of regret about his injuries; in fact, Marco's larynx remained semi-paralyzed for weeks. He required nebulized steroids to clear mucus and intravenous dexamethasone to reduce the edema. To my surprise, though, I didn't apologize, and neither did he. I couldn't fathom where this viper instinct came from, the force of it, or whether my fingers simply obeyed what I'd been thinking all the time. There was no resolution, no way to puzzle it out. We didn't speak for weeks, then months.

*

By winter, I'd moved on, at least I thought so, focusing on my academic and *Logoharp* preparatory work, spending days and nights reading up on my future. But surprise again, Marco came around to an anatomy laboratory wanting to talk to me. Wanting to "work it out" between dissected pig guts and the slithery leg pumps of decapitated frogs.

We reconciled. He was gentle and so was I; we went to bed, it was probably the brightest night of lovemaking we ever had. So brief.

In the next few weeks we went back to Bryce and Zion for hikes, and then to Breckenridge for skiing. On the two-day excursion to Zion *Guojia* Refuge we decided to marry, trying to repair what we described as "the broken throat" of our relationship. A few days later we sat on a bench beside an icy river beside the Zion Cliffs. There was no blue sword reaching down from the sky, no carpet to Elysium. Both of us twisted our jade wedding rings round and around our fingers. We tried flash cards, exchanging written criticisms of each other with coded numbers for this or that infraction, but there were too many. Nothing worked.

More and more time was spent apart. Few, if any, Aeolian vibes or visions visited me. On the ski slopes Marco got lost in crowds of Chinese and Japanese tourists who thronged the lift lines and dove down the slopes in bunny suits and Astro Boy throwbacks. I could see the western horizon sinking in his eyes, all the skiers dipping down the mountain like wasps headed toward a red sun. In our room after dinner, I caught his eyes flitting back and forth wildly as he scanned his computer, as though searching for something, reading bar codes, but which codes? He lay glued to his devices. At lunch, and sometimes at tea, he talked about returning to China for his internships, saying it was his duty to be a medical man in Mother Country.

"In China? I thought you hated the place."

"No. It's how Ameriguo kowtows to China that I hate."

My voice left me. Picking up a glass of water, I gulped, hiccupped. He watched me. I asked with my eyes. He seemed older, not terribly concerned.

"Naomi, you're from True North, where you belong," he said, touching my arm. "Here you'll be free to pursue your own interests, maturing, perhaps going to medical school or studying cosmology or aerospace."

"Don't go," I pleaded. "I love you. Please. We love each other."

He reached over to me, squeezed my hand, then paid the check. Outside he hugged me hard, my head pressed against his chest.

When we returned from Zion to my parents' flat, he left without saying goodbye. My father, Deddy, a musician, noticed tears, but he was distracted, pulling at his mop of wiry black hair, doubled over, groaning, running to the toilet. The next morning, he announced that he had a blood disease, perhaps leukemia. My mother placed hot oatmeal, orange juice and coffee on the table and asked a few cautious questions about our ski trip before retreating to the bathroom to put on her makeup. Mom didn't seem too interested in my Marco drama anymore; she was already familiar with it, blow by blow. Besides, she was getting ready to leave my father, though I wasn't sure when. Her judicial style and impeccable speech have always put me off balance. But now she seemed a million miles away. Her only admonishments to me, besides "Do you have enough money?" and "Stand up straight!" were to focus on my pre-medical studies, not men.

Neither knew Marco and I had married, nor did I say a word. At the breakfast table my father finished, belched, then took me out in his turbo. An ugly day, overcast and dark. We revved just above the tree line as I studied the ruts in the road and dirty melting snow.

"What are you doing wasting your time?" he said, his voice dropping low as he gagged, then swallowed his belch down.

"Maybe this boy means well. But you're going to be a doctor or researcher, or whatever. Focus on your sciences, not Chinese or that ridiculous boy."

I breathed again, not wanting to contradict.

"He's being cavalier toward you," Father said.

I didn't know exactly what *cavalier* meant, but it sounded bad. I thought it had something to do with the Puritan Roundheads. But no, my father's hazel eyes flashed, dilating, as though throwing sparks at me. He had a ripe, sensitive mouth, telling me in no uncertain terms that I was deviating from my chosen path, my love of bodies and planets, my devotion to learning more about Asian hegemony. He said I'd be a better physician than Hsu Yang ever would be, given his restlessness and inattention. But I'd have to make my own choice.

"You're like a bubble of hot blown glass, not quite annealed to final form," Father said. *Annealed.* I didn't know that word, either. My parents had spoiled me, assuming I was some kind of Brancusi sculpture twisted into weird cognitive shapes. I could never do anything along a straight and narrow path, which frustrated them. I had weird high cheekbones, unspoken ambitions, if only they knew—or I knew—what they really were.

*

Becoming a physician was somehow too predictable to me, too dependent on rote learning because...well, Hsu Yang had indoctrinated me. By that time, too, I had begun spending dozens, then hundreds of hours practicing Chinese characters in my displays. Every character seemed alive to me; one character led to study of the next. I probed history, origins, *jiaguwen* bone script (甲骨文) and grass script (草书), ordinary colloquial *bai hua* (白话). I tried to parse Chinese traditions and a framework of time and social indebtedness, the way the masses were meant to serve the greater good through personal sacrifice, patience, poverty. The way Confucius looked at time past as something tangible and superior, while the future was spotty, unpredictable, a decline in fortunes. After the Tian An Men Square massacre of 1989 and China's economic rise, Mother Country's sense of time inverted. The future is everything now, the past looks out of date.

"So you're learning Chinese, but what will you do with it?" Marco asked me on a Saturday afternoon, having promised to pick me up the night before.

"To understand you better," I stammered.

He scoffed. I knew I was on thin ice with him. If I could only learn his language, he might accept me as legitimate, permanent. I tried to believe our future wasn't determined, that I might see him and he would love me again if my premonitions proved true. Yet I understood our separation. We both had to go to Mother Country to clarify what tied us to her power.

*

In two more days, Marco is scheduled to leave. He's reporting to a hospital in Beijing for a full-year's senior residency. His grandmother wants him to meet a Chinese girl from a good family, hoping they will hit it off. The important thing, the best "cure" for the temptations of a paperweight foreigner is arranging a senior year abroad during which time he will meet the right marriage prospect. Marco agreed to this without question.

"You're kidding," I said, having waited on my dormitory steps two hours for his arrival. We were supposed to meet for dinner.

"No, I'm not. My grandmother and my mother want me to go. I have to respect my *Lao Lao* (姥姥). She's old and this is probably her last wish."

"What about me?"

"Naomi, my family thinks you're a loose screw."

"Who cares? You haven't told them about our marriage."

"Or my punctured throat?" He rubbed it. Master of hyperbole. "Marrying an *Ameriguan*, especially someone so young and unformed as you, can't be legitimate in their eyes, regardless."

"What about your eyes, Hsu Yang? You're an *Ameriguan* now. You married me."

"I'm also *Chinese*," he intoned, again, that italicized authority. "*Lao Lao* raised me." His fingers slid back and forth over his chapped lips. "It's hard to explain what that means."

"I know what it means. Stop the turbo and let me out."

He turned to me, startled. Had I ever issued a command to him? He hesitated, then downshifted, slowing and skimming to the exit lane above the tarmac. Turbo traffic was light in the air.

"We can't stop here," his voice dipped, pleading a little.

"Pull over in the next sequence."

I stared ahead. Then down between my knees, trying not to gag. I was calculating how I would get back to my school by hitch hiking.

"I'll get a sky taxi."

"No sky taxis near here."

"I'll hail one."

We debated a few minutes more inside his VTOL. Then he braked, lurched, took several seconds to stop. Lifting the latch, I threw my pack onto the tarmac, stumbled to a ditch and tried to vomit, but nothing happened. Below me, a gulley—an abyss below—and I could see almost nothing. When I finished, he held me stiff in his arms.

I was lying down curled up in the back seat of his turbo with a dirty coat under my head, all my study modules and ski taxi tokens thrown onto the floor. I could actually see the causeway below because of striations of rust in his turbo that had fallen away next to the throttle at his feet. Through the undercarriage the painted lines led all the way to Taiwan, and then China.

Two weeks later, Marco climbed into his VTOL and disappeared. For two seconds, he kissed me *staccato* on both cheeks, the Continental way, as though nothing between us had passed except distant friendship. He stared directly into my eyes for a split second, then turned away. I recall he wore a beaten-up leather jacket, like a mafia hit man, mounting his sky luge with mirrors, stuffing playing cards into a side pocket along with some light clothing and a stethoscope.

I could see from his Nav bar that he was heading directly into the Xpress tubes, hopping the Molokai Slip Luge at speeds of Mach 3.2, much faster than the speed of sound through air. Since the mid-Pacific tube traffic moves faster than the route skirting Kamchatka north along the Ring of Fire, Marco preferred Xpress. He was still receiving generous stipends for a surgical residency from the Commission for Discipline Inspection and Physicians Vigilant Harmony Association, a branch of the Beijing paramilitary. His scholarship gave him the wherewithal to double his speed past anything we had known.

I don't remember too many more details about his departure. Without him, the first night rolled away, warm and cloudy, into turbulent dreams. I returned to my dormitory pod, ignoring the girls around me. My legs and arms lost sensation; the numbness spread into my chest and throat. Before sleep I traced his tunnel course in my retinal display; the green and red blinking lights of his vehicle seemed like cartoons in a video game.

Eventually I curled into a ball, wiped my eyes and nose, shut off all the lights while I lay awake, thinking of Marco's future and my own. I stuck out my tongue, too, something stupid, as though I'd lick the pod glass to clean out all my memories.

Do condors cry? Strange thought. In my pod I felt defiant, rising, swooping, a condor searching for prey, my wings twice the size of human arms. Condors don't cry, of course, but they hiss, snort and grunt while defending the young in their nests. You can hear their flapping wings from kilometers away.

I know this now; I researched it. I also know that Marco was never mine. But to this day, if I close my eyes, I can still swoop down, brushing by him, pecking and tasting the salt and cabernet of his skin.

3

NOVEMBER 2115

THE NULL HYPOTHESIS OF LOVE

爱
的
零
假
设

’m speaking into my nanorecorder that tokenizes dictation into 104 human languages. At any time I can decode my entries to enhance supplemental knowledge. My recorded notes give me access to a tokenized (quintillion) AI database of political events and crowd reactions, the foundation of my training as a multi-channel linguist and scribe.

I've been accepted as a candidate for *Reverse Journalism.* An RJ researches, extracts and reports the most likely scenarios of the future that will benefit Mother Country, its "children" (the masses) and, at times, the Ameriguan subsidiaries. Of course, I have to jump through lots of academic hoops to advance beyond the lowest RJ internship tier. Ultimately, I have to understand and speak all 104 languages fluently. In a few weeks I'm headed to Taiwan for further training.

Though I've heard from Marco only occasionally in these past years, his face still appears in the mirror. Summers, especially, I see a pale oval reflection of his face against mine. In winters, I still see a cloaked amateur wearing a knitted cap as he dives down the Breckenridge ski slopes. In each season, I long for its opposite—summer changing to winter's cold, winter into summer's heat, spring into fall, fall into spring. Why is that? I can never be satisfied with just what is.

The *Logoharp's* life and its reception of signals and spirits takes precedence now. To increase exponentially my quotient of understanding, of empathy for all others, one of my graduate research projects is to map out and publish a *Null Hypothesis of Love*, a theory based partially on the writings of D.H. Lawrence and Carson McCullers, both of whom wrote about the dichotomies of feeling between *lovers* and *beloveds.* Self-modifying this theory to account for cross-cultural and gender-robotic transformations in our times, I aim to post my theory on social media if the academic journals won't accept it. Internalizing this null hypothesis as I undergo transition to human-cyborg status, I'd like to reshape our social skin.

Deliberately, willingly, I've decided to pursue this career instead of medicine. The title, Reverse Journalist, sounds glorious and backward, like a Reverse Engineer. RJs deconstruct reality and remake it in pleasurable form. We're not like conventional journalists who haplessly report and announce random social and political events of yesterday or today. Instead, we seek the truth of *probable* outcomes, scripting events to glorify and sustain the health of the Party and its constituents.

RJs extrapolate the future based on algorithms enabling us to analyze millions of social scenarios from a *Database of Crowds*—a repository of historical events, survey data, political messages and crowd responses to them. Extracting the most likely scenario given a particular convergence of prior events, we ensure the events happen as we prescribe them—that is, if all the social conditions and political strategies of our bosses/ leaders are properly aligned.

In Ameriguo, the subsidiary Directorate has already given me permission to begin physical preparation for the *Logoharp*, my universal translator. This is an essential tool of Reverse Journalists, but only the ones elevated to the highest levels get the full installation. My first surgeries will entail implants of programmable logic from *The Laws of Ice* and *Critique of the Frontier*, two Chinese classics about the fate of modern civilization. The logic incorporates Mother Country's specific instruction set to remake and spread harmony across our societies and a small group of planets outside our solar system preparing for colonization.

*

I realize I'm immature and need rigorous training. Yet my superiors understand I have a gift, sensing what might happen for better or worse to a politician or a scientist or a whole country before the experts do. As an example, at age 15, I started a Citizen Live! nanoblog, forecasting the outcome of the 2104 Taiwanese elections. I predicted *Falun Gong's* doom in Taiwan; the Independence Green party would lose badly again to the Blue Party's *Kuomintang* loyalists swearing allegiance to *Zu Guo* (祖国), our Mother Country. I foresaw the downfall of decarbonization on both sides of the Pacific in favor of those who would chop down and bury our trees, claiming the carbon release was actually less than wildfire burning. And now we have the Domers, those who argue that fossil fuel exudate can be scrubbed and recycled to the upper troposphere without raising planetary temperature. It doesn't work.

The Directorate never applies the terms "propaganda" or "disinformation" to describe RJ's work, which always contains grains of future truth. Not for a minute has it occurred to me to question either the Directorate in Ameriguo or the training institutes I'll attend in Taiwan. The whole world demands my focus far more urgently than any selfish ambitions or plays for romance. I've wanted, most of all, to produce contentment and insight among the multiple publics who read or listen to my *Citizen Live!* nanoblogs. With the *Logoharp*, I'll foresee, broadcast and monitor the laughter, sufferings and unselfish sacrifices to our State of millions. (I don't think my parents would approve. Perhaps I do need to get away from them.)

*

My father disappeared about a year ago off the coast of Japan. Most likely, he was in search of a cure for his blood disease. No letters or video messages, either, though periodically I try to locate him, tracking available surveillance videos from drones skirting Mount Yotei adjoining Sapporo. On one of these videos, I watched a man bulked up in ski gear trying to snowshoe down and up a U-shaped hanging glacier. Dad loved unspoiled nature, and I'm guessing he must be settled in Hokkaido. I keep hoping to catch a glimpse of his bear-like body, his hairy chest, a mop of black springy hair that would distinguish him from native Japanese. He has a wide-legged shuffle, wearing down the outer heels of his shoes as though he's Charlie Chaplin. But so far, I can't locate him.

Marco's absence is clearer to me. In the middle of the night, on occasion, when I don't block out my thoughts, I'll wake up, believing my lover is rapping on my door. The thermostat inside my body goes haywire as I think of him and the days grow hotter and hotter. With multiple surgeries planned as a State-appointed RJ, of course I'll remember less and less. Ablation will reduce the normal seven trillion nerve endings in my human body to half that number. I won't have normal emotions. Transformation to cyborg status will satisfy the Singing Directorate and provide relief for me. With the exception of a rare stinging in my right temple from *Logoharp* overload, or a pounding in my chest during combat or media assaults, I'll feel little, if any, conventional human pain.

*

Here's my current null hypothesis of love. I still can't quite get the words right, and I suspect it's really two null hypotheses, if I can only figure out how to put them together:

> H_0: *There is no association between the intensity of romantic feeling and the length of time each member of a couple perceives the intrinsic "worth" or "value" of the Other.*

Therefore:

> H_{01}: *The concept of Love and Worth in relationships is based on a skewed perception of lack and desire; i.e., the beloved has qualities the lover "lacks" and therefore desires in the beloved.*

Most likely this is a temporary condition. I can't think of an alternate hypothesis right now.

My analysis:

Worth is too subjective a concept. It requires interpretive details, definition. One can be worthy in character or value but not fitting to a partner; one can be fitting in character, beauty and values, but not sufficiently prized by a partner who feels suffocated and seeks escape. Perhaps the *perception* of value is the only thing about Love's currency that actually matters. But value is like cryptocurrency; it's changeable according to a ledger of supply and demand—that and whichever wounds each Lover is trying to staunch with expectations of Love from another.

Shit, I still sound human.

I received this note from Marco Hsu Yang letting me know he plans to marry another. I'm trying to respond objectively, as though I've already become robotic.

> *Dear Naomi,*
>
> *How are you? I've filed the papers to annul our marriage rather than seeking formal divorce. I'm able to do this here in China with retroactive application to the Zion Refuge because I gather informal "marriage" isn't legally recognized in either place. Though I cared for you, I couldn't tolerate the arguments roiling up from your stormy personality. I*

believe you lack confidence and try to cover it up by being combative. Perhaps it is your father's disappearance that makes you so.

My fiancée Jing and I wish you well. —Marco

My reply:

Hello Marco:

Thanks for your note. I think of you every day.

The news here is that the Directorate has given permission to implant my Logoharp in the portals linking my voice and brain. This will be a full installation, but I'm not sure of the dates. The harp isn't strictly musical like a Chinese harp, the Guzheng, zither or even a Western-style Konghou harp. It's designed as a direct extension of my thoughts, feelings and visions. It receives messages from the Singing Directorate. It dings like a conventional neck phone when it receives a message, but when the harp speaks through my voice, it sounds deeper, playing in an alto clef, its middle line a "C."

Once installed, I understand the harp's antennae portion on top of my head grows for awhile like a wild sapling. Full grown, it acts like the oversized antennae of longicorns (long-horned beetles), deep teal in color, adapted beautifully to extremes of sensation and sound, whether extraterrestrial or earthly. The weird part of it, Hsu Yang, is that this **Logoharp** *isn't just for government order taking or language translation. Instead, I can navigate with sound itself—something like echolocation, in other words—much like a leaf-nosed bat. Since most bats produce sounds by contracting their larynx (although a few click their tongues or emit noise through their nostrils), the harp contains multiple structures both to emit and receive information across a range of frequencies. Sonar to satellite. Normal hearing tops out at 20 kilohertz. My hearing will exceed communication satellites on the X-band (8-12 Ghz), K_u-bands (12-18 GHz), K_a-bands (26-40 Ghz). The highest frequencies are known as* **Logoharp L_h-bands** *(40-100 Ghz). I've heard the harp can also be tuned to extraplanetary sources; I'm unclear how this works.*

Becoming a harp recipient scares me a little; it scares most people. But eventually I'll understand

and speak every human language. By implication, your language, your mind, should become clearer to me, especially your distinctly Chinese perceptions of Love and gambling—for example, your idea that the average "loser" snatches defeat from the jaws of victory by focusing too intently on winning. Hence flubbing it!

Perhaps I tried too hard to win you. Hence, flubbing it!

As for you, Marco, I foresee a glorious rise to fame in Mother Country as an exterminator of excess human talent. But soon after, bitter partings, divorces and disgrace before the tribunals of the State. —Best wishes, N.F.

4

FEBRUARY 2116

BLUE-NOSED BASKETBALL RECRUITER

球
探

A recruiter for the Reverse Journalism *Elites* program has found me at a university coffee shop. She's wearing an oversized basketball uniform and notices I practice mirror writing like Leonardo da Vinci.

The recruiter's name I can't recall, but she's gigantic and gawky, 2.0574 meters tall. She has no eyelashes, either, and her irises are transparent. The skull cap she's wearing on her head hides two retracted prongs, most likely antennae. Her body appears to cast a radioactive, teal-colored aura, spreading to my skin.

"What are you studying?" she asks.

"Mandarin, French and Acadian Volk-Sprache, the latter a Maritime dialect spoken by German contractors working in the ice mines in Aitken basin, the largest and oldest impact crater on the far side of the moon."

"You like space travel?"

"Any travel."

"Why are you practicing mirror writing?"

"To avoid prying eyes." Across the aisle, a teenage couple, probably freshmen, give us the once over. I turn around and grin back, shrugging, as though nothing about this teal-blue giant appears weird. From the couple's cheek chewing and repeated use of word "like," I suspect neither can be more than 16 or 17 years of age.

"Leonardo encoded his language to keep his thoughts and plans secret from pretenders and conspirators. A useful skill given the amount of unauthorized surveillance in our worlds."

Recruiter nods, apparently impressed. She backs up a little, complimenting me on my meticulous penmanship.

"Actually, Leonardo da Vinci was our first Reverse Journalist," she explains. "Have you ever studied da Vinci's air screws and ornithopters resembling giant bat wings? Just the way you might fly if you become one of us."

"You fly?"

She meets my eyes with a gloomy stare. "You know about the Elites?"

"Not really," I lie. "But I have applied, and been selected, for low-level RJ training."

"Flying is one of many exceptional traits. The Elites have da Vinci accoutrements, like rotary bat wings, which we deploy when needed. Detachable air screws work like parachutes when we're forced to jump from ships, mountains or skyscrapers."

"Why would you do that?"

"To escape spies and terrorists."

"Oh."

"Let me explain," she goes on, drawing closer, glancing over her shoulder. She whispers: "We're a hybrid life form, superior to ordinary humans, but vulnerable. Our task as scribes and interrogators is not to report conventional news. We leverage a vast cache of auxiliary, privileged data to extrude favorable futures, at very least the timing of future certainties. Our job is to calm the masses, to smooth their social skin. We leap over the boulders of human objection—"

"What? I don't understand—" (Actually, I do. The woman seems kind, but freakish with her height and teal-blue lips, transparent eyes, talking about "future certainties.")

"We're targets," she continues. "Sometimes we project a future no one likes. The Directorate makes us into a distinct gender, half Borg, half human, BluePOC, taller and stronger than average human *females* to resist terrorists who wish to alter the futures we present."

"You're built to fight, in other words?"

"We resist. To protect the knowledge in our heads. Terrorists will launch bombs, strafing and radioactive attacks, randomly, it seems, within the air tunnels or underground sub-stations to ruin our predictions. When necessary, we escape. But every year a few of our RJs are lost in the field."

"I had no idea."

"Do you want to know more about us? We're Elites. I have an e-chure—" She pauses a moment, waiting for my signal. No signal.

"I'm just starting out. You're way above me."

"I don't think so."

"But you are."

"I have a sense about you." She loosens her cap, revealing a naked skull shaped like a Chinese pipa: gourd-like body, strings, frets, long neck, tuning pegs. "This is my installation. But I was always tall. Now I'm even taller."

"But what about your harp?"

She gestures majestically, flicking her antennae, her arms so long she appears rubberized, like the Gumby figures I used to play with as a child. Facing the café windows, as though drinking in the light, she seems focused on a distant bell tower while preening in her silky blue and gold uniform. "Of course. The *Logoharp* is a given, but only the Elites have access to its higher-order receptions. You might surmise we're both male and female in nature; our sex organs are distinct, but discreet. We do experience a magnanimous love for all human genders. But we're wired not to fall in love with individuals. However, very rarely, this happens."

She eyes me up and down.

"I see," admiring her gall just a bit. "Are you coming onto me? By any chance?"

"No. I'm trying to recruit you."

"I guess being magnanimously bi-gendered makes life easier—"

"Not easy," she corrects me. "Our recruits put emotions aside. We build structures of probability—lattices of numbers and scenarios that we envision and fantasticate on screen and in the air, then the real world—anticipating the next interlaced political event so that the public can understand, in simple terms, what's going on—and what will happen."

"No," I shake my head fervently. "Probability analysis doesn't equate to prediction."

"Hey, listen!" She touches my real hand; her freakish giant hand goes navy blue. It's twice the size of mine, but with no freckles, veins, flesh spots, hair.

"What are you doing, Comrade?" I interject, withdrawing my hand. It's as though she's taken tactile liberties with me, assuming, naively, that sensory information communicated from one to the other is more appropriate than verbiage right now. "With all due respect, no one can truly predict the future," I observe, my voice rising, resistant. "There may be factors that escape logic, that no one foresees. Besides, the masses never really understand what's going on behind the scenes."

Her voice contracts again to a whisper. "Are you sure of that?" She grins, kind of a "gotcha" crease in her upturned lips and skin surrounding her clear goblet eyes. "Have you ever taken a poll? Conducted a survey?"

"No, but I might in the future."

"Depending on your employment," she rejoins. "Of course, your employment, employer, will matter. You've heard our broadcasts, haven't you? We extrapolate the most likely impact of Directorate actions on public behavior—something like calculating the explosive trajectories of a warehouse full of billiard balls. Our projections help narrow down public expectations for change, a gaming strategy we call *winnowing*, which impacts earthly survival. Our task is to shape—"

"Who's '*we*'"?

She pouts, then discharges a bluish o-shaped funnel of air.

"Who's '*we*'?" I repeat. "Who is supporting you?"

"The Elites!" she fires back. "Our job is to flood the masses with tweets and images, moving and still, which everyone absorbs both consciously and subliminally. But we also have direct contact with the highest official levels. Our job is to implant messages in sub-second intervals in our media so that no mind can refuse to absorb them, yet they are there, feeding the subconscious. Simply put, we stimulate or suppress, as appropriate, the fight-or-flight impulse that lies dormant in all of us."

I put my pen down, trying to signal her to go.

"Listen, there are many layers of authority," she goes on, ignoring me. "Our assignments go right up to the Directorates in Beijing and New York. We have the greatest influence on executive decisions. You should think about joining—"

"I've already made plans for Taiwan."

"Sure, that's fine. But read about us, anyway, please? Can I have your neural address?"

I agree, reluctantly. She reads it on my prosthetic palm turned up; my ID is stamped in the flesh. Through the window, I notice the afternoon sunlight touching her cheek, turning her skin gold.

"You should apply," she says firmly. "We need linguists and cryptographers like you."

"Thank you," eyes narrowing, locking on her retinal displays which show nothing but bold black numbers.

"Oh, yes! My heads-up display shows your neural address. That's part of our transformation. Skin turns dark navy at night or under threats of violence. Retinal displays in multiple spectra: visible rainbow, infrared long waves, ultraviolet short waves, and black and white as appropriate. Gold tinges in sunlight, giving in to our emotions of joy and satisfaction. Have you caught our games?"

"Not yet."

"Well, tonight we play against the Red-Skinned Magpies."

"A boys' team? Why bother? If you're prescient, you already know who'll win!"

"The score will be close, but we'll squeak by—"

"But why?"

"It's more fun knowing! All those slam dunks and guys sweating and falling on their asses!"

"I see."

She high-fives me so hard my hands sting. Resuming my mirror writing, I confess I'm not completely clear about the nuances of Elite RJ reporting. I'll learn more during the training period.

5

SEPTEMBER 2116

SINGING FALSETTO WITH MR. BAI

白
老
唱
腔

After Marco Hsu Yang sent me his kiss-off message, I immediately reconfirmed my acceptance at Taiwan Normal University Language School. I have to graduate with honors from there to enter the Boccioni Institute of Futurism in Taipei. My goal has always been to learn Chinese and to perfect the translation and reporting skills I'll need for a chosen RJ career, whether Elite or Standard.

At first, I reasoned that I might try to stop in Japan to search for my father; however, I was warned that my orientation and lecture schedules in Taipei can't be altered. Training at the Boccioni Center will ensure my basic skills as a Futurist, but to become an Elite would mean many more months, even years of training elsewhere. The initial step is to do everything in accepted sequence if I want this chance. Japan will have to wait. This saddens me.

By definition, an RJ reports the future as though it has happened, and then, paradoxically, it *does* as scripted despite the denials and incredulity of crowds. That's a strange idea, I know, but in essence, RJs are co-authors and guides to political and social events not yet come to pass.

I've learned that the Singing Directorate officials in both Beijing and Ameriguo need RJs to help neutralize (by pre-empting) the threat of international spies and social misfits, dissidents, terrorists and old-style journalists eager to disrupt Party order. They monitor the RJs of North Korea, Russia, Saudi Arabia, Ethiopia, Central African Republic and other empires. While RJs are certainly equipped with enhanced mental powers, their physique is transformed, too: joints as hard as diamonds, rotorized wings that fly short distances; and with infrared and ultraviolet frequency detection and the unique *Logoharp*, their true value lies in executing a not-yet-tangible vision. As the lady basketball recruiter told me, "Both in our eyes and minds, we see a path through the boulders of human objection, guiding our subjects to behave as our algorithms predict while we remain safely hidden from public view."

Maybe not so safe. But hidden most of the time.

Though it seems reasonable to start my training according to this Elite agenda, I've decided first on a somewhat more comforting curriculum. Taiwan, in other words. I've wanted to visit Taipei because it's entirely unknown to me, an island of rebellious habits and extraordinary appreciation of Nature. I've seen images of the white trumpet shapes of the *Yangmingshan* (阳明山) calla lilies; the sulfurous fumeroles pouring crystals out of Seven Stars Mountain; the giant rock face of *Guan Yin* (观音), the compassionate Bodhisattva, occupying the Western silhouette atop Taipei's northern mountains, which I've resolved to climb.

Also, I've heard about the steaming vinegary *baotzu* (包子) dumplings and my favorite spicy pork noodles, *zha jiang mian* (炸酱面), along with the kindness among locals toward visiting foreign students. The old Taiwanese actually remember their ancestors talking about the twentieth century: the Japanese invasion, the Red Armies and the Civil War, how ordinary citizens tried to support the Kuomintang Army despite all its renegade corruption and failed campaigns. Even decades after the Civil War, I recall seeing videos of Taiwan shot in the 1970s, one of them showing a group of blond Mormon men dressed in three-piece suits riding around Taipei streets on Penny Farthing bicycles. These Mormons never seemed to fall despite the height of that big front wheel. They were in steamy Taipei to preach and complete godly missions.

Though I've no idea what modern Taipei looks like today, I've seen adverts for multiple language institutes that circumvent the stricter rules set by Mother Country. After a year spent in a Taipei Normal University Language School, for example, I can enroll in Boccioni Futurism, named after Umberto Boccioni, the great sculptor. The institute offers a radically accelerated program on behalf of Taiwanese Universal Languages Commission (modeled after Umberto Boccioni's Futurist artwork, *Unique Forms of Continuity in Space*). I plan to take a hypersonic transport to Asia as soon as I finish preliminary language exams.

Though I'm excited about my new identity, I miss my parents. Ostensibly they're remnants of the forgotten past. About nine months ago, my father made the Missing Persons report. He disappeared somewhere in Japan. I last saw a fuzzy glimpse of someone who looked like him in a poorly circulated news video which I magnified on my pod display. I'm not sure it was he—although the figure seemed tall and bulky like a cave man, so it could be. He was reported to be on a clipper ship bound for snow-capped Hokkaido, ostensibly to visit Japanese healers who use native herbs to treat blood cancers.

In truth, I believe he went into hiding near Hokkaido to avoid my mother, his doctors and creditors. Still no messages, but he keeps reappearing in my dreams.

*

It's been many months and I long for completion. I've done well with Mandarin language studies thus far. At the Boccioni Institute I've met a Chinese teacher named *Bai Lao Shih* (百老师), which literally means Teacher White. Guessing he's about 70 years old, poor and well-worn, dying his hair shoeshine black and wearing 2040s Chinese woolen Xi tunics with lots of dandruff falling to the shoulders. Apparently, he's excused from mandatory retirement because of his special knowledge of classical Mandarin. His speech, has no *er hua yin* (儿化音) Beijing accent that sounds to me like trucks sucking sewage from manholes. Mr. Bai can mimic the most delicate Chinese intonations in his speech. He also writes pictograms and ideograms carved originally as Oracle bone script from thousands of years ago. He applies thin or thick brushes to paint poetic characters on long linen scrolls, perfecting the styles of *cao shu* (草书) grass script and *zhuan shu* (篆书) seal script, plus *jiaguawen* (甲骨文) bone script for all to see. These styles are fast-disappearing in Taiwan's historical archives.

Oddly, though, Teacher Bai is the first instructor I've met who actually stumbles over the Mandarin translation of Reverse Journalism; he seems to know nothing about it. In Chinese I attempt a translation for him: *fan xiang xinwen* (反向新闻) or *wei lai de xin wen xue* (未来的新闻学), *futuristic journalism.* But maybe there's a better translation. He seems to have doubts about the idea; unfortunately, some doubts have rubbed off on me. For example, he says we can't extrapolate which political leaders will rise or fall in the next election, much less who's going to live or die or be crowned an imposter today.

"Na$_2$O$_2$ *MeiMei* (妹妹)," he quips, calling me "little sister sodium peroxide," referring to my hot chemical disposition ready to disinfect anything tossed dirty in the streets. "There's no rhyme or reason to our political circumstance," he snaps. "Perhaps we should just draw lessons from the female impersonators in past times."

"Female impersonators? Why do you say this, Mr. Bai?"

"I say it because the impersonators spoke truth from their hearts. In falsetto, of course."

By "impersonators," I don't think he means patriarchs like Confucius or Lao Tzu. More like Mei Lan Fang, the "Queen of Peking Opera" in the early twentieth century. Mei Lan Fang, a man, is best known for his operatic portrayal of florid-robed girls—women of extraordinary grace and refinement. Bai likes to mimic Mei Lan Fang's recitatives from *Kunqu* (昆曲), the oldest form of Chinese Opera. Nearly every evening, when we both arrive at the institute by navigating the smelly back streets of Jinshan (there are still rats rummaging the sewers), he sits across from me at a decrepit classroom table, coffee and tea stains never wiped clean, his lesson books open, no wireless devices allowed. Humming in a scratchy falsetto, keeping time waving his fingers, he extemporizes, singing his truth. I'm swept away by swirling crescendos of romance and lost loves in battle, divided empires, the presence of ghosts and concubines. His singing seems decrepit and lonely, as he is, as I am, but just right today.

"Teacher Bai, your singing is delightful. Why do you make me so happy?"

He keeps singing.

True, I feel light-hearted to be united with an elder who doesn't mind my weird appearance, neither the unicorn shaped sensors protruding from my nose clip nor the proto-antennae implants coming out of my ears. Bai always carries a flask of hot tea with him, which we share, drinking from dirty cups; and occasionally we'll walk out to the food stalls in the alleyway behind the institute, grabbing a cup of hot-and-sour soup (酸辣汤) mixed with duck blood and spicy bean curd. This keeps the winter chills away. Bai has a sallow appearance and never wears an outer coat, even in the freezing rain. He brushes his slicked-back mound of hair and giggles when I compliment him on his youthful appearance.

"I love these songs," he says. Slurping his soup, a spoon held by dirty fingernails caked in black (he has no shower in his flat), he tells me he goes to a public shower twice a week. His face seems very clean.

"You're shivering, Teacher Bai. I'll get you a coat."

"Not at all! It's a palsy. Runs in the family. I take herbs for it."

"You're shivering. Let's go back inside."

A few days later, I buy him a new woolen scarf from Scotland. Its weave is tan-colored, red and white stripes, plaid design, and he loves it. Stroking the soft fabric again and again, as though he's stroking a cat. We open our textbooks and he asks me to read this passage in English and translate it as closely as possible.

"Reverse Journalism refers to the act of scripting, then reporting an event on paper, computer or holographic screen, then seeing it acted out with complete fidelity in the real world."

I try with fractured Mandarin.

反向新闻是指脚本操作，然后在纸，计算机或全息屏幕上报告事件，然后…

Fan xiang xinwen shih zhi jiaoben caozuo, ran hou zai zhi, jisuanji huo quanxi pingmu shang baogao shijian, ran hou…

I can't finish the translation.

"Is such a talent possible? he asks. "This RJ role seems like playacting in Beijing Opera."

"It's social science," I reply. "At least that's what we're taught. This type of predictive journalism was practiced more than a century ago. Journalists reported an event, claiming objectivity, but really cherrypicking certain details, amplifying others, forgetting to mention a few more, speculating or going 'wide and low' in their interpretations according to the flavor of the partisan media, right or left, but mostly right, hiring them. Beneath the words and severe expressions, women reporters on camera pitched their voices, even questions, into 'downreadings' at the end of their sentences, all the while meaning to sound authoritative and serious. Male announcers practiced machine-gun monotone or querulous upreadings when they wanted to cast doubt on suspicious interviewees. Always mindful of audience ratings, of course. Reporters anticipated the crowds' naïve ping-pong reactions with glee, as though the event or political repartee quoted had actually happened or would happen exactly as they reported it. But no. The picture in people's heads, their confusion, their incredulity and anger at being left behind, came to pass from all the *filtering*. Therefore, the news became propaganda, foreshadowing who would win or lose, and how."

"But today, is it any different? Perhaps someone else has scripted these events long before?" Bai queries me. "Isn't it up to you, the reporter or broadcaster, to write them out and interpret them as your bosses suggest, in memos?"

"Well, not exactly. In our modern times, we journalists are returning to our reporting roots, trying to correct the mistakes of the past. Our mission as RJs, for instance, is to tune out unwanted influence, distortions, partisan branding with saturation messages (i.e., we call these messages "*logo harps*" of the wrong kind). My job will be to delete the garbage messaging of trolls and extreme political foundations. Breaking news will be cleaned up and neutralized via AI censors so that social media influencers don't get the final say."

"Okay, but who gets the final say?"

"Algorithms. Numbers. Big data. Generative AI may incorporate the racial/ethnic bias and lack of transparency of its trainers. But undeniably, eighth generation AI produces balanced results. RJs can now calculate what the masses really want, what they actually need (not at all the same) and a probable timeline for solutions. Then we script the events and likelihood of a desired outcome, winnowing down our scenarios to just a few."

He blinks, starts to hum, his eyes glazed over.

"I was a budding actor once."

"Like Mei Lan Fang?"

"Yes, in the Mei style. I once perfected a woman's voice."

He gulps his tea a moment, takes a breath, then starts singing in falsetto, up and down. I can tell, watching his eyes tearing a little, that's he's already traveling backward in time.

I can see Bai's Adam's apple fluttering, throaty and off-key, as he scratches through a *White Snake* melody.

"Oh, Mr. Bai, your singing is pleasant but may I steer you back to the moment?"

"Of course."

"Haven't you been trained to translate the important terms of Reverse Journalism? Isn't it a requirement to work here?"

"No, sweet Naomi. I'm an antique. More of the old school—"

He says no more. In our silence I revert to the archives, reading out loud and translating as I go.

> *Our authorities guide the formation of events to con-*
> *form to the Singing Directorate's vision at time T_1.*
> *Scripted events culminate when our political actors*
> *take their places and carry out the script in time T2.*
> *The unfolding of actual events may be postponed due*
> *to unforeseeable interruptions...*

"Which interruptions?"

"Someone or something going rogue," I reply, "not acting according to the script."

"Has this happened?"

"Of course. Historically, for example, in Ameriguo, in the early days of the Civil Rights movement, Ms. Rosa Parks wouldn't give up her seat on a bus to a white person. Brave of her."

"Another example?"

"Bantu Steven Biko, an anti-apartheid activist in South Africa. Beaten to death by police in jail."

"Another?"

"Liu Xiao Bo," the disgraced poet and author of Charter 08, a petition for human rights in China. Liu actually won the Nobel Prize for his work in 2010. When he was active, he celebrated the United States and its interventions abroad for the avowed sake of democracy, including wars in Kuwait, Afghanistan and Iraq. Eventually, though, before his final imprisonment, Liu repented."

"But why?"

"He decided his ideas about democracy were as useful 'as a paraplegic laughing at a quadriplegic!' When he was invited to New York to speak and tour, he visited the Metropolitan Museum, but after getting a look at paintings like the *Rape of the Sabines*, Caravaggio's grisly *Salome with the Head of John the Baptist* and umpteen crucifixions of Jesus Christ, he decided Western civilization was so violent, misogynist and royalist that it could never save humanity from itself. He then resolved to criticize both China and the West, and was detained and incarcerated multiple times until the end of his life in 2017."

"Oh."

After a few moments, he speaks again. "I was not familiar with all these historical examples, Naomi. But do you think any leader has the option to 'go rogue,' as you put it? To modify events and policies in order to make life a little better for our citizens?"

"I hope so, but not sure. As for me, I want to participate and help co-create what's to come. I want to create a positive outlook. Recently, for instance, I've dreamt of my parents waking up from torpor, death, wherever they are. Their eyes suddenly pop open because the world is so fresh and clean, and they rise from their coffins, renewed, looking around. I see joy in their faces, like toddlers discovering the world for the first time."

"Lots of elders rediscover the world," Bai says. "Look at me! But are these events you're describing real?"

"I foresee things happening. I foresee rogue events, too."

"Naomi?" He seems doubtful again. He shakes his head, mumbles to himself. We take a break, watching the holographic TV set in the school lobby. A newscaster announces that Beijing police are arresting prostitutes who pull jackets over their heads to avoid the cameras. Another newscast features the Ice Festival of Harbin, in Manchuria, where hundreds of children are pushing "ice sleighs" on runners gliding over the Songhua River. "The winter ritual brings families together to ensure ancestral continuity and pleasing harmony," a news-caster announces.

"I like harmony," Bai says. "Will Reverse Journalists en-sure a harmonious future?"

"Yes, I believe so."

He reaches out for my soft left hand, stroking it too many times. Politely, I withdraw my hand, making excuses that I've been bitten too many times by local mosquitos, fleas and cockroaches (*Zhanglang* 蟑螂). I'm reminded, as I try gingerly to withdraw my fingers, that Teacher Bai smells of boiled herbs.

"I'm proud to be selected as an RJ candidate," I tell him. "Our mission is to improve health, *bonhomie* and equality of all peoples."

"Very good! You practice magic tricks, too?" he asks, eyebrow raised.

"No, we act in accordance with our leaders' directions."

"You haven't met these leaders yet."

"But I've already received my first instructions; they've asked me to finish my training as rapidly as possible so I can get the *Logoharp* in full installation. Even without most of the hardware, can you feel the portal in my throat? It resonates. I'm receiving dings, the Directorate messages, though I can't make out the encrypted meanings."

He reaches for my larynx, placing his fingers very lightly above my suprasternal notch where the instrument hums, pulses, goes silent and hums again.

"I'm told that during public emergencies I'll hear sounds like stentorian laments of cellos, drums and clackers loudly striking wood!"

"You'll hear all that?" he asks.

"Some of it."

"But how does your *Logoharp* sing, exactly?"

"I don't understand the mechanics yet. But it's a harp, with ultra-sensitive *vibrato* to translate all signals and moods. It takes instructions from the Directorate and measures the reactive pulse of the people. A full-duplex conversation in musical terms."

"Sounds complicated."

"It is."

Bai stares at me, a blinkered expression I've never seen before. He withdraws his fingers from my throat and places them on the table, drumming rhythmically.

"Naomi." His voice wavers a little, as though to chide me. "Before you take the pulse of the people, take your own. Is your human heart beating? Is your conscience still alive? Remember your parents and the lessons you've learned. Above all, be careful with assassins and pretenders, even people you trust."

I nod faithfully, not sure what he means. He kisses me on both cheeks as we end the session.

6

MARCH 2117

ROUTINE STUDDING PROCEDURE

植
入
手
术

I'm back in snowy Utah trying conventional and Volokopter skiing, where the copter drops you off at Mt. Nebo, the highest peak, 3,755 meters, and you have to find your way down without radio or other human guidance.

In winters, I think of summer. I remember the sand dunes of Southern Taiwan, my lookout for Chinese sharp-nosed vipers, and then the face of Teacher Bai singing in cool Mei Lan Fang falsetto. Though thoughts of the *Logoharp* buoy me up these days, I dream of hikes up Guan Yin Shan into cloud-fall, the fog and thunderheads, lime trees, tea terraces. I'm always thirsty on these hikes because I frequently forget to bring potable water. Also, some doubts about my future career disturb me, yet I leap forward regardless.

The *Logoharp* preliminary surgeries are finished. You could say I'm neither cyborg nor fully human, just a transitional creature without power. Right now, I'm situated at St. Francis the Oracle of Zion Medical Unit, Salt Lake, Utah, awaiting another install. I suspect even after this implant I'll require firmware upgrades.

*

Dr. Jens Remker, chief of the surgical unit here, is meeting me in a few minutes to discuss a routine studding procedure, my third and most extensive. Diamond studs and rotors will be implanted in all the critical fighting joints, especially the knees, elbows, wrists, ankles and fingers, part of my body armor. There will be some additional repairs and cloning of cardiac and neural tissue. This is for my own good, my transformation, they say. When I pass these hospital walls without paintings or proper signs, just puke-green color with little sperm-shaped splotches of pink rendered with white corkscrew tails that go off in all directions, I'm uneasy. This is supposed to be a distracting image.

"You're Naomi?" The question hangs in the ether. Under twilight anesthesia, I catch only a silhouette of a tall blond Aryan leaning over my bedside. He carries an old-fashioned digital tablet.

"Doctor Jens Remker. Pleased to meet you. I've looked up your records."

He takes my natural hand. This, I understand, is prelude to the final step. I've read all the caveats: loss of personal femininity, at least its human form. Whatever sexuality I have will become diminished, absorbed, into cyborgian agenda. My life span will shorten with this surgery, but frankly, I don't know what I'd do without it. Perhaps, in Marco's absence, I need to feel exclusivity, a power and distinction in body and mind that very few possess.

Dr. Remker, Austrian by birth, has frosty blue eyes that magnetize me. He seems kind. He has high cheekbones and a narrow square jaw, hints of gray at his temples mixed with abundant thickets of blond. Thirty-eight years old, a triangular muscled frame, one dimple, a disarming smile so intent I can hardly believe he's survived 12 years of surgical training, which tends to turn physicians into dissectionists.

"You must be an athlete?" he asks, eyes widening, scanning me up and down.

"I pole va—" I meant to say "vault" but my speech is slurring.

Remker's natural inclination is to put his patients at ease. His touch and reluctance to touch tell me this. He waits for my signal. I turn my left palm up, natural fingers opening just a little. Slowly he squeezes the left as he inserts several feeds in the right forearm and thigh, explaining what he's about to do. His team will inject stem-cell foragers followed by nanoseals to augment growth in my organs—heart, lungs inner ear, gut, larynx, sensors and eventually my joints and skin, which will color gold in the sun and then teal in waning light and dark ocean blue in the evening.

"You know," he begins, as though preoccupied with a question, then withdrawing it. "You have a lot of beautiful hair."

He's brushes it back as I watch him with one eye; he's tucking it full and thick into a blowsy surgical cap. "Your physical appearance, by necessity, will change with this surgery. Your hair, your cheekbones, the natural curve of your fingers and hands."

"I'll still have my hands, won't I? At least my one natural hand. I'm told I'll fly, zoom anywhere above everything."

"Mostly hopping and skipping in short-haul flight. Like pole vaulting, only higher and faster—a bit like vaulting long distances in mid-air."

I close my lids, feeling the wings spreading from my back.

"I've signed the paperwork already."

"Naomi, you'll lose something."

"My fear, hopefully."

"Your hair, your natural skin color. Your girlish appearance."

The nurses enter behind him. Their dress is weird; they wear clear polyimide helmets, apparently to protect from cautery sparks. Two are dressed in black leather jerseys, aprons and pantaloons, as though they work in a foundry. I hear them revving a high-speed drill, tapping hydraulic hammers, gathering up wads of instruments and cotton batting.

"You won't feel anything," Jens assures me. "Doping is incredibly effective."

"I feel everything physical. Even under anesthesia."

"Well then, you'll be so enhanced I won't be able to talk to you!" He smirks, then breaks into a Cheshire-cat smile. Perfect teeth. "Just want you to be fully aware."

"I am."

"Your personality and memories, at least some of them, will disappear," he says, unkinking the IV tubing. "The chemicals affect the follicles of the scalp, too, like chemotherapy, but eventually some hair will grow back. Besides, you'll be wearing the standard Argonaut cap and body suit most of the time, covering everything but your face and the *Logoharp* antennae, which, when mature, will resemble ablated antennae of a longicorn. Your epidermis will feel smooth; other times it grows scales for your protection."

"I've been told my facial contour and eyes will appear more 'Chinese,' at least mixed blood, thanks to the surgical transformations. Is that correct?"

His speech slows. "I can't tell you exactly."

"Please answer my question."

"I can't tell you." He whispers, "Every patient is different."

Is he afraid? Am I? Out of the corner of my eye, I detect each IV starting to drip. Remker's long fingers are gloved, all fluids dripping now. The cold currents in these chemical streams fill me up as though I'm swimming in an icy river. All the fluids swell my visible veins, but this is expected given volumes of blood and Ringer's lactate required for surgery.

"Naomi, you've read the fine print, right? Your metabolism and aging will accelerate, as will your cognitive capacity. But you'll have virtually no taste in your mouth, and limited sensations of touch. Aging is much faster than normal. Expect to live roughly half the length of a normal human life span."

"I understand. Worth the sacrifice?" I suddenly flash an image of ruddy Jack London, who said he wanted to be a "meteor in magnificent glow," not a permanent planet.

"Why must I wear this Argonaut suit? It makes no sense to me! No one will ever see me work."

"On the contrary, Naomi, scribes and interrogators accompanying our dignitaries in the ocean luges are seen and critiqued in social media. Your face will appear in phones and holo-screens."

"I don't like that. I like privacy."

"Why? If you're going to be a journalist, you'll be so exposed you'll grow weary of it. Besides, you're still beautifully formed."

I don't know how to take his compliment. He sticks me in the thigh with 10 needles at once. A surgical gatling gun, wheel within wheel.

"Can I trust you?" I ask.

"Do you have a choice?"

He turns away, but I can't help tracking his every move. His face is pure Brancusi sculpture, angular, futuristic. Tapping on the tubes now, the valves fully opened. The anesthesia smells like powdery pink bubble bath, a disgusting inhalation making me gag. "This isn't supposed to happen," I muse, looking into the glaring operating theatre lights. "There's a dead armadillo on the street."

"Your past life," he laughs. "Did you run over one on your Volokopter?"

He lifts me from the waist, pushing a spittoon tray in front of my mouth. I vomit hardly at all, but then multiple arms come out and gently push me back down. "There's an armadillo run over by a passing VTOL, don't you see?" I plead with Jens, but he doesn't see it. "His beady eyes are popped. No amount of armor can protect him."

"Relax," he laughs.

"I am."

"You're not changing your mind, are you?"

He mumbles something about nanoseals and diamond studs, then the new cardiac and neural implants, making my core even stronger. A hint of alarm in his voice, although the question is moot because all the permissions have been signed.

He waits.

"It's okay. Go ahead. Just go ahead. Please."

The blond Aryan with perfect aquiline nose nods, signaling his crew, squeezing my left hand and leaning closer to me.

"You'll be bruised all over when you wake up; your head will spin for a few days, so you won't be going anywhere."

I tighten my fingers around his.

"No speech, either. Your larynx will be spliced and re-shaped to accommodate the last modules for your harp, though frequency synching won't happen this time. You won't like the noise at first. Some soft switches will let you turn down the volume or change channels."

"What's your name again?"

"Jens. Just call me Jen."

"No, Dr. Jens. I prefer your name with the *s*. You're a plural kind of guy."

He nods. His mining light is the last thing I see.

*

A drawbridge opens—a jaw, amazed. In the gray din of the operating theatre a skiff rises; we're rowing down a tributary that leads to Lake Superior. The oar in the water makes a dipping sound; I hear droplets against the wake like diphthong music to me, interrupting the screams of a hacksaw and rotary blades. My sternum cracks. I feel buzzing stabs, a zipper of flesh cut lengthwise. Defenseless since my limbs are bound against the stretcher railings. No one touches my primary organs except for the heart. But I do feel the drilling; a robot takes a high precision drill to my ankles and knees. It doesn't hurt too much. Nerve ablation has taken care of that.

Marco Hsu Yang bobs in our canoe less than a meter away. I try to reach him, lifting arms that won't lift, knees that won't bend, wading up to my neck in the water, like a child thrown overboard and not knowing how to swim. He stares at me, doesn't move. Someone has given up on me, and I'll drown. The surgeon takes my heart in his hands—is this Jens? I breathe without breathing. Believing all is well, yes, my parents will rescue me. A miracle is about to happen. I dream of blue-skinned giants playing basketball.

*

It's morning again. Pale pink light pinches my face, streaming through the windows, and no surgical reflections. Dr. Jens Remker comes to check on me. He tucks my remaining thickets of hair into a surgical shower cap.

"A torrent!" he exclaims, his lips curling into that smile as he arranges my hair. Jens tells me I'm healing fast and will be assigned for work someplace remote and cold, maybe the lunar South Pole where he's going for work. "The South Pole-Aitken basin on the far side of lunar surface is where Mother Country maintains its research base," he says. Jens plans to serve as a biophysicist there once his surgical duties at St. Francis are up.

"How much Chinese do you know?" he asks me.

All I can do is stare at his face, those cheekbones, his mouth. And though I register his questions I still can't speak.

Not enough, I sign, though my academic records indicate advanced conversation.

"Maybe I can borrow your recordings?"

I nod, but we're distracted by children staging wheelchair races down the green and white-tiled hallways. With my mind I push the chairs.

"You're recovering," he tells me. I explain through a laryngeal surrogate that I was in wheelchair races at seven years old, just a week or so after the surgeons repaired my half heart. I can still feel the wheelchair again, my hands wrapped around the wheels, pushing so hard the chair rockets down the hospital hallways as my fans squeal in delight.

Jens reaches for my neck phone, taps in a code (perhaps his?) while he readjusts my tracheal tube. He rewraps the balloon prosthesis around the right wrist stump.

"We'll restore your prosthesis in a few days with a new model. It won't break. You feeling any better?"

A flutter in my throat.

"We should talk more about the situation on Aitken; miners are striking there and nothing gets done. I'll need orientation, especially adapting to plasma conditions. We should speak offline when you're better."

For a moment he presses my left hand against my cheek so I can feel the abalone and steel nanotiles he's installed—another mode of protection for a broken jaw. He stares through the mirror of my eyes. Is it pride he feels? I count—at least part of me—as a monster, the new Bride of Frankenstein.

"I hope I can speak with you again," I rasp, a bare whisper. "With my own voice, and not with the new *Logoharp*, though I'm dying to try it out."

7

MAY 2117

THE ALTERNATE HYPOTHESIS OF LOVE

爱
有
新
论

Weeks later and I'm back in my pod at night. Missing the comfort of the nursing team, the familiar blips, my vital signs displayed on the nanotiles. Alone, I can't help feeling a twinge of happiness, emptiness, having briefly encountered Dr. Jens Remker. No messages though; I guess he's too busy with other patients. Late at night, I still dream of Marco. He's what's left of my memories, at least the remnants of skiing together. Also, physical things: flesh tones, my pulse under fire, blood flow, temperature, metabolism; it's hard to forget any of it.

In the mirror I see changes. My scalp grows peachfuzz now, soon to be hair of ambiguous colors. My larynx is bruised and my voice just coming back. Scratchy. As predicted, the skin of my body is turning a pale venous blue, just a shade or two darker than that of a pit viper, although I'll flare gold in sunlight. The veins in my hands and arms look weirdly flesh-colored, as though I've been irradiated and turned inside out. And the antennae, of course, my wild saplings, look clipped now. There are suckers (tuners), organic growths lining each appendage up and down. Apparently, these tighten or loosen to receive alternating frequencies; as my capacities grow, I will detect microwave background radiation, hydrogen spectral octaves and the bullshit *patois* of this or that politician.

My *Logoharp* nears completion.

To clarify, the Directorate demands metamorphosis of all humans-turned-cyborgs. We're re-architected to support rotary percussive drilling and cutting. Charging repositories, essentially nanoplugs, fit inside our scapula, knee and ankle joints, all outfitted with thorium-oxide fuel cells to sustain short-distance flight. Further, with my *Logoharp* installed, I can detect everything from dog whistles 10 blocks away to the eruption of sun spots. So too, my harp enables direct reception of Directorate instructions, encrypted or not, at any time, since I've opened a new channel to the State's collective brain.

This is prelude, of course; now I join a new class of Reverse Journalists, though not the Elites as yet. Over the years scientists have studied our "second sight" clairvoyance, our ability to recover from mortal wounds to which an ordinary human would succumb. Alarms have escalated lately because of multiple assassinations of journalists and even RJs who try to expose not only petty acts of corruption but also conspiracy schemes among election deniers. RJs who *write the future* to foil these malefactors are considered essential nodes in the Intranets of Power. But even with network redundancy and rerouting worldwide, the murders of multiple RJs threaten the entire network. Therefore, we're built resilient, with hidden neural net processing layers and obligatory body armor.

I have no opinion about our enhanced construction one way or another, but I'm glad I'm as tall and stronger than most men.

*

Jens Remker still hasn't messaged me since I left St. Francis and I haven't contacted him either. I'm reluctant because of my scales, my height and blue skin and, of course, the hair loss and tuning appendages. Technically he's my Frankenstein who should love his "Monster." Yet I fear, as a man, he'll be repelled since my girlish expressions are all gone.

I've formed an Alternate Hypothesis of Love. It's girlish and imprecise, but it can be tested. In the subgroup defined as "romantically inclined couples":

> H_1: The intensity of passionate feeling and the perception of "worth" that each individual holds for the other is inexplicable outside the shared triangle of love.

It also follows:

> H_{1a}: The shared triangle consists of three vertices: the lover, beloved and the unstable third point, which may be an in-law or the lovers' skewed perception of lack and desire. In other words, the beloved has qualities the lover apparently lacks and therefore desires in the beloved, but only for an undefined period of time.

Is this tautology? I'll test these hypotheses when the opportunity arises.

*

Directorate bots have outfitted me with the argonaut cap and black body suit. Most of the bruising has healed. I'm taller by 21 centimeters, more than eight inches, noticeable in any crowd. I haven't tried to fly. There is an incessant, annoying ringing in my ears, which I'm told I'll get used to. My lips swell a bit. I can't think of a thing Jens would find physically or emotionally *attractive* about my new appearance. Perhaps he was right to ask whether I wanted to postpone the surgery because he liked me the way I was (stupid teen babbling inside my cyborg skull).

Forget it, I'm back at my exams, a new creature. In daylight I flash to Dr. Jens and his gentle, curious manner. At night I'm spooning with Marco Hsu Yang, though too often he's got his brains elsewhere. I'm surprised that my memory still touches his dark shoulders, feeling him by my side. What good are these thoughts? I want to tell him, right now, that he should have loved me. Why do we abandon our first loves, and why do they abandon us?

In these healing days I've formed no other alternate hypotheses of love; my data are scant, my sampling size too small. But I might venture a hypothesis about Creators and Monsters, or Monster Brides, that there is direct association between a Creator's drive for perfection and his or her achievement of near perfection in the Monster. Alternately, a direct and loving association exists between the Monster (or Monster Bride) and her intense feelings about her Creator giving her everything—including the gift of life.

This is also a testable hypothesis. Perhaps I'll create a new one about Love once I'm traveling in my luge through the

Pacific Ocean tunnels. In the meantime, I hope I'll hear from Jens Remker, or kind Creators like him.

8

OCTOBER 2118

MILK OF AMNESIA

遗忘之乳

Beijing's Singing Directorate has asked me to take part in the Exchanges. My Singing Directorate bosses here tell me I must go. It's nearly time, and I'm traveling to set an example. My *Logosharp—Logoharp—*is fully installed and operational.

The last few years I've been stationed at a media laboratory which operates inside a cavern, an underground securitized facility not far from the Bryce Canyon hoodoos. On my half-days off once a month I hike and fly around the hoodoos for sport.

Occasionally I'm assigned brief tours to Mother Country. Back home, at Bryce, I love the reddish sandstone of the hoodoos, especially when they're covered in fresh snow. The hoodoo rock people are taller than most moderate-sized cyborgs and remind me of the reclining figures of Henry Moore, the late sculptor. He created the Harlow Family Group, a three-headed "hoodoo" showing a husband, wife and child bonded forever. I converse with this group when I visit the stones.

Inside our Bryce facility, one rarely sees a human beyond a security guard or two. In the antechamber there is nothing but an Aeolian pipe organ that operates 24-7 using an electronic bellows. Decisions of the highest presumptive directorates or their committees stop the music; they are always rendered in a vibrant *a cappella* chorale, improvised from themes by Zoltan Kodaly and Stephen Foster. One doesn't hear the singing *per se* because the transmissions are pumped directly through the *Logoharp* into the participant's aorta, much like sonar at very low frequencies signaling across the ocean. Obedience among RJs called to the Exchanges is considered *heartfelt,* and no one ever questions orders or outcomes, though sometimes I fear my exceptions.

I was born with a hole in my heart. My mother, a human, smoked, and the hole (which grew larger, reducing my heart to nearly half its normal size) was sewn up with surgical catgut followed by sonic ablation, causing the tissue around the repair to collapse and scar. Even though the surgeons were meticulous by rebuilding missing pieces with synthetic parts, the prolapsed valves and minor leaking across the ventricles continue today. This is why Directorate assignments absorb quickly through the right ventricle but leak out through un-plugged calcium channels in the left. Consequently, when I visit the Exchanges, I forget most directives after a short time. They simply disappear from my *Logoharp* "pegbox" and I can't voice the proper "copy, confirm that" automatically. To compensate, I take copious notes to preserve instructions with a pop-out nanostylo embedded in my wrist, but sometimes I forget what I'm doing. That's when I resort to lessons my parents taught me. I vaguely recall our talks at the dinner table about choice—*Logos, Ethos, Pathos*—the alleged difference between right and wrong and how communities discern and even *feel* the differences.

I'm not supposed to remember any of this. The Directorate teaches Sophistry, or the contemporary equivalent of moral relativism; that is, what lawyers learn in school to twist the truth cleverly with words.

Don't forget the Greek philosopher Protagoras who started it all. He believed that "Man is the measure of all things, of the reality of those which are, and the unreality of those which are not," insisting he could make a weak argument sound strong. Protagoras also claimed no one could prove the existence of the gods (making Homer upset, rest his soul). Yet as a child I learned about God as an "invention" of humans, much like religion, the opiate of the masses to prevent people from going apeshit about their diminished lives.

Secretly, I hear a goddess speaking to me in disguises, urging counter-instructions, words about second chances and subtle acts of rebellion. One goddess (Leila Pallas, I call her) tells me, "Don't listen to those dirty old gods, their avatars or their Truthiness. They lust for vengeance and territory, even when they don't need it."

I understand. Leila's voice, a deep contralto, speaks to me especially when I dream. In one recent dream, I've risen up through the exposed rafters of a giant barn (or is it a theatre?), holding the hand of Jesus (or an actor who looks like him). There's no thought of rebellion on my part, either, just rising up, resurrection and happiness holding His hand. I don't know what the dream means; I won't tell anyone.

Because of my impairments, the lower-level directors have always been indulgent toward me, patiently reminding me of my duties. I'm supplied with extra memory and pump support to staunch my "Milk of Amnesia," as the Elders call it. When I was assigned to Bryce, the Singing Directorate recognized my talents for thinking out of the box, so much so that I've turned every holographic problem into a 22-sided origami resembling a crayfish. Elders equate my origami with foreseeing extra political dimensions they haven't thought of—for example, the time I blocked a decision, contrary to *Logoharp* instructions, to cut water and meat rations to constituents in Texas, Oklahoma and Inner Mongolia during severe drought.

> *Dear Citizens! In these rainless times the Directorate has increased rations to alleviate your hunger and thirst. Every family will receive an extra two liters of water and 1,000 more calories of delicious meat, fruits, and veggies each day! However, to stretch available resources, women will be barred from conceiving more children for at least three years, contingent on climate recovery. A Directorate No-Child Policy will be announced shortly.*

My bosses flipped, of course, citing disaster budgets, but when I showed them statistical and PR consequences of alienating or killing off whole segments of the population, they reluctantly agreed.

My superior, Dr. Cheung, chewed on her cigarette, coughing up bloody phlegm but admitting her error. "What fucking choice do I have?" she said. "Naomi broadcasts a *reverse* decision before we can catch her making it!"

After that my superiors showed me a bit more respect. The masses in Mongolia, Texas and Oklahoma began to show genuine appreciation in their neural posts, saying how many existing babies and elders had been saved thanks to Directorate generosity.

But why was I chosen? Why does everyone think I'm prescient? I'm probably not—just a good guesser. Penning a first-grade essay shortly after I learned to read, I predicted the demise of Ameriguan democracy, arguing that it had happened *de facto* a century earlier (the Directorate took note). At age 10 I wrote a letter to the W.H.O. Directorate in Davos, Switzerland, arguing that lethal zoonotic viruses would kill three to five million humans predictably every five to 15 years when global temperatures spiked another 1.5°C.

Correct.

Now the Singing Directorate chooses me for specialized training consults. Today I'm headed to the mid-Pacific luge tunnels to oversee my part in these Exchanges, our Conference entitled "Human Flesh Search—How to Cushion Shock." The tunnels are part of a large network of undersea bypasses facilitating cross-border trade and chat. Mother Country built most of the tunnel infrastructure 50 years ago without partisan backtalk. And to its credit, China has paved the way for access to the world's largest free markets for consumer goods—Ameriguo and Baltica. (Other countries such as Russia, the LatinX South, Sino-Africa, Australia and Oceania are considered secondary markets.)

Our Ameriguan dock workers stationed in ports from Seattle to San Diego inspect these imported goods to weed out corrupt product (mostly drugs, faulty electronics and spoiled food) before sending remainders to assembly centers in the interior, where workers in 10-hour shifts get a wage for making logo and labeling adjustments. Each product gets a stamp: "Processed in Ameriguo 2.0." Only citizens ages 19 to 50, "The Golden 31," as they're called, actually purchase these goods. Teenagers and elders awaiting their respective lottery tickets use proxies for purchasing, as necessary. Underage children, wards of the State, are barred from purchases. However, a robust black market exists, run by teenagers, especially for medical marijuana, human organs and painkillers.

9

NOVEMBER 2118

LUGE BLINDNESS

雪
橇
暗
途

Luging just south of the Molokai Fracture Zone is risky. In the ocean tunnel anteroom just before departure, the Launchers have outfitted me with a decompression helmet resembling a Jules Verne diving hood, one equipped with a digital squawk box to send and receive alerts. The transformers attached to my digits direct the luge along the tunnel switching tracks. I see nothing but dark marine blue without much sea life except for the occasional red waypoint tunnel lights illuminating schools of sardines and Pacific jack mackerel.

Luge blindness (I'm subject to this) is like instrument training in hypersonic flight; the body can't rely on external visual cues for navigation at these speeds. Only pressure readings, depth altimeter, and turn coordination apply. What's more, a traveler must enter a state of near-torpor to produce enough muscle flaccidity to withstand pressures at a half mile below the ocean surface. Sensors monitoring vital functions report to a Molokai Fracture Waypoint, but only when the craft switches to a higher track in emergencies.

To a degree, experienced travelers can control speed by *wishing it* slower or faster. Our wired digits help, but strength training is needed to maintain complete speed control. Steering to alternate tunnels is done by flexing the sled's runners with the calf of each leg and exerting opposite shoulder pressure to the seat's back runners. This is much like the luge sport from Norway. Using G-force rebalancing, we endure steep descents and ascents on our tracks to avoid the mid-Pacific volcanoes and the more dangerous tectonic activity along the Pacific Ring of Fire. The northern luge route takes a traveler from the San Andreas fault to the Aleutian trenches, skirting Kuril-Kamchatka to the Sea of Japan and landing in the free port of Shanghai.

The mid-Pacific route (my route, risky but faster) goes directly through the Molokai Fracture Zone and Necker Ridge past Hawaii *en route* to Magellan Seamounts, the southwest spur of the Mariana Trench. I'm glad I can avoid the spongy dark cyclones roiling over Hawaii and the Philippines. Tunnel traffic has eliminated that; we lie on our backs strapped into our luges, and the network propels us forward at unimaginable speeds.

Even in these luge states I can hear instructions. The Exchanges, I'm told, will feature hundreds of Information Sentinels (the "Ones") from around the world and a few other worlds, too. The exact content of the programming hasn't been announced as yet. Unfortunately, Jens Remker won't be there. Under water I find myself wishing Jens were with me. I love his kind voice, and all his facial angles, triangular lines and Cheshire-cat smile flashing in my mind.

Just now I've received a holo-mail from Jens, a relay of 3D videoclips, documentary style, and, for my amusement, a spongy hologram of the space surgeon himself bouncing around the moon's Aitken basin. The little spaceman cartoon fits inside the palm of my hand. I know he wants to entertain me because he speaks directly in Volk-Sprache, the dialect I'm learning for a possible reassignment to the South Pole lunar mines.

"Hallos Naomi, *ich bin wiederlagen Biophysiker!*"

"Naomi, I'm biophysicist again! Researching far-side lunar plasma and its effects on cellular metabolism." I see his handsomeness in my heads-up display. "How are you, Ms. Gold as Day, Blue as Night?" He's so exuberant, even when his deep baritone wavers during undersea transmission to my headset.

"The moon was supposed to be sterile plate, yaah!" Jens voices, doing a little holo-trick so that the full moon bounces like a yoyo in his avatar's hands. "But instead we've got a swarm of photons from solar wind and distant galactic objects all over the atmosphere. Especially in the South Pole's deep craters ice forms and never melts, so ideal for the miners extracting the titanium and rare earths we need for Jupiter and Titan missions."

He cuts in and out again as my luge tilts 75 degrees toward the Mariana Trench sidewall. Going deeper and darker, his voice strikes me like thunderheads breaking into rainbows. With Jens, I feel a twinge, submerged and half-aware, as I dream of bodily contact. He mentions the discomfort of his space suit in the extreme Aitken cold that dips to -35°C and lower in the caves. Yet all I can think of is bouncing alongside him in my spacesuit, the moon's scant gravity letting me leap 10 kilometers high in a single bound as he grips my hand.

"Miss your amphibious blueness," he messages me.

"I miss your one dimple and square jaw," I reply. "You having fun up there?"

"Better if you come up here."

At Aitken, his team discovered strange spheres of magnetic force, possibly remnants of a comet that slammed into the moon billions of years ago. Perhaps these magnetic forces intensify desire and inclination, a need to merge with others. But this is just speculation on my part.

Jens transmits a video of himself bouncing around Shackelford Crater in a white spacesuit. Though I'm half-dazed with the speed and depth of the water swirling around me, I assume it's really Jens, but maybe not, just an avatar jumping across crevasses on a pogo stick, then plunging into the icy lunar ravines below.

The sight of Jens disappearing disturbs me.

"Naomi, have you tried to fly distances yet?"

"A little. A few leaps and bounces above hoodoos, soccer fields and low-lying buildings."

"Do you think you could ever make it here, to Aitken basin?"

He's so direct. "I hope so Jens, but not right away. The Mariana abyss is approaching, I'm assigned to the Exchanges and I've got to get off."

His breathing interrupts; I hear a catch.

Steeling myself for the absolute darkness—a looming crustal ridge 11,000 meters undersea at its deepest point—I sense the liquefaction of magma, an undersea upwelling of basalts and coarse-grained gabbros, the latter slow-cooled and blackest black. No beginning or end, it seems. The Mariana Trench takes the shape of a crescent scar stretching 2500 kilometers in the western Pacific without traces of life. The luge is flipping me on my side, following a cliff track that stretches 100 kilometers or more. I'm silent, focused on the NAVs, the waypoint lights, the feel of my left shoulder pushing against the backrunner of the luge and my right leg steering opposite hard right. I want to go faster, but feel uneasy with tilting the luge nearly upside down.

Twenty-five kilometers more. Twenty-two...18... I'll message him back on a secure channel, my voice unsteady, when I'm righted again.

Transmission starting in two minutes.

"Jens? You there? At the Exchanges, we have little freedom of movement. Besides, you might be put off by complexion. I show snake scales under stress."

"No worries! Let me know when you arrive safely, Naomi."

He sounds cheerful, signs off.

*

Our Convocation will be held over three nights inside an underground hardened site in Xi'An, home of the terra cotta warriors. We're meeting in a cathedral-sized tumulus and museum known as *Han Yang Ling* (汉 阳 陵 博物馆). Once the afterlife abode of Western Han Emperor Jing Di (景 帝, 188

BCE -141 BCE), the excavated city is 20 kilometers in size and contains 81 underground tunnels. Massive. Aside from his funerary extravagance—he commissioned armies of clay soldiers, farm animals, craftsmen and elegant courtesans to accompany him in death—Jing Di is most famous for putting down the revolt of 154 feudal princes. He subdivided each fiefdom among the princes' sons, who were barred from hiring their own administrators. This re-centralized Jing Di's power. The site today has been hardened to withstand a terrorist attack. Its reinforced steel encasements, doors and valves are designed to relieve bomb blast overpressure, along with filtered ventilation and airlock systems to save those inside.

I suspect the Masters decided on Han Yang Ling to remind every diplomat to seek negotiation with hostile forces. Our Convocation theme this year is "cushioning shock," but the real issue is talking down the excesses of Mother Country's flesh trolls in social media. Many of these trolls are government-inspired vigilantes and doxxers who aim to "out" corrupt celebrities and politicians. I'm watching the first night of the conference on my luge displays now.

Sentinels are gathering inside the atrium. These are a different species altogether, not Reverse Journalists, per se, but champions of fact checking and data accuracy—in other words, researchers who protect State secrets. The early arrivals walk proudly down the tumulus ramp, each one sporting a native hairdo and costume. Some are dressed in armor and silks, outfitted with corncob-pipe headdresses, fruit baskets, peacock feathers and baubles reminiscent of Beijing Opera. Others carry laser swords and scabbards to indicate their military preparedness. Arms held wide, palms up, toes pointed, torso facing front, head rotated to the side, each sentinel adopts the "Egyptian style" of presentation for the cameras. Lively *hu chin* and *pipa* music is piping up; singers and instrumentalists play a Chinese *canzonetta*. Each sentinel hops, skips and jives to the beat, their dancing silhouettes reflected against the museum glass displays.

Wait a minute.

Police have descended on Mr. Jerzy Chao, an environmentalist well-known in Jiangsu. He was supposed to be one of our chosen speakers, describing how RJs and sentinels can responsibly disclose the crimes of corporate insiders feasting on government "sweets" (bribes).

Apparently, the trolls have doxxed him again for some new crime. They're spreading "evidence" that he's been extorting local chemical polluters by threatening to expose them. Never mind that they've turned Lake Tai, a source of drinking water for 10 million people, into a scummy pond. "Chao has confessed," my sources message me. "He's likely to reveal even more information when he's deprived of food and water for five days."

My *Logoharp* hasn't register this reversal of fortune in detectable tones. If it did, I'm too distracted to pay attention.

I'm guessing Chao is partially innocent (maybe he took *some* money), but he's an easy target. The police drag him out of the mausoleum while the doxxers have their field day, "skinning his flesh" with nonsense verbiage and undocumented claims online. Conference attendees stoically watch the giant digital screens. A few murmurs. We're seeing naked text and emojis from the doxxers scrolling across the screen like it's the end of days.

*

I feel nauseous, a little unsteady. Perhaps it's the rapid lurching of the luge along these upside-down Mariana cliff tracks. Or it's my feeling that the doxxers will win again despite our efforts to calm them down.

Sure, I was hoping once to report about political events and personalities *after* they were given fair analysis and vetting. But now "news" has lost its sense of contingency. It's all projection, gut reaction, crowd panic, venom, making our jobs even harder.

My work—the work of all of the RJs and sentinel researchers who back us with data—is to assure that every political event seems true, believable. Our scripted events proceed with such organic force that all social actors, even those unaware they are participating, become shocked, then incredulous, as the events unfold. Those who read and view the event as "news" swear it could never have happened. Yet it does. Okay? Then why wasn't I informed in advance about Jerzy Chao's demise? Who is responsible? Apparently, there is so much infighting among our media groups that it's nearly impossible to trace the source.

Illusions die hard, of course.

For example, even before Reverse Journalism was created, half the world mused/believed the American moon landing of 1969 "never happened." (It did, of course, but quite a few conspiracy theorists argued the "landing" took place on a Hollywood soundstage.) In 2034, the second Tian An Men democracy demonstrations "never happened" because State-sponsored hackers and doxxers wiped out every trace in social media. Vaccines designed under emergency conditions became "works of the devil." Another example: In 2013, North Korea's Kim Jung Un, called "Fat Boy" and "Rocket Man" by Western politicians, never had his China-savvy uncle executed. These historical reports were false, just stupid inventions of the global media, people said. However, all the actors in these non-events eventually behaved in exact accordance with the script. How did this work?

Shortly after Kim Jong Un and his tribunal allegedly executed his wayward uncle Jang Song Thaek, Thaek, branded by Kim as traitorous scum worse than a dog, inexplicably reappeared at a Pyongyang benefit for starving dogs. He was alive, and the rumors of his death were obviously untrue. But by the time the press noted his reappearance, Kim Jong Un had decided to *feed* Thaek to the starving dogs, many of them Rottweilers and Greyhounds. The Rotts and Greys feasted as children attending the event jumped up and down to see the dogs slobbering and fighting over Thaek's tough meat and bones! The event drew millions of witnesses through pre-scribed video channels, and the script held true. The electorate, at first skeptical of Jang's death, soon celebrated it, writing big-character posters and staging dance contests featuring children and dogs dressed in matching glittery boots. At last, the starving mutts' health and nutrition were partially restored through donations at the contests. Kim Jong Jun satisfied his beloved citizens with "moral entertainment."

These "non-events" that become actual events illustrate our new reality. Following the Directorate's theory of *unintentional contradiction*, the actors in every story, both elites and minors, routinely perform just as the reverse algorithms predict.

I realize my ability to understand the rationale behind these *guided* predictions is limited. I'm sure there is one—a rationale, that is. My job is merely to ensure the smooth progression of history without asking trivial questions. Steering events as my *Logoharp* envisions them helps maintain our society's shockless cushion.

At times I feel ashamed, contaminated by the work I do. Teacher Bai's words reverberate inside me. How do I explain to Jens or anyone else what I do? Won't they want details? How do I manage these flesh trolls and doxxers, or just ordinary citizens unaware of what's going on? I truly want to reason it out, but have no adequate explanation while I'm luging in this bottomless sea.

*

I'm nearing the end of my journey above the ocean crust. I'll be late to the Convocation; maybe I'll just have to chime in virtually. At Magellan Seamounts, my luge swings north, catapulting me to higher ground in the Philippine Sea, bypassing Taiwan, my old haunt. Yet with the century's sea level rise and the presence of the ocean levees outside every major port, even the fittest luge traveler emerges exhausted, shaky. At Shanghai Port I decompress for five hours before my weight and synaptic composition return to normal. Only then am I free to remove my helmet and take the elevators to the surface.

10

DECEMBER 2118

MEETING MIRANDA IN SHANGHAI

亲
爱
的
朋
友

Miranda—her given name is Qian Shuai (her given name "*Shuai*" 帅 in Chinese means "handsome" or "graceful," and she is)—is my accidental friend in Shanghai. She waits for me in the cloak room five levels above the Free Port Hyperbaric Chamber. Shuai always arranges a parlay and meal for us in a Shanghai *hutong* (胡同) when I come to visit. I always see her at least once, even if I'm supposed to show up on assignment elsewhere.

Lithe as a string bean, Miranda is always running toward sunsets. Her loves include old-fashioned bookstores and Chinese *hutongs* still out of sight from the watchmen with their noodle stalls. The modern antique of a Greek–Chinese restaurant she chooses this time has teak staircases decorated with tacky paintings of Mykonos windmills. The WC boasts a porcelain sink and flush toilet. The place smells of cedar shelves heaped with Swedish coffee, treats and stuffed animals (mostly koala bears and pandas). When I meet her there, I relax, feeling I've arrived safely under her watch. Yet in a few moments our dinner will be interrupted; directives bubble up red in my retinal display. I'm shortly to see my colleague, Dean Cheung, who has plans for me in Hong Kong. I may never get to the Xian Exchanges after all, but I'll be required to screen all the "Cushioning Shock" seminars and recordings to determine how to "play" the Jerzy Chao incident to the masses.

"What have you been up to?" I ask her.

"Writing bitterness," she teases, dividing up the moussaka and pineapples that we share, though normally I don't eat much.

"Last time I saw your byline, you'd written about capital redistribution in small Hunan and Hubei villages, yes?" She smiles, acknowledging my attention. "The story was about landlords forced to give up fifteen percent of their property to the poor. Also, villages holding local elections, even chasing corrupt managers out of town with baseball bats."

"That was the past," she replies. "Everything's been replaced by lotteries. Remember? You gave me that Shirley Jackson play, to teach me about *The Lottery.* Then you broadcast the baseball-bat story for your Western readers."

"Yeah, I loved the antic violence," I tell her. "It sounds like the Directorate is endorsing something like true socialism. Or rule by committee. Which almost sounds like someone is endorsing free will. I thought we were supposed to make free will seem unattractive in our news stories and announcements, right? To expand the influence of the National Council."

"We only have to make unattractive the folks who try to speak against the Council," she says.

Miranda likes to challenge me; she can be a little harsh sometimes. She once said that I had been rude and even cruel to Marco Hsu Yang, not understanding him, and that this was why he left me.

"What are you writing about now?"

"Monsters," she said, sipping her tea.

"You mean the renegades opposed to the ideals of Great-Great-Grandfather Xi?"

"No! The monsters of Shanghai, Beijing and Heilongjiang."

"The kind that forces others to burn themselves alive?"

"The kind that sees no other way to get their points across."

In the late twentieth and early twenty-first century, Miranda went on, her long hair remarkably jet and shiny in the candlelight, rural people were setting themselves on fire when local governments and real estate barons had grabbed their homes and farms to build condos and shopping centers. More recently, *chai* (拆), the demolishing of rural homes and property without owners' consent, along with self-immolation as protest, have become rare events. However, last week Miranda was summoned to the bedside of a girl who nearly burned herself to death when her parents were taken away. For five days Miranda sat at her bedside, recording her story. Shanghai officials said that she would be sent to work in the Kamchatka tunnels. Even with her easy job as a token taker, she didn't want to go.

"What happened to her parents?"

She grimaced. "No idea. She regrets what she did. Realizes she was spoiled, and shouldn't have taken it out on herself. She wants others to learn from her experience, so she agreed to let me write her story."

Miranda cocks her head and swings her long neck around to glance behind her. Fortunately, the outer tables behind us are empty, so we're reasonably sure not to be overheard.

I stare into the candle flickering on the table. She offers me a stuffed grape leaf dolmade, her crooked-tooth smile bursting through a tiny window in my heart. I think of a picture we took together, the two of us at a Christmas party during her appearance a few years ago at The Culture Playground, one of her favorite foreign haunts, my arm encircling her tiny waist.

"Your hair's longer than I remember."

She squeezes my natural hand.

"Lighting matches doesn't solve anyone's problems," she says pointedly.

"Are you still smoking?"

"No, I've reformed."

"How can the girl talk? She must have been badly burned."

"Her speech is fine, but she's blind. The firemen smothered her with chemicals and put her in a hyperbaric chamber. Like you!"

"Like me?"

"You're always too eager to get here, Naomi! I've watched you nearly pass out because you ascend too fast."

"I'm a little claustrophobic," I tell her, lifting my face plate to take a mouthful of food. "I don't mind the joint pain or a few bubbles in my blood stream."

She frowns suddenly, bites her lip; my *Logoharp* registers a dissonance.

"What are you doing about the flesh trolls, Naomi?"

"It's a new responsibility."

"You must rein them in."

"The Directorate sanctions them."

"They go too far. Eating people alive, their reputations, at least."

I stop eating. Take her hand. "You're a real journalist. No one will harm you. Not if I have anything to say about it."

She gawks at me; I sound stupidly, falsely heroic. A ding in my ears, as though a message should arrive, but doesn't. Watching her endlessly upturned mouth and eyes, I envy her. I fear, too, that someone will condemn her liveliness in ways that can't be named.

She gets up, sweeping the floor with thin spidery legs as she heads to the condiments table. She wears a body stocking, a pert Scottish kilt, a heavy sweater; she's Chinese Modigliani.

"I can't figure out why the government would throw so many resources at recidivists like this girl when so many otherwise healthy ones just disappear," she says.

"The others are of age."

"You mean 50 years and above?"

"Yes, according to the law. Fifty-five is elderly, beyond retirement. It's true in both our countries. Besides, I haven't seen you in three years," I remind her. "Do I look old? I'm almost 26 in Earth years. Hybrid cyborgs age much faster."

"You're not old!" she laughs. "Except you have a few lines around your mouth when you frown."

Touché.

"You're a cockeyed optimist," I rejoin. "But I'll be decommissioned soon enough. Most of the old Ameriguans are getting camping kits and archery sets or shotguns when they reach retirement age. They're instructed to disappear into the northern forests. They'll take trains or transports in the air tunnels. Me, too, I expect."

"Oh, no! You'll get an extension! At least five years," she retorts. "You're not going anywhere yet."

I study her flawless skin.

"How do you manage to stay so youthful? You haven't aged at all," I tell her.

She giggles, shyly. "My boyfriend Liu left for Urumqi since two years," she says, stumbling. "I mean two years ago. When he came back he took all of his things."

"But you have this Gua Gua."

"Yeah, he looks like a squashed melon."

"You should go to Baltica."

"No, it's okay. I like living here."

I'm reminded that Miranda is making a reputation in China as a filmmaker. Most documentarians create fictional stories taken from a government-approved script, incident or personality. She attempts, at least, to insert tidbits of factual history to make fun of her critics.

The first time I met her in a Beijing bookstore literary event, she wasn't happy, between jobs, and feeling unrecognized. She surprised me with nearly fluent English and a knowing laugh, so much so that I knew we would become friends. At the book store her friend Maya got into a shouting match with a British author discussing his Gaia hypothesis. He claimed Gaia (biological systems of Earth) would easily absorb all the trash and shit that nine billion people had spewed into Earth's water, land and air. Mind you, this conversation took place in the second most polluted city in the world (Delhi is still the first). Every night the stars are obscured by boas of diesel exhaust, coal dust, sulfur and oils, where the smell of rotten eggs and sewage is often so pervasive it infiltrates the trains coming in from Tianjin.

Miranda is only mildly concerned about pollution. But when I met her, she was distracted by her breakup with a long-term boyfriend who bit his nails and refused to marry her on "principle."

With me, and I assume most foreign cyborgs, she never stops laughing. The second time we met, again at the bookstore, we walked to the train to meet a 11 p.m. Beijing curfew. "Gua Gua is my newest," she told me. "He's a White Tigers inspector sexbot nine years my junior. Don't forget, I'm a *sheng nu* (剩女), *leftover woman*,'" to which I shake my head, then hug her tightly.

"Your crush won't be your last," I assure her.

In truth, Miranda is hopelessly devoted to her craft. She plans to take me to Harbin's City of Ice, its annual festival that began 200 years ago. Harbin in winter is still a wonderland of ice sculptures, pagodas and snow penguins. Artisans make exact replicas of galleons made of ice, along with medieval Scottish fortresses right out of *Ivanhoe*. I check my monitor; tonight it's -25°C in Harbin, a temperature ensuring the festival will run for a few more weeks at least. Miranda shows me the digital read-out on her Iris pad. She plans to film the festival and all the displaced souls inhabiting Harbin throughout the winter.

"We can go to the river and watch the families skating and pushing the carriages of the elders," she said.

"Please explain this to me?"

"It's part of a ritual, families giving offerings and saying goodbye to old ones who ride in a cryopod, a kind of ice carriage, as though they're babies again," she says.

Miranda Qian Shuai has heard rumors that some of the elders get up and walk away from the pods, escaping across Harbin's frozen river, the Songhua, to the other side, traipsing North to *Mo He*. I'm not sure any of this is true, but she plans to take me to the Ice Festival soon.

*

After dinner we stroll for an hour along the freezing Bund and take selfies together with Pudong and the Huangpu River in the background. Her silicone-gray pea jacket and Russian toque are warm against my heavy latticed armor. For once, the Shanghai night is crystal clear—a rare event—and the Pearl of the Orient TV Tower thrusts upward like a spaceship on fire. I realize Miranda is the journalist I wanted to be. She is only mildly critical of her environment and, most important, she's human entirely, not a transplant mash-up.

We hug goodbye. Lingering a moment. In the darkness I wait for a transport that will take me across the Huangpu to the whirling needle of the TV tower. There's a heliport/VTOL port at the top, making it possible for me to fly direct to cities all over China, including Hong Kong. I'll fly in a compression cockroach skating along the Huangpu, seeing never-before-seen-chunks of ice on the river. Both the east and west banks, Pudong and Puxi, are covered in white. There's no mistaking these fluctuations in the atmosphere.

11

DECEMBER 2118

THE CHINESE MACBETH

黄
土
王
冠

Soaring over Fujian, Xiamen, Shantou and the flats of South China, I see thousands of white windmills, all suspended on top of soaring vertical piles of steel. The mills seem to chop up the sky. Presumably thousands of white gulls have been chopped up, too, though I see no swarms; perhaps the gulls are getting smarter.

Revving south, we pass a string of green pearls and sand-blasted islands, the remnants of Hong Kong—230 islands in all; though more than two dozen of them have disappeared beneath the rising seas. The most important islands have been shored up, their centers entirely airborne thanks to the network of supporting piles and vortices allowing the rising seas to flow underneath the islands but not to engulf them. The districts in the peaks of Hong Kong—Sunset, Lantau, and Victoria Peak—have been flattened and extended into floating farms and skywalks with green rooftops. No more conventional hills or roads on the main island. Escalators and VTOLs move millions of people up and down as needs dictate.

Dean Cheung Yuen is waiting for me in her offices at the University Forum overlooking Victoria Harbor. Retired, she still has direct connections to the leadership in Beijing and Shanghai. Soaring on her past reputation as an investigative reporter, she likes to party in Budapest, Rio, New York, Cairo and Johannesburg. Everyone loves the tiny windblown journalist who ties a rainbow of strings around her assistants' fingers to remind them of all the things she's asked them to do.

She greets me with a bear hug.

"Naomi, 你还是那么年轻! Amazing! You look so young!"

I bow and thank her. "You look very young, too."

"I doze off five minutes every hour!"

"Maybe that's your secret."

"Maybe...but I'm an insomniac," she says. "I do diligence twenty-four-seven but never sleep except on jets!"

I try to imagine a sleepless wolverine.

Dean Cheung crinkles her nose and waves her hands above her head to express important thoughts, as though she is twitching in a hip-hop rave. She has impeccable rhythm.

"I have two possible assignments for you," she says. "One, conventional; the other a little more imaginative."

"There's a choice?"

"We'll talk about it later."

"Later? Why not now? How's it going here?"

"Fine. Except a gazillion people want to get into our program."

"Well, people have wanted to get into Hong Kong universities since forever."

"No. I mean our program. It's specialized, very popular. Lots of young people want to get into our field."

"Why not? We're specialists in 'He said, she said' journalism."

"That's not what we do. That's not all that we do."

"Of course not." I find myself feeling brave enough to confront her. Something about this 4-foot-11-inch journalist celebrity and her globetrotting reputation cows me, but I go on. "Cheung Yuen, real journalism ended seventy-five years ago."

"What do you mean, Naomi? Journalism is being reinvented. We're reinventing it right here to work for our times!"

"Oh, you mean reporting events that never actually happened, but will, like the dissolution of my country."

"No, not at all," she says, shaking her head, then pulling on little hairs at the base of her chin, a gesture that makes me want to whip out tweezers. "We never describe our RJ program that way. We call it 'Ob–Sub reporting.' Objective and subjective. Times past shape the future, of course; and the future revises our outlook on the past. Young people believe their journalism still has an impact on people's attitudes and even their defense of human rights. Only the elite learn how to script probable outcomes in the second half of the program."

"You mean, what I do."

"Something like what you do, when you're not too intense about it…not letting those atavistic emotions get to you. What are you working on now?"

"Reviewing a revisionist history projected forward, as you instructed me in advance of this meeting. About a love triangle—a fallen leader and his wife and her lover who arranged the murder of a powerful foreigner."

"That's an old story, but relevant to our thinking today. One that keeps repeating itself."

"Maybe because people haven't gotten the point."

"People get the point," she says. "But they like an *entertaining* story."

"Okay," I accede, feeling a jamming in my heart. "I remember, Cheung Yuen, a bunch of the students signing a petition saying that I didn't know enough about holographic journalism so why the hell was I running your simulator."

"They said you didn't know enough technology."

"You gave me that assignment. I didn't want it."

"You had technical assistants to help you. Some of the evaluations were devastating."

Cheung Yuen never minces words.

"You've reminded me of my failings before. You fired me for them, remember?"

"I had to at the time. Still—"

"Still what?"

"You're not afraid of making adjustments; you're good at perfecting those dithering translations and adjustments of crowd behavior the scripters have to make up. The older students, especially, grow cocky in their prime, dismiss you as stupid and old hat."

"I am old hat. The surgeries advanced my time line. I'm older and crankier than I was."

"Naomi, dear!" She strokes my latex cheek. "I've passed my time and I'm still here! You can, too. But I think you would've had a better experience in teaching if you'd stuck to the script. At least some of your students praised your skills... the conceptualization, use of pyramids. They said you're a caring teacher, except when you go off half-cocked with your historical theories about dictators and their vendettas! Anyway, some of the students felt cheated. You read their reviews."

"No actually, I didn't."

"You should."

"I'm aware of my ratings. What do you want of me?" My eyes harden. "I'm tempted to say you're working me for a lower price."

"Not at all!" Her eyes go soft, as though she can absorb all my *qi*.

"You told me yourself, you have to be rich to come here," I remind her. "All of these kids have parents who work for the National Council or the higher-level Directorates. These folks get cushy subsidies so their kids can also work in the same positions they have. The less successful ones work for nanotech journals or do corporate service for the thirty-odd years before they're put on ice."

Cheung Yuen nods. She's good at patronizing me.

"Until they're supposed to be put on ice, but somehow stay warm. They get vacation time," she says. "Usually in Hainan, Tibet or the Italian Riviera. Extension time! Thanks to our system, they end up doing exactly the opposite of what they intended to do at first, yet feel very satisfied. That's how Reverse Journalism works."

"They have a purpose, in other words."

"Naturally. They shape our public events."

"Desirable ones. The past is reverse-engineered to create a future of acceptable memories. Then we project forward."

Cheung grabs my shoulders. "You sound like one of those 'democracy drones.' Stand up straight, Naomi! Why such resignation in your voice? Come on!" she says, now patting me lightly on my gloved synthetic hand. "I wanted it to be otherwise many years ago. But you can't fight City Hall. Are you upset about your parents? You should pay them a visit."

"I won't have time. My mother's gone now—you know that? Last I heard she was reassigned to a reeducation camp in Aleutia. I guess because of her 'rebellious' thoughts. My father, too, reported dead, thought I don't believe it. Both my parents had the uncanny ability to infer many sides of a story. My mother had an accident before her relocation."

"What kind of accident?"

"I wasn't informed."

"Your father?"

"Living in Hokkaido. Not sure where in Hokkaido. He's reported missing."

"Perhaps you can bring him home with a little help." She raises a brow, checking my reaction, which is null on the face of it.

"I have something more urgent to discuss with you, Naomi. There's considerable unrest around Heilongjiang, in Manchuria," she rejoins. "People are starting to complain."

"Ah." A pause. "So that's why you called me here?"

"Maybe. But you might recall the two indispensable catechisms. I can't have any journalist, even a senior RJ, who forgets." She pauses. "The two catechisms are—?"

"What? You're asking me to recite them?"

"Yes, please."

I stand at attention and put my hand over my half heart, the *Logoharp* speaking for me, pre-recorded:

"Catechism number one: All stories are framed and scripted before the event takes place in order to ensure the best of all possible outcomes."

"And two?"

"The responsibility of the predictive journalist is not to seek the truth in random events, but only the truth of probable outcomes. A coin toss—"

"What's this 'coin toss' part?"

"My statistical training."

"There!" she smiles. "Don't you feel better?"

"No, not really." I clutch my throat. The Directorate no doubt is jamming my *Logoharp* to quell resistance.

"I have no other suitable candidates for these jobs right now," she said. "I have to decide if you'll do." She thinks a moment, pulling those chin hairs. "Anyway, there's been a lot of unrest in Manchuria, as I said. The State is reporting an imbalance between the numbers of children born and the elders in the lottery. Not enough elders, in other words. Too many have been getting merit awards and life extensions. Lots of whining in social media."

"You've called on me to fix it?"

"I'm sure you can! But this may not be the best use of your time. The rebellious elders with open mouths end up being quite cut out."

"You mean they get ice therapy."

"For most. It chills their resistance!"

She yucks. Big yellow-stained cigarette fangs exposed in a tiny O-shaped mouth. Pausing a moment to see my reaction.

"I've had a similar experience," I nod, inviting her into my story. "The other detainees carry it out, never the police. They force you to kneel on the ground next to the toilet while your cellmates drip freshets of ice water on your head so it's drizzled down your back until your body completely locks up. Then they make sure your head is slammed against the sink. In most cases your front teeth are shattered."

I open my mouth.

"That's what happened to you?"

"Yes, my teeth, now repaired. I was disobedient in very early training. Of course, you can read all about these punishments in *The Beijing-New York Times*."

*

For me, reviewing the archives is just a matter of inserting a nanochip inside my left ear and flipping sonically through microfiche. As RJs, we have these privileges.

"If you don't cooperate after punishment, you end up in a frozen fort in *Mo He* at −35°C with a couple of army blankets and rancid oil for your gruel cooked on a Bunsen burner."

"You speak so bluntly," Cheung Yuen says, wagging her finger at me. "Have you never learned the art of nuance? No one's blunt here! I'm as Chinese as anyone, but we never say things so bluntly! Don't oversimplify what you can't understand."

"I do understand, Yuen." I try to breathe deeply; a pause in the rhythm of argument. My *Logoharp* is interfering with the deep action of my left lung.

"Dean Cheung," I manage, "you know me well. You value my bluntness. It's such a foil for yours! And you're also Ameriguan. Remember, 'Ameriguan' in Chinese roughly translates to 'Beautiful Crown' *Meili de huangguan* (美丽的皇冠). You reported the transition of our country three decades ago. China is still so complicated that no one can ever begin to understand all 5,123 years of its history."

"How much do you know?" she challenges, clicking her tongue a little, a habit I find perturbing. "How much history?"

If you mean which dynasty or emperor waged war on whom, and the concubines he acquired, I know the basics. But lately I've read more literature than history."

"Good, then you're familiar with the tragic story of Macbeth."

"*Macbeth*?! Of course. As young people, my parents were actors. They read me Shakespeare and I must have seen at least ten versions of *Macbeth* on old reels. But that's a Western story. What does it have to do with Heilongjiang?"

"It doesn't." She lies.

"What about the ice fields? Do you have any news?"

"Table it for awhile," she says, glancing down at a plastic container on her desk.

I see half a dozen splotchy blue eggs with chicken cloaca crusts on them. "Here, have a couple!" Cheung offers, picking out the two fattest ones. "They're delicious, from a student whose family has a little farm in Guangxi."

"Cheung," I sigh. "I can't carry them back to my hostel without breaking them."

"You break everything!" she laughs, forcing the eggs into my open hands. "This priority assignment is about 'Chinese Macbeth.' We must improvise on this story to make a political point. One of our algorithmic leaders has to be removed from office and tried for his crimes. Are you familiar with the 'model' story of a rising political hotshot and his loony wife who murdered a foreigner?"

"What?"

"That's Chinese Macbeth!"

"And what about Heilongjiang?"

"Save it. Just wait."

"The two are related, of course. Why pretend they're not?"

"You need to focus all your attention on the new Chinese Macbeth! Your task is to unveil his criminal record and chaotic thoughts. He's an addicted gambler and has a sordid history with women. We need your flesh trolls to out this bastard before you can tackle Heilongjiang. The latter is complicated."

"Not as complicated as you, Dean Cheung!" I gasp. "Yeah, I've heard rumors. But what about this 'Chinese Macbeth?' Wasn't he modeled after the dead princeling 'Beaux' as we called him? He lived in Dalian a century ago and was rich, daring and Westernized. Actually, his story is more or less the substrate for the historical project you asked me to review. But what does this have to do with me?"

"Play a game of holo-dominoes and you'll find out," Cheung replies, snapping her tiny nicotine-stained fingers. "Seems you display deep-seated sympathies for Chinese elite men who seem like Western gamblers to the rest of us."

She's researched my history.

"Start tomorrow," Cheung continues. "Please stay in the dorms tonight and for the next week or so. Rest. You'll get further instructions in the holo-cave. I believe you're well suited for this assignment!"

12

JANUARY 2119

THE TRAGIC TALE OF BEAUX AND GOO

悲
剧
故
事

New Year's has passed. Everyone here has family, bustling to-do lists. I have Hong Kong's clouds, an advancing knowledge of how *The Logoharp* alters my brain. The harp relies on Universal Augmented Intelligence (UAI), its state-of-the-art Large Language Models (LLMs) and the more mysterious musical compositions whose sources I can't identify. I've seen the MRIs of my brain, now expanded to nearly double the nor-mal size. Machine learning is like an army of intelligent worms invading, altering my thoughts; a sense of reality and dreams beyond ordinary imagining. But not always distinguishable.

I have headaches. Throbbing constantly. Too much noise in the available channels, insufficient filtering. Too few simple melodies and lines of code.

I long for the clarity of turquoise and sunset skies over Bryce, my home, or wherever home is supposed to be. Perhaps I miss Miranda and Jens.

I don't play with holo-dominoes anymore, either, and haven't since the age of six. Dean Cheung is talking in riddles. She's forcing my *Logoharp* to envision personal dominoes in my past, watching the younger dominoes fall in juicy little wavelets and s-curves until the last piece drops and I reach an acceptable conclusion. Acceptable, that is, to her.

Confession: I've never watched a titillating episode of holo-dominoes on video that ended up fulfilling a dramatic purpose. Never. But I've seen, even created, titillating episodes that ended up ruining people's lives.

A memory. When I was an intern reporter in Michigania, I got a little town riled up by describing how the locals welcomed a clutch of Southeast Asian war refugees by donating housing, food and paper flowers to add "spots of color" to their dreary apartments. As a budding reporter, I described the "anytown" appearance of Pleasanton's streets, squat little groceries, drug stores and beaten-up roads as typical leftover

Ameriguo, somewhat "podunk" (my word) in tone. When the migrants finally arrived, I announced that the "real town" of Pleasanton was actually a paragon of generosity, kindness and local spirits. But the townspeople never forgave me for that one word, "podunk." It was a naïve, stupid choice, one of many I'd come to regret.

*

Media titillation is like dropping a pebble in a lake and watching it produce concentric wavelets, little molecules of gossip that become memes. A crescendo of memes acts like a transverse wave eventually breaking on the shores of public opinion. Citizens react with denial, jokes, criticism, flippant dismissal or approbation. The effect becomes pounding, then intrusive.

Resurrecting a story about Chinese Macbeth or other fallen heroes is a case of media titillation. But when Cheung Yuen summons me to her holo-cave and its wrap-around media room (the hexagonal screens resembling the compound eyes of a fly), I feel especially uneasy.

Two images: a quizzical, handsome dude with thick black hair and eyebrows titled "Beaux." He's pictured hugging his Jackie Kennedy-lookalike wife, Goo, an attractive, clever Chinese attorney. Another figure on the screen to the right is partially blurred out. I believe he's the current target. Cheung says he's a disgraced "algorithmic architect" who has violated National Security protocols. This figure seems to have cords

135

of gray hair, a sly smile and a triangular, high–cheek–boned face pitted with acne.

I suspect the architect is typical cannon fodder for warring officials who want to defoliate the opposition. But why drum up an old story of greed, murder and romance to service a new one? Maybe someone thinks historical tales of corruption uniquely entertain the masses. This story is recounted in our archived obituaries.

Rise and Fall of the Jack and Jackie Kennedy of China

In the early 21st century, a Chinese politician dubbed "Beaux" for his good looks and bespoke style of Western dress quickly rose to become a New Left Star.

As governor of Liaoning Province, Beaux played a critical role in the Northeastern Revitalization campaign and earned membership in the Central Committee of the Communist party.

Beaux staged anti-corruption campaigns with his wife, Ms. Goo. Goo was beautifully put together, so square-jawed and stylishly dressed she was nicknamed the "Jackie O of China." The couple appeared with groups of children at Red Rallies, singing patriotic songs and extolling Chairman Mao and the virtues of uninterrupted revolution.

Meanwhile, political opponents claimed Beaux had implemented a sweeping, involuntary organ-donation campaign targeted at *Falun Gong*, a rogue spiritual group reported to number as many as 70 million Chinese. At one point Interpol indicted Beaux for crimes against humanity, but he was never caught or brought to trial. In 2012 Beaux was on tap to become a member of the elite Politburo Standing Committee in the Party's 18th National Congress. Some thought he'd rise to the top post as Party Secretary.

But then Goo, reputed to be jealous and extremely volatile, having suffered extreme poverty and humiliation during the Cultural Revolution, engineered the murder of a "fixer" in her employ, Mr. N.H., a British businessman. Allegedly, foreign businesses had to go through N.H. and Ms. Goo's law firm to gain access to China's coveted markets. Goo's firm charged extravagant fees for privileged access.

When police arrested her, Goo claimed N.H. had threatened to hurt her son, Gua Gua, when she refused to pay an unspecified bribe for his child-minding services in Oxford, England, where Gua attended university.

The Briton had apparently agreed to be a front for Ms. Goo when she purchased a £2 million "corruption villa" on the French Riviera after leaving husband Beaux for good. (Beaux had a reputation for chasing everything in a skirt.) In addition to taking 800 million yuan from high-brow clients and public coffers, Goo signed over half her interest in the French villa to N.H. in 2007, allegedly to protect her husband's anti-corruption reputation. But when rental incomes ran low, Goo wanted full villa ownership back, and N.H. refused, demanding a £1.4 million commission for his half of the sale. Goo testified he threatened Gua Gua's life if she didn't pay up.

Goo and a bodyguard agreed to meet up with the Briton fixer at a hilltop hotel in Chongqing for negotiations. When N.H arrived, Goo allegedly served him drinks laced with potassium cyanide. Investigators called to the hotel 26 hours later attributed the foreigner's death to alcohol poisoning, but no autopsy ensued. Media reports suggested a former police chief under Beaux, Mr. Wang, had taken heart blood from the victim's body and realized the Briton had been poisoned.

Goo was arrested and Beaux was also placed under house arrest. When Inspector Wang confronted Beaux, his boss, with evidence of Goo's involvement in N.H.'s murder, Beaux slapped him in the face, accusing him of lying for political advantage. The police chief, said to be in love with Ms. Goo and already under investigation for hiring a cadre of mini-skirted police officers for personal protection, ran to the local American consulate pleading for his life. The consulate turned him back to the Chinese courts. Wang divulged many details of Beaux and Goo's crimes, and the fate of the three was sealed.

Poor Ms. Goo! Her hands shook constantly, allegedly from drinking poison delivered in her tea from unnamed co-conspirators. Pleading for leniency, Goo confessed. She murdered N.H. and testified that Beaux knew all about the family's extravagant overseas businesses. Beaux denied everything, accusing Goo of being completely crazy, a liar under stress.

*

I regard Beaux as a tragic figure—in many ways a "Chinese Macbeth," and Goo as "Lady Macbeth," as Cheung suggests. Sadly, Beaux, a Princeling son, had been tortured and beaten during the Cultural Revolution. He bore scars on his hands and back. Ms. Goo nearly starved to death, begging on the streets in the 1970s and working for a butcher before her luck changed and she was able to attend university and law school thanks to powerful friends.

But why would Cheung want me to model the downfall of an algorithmic architect with the story of Chinese Macbeth? Was there a murder? An ambitious woman? A police inspector?

I have nagging doubts. First, historically speaking, I've read that the original Beaux was a convenient fall guy, the victim of a sudden paroxysm of group conscience leading up to the 18th National Party Congress. As in every other Congress, the Party performed a thorough house cleaning to streamline its ranks, particularly to belch out dissidents and outliers.

Though I can't argue with history, I don't want to create trumped-up charges for nothing. I have to pore through thousands of holo-files, speeches, recordings and wiretaps, assembling a dossier of this new character's papier-mâché accomplishments, his 3 a.m. nightmares and sexual trans-gressions. The flesh trolls on social media will follow my instructions and strip him bare. I'll *prove* he's taken massive bribes, parked his villa in France or Qatar, murdered a for-eigner—or at least his wife or mistress has. Even worse, the architect (I'll call him Beaux II) has secretly devised a flaw in a system critical to Mother Country's security, but why? He's hiding, I'm told, a fugitive who disappears in and out of hats and alternate dimensions. Perhaps accused of crimes that haven't even happened yet?

I feel dizzy, sick to my stomach. The holo-cave is spinning in circles.

In truth (I whisper this to myself), I am attracted to Western-style cowboys and gamblers. The historic Beaux was smooth, animated, impressive in his expensive bespoke suits, not like the typical party hacks. I wouldn't like Jens to know about Beaux or this assignment. He will be disillusioned, although maybe he has an inkling already. Why can't I shield him from my dirty memes?

Dean Cheung tells me all memes are irreversible. I know she'll provide a few more details but won't say too much, en-couraging my creativity, shirking interference with my harp's predictive powers so that my vision remains absolutely clear.

I hate this. First, she tells me to investigate the algorithmic architect, but now I've gotten a message to check out the Harbin Ice Festival. Apparently, there's a connection between the architect, the *Laws of Ice* and what goes on among Heilongjiang (Black Dragon) ice worshipers.

I wish I knew exactly what Cheung was talking about.

13

FEBRUARY 2119

ICE SWIMMERS

冰
泳

Miranda Qian Shuai is messaging me. As an *RJ* with connections to Dean Cheung Yuen, I've been cleared to accompany her on assignment to describe the winter rituals at the Harbin Ice Festival in Manchuria. Another diversion. Miranda has gotten her wish; she says she can't wait to host me.

The seat of activity at the Ice Festival is the frozen Songhua River, the biggest branch of the mighty Heilongjiang "Black Dragon" River extending 1900 kilometers. This evening Songhua's shores appear frosted, layer-cake white, on my screens; even the stands of blue spruce and pine are frozen in glittery rime. Miranda tells me that her best friend Lang Fei, from

Computational Security, will meet us to explore, though she's not sure exactly how or when.

"How do you know Dean Cheung Yuen?" I ask.

"I'm a reporter, remember?" she replies.

There are so many links between the Directorate and leading documentarians and reporters throughout China that "pairings" of assignments and desired locations are automatically made.

"So it's not a coincidence?"

"No," she replies. "It's not." She says no more.

*

"Lang fei" (浪费) in Chinese means "waste," or "waste of space." Miranda giggles when she explains this to me, dragging a suitcase behind her as we descend from a Volokopter ramp in face-numbing cold.

"Fei likes to tell bathroom jokes about failed attempts to mount girls who are as pretty as 'little Capuchin monkeys,'" she says. "He's told me, 'There are times I try to climb on top of a monkey woman with my package the size of an ice pick.'"

"Ice pick" is supposed to be a boast. Miranda's struggles with her bag and I carry it for her. Everything seems lighter when she's near me.

I realize in clouds of memory that I met Lang Fei once before. Miranda and I toured the Bell Tower of the ancient city of Xi-An (City of Western Peace). We rented bicycles to tour the surrounding guard walls. And yes, Lang Fei was there, agile as a Capuchin monkey scooting on all fours, rocketing up the stone steps to the Tower's main vestibule. Lang Fei is bow-legged because his parents couldn't afford proper vitamins and surgery during his infancy. Today he wears braces on his legs and big horn-rimmed glasses, just like those cartoons of buck-teethed Nipponese soldiers depicted in American newspapers during WWII. (A picture also comes to mind from Japanese and Chinese pillow books...the Japanese men have gargantuan penises; the Chinese men's penises are no bigger than acupuncture needles).

Lang Fei boasts of defeating systems. He's trained as a doctor, but Miranda tells me he left medicine to become a free lance croupier in Macao and then Vegas during the *Ameriguan* handover to our Mother Country. During these turbulent times, while millions in my country went on the road with shopping carts searching desperately for food, Lang devised a way to defeat casino dealers at blackjack, the game of 21. Several times he played his crooked system and was thrown out of casinos for counting cards, though technically speaking, he wasn't counting. Miranda's explanation of his activities wasn't quite clear; it had something to do with a card reader and dark folded edges.

At first Lang Fei worked part-time as an emergency physician, gambling on the side. But when money ran out, he went back to Beijing United Family Hospital and Clinics—this time as a security analyst managing the IT department. His position in IT gave him access to all the medical records, including those of the elite officials who could be useful to him—the corrupt and greedy ones that Lang, a cripple, despised. His chosen weapon was a few well-executed hacks from unnamed sources, dumps of thousands of records to his personal archive which he fed selectively to the Chinese media, revealing one or more dirty secrets. The pustulant health pretenders from the Directorate's top tier could no longer be saved with cosmetic surgery or even a digital darkroom. Yet these celebrities kept up the image of youth with skywriting, fireworks portraits and even iconic (and retouched) photographs of themselves speaking earnestly to constituents in bistros, large shopping malls and Tian An Men Square. After Lang got through with them, these undesirables were carted off to Heilongjiang for decommissioning and a ride in the ice sleighs. No family worshipped them; and no friends of ancestors came to their funerals.

Eventually the Directorate tapped Lang Fei for his unique talents. Assigned to work on an algorithmic challenge of unintended consequences (I call them unintentional contradictions, 无意的矛盾), he was considered a key engineer of desirable Party outcomes. However, the leadership didn't quite trust him because he was doubly perturbed by the fate of his grandparents.

He was, Miranda told me, a mama's boy, and particularly attached to his grandmother, a trait he shared with Marco Hsu Yang. Lang Fei was supposed to have had a son with a wife he no longer sees; he was never available when his wife needed him. But he was always available when the crowds gathered with stones or potatoes to throw at celebrities he disgraced for being depraved. In short, Lang was the perfect man to break anything or anyone undesirable to him or the Directorate, providing his higher ups could catch him in an amiable mood.

*

I tell Miranda, as we descend to the buggy station, that I'm excited to meet Lang Fei and see Heilongjiang at last. Except now that Mother Earth is 2.5 degrees Celsius warmer than it was 100 years ago, the Ice Festival generally lasts no more than six precious weeks. Festivities require extra refrigeration while 15,000 artisans and laborers use hacksaws and drills to cut ice from the Songhua River each December to build fairy forts, Celtic castles, cartoon penguins and angels, the Forbidden City, and occasionally, the bygone World Trade Towers of New York City, now depicted simply as two lavender beacons in the night sky.

"I've heard rumors that a few elders manage to wake up from their ice sleighs on the river and escape. No one knows how," Miranda whispers to me. "Some are even said to have escaped by sledding and boating, perhaps with help from

family, thousands of kilometers north to Mo He,
Kamchatka, and then Sakhalin and Aleutia."

"The perfect escape?" I shout over the wind.

"It's -40°C in Mohe!" she shouts back.

Miranda reminds me the ice sleighs are comfortable and climate-controlled, part of a ritual send-off for elders, so that when someone old lies down into its snug spaces a final time, the ambience feels warm and inviting.

I listen, say no more. All I can feel is the extreme cutting cold into my chest, despite my Russian sheepskin coat and Yak hat, as I drag our optics and bags up and down escalators and long hallways, eager to start our adventure.

Miranda and I take a sleigh to our cheap Ibis hotel around the corner from St. Sophia Cathedral. We sleep a few hours in hard twin beds, throwing our sleeping bags over our bed-clothes for extra warmth. By mid afternoon we arrive at the Ice Festival gates cordoned off with lanterns and parking lots for all the sky taxis arriving from the city. The first thing that attracts our attention are a bunch of *dong yong zhe* (冬泳者)—winter swimmers—beefy Russians and hairless tubby Chinese dressed in swimming tutus and briefs, sandals and bathing caps, plunging into an Olympic-size pool cut from the two-meter-thick ice of the Songhua. A ductless fan nearly the size of an aircraft engine keeps the pool water from icing over. It's Spring Festival, ostensibly, so the light creeps in longer each day. The Russians, all middle-aged and ruddy, are there to charm the Chinese crowds; a couple of men do handstands on the diving platform caked in ice before plunging into the icy pool and popping up to applause. The females wear bathing caps and tutus covering ample thighs slathered with seal fat. They work the crowds with jokes and come ons.

But wait, a graying Chinese swimmer appears at the high dive dressed in a sheepskin coat. He strips, displays his soft middle-aged body to the cheering crowd, focusing on the abyss below. Three steps off the board and trying a one and half pike he freezes mid-air, hits his head on the board and belly flops into the pool.

Wait. Wait some more. Chinese swimmer disappears. The crowds start to chatter, then wail as one of the Russian tutued swimmers starts to shout to her compatriot dressed in hammer and sickle briefs. The guy does nothing. She dives in, comes up to catch her breath, dives again. Miranda turns to me, her jaw slack. I shrug; rescuing tubby divers isn't what I'm here for. But I realize how terrible it would be if I let these two drown. My skin begins to react in snake scales, my coat thrown off. Shit the water is a blue slushy murk. I cork screw feet first to the frozen bottom, a pencil dive, arms swooping up, water cold as death. Grabbing two bodies under the armpits, their eyes popped, their limbs floating without movement, I kick off the bottom, pushing them up to the surface. Screaming "get the backboards!" but no answer, no boards. At first the Russian in the red briefs hoists their lady swimmer; then the Chinese guy, his scalp torn and bloody. The crowds whip out their phones. Lying side by side on the concrete, bear rugs and rough army blankets thrown over them, the victims seem peaceful. But the Russian lady starts to breathe after a chest thump; the Chinese guy requires prolonged CPR while Miranda provides traction for his neck. At least five minutes go by, then 10; he breathes intermittently, then stops. I thump his chest again, turning him on his side to clear all that water. More CPR, more thumps. He coughs, then spews a fountain of scum. I'm surprised that no one here seems prepared with minimal equipment like respirators or defibrillators. Eventually an ambulance shows up. The EMT bots appear lackadaisical, lifting him into the truck like a sack of potatoes.

Though the guard house is layered in ice and green mold, there are heaters so I strip and shower. No one has extra clothes my size. I wait for a Russian launderette to warm my things in a dryer.

Presently we move to the open river. Miranda leads me gingerly on the ice, as though I'm too old to walk. I reply by firing rockets from my ankle plates, just to see if they work, levitating both of us off the ground.

"Harbin is the cold of another planet," she says, philo-sophically.

"How would you know? Which planets have you been to?"

"I was competing for Mars-colony status, but my height disqualified me!"

I wonder at her beauty. She turns away and we watch the skaters. The golds and reds of the setting sun bathe us in eye-stinging light, and I adjust my visor, pulling hers down as well. There are kids wearing old-fashioned Minnie Mouse get-ups and peasants pushing sleighs made up of ordinary classroom chairs. Someone sporting a Monkey King body suit skates in circles around the crowds.

My brain flashes to the image I wish to see. It's Beaux II, skating, pirouetting sloppily around all the others. He's a dervish, committing no crimes. But precisely the one I have to take down.

Miranda communicates without speaking. I receive her thoughts as input tokens: the Directorate is aiming in Harbin to emulate the wintry fairyland frolic of Pieter Bruegel or Hendrik Avercamp. Six hundred years ago, the Dutch painters depicted commoners hunting or negotiating the deep snow and skating along the frozen canals of local villages on the Zuiderzee. Today it's the Songhua, and all around us are a menagerie of kids dressed up like cats, goats and wolves, all of them showing off, the better skaters competing for prizes and the crowd's attention.

"Since when did you study Bruegel and Avercamp?" I ask.

"Before I met you," she tells me, reminding me of her superior education obtained by hanging out with foreigners in Beijing's Culture Playground. "But I studied harder after I met you," she says, breathless.

We touch down. I pet a husky attached to a peasant's sleigh. He's for hire, and though I try to feed the gentle creature some bacon from my pockets, the owner refuses, saying his charge is on a strict diet. I wonder if the animal has enough strength to pull even me. So I slip into his sleigh and breathe upward, to lighten the load. Miranda suddenly plops down beside me, though I can no longer see peripherally thanks to my helmet; I'm not entirely sure she's beside me except for her voice.

"It's all right. She weighs nothing!" I tell the driver. My molecular density readjusts to a lightness I generally deplore.

Miranda shoves me a little with her shoulder as the husky digs in, pulling us forward away from the Songhua riverbank, a struggle for him, so I breathe upward even more, encircling her waist with my arm until we're practically levitating off the seat so our dog can look mighty and powerful gliding quickly past the skaters toward an ice palace. It seems styled like a filigreed Xanadu pleasure dome, decorated with mirrored glass and long vertical wooden panels depicting cartoon ballerinas and he-men lifting barbells. "Isn't it sublime?" Miranda shouts. "Because there's nothing more sublime than freezing one's *pigu* (屁股) off at -29°C as a husky pulls us to nowhere!" She giggles, shouting further erudition. "These oversized ice angels and sleigh dogs express the unbearable lightness of breeding!"

"Being!" I shout back at her into the wind but she doesn't hear me. I wonder whether Miranda has also read a translation of Milan Kundera's *The Unbearable Lightness of Being.* I quote him from the archives:

> *The heavier the burden, the closer our lives come to the Earth, the more real and truthful they become. Conversely, the absolute absence of burden causes man to be lighter than air, to soar into heights, take leave of the Earth and his earthly being, and become only half real, his movements as free as they are insignificant. What then shall we choose? Weight or lightness?*

She pulls on my prosthetic right hand, gloved thickly, as we jump out of the sleigh. Immediately I adjust my molecular density to ground level again, but with Miranda I still feel lighter than air and, ironically, grounded and completely happy.

*

A few hours later Lang Fei greets us at the festival gate; he's coming directly from the airport. "Lucky that the aircraft engines didn't freeze this time," he says. "Otherwise, I'd have to go back." The late afternoon sky paints us in cerulean colors, then violets. It grows darker. He warns me that any synthetic skin of mine exposed will become frost bitten in Harbin twilight.

"I'm well insulated," I tell him.

The three of us lock arms and together we fly low above the river along snow fog and violet dark. Pines and larch adorned with white festival lights shimmer as I catch a horseman and pony below on the riverbank pulling a sleigh filled with giggling children. Down the riverbank Miranda gestures toward a gate; we descend and settle into an ice shelter warmed with a tiny brazier as nighttime crowds gather around us. She points to the darkening water. "If you follow Songhua on the map, it twists and turns like a dragon from the *Changbai* mountains. Then it becomes Heilongjiang, Black Dragon."

Lang Fei translates. "Songhua waters don't appear black except in nightfall but that's when the river comes alive."

"Songhua flows from Harbin northeast through Russia's Khabarovsk to the Straits," Miranda rejoins. "I've heard it's a forbidden escape route with many falls and plunges, even a few dams, so no one can properly use a boat, though a few try."

She tugs me as though I'm a child.

"How would you even think of these things? Who would try to escape?"

She clicks her tongue. "Not now," as though no further explanation is needed.

Miranda gets up again and hurries down the shoreline. Lang Fei struggles to keep up with us. He walks on the balls of his feet, pigeon-toed, and I'm tempted to pick him up/ Miranda commands me to sit on one of the little stools next to the riverbank. In the chill and the whipping wind I boost my optics to detect the boats, human figures and skiffs sliding along in perfect darkness. She points toward the orange gleam of sodium lamps a kilometer upstream belonging to the Guardhouse. There are groups of black-coated soldiers shuffling about, changing guard. They wear the traditional Chinese Red Star hats. Two climb up to a watchtower. Each is holding, no doubt, an AR-37 or a laser-guided harpoon. I assume it's to catch animals or curious humans. A searchlight sweeps the river but fails to illuminate our party.

"I'm getting numb," I announce finally. "We'll have to go soon, but please tell me more about the skaters and the elders. I really can't see them very well."

"I thought cyborgs never got cold," Lang says with a cluck, lifting his brows.

"I'm a hybrid," I say, raising my visor in the darkness.

"We'll come back here at sunrise to see the cooking stalls and igloo sleighs," Miranda interrupts.

"Igloo sleighs? Ice coffins?"

"Not sure of the words."

Her facial muscles go tense a moment; her mouth opens as though in a fit of confusion. I know how frustrated she feels sometimes, not being able to come up with just the right words in English.

Lang Fei explains to me that "igloo sleighs" or "ice sleighs" or "ice coffins" are actually the cryopods that elders lie in. "It is part of an elaborate ritual," he begins. "The highest honor—"

What's he talking about? I ask her without words.

"Naomi, you've already got the gist. Besides, this isn't the place." She shakes her head back and forth, slowly, a warning.

More winter visitors press in on us. For a moment we gather the heat of the crowd. Then a sleigh driver comes by in an open wagon led by a white pony scarred with crusts of blood. I shake my head slowly; my *Logoharp* voices in deep masculine mode: "Put your switch away."

He listens; the pony perks up, shaking his harness bells as though to thank us. As we mount the sleigh, a fat peasant dressed in another red-starred hat pulls alongside the cart, displaying his shivering puppies kept uncovered in a bicycle basket.

"Those puppies are freezing to death," *Logoharp* warns him in Mandarin. I repeat the warning: "They'll die without covers and you'll lose your investment."

This stirs him a little. I remove my scarf and outer hood, covering the puppies as best I can, adding a hand warmer to the basket. Miranda grins. The puppies are the Chinese kind—baby pugs, a few mutts and retrievers, nearly hairless, shivering and squirming with cold.

I grab two of the mutts and put them inside my coat, throwing coins in the basket. Our driver waits as we seat ourselves once again; he snaps his switch against the carriage's frame. Shuai winces. "He wants to please you, maybe a bigger tip." She points out the merchants cooking in firelight down the road; we see braziers offering sausages and steamed dumplings in stalls on the road next to the bright storefronts. Lang Fei seems buried inside an oversized coat, turning toward me, shaking his head in protest about my sympathy for puppies. The driver stops so we can buy *shaobing* and sausage for a late-night snack to feed the puppies I resolve to keep.

At the Ibis, the rotating door is still frozen shut. I pay the driver, push open a side door and head straight for our room, shielding the puppies in my cloak to elude the curious concierge. Lang Fei grabs a handful of *baotzu* and checks into his own room. Miranda opens our door, turns up the gas fireplace and places the puppies on the floor, pulling a blanket off the bed to warm them. She makes me some Oolong tea while the pups wolf down the food and water and we drain our cups and curl up on our pillows. I sit on my bed, and can barely pull off my boots. She bends down and helps me.

"It's hot in here," I tell her, finally.

"I'm still cold." She shivers before the fire.

"What is this ritual, exactly?"

She grabs her translator and searches for the correct word.

"Oh...the sleigh is a containment pod. A sarcophagus for those who still live."

"I'm not clear."

"A sarcophagus carved with outer layers of ice, with runners. It can be pushed. You push the elders down the river as they're dreaming. The families worship them."

"I don't understand."

"Chinese ancestors are always worshipped. Because they're still dreaming, you're in their dreams, and they're in yours."

"I thought the ones in the cryopods were already gone, or nearly so."

"No, they're not. The parents and children are a bit like corpse walkers, only they skate along the river with the elders lying in ice carriages on runners. I'm told the 'corpses,' though they're not dead yet, are dreaming of some journey or romance they once had as you push them along the river, but they can't wake up. They're in a state of—how do you say it?"

"Torpor? Hypnagogic sleep just before death?"

"Maybe," she nods. "The elders, and a few of the disabled are mercifully put on ice before decommissioning and recycling," she whispers. "All these souls return in their dreams to an earlier time in their lives. I've heard they search for someone or something lost to them. It's an option within the Recycling program."

"Oh. That's the 'Harmonious Recycling,' program. Isn't that what it's called? How are they recycled?"

"The coffins end up on stilts upriver. Families can worship the elevated coffins for ten days during the dreaming period. Then they're washed away somewhere. I don't know where. It's a humane way of recycling oldies who take up needed resources. The Directorate program gives them satisfaction before they die," she explains.

"I'm not quite familiar with the details," I respond.

"It's a relatively new program. Just about a year old. Still in beta."

"They're taking neural journeys? You mean accessing un-trafficked channels? Journeys not taken before?"

"I'm really not clear," she says. "I get some of this from fellow reporters. I've heard a few elders return to journeys interrupted in earlier life. Sometimes early loves. But no one has recorded what they feel or see."

"Doesn't someone want to?"

"The program isn't fully tested. To our external view, they're suspended. Inside, they dream a journey that may be incredible."

I conjecture. "There are neural gateways where significant or unfulfilled memories veer off, leading to alternate reality. For example, a Laurentian fishing trip I planned to take with my father, but never did. And your dad, an outing to the ice rinks you wanted to take with him?"

She sighs. The wind outside dies down.

"Miranda, perhaps your recycling system is far more sophisticated than anything tried in my home country. Are the elders injected?"

"The monied ones get a tranquilizer recombinant, and then, the extreme cold does the rest. There is a sleigh worship period of ten days, at least, which most families elect to take."

"I thought the elders got a survival kit and a few days' rations to head North."

"Very few make that choice. Cryopods allow you to forgo the kit. Many forgo the kit and the trials."

She stares at me, affecting an earnestness of expression meant to corroborate my silence. "The reasoning is that it gives everyone in a family a chance to contemplate the next step."

"Next step?"

She nuzzles the puppies.

My *Logoharp* registers dissonance. "We're not supposed to die before our time," she explains, a bit wistful. "Yet this system is created to smooth out the death cycle."

Slouching on my bed, mentally I re-log and encrypt, counseling internally not to judge Miranda or anything she says.

It seems that China and Ameriguo have a similar approach to human recycling, but Mother Country is much more advanced. The attempt to find a humane recycling solution began a decade ago because there were too many elders and not enough young souls to sustain the economy. Not enough land to bury the dead. Now there are too many young souls, and still not enough resources to sustain everyone.

Accessing the archives, I've learned that in another past, there was a plan to inter corpses in stacks, in skyscraper-size tombs buried miles below the remains of fracked fields. But the burial costs and waste of human muscle were too high. In addition, *The Laws of Ice and Critique of the Frontier* redirected government efforts in a more sustainable technique. The Physicians' Vigilant Harmony Association, one of the groups overseeing human recycling, assembled cooperatively in the United Nations to devise a solution. It was decreed that after fifty-five years of age, neither Ameriguans nor Chinese, much less denizens of other countries, could be integrated successfully into regular employment ranks. Economic welfare aside, no system for 9.5 billion souls would enable the full breadth of living talent or experience to flourish on any continent. Massive flooding of coastlines, droughts and violent dust storms in the interior made things worse.

It wasn't long before Mother Country officials ordered RJs like me to generate public information about end-of-life recycling, though the exact nature of the system remains undisclosed. Today, only a select group of elders—Directorate top dogs, a few stellar scientists or academic dignitaries with big reputations, plus leading actors and other celebrities—are permitted to work until the age of 60, when they too are forced to retire, but not necessarily to enter cryo-sleep.

Some live out their days in Yellow Mountain (*Huang Shan*) in Anhui, the subject of Li Po's drunken poetry. The Directorate has also dispatched military leaders in good health to Urumqi and Lhasa to assist Han soldiery in keeping order, although both regions were pacified decades ago through a voluntary intermarriage program.

My Logoharp nudges me to dismiss my misgivings. Perhaps Harmonious Recycling is a humane solution after all. The doxxers haven't touched it yet. I wonder why? As I watch my sleepy journalist friend fall softly onto her bed, still in her coat, nuzzling the puppies to her chin, they exchange kisses again and again. Anhui seems like a dignified way to spend last days. An elder can sit in a deck chair overlooking the valleys below, steeped in memory, in mountain mist. The heaviness of earlier days lightens. There is, of course, the waste of experience and expertise among the masses; particularly those individuals who are not quite old enough or famous enough to escape recycling. But the elderly must make way for the young. And there are social programs that give a boost to young ethnic minorities. For example, the offspring of the mixed marriages in Tibet get Han Chinese pedigree, plus other perks. In Ameriguo, the offspring of mixed marriages are treated like everyone else.

"For generations Tibetan-Han children have been admitted to colleges with lower high school exam scores and discount tickets to sporting events and movies," Miranda says. "The Xinjiang Muslim youngsters have been separated from their parents for generations. They're placed in orphanages and schools the size of football fields to be reeducated as loving, patriotic Chinese. As each decade goes by, the minorities are less inclined to pursue acts of political resistance or violence. Most of the Uyghur parents who've survived the camps and fled to Turkey never see their children again."

"This is a solution?"

"It certainly beats angry Uyghurs slashing up passengers in train stations," she says, wryly. Miranda responds without emotional judgment, handing me the puppies as she heads for the bathroom.

"You Ameriguans!" she calls after her. "You're a different breed. Every soul is entitled to do whatever it pleases, good or bad!"

Before bed Miranda asks me to research *Citronella*, a recombinant of the *Neisseria meningitidis* bacteria laced with lemon scent. The injection produces hallucinations in sepsis. Combined with cold, and injected without pain, the virus in China is used effectively to transport elders or disabled dreamers into a chosen marker of the past. That marker is private; the authorities cannot exactly trace where each dreamer goes. During a 10-day period, sleepers are said to journey to the ends of the earth, returning to something or someone they miss or have lost. At the conclusion of the 10 days, the dreams end; the ice sleighs are winched up, removed by crane from Songhua banks and transported to a flood zone. Again, it's not recorded where this flood zone is, exactly, though some families claim it lies far north. Families can journey to say farewell to their loved ones at their own expense. Some following the caskets, faces of the dreamers still visible in their pods. Finally, some caskets wash out to sea by storm, after which large collecting ships recycle them into chemicals on demand.

*

Most Ameriguans will still elect the cryopod option. My algorithms tell me so. "True North Survival kit" will be less popular, though Ameriguan Survivalists who enjoy hunting are free to pursue this frontier option till the end. They get a Damascus Steel 8.1 Full Tang Deer Antler Knife to hunt for food along with a Remington semiautomatic shotgun Model 1500 with a few rounds of ammunition. Either way, the style of weapon doesn't preclude accidents or the madness associated with fending off predators in extreme cold.

For the majority, the cryopod dreamers, I think, these last days may be best of their lives.

Why not go back and live the romance you never had? Or find the child or lover lost by medical incompetence or a hospital strike? Or the dream to become something or someone you truly wanted to be had you not made those stupid mistakes in your tadpole youth? These early decisions weigh heavily on most of us, but the cryo-dreams are supposed to be light and in full color (though rendered in less than high definition). The objects of affection seem accessible yet remote so that no one actually touches them. Dreams have no physical reality, no body, no atomic structure other than flashes in the brain.

What then shall we choose? Weight or lightness? I know what I would choose if I had the chance.

In China, elders respectfully board high-speed trains to Heilongjiang and the Songhua, a journey accompanied by fam-ilies. This journey confers worshipful dignity in the transition from life to death.

"Western media doesn't publicize the Heilongjiang exercises," Miranda says. "But I believe the Chinese way is better."

"How old do you have to be to take the journey?"

"Well, my dad's turning fifty-one," she says. "My mother, I don't know exactly."

"Your dad. Is he ready for this? Do you care?"

"Of course. I care."

"But you've told me he abused you when you were growing up. He scarred your trachea when he grabbed you by the throat." I'm whispering this in her ear. "Sometimes you can't talk because of it. The words come out strangulated. Numerous times he choked your mother. At least twice you jumped on his back and fought him off."

"Are you spying on me? How do you know this? I don't recall saying anything."

"When I pull out the stops on my *Logoharp*, I share your dreams."

Miranda turns about face, striding away. I can see from behind; her neck and back tense as she composes herself. Through a large picture window in our room we see a stone sculpture of Confucius, at least three metres high, placed in the hotel garden down a heated walkway leading to the Songhua. Miranda's voice is scratchy now, like a *hu chin*; she touches her throat.

"It's peaceful here," she whispers. "I like to watch the processions of sleighs and the children pushing their grandparents around. The elders lie peacefully like babies in carriages. I wonder where they go?"

"Babies are only peaceful when they sleep! Miranda, I doubt this is a topic you'll be able to write about extensively."

"Why?"

"It isn't news, anymore. The system's already in place."

"Yes, but as long as you can seriously report anything or make an incident or practice seem legitimately fresh?" She pulls on her fingers, as though trying to remove a ring. Her voice becomes a little shrill. "Maybe we can add some new dimension, especially if there's a future altercation or custom or gesture of piety that the leadership must create. Isn't that possible?"

I touch her shoulder.

"Well, maybe I could tell this story in my future memoirs?"

"Shuai—"

She shakes herself loose, heading for the sink to wash up. She calls back to me. "You'll see the ice sleighs tomorrow!"

14

FEBRUARY 2119

WORSHIPPING ON THE SONGHUA

江
畔
朝
圣

It's 1 a.m. and I'm not sleepy. I watch her in her cocoon of bedding, her breath rising and falling. I try to recall how a real journalist would write about a termination ritual of the kind we're about to see, but then my brain slices into a question: How can someone like Miranda, with her beauty, writing ability and infectiousness, not command the highest attention in Chinese media circles?

I see a million suitors for her, hundreds of job offers, the opportunity to be interviewed and broadcast on every SkyView, CCP and GlobalFox channel worldwide. She's a cosmonaut returning to earth, a journalist, a democracy crusader. Remembering how she leaned her head on my shoulders for a photo at a Christmas party a decade ago, how I looked human, allowing my real blond hair and complexion to show, wearing conventional glasses, smiling as I wore my antique gray Ralph Lauren suit sporting a polka-dot bowtie. I looked at the photograph years later recollecting how I must have been something like her older sister, confessor, lover, so much so that she seemed utterly content to lean on me, enjoying a brief hiatus from whatever troubled her.

Miranda wakes me. In the dark we wash and dress, have a cup of Oolong tea, then hurry to the ice city. Her cochlear implant rings. It is Gua Gua (she whispers, derisively, "Foie Gras"), her boyfriend. I hear argument and then sweet dulcet tones of tolerance bordering on condescension, barely masked, because obviously she prefers to have an attentive lover than not to have one at all. I suspect he's another *fu wu dai*, a rich fifth-generation Chinese. His callow ways and priapism serve her purposes, I guess. She's explaining to him in Shanghai dialect how and why she had to leave her city to accompany her old RJ friend, Naomi, assigned to algorithmic interventions. I can hear his tight hysterical whimpers, *the jeezus-christ oh fuck* ejaculations, then silence, her giggles, then her mock kisses, which stop him cold. While she's talking, I leave bowls of cereal, minced beef and water on the floor for our puppies, still sleeping rolled up on our pillows. I spread sheets of newspaper and Tyvek3 on the carpet, which I've grabbed from the bones of a new hotel wing so the puppies have a secure piddle place.

We depart at 6:30 a.m. As we arrive by carriage at Stalin Park, we walk through an Ionic column portico carved in ice. Tourist officers greet us, gesturing noisily at a spectacular modern entertainment center fronting the ice on the shoreline. It's the same Xanadu pleasure dome we saw on our sleigh ride. Sunlight pierces the fog along the riverbank now, the winter swimmers stretching, doing handstands, plunging into the lanes of the Olympic-size pool, aka frozen abyss.

Since the guards aren't patrolling yet, Miranda and I walk past the concrete barricades covered in red flags. We buy some fritters and hot porridge from the food trucks and keep eating while walking downstream toward Xanadu.

One by one the worshipers of the Songhua appear like slow-moving tortoises. There are groups of skaters, many of them small children, pushing sleighs and pods on the frozen Songhua from Sun Island Park, where the majority of ice sculptures are kept. Others appear further away, from a launching point somewhere in the northeast. First tens, then dozens, then hundreds of worshippers: children, fathers, mothers, all dressed like harlequins in white, pink and black parkas, pushing the sleighs on cryopod runners, their movements a whoosh—a smooth propulsive motion, as though the friction and momentary heat the runners make produce an easy, wet glide.

I see a teenager backing up four or five meters behind one igloo sleigh, charging hard with his skates and pushing on the handles so that the momentum of the dreamer inside carries far forward. Then the children squeal and fight to catch up to the flying sleigh until their hands grip the carriage handles tightly, and they're dragged along. The children push in spurts and sing nursery rhymes and songs of praise while the parents skate beside them, each a small entourage, celebrating and often talking loudly to the dreamer inside, hoping they can be heard.

The light is harsh, and I can't see the faces inside each pod, only the shadow of bodies nestled inside, each dreamer lying prone with a face to the sky. Almost every family drapes a colorful flag with a symbolic crest over half the pod holding their precious cargo. Neither Miranda nor I move while the procession of celebrants passes. My face freezes like marble in the icy glare. But her face looks warm and pink beneath her white Russian fur toque, as though she has already entered a dream.

"Give me your hand." I hear her command me as she reaches out. Dutifully I unscrew my right hand and place it on high heat, handing it over to warm her.

"No, damn it!" She pushes me away and my synthetic hand falls to the icy ground. Rushing, Miranda slipslides on the ice, moving toward the families as though to welcome them. I see no tears. It's all upturned mouths and eyes, luxuriant welcoming. I pick my hand off the ground and re-dock it.

"How are you feeling today?" Miranda Qian Shuai asks a worshiper with her microchip amplifier.

"Happy!" the young mother responds, grasping her toddler's hand. Both are dressed in bright pinks matching their cheeks. "This was my mother's last wish! I'm sure she's going home to her first lover, the one she really wanted to marry. It was wartime and he was sent to the front. Maybe she's writing the letter she couldn't bring herself to send to him. My mother rejoices in her dreams! It is a great lesson for the kids, and for all of us."

Miranda nods in agreement, with compassion; she's a broadcaster recording the joy of these families, asking me to hold the camera as she dances and skates on the ice, revving up for each encounter. Slipping and sliding, she falls once or twice, but someone always rushes over to pick her up. She thanks them, holding out her index finger to which a digital recorder is attached. I can't recall exactly how or when she had the nanorecorder implanted—time stands still. I forget everyone as I watch her. Yet soon—sooner than I realize—the show is over; waves of sleighs and runners slacken and she signals me to head back to the festival while the guards in the towers resume their positions. Weapons are mainly for show, to assure that no one heads off in the northerly direction.

"Where exactly do the elders go after the ten-day worship period?"

"The barges come and round them up like ponies," she said. "One source says they tug the sleighs northeast on Black Dragon River to Khabarovsk, where they're quarried at port and displayed on stilts for a few days before being recycled."

"Ice coffins on stilts. Hardly seems real."

"It's a lucrative business, especially for the Manchurians and a few Russians. Each family must pay a very high export-and-recycling fee," Miranda says. "Apparently there is an arrangement for pharmaceutical laboratories and hospitals in need of natural products."

"So that's it?" My palms upturned, empty, talking for me, a sudden semi-hysterical up-reading in my natural voice. "Do you want the icemen to turn you into a 'natural product?'"

"I'm entirely natural right now," she retorts, arching her brows. "But if I come back as a 'product,' I prefer to be a Lancôme Concealer."

She sings in a lilting soprano:

*Oh, skate me down the river, let my runners skid
and glide,*
I will skate to you, my darling, in one fantastic ride.
*No wavering, no questions; we've met but once
before,*
*Come back to me my darling, I'll ride with you once
more.*

I feel a breeze, then a hand tapping me on the shoulder.

"I'm Lang Fei," he voices, too loudly. "Have you been waiting long? I'm just able to arrive."

15

MARCH 2119

SOUL THROWING

夺
魂

Lang Fei can make or break systems—card games, computers, families, criminal gangs—although he likes to describe himself as a slacker, which is what *lang fei kong jian* (浪费空间) means in Chinese.

On the icy steps of a Chichen Itza ice pyramid that rises in the early Harbin twilight Lang Fei scoots on all fours like a Capuchin monkey short on vitamins. He makes no bones about his weak limbs; his parents had no money to treat his polio, so he hunches with unnaturally long arms trailing on the ground. As he tries to climb to the top, launching himself two steps at a time, then slipping and sliding back, I give up watching, lift him up in my arms, carrying him like a baby. We're levitating just a bit; I'm firing bursts of hydrogen flame from my ankles to speed the ascent. I try to avoid the stares of spectators, most of them wrapped in black woolen scarves and hats, giving them a menacing look like Ninja bandits. Lang Fei is placid and inquisitive in my arms; he has no lines on his heart-shaped face, though his cheeks are pock-marked, his black eyes turned up at me as though believing (inaccurately) in my godliness.

"Your face seems unaltered, but it's naked, no facial hair," he says.

A consequence of radiation, I remind him.

"But the rest of you is nanocomposite, carbon fiber, silicon, abalone, flesh and steel?"

He lets his arm drop, his paw brushing against my pelvic armor.

"Stop it."

"I'm sure you're well-built but not invincible. You need lubrication?"

"I don't menstruate."

"You seem stiff!"

"Correct. My body naturally tenses in the cold."

"Maybe watching these ice sleighs and the sycophantic naïve idiots following them around makes you tense?"

"A little. Besides, children are children. They're innocent."

I greet his face with frowns, a wrinkle of my hairless brow, my visor closing over my eyes. Fei chuckles. "You're too fierce, Naomi!" Then he springs from my arms, zipping inside the ice pagoda, climbing on all fours to the observation deck. I follow him, just to make sure he doesn't slip and fall. Entering a darkened anteroom, a life-size Shakyamuni in contemplation, lit in pink, its long curvaceous fingers assuming the *abhaya varada* mudra of charity and protectiveness. Lang Fei bows, *baituos* (摆脱), finding a fur-covered seat, pulls a pack of playing cards from his coat pocket, shuffling the deck with a zipping motion, the cards flying and interleaved in air.

This moment he reminds me of Hsu Yang. Fei whispers, too loudly: "I can figure a way to break open the cryopods! But no one seems to care about escaping. Everyone acquiesces in the Lottery and just accepts Fate. Bunch of sheep!"

Lang Fei tells me that he's heard of crotchety old elites paying piles of *yuan* to scientists in the hope of isolating an immortality gene—allegedly a pair of extremely rare polymorphic genes responsible for boosting adaptive immunity. The genes not only code for proteins that stimulate T-cell-scavenging to ward off infections in the body, but also activate the gene sirtuin 6 (SIRT6), which is known to stimulate DNA repair, conferring long life to the lucky ones. "Fortunately, no one has succeeded in perfecting anti-aging therapy!" Lang Fei exclaims. "A few old coots register their whole genomes, play the polymorphic game and inevitably (ha ha!) lose like everyone else."

What's he talking about? There is a provision in *The Laws of Ice* that an "Immortality Gene" confers freedom from death—or at least, systematic decommissioning—if anyone of 9.5 billion souls actually has it. We're taught to revere the *Laws*, though too many don't understand them.

I recite the relevant *Laws* for Lang Fei just to remind him how little control we have:

1. *From Cosmic Ice and Dust our lives were formed, and to Ice we must return.*

2. *Cryo-genesis and cryo-destruction maintain earthly balance. Our social skin demands government-directed recycling and cryo-destruction to sustain human life.*

3. *The rarest Immortality Gene confers freedom from Death, and thus freedom from cryo-destruction.*

4. *Immortality is conferred only on Sentinels and Scribes of the State gifted with Genetic Prescience and the deepest understanding of our Laws.*

5. *The disappearance of Ice will spell the destruction of earthly life. As long as our world sustains Ice, Harmonious Recycling will preserve the testaments of humans in their final journey.*

How do genetics relate to Lang Fei's game of cards? How can he open the cryopods? Lang Fei is full of secrets. He's grasping my gloved synthetic hand. But I notice his knuckles are scalded, scabby, like chopped up worms, as though a thug has just rapped them repeatedly with a bamboo pole.

"You were tortured, Fei?"

"Occasionally," he says. "They thought I was *Falun Gong*."

"You're not?"

"That's *none-ja*," he replies, as in *none of your business*. "Because I move around on all fours my hands have toughened up."

I nod, affirming his connection to monkeys.

Lang Fei studies me. "You're pale, Naomi. Do you need a transplant, perhaps, or a transfusion?" He tries, unsuccessfully, to push his hand, and mine, lower against my pelvic armor. I slap him off.

"I can get any organ you want; the teen black market is full of them. All the elders with life-extension badges get their organs from involuntary experimental subjects, mostly common criminals and *Falun Gong* kept in black jails."

"The *Falun Gong* were exterminated long ago."

"No! A few survive in Taiwan and in the jails. A few in Ameriguo. Some go *incognito*. *Falun Gong* are lifetime believers in soul throwing, meditation and body healing; they have a witchy way about them, throwing their souls into each other.

But in our country, we don't share souls easily. If we seek to share, we obtain permission from ancestors, and only in extraordinary circumstances."

"Such as?"

"When we love children and wish to save them. When one is sick or dying from viruses we can't control."

"You have children?"

"I've a son. He's got big searching green eyes. He cries all the time when I'm gone."

"How often is that?"

"Most of the time. Have an Auntie who cares for him."

Silence. I refrain from asking any more questions. I imagine what it must be like to sacrifice the touch and trust of a child to someone else—say, an appointed Auntie of the State who despises you. On the other hand, why does Lang Fei spend so much time away from his child?

"Teach me more about soul throwing. I'm guessing for any RJ working with crowds, soul throwing would be very useful."

He rolls his eyes. "Naomi, I'm told you can master any skill in the book and not in a book. You could cure whatever ails me, if anything did ail me, with your mind."

"Soul throwing is beyond my programming. Tell me more."

He doesn't—at least not now. Lang Fei is goading me. He knows my brain is wired to accept scientific method, not transmigration of souls. I'm programmed to evaluate data and human behavior based on evidence, reality, not unproven beliefs. I recollect an experience in the Sulawesi caves of Indonesia when I was in early training after high school. Scientists found handprints of long-fingered hobbits, or perhaps aliens or Homo sapiens imprinted on the cave walls at least 39,000 years ago. The artists blew red ochre dust on their hands to make these prints—a bizarre language I'm sure was meant for advanced civilizations to interpret—maybe an imprint of their supple hands reaching beyond the caves to the stars. Prediction, in other words. Desire. Centuries of limestone deposits preserved these ochre hand prints.

"If little elves can leave their fingerprints behind," I tell Lang Fei, "it's just as likely that shamans throw their souls into the dead and make them walk again."

"You've seen the walking dead?"

"I've heard about them, but no one in Sulawesi could locate a proper ceremony for me."

"Shamans are superfluous. At least people's belief in them."

Evidently Lang Fei reads my opinions in the archives.

"You're supposed to be a digital shaman," I tell him, sizing him down. "Do you throw your soul into the sleepers? Do you know how to break the codes to wake them up?"

"No one can break the codes alone, Naomi! Even shamans of science require a deeper understanding of our DNA and belief systems. I don't get the astrological explanation, but ordinary shamans say a child born under a certain configuration of stars might experience a bounce in the space-time curve—a "defect" or *altered state*, you call it—perhaps a heart murmur or the ability to count cards or remember complex logarithmic tables flawlessly. All because one gene has been expressed or deleted. Alternately, one is born in that split second interval in which the clock of the universe suddenly halts. This happens in the cosmic game of 21, alterations that change the character of protein synthesis through one or more altered codons."

"Are you talking about an 'immortality gene?' Can a rare mutation confer wakefulness or even immortality?"

"The system seems to operate this way. The immortality gene most likely exists either as a consequence of deletion or an extremely rare mutation contributed by a 'God Source,' someone or something long lived and other than human. Alternately, a hiccup in the timing of Mother Country's recycling system causes certain elders to wake up."

"Are you a geneticist?"

"I was. Barefoot doctor, too."

"I thought gene deletion brought deformity, at least in most cases. Like firing a gun and watching it backfiring in your face."

"No. Deletion *is* freedom," he repeats, "at least in this special case." Lang Fei's speech slows, ejecting words with long pauses, as though I'm a foreigner learning to decrypt his code. "But Naomi, it's not you who pulls the trigger. You engineer the outcome."

"You're talking nonsense!"

"I'm not! Why can't the system be modified, or at least broken and rebuilt to allow more of us to live out our lives? We surrender ourselves to dreaming when there is so much more to live for."

"Fei!" I nod, forgetting myself, stroking his hair with my natural hand. "You sound like Chekhov! 'We must work! Just work!' I remember this play. The only cure for the ills of our minds, to make a beautiful world, or to get a glimpse of it at least, is to work non-stop for it now. But why should you care, Lang Fei?"

"My grandmother—"

He reaches up and takes my natural hand.

"You miss your grandmother?" He shakes his head, a tear forming behind his eyes. "I'm sorry about your grandmother—"

"She was wise. She guided me. She died—"

"Truly, I'm sorry. The system is a waste of human kindness, talent."

I check my pulse, my watch. "I have to go. Can't imagine a shotgun backfiring in one's face."

"A gruesome ending," Fei says.

"I suppose so. But what happens if the bullet arcs high, landing in some unexpected place?"

He shrugs.

"My programming blocks the image."

"You and your machine learning, stupid stuff!" he says. "Rely on your instinct. Your tenderness, exactly. The recycling system is already demonstrating its flaws. You can fix this."

"How? My programming—"

"Fuck your programming! You're still half human, aren't you?"

He stops.

"I have to go," I tell him.

"You understand my meaning?!"

"I hear your words, but not the true meaning."

"I'll try again."

"No, Lang Fei, the Singing Directorate calls me."

He hangs tight onto my left wrist. I'm forced to rotate and twist his palm backward against its natural hinge; he yelps and falls to the floor.

"Naomi!"

"Sorry, Fei. You may be a shaman, or want me to be one. But I'm not wired for intimacy or undue persuasion, emotionally or physically for that matter."

"Don't you regret that?"

"Yes, a little."

He grunts as I lift him to his stunted feet. Asking him with my eyes, the tilt of my helmet, should I carry him back down to the icy fairground, or leave him? He doesn't answer, just stares at his feet, dejected.

16

DECEMBER 2119

LUCKY LIFE LOTTERY

命
运
摇
奖

The elders are queuing up outside the registration centers of every major city. I see them now on my screens.

In Ameriguo, registrants are of every color and size; many seem young and fit, as young as 50 years or less. In China, they are, almost without exception, the polyglot of ethnics: Han, Zhuang, Hui, Manchu, Miao, Uyghur, Naxi, Bai, Mongol, Meng and others. Each individual clutches a packet of tickets; several of the women are dressed in silks and woolens, layers upon layers to protect their bodies from the cold. The men are mostly wearing lighter jackets and fedoras, apparently convinced that the system will provide all necessary accoutrements for their journey. Someone takes a photo; the men look unspeakably casual, several smoking pipes, as though they're headed to a hunting resort.

All registrants form three lines. Everyone has the option of choosing which line, which extinction option they'll pursue. Alternately, the Lottery will choose for them, though very few want to be randomly assigned. Early arrivals crowd into the warehouse space while latecomers form queues extending five or six city blocks outside the building as they wait.

Where are the renegades? Where do the unwilling ones hide?

The train conductors organize the crowds into paddocks. Those who elect the True North Frontier option are assigned to Queue #1. The second group elects, or is assigned to Queue #2, the 10-day Heilongjiang Paradise Dreaming option. This group forms the majority; they're shepherded into the largest paddock, filling half the warehouse space. A third group forms Queue #3, the smallest line. These are the adventurists who don't care where or how they go. But this group has one single, slim advantage. Someone may be lucky enough to draw the *Deletion* ticket, the one-in-a-billion free pass issued every few years. I'm not certain whether these lucky ones win the ticket because of a corresponding deletion in their DNA. Chance tends to favor biology. But once these lucky few draw the ticket, they never sleep. They can't die, either, at least through conventional methods. Immediately they're set free to live for eternity just as they please. Publishing their names on city billboards, the Directorate automatically provides a generous life stipend, something like hitting the jackpot. But for those who elect Queue #3 and don't win, the State expedites the decision. They're the first to board trains to True North and all say goodbye beforehand. This is a relief. The drones take them away immediately.

Perhaps not so surprising is that this third group is composed mostly of loners, chancers and misfits. Few have ties to family or society; many steal or kill for a living. It's easy to see their lifestyle written on their faces. *Play the lottery. You have nothing to lose.*

On the other hand, the respected oldies of our society overwhelmingly favor the *Citronella* and cryopod option. Why wake from Paradise, which paralyzes them in their dreams, yet makes dreaming so pleasurable?

I asked Lang Fei: "So if they accidentally awaken and escape, where do they go? What'll they do? Survive in a cave or colony? Who would receive them?"

"Dunno!" He wavers. "Maybe nuns, gnomes, families or caretakers. Really not sure who receives them."

Lang Fei is fibbing, of course. He believes the Citronella option is like Blackjack; playing a "soft 17" means that an ace can act as either an 11 or a 1, allowing the player to double down and outwit the dealer, especially if the dealer's up card is low, between a 2 and 6, forcing him to hit again. The cards are rigged in the dealer's favor, but there's always a slim chance that a player will win, waking up from ice dreams and escaping North. I can't help savoring the idea of seeing a few of them break free.

17

FEBRUARY 2120

LIJIANG INQUEST

丽
江
审
讯

Am I human or cyborg? Am I capable of more than the State has set out for me? What Lang Fei suggests continues to disturb me. *Logoharp* dings, suggesting, in a low-volume *continuo*, that I can win at cryopod Blackjack. But how does anyone learn to spy or infiltrate, much less disable, a recycling system protected with the equivalent of the Enigma Code?

There was a time I wanted to return to a fully human state. My thoughts of Dr. Jens Remker and what could be—and what can never be—almost make me believe in another future.

But duty calls. I'm headed to Lijiang headquarters for yet another official confab. Why do I keep toggling back and forth in my mind between Jens and Marco Hsu Yang?

Perhaps because Jens has contacted me again, this time entreating me to take the earliest shuttle to his lunar station on South Pole-Aitken. I imagine Jens not there at all, but standing alongside me in earthly paradise—perhaps the cliffs by the Irish Sea, clear and fresh, too cold to swim. We're fishing for mackerel, his favorite. He cooks for me inside a thatched cottage, otherwise damp and dark, which we've rented for a long, luscious weekend.

In these moments we will never talk about breaking systems. Jens tries to reassure me instead, to calm my confusion. He knows I've expressed a desire to shape the future as a Scribe, a One, an Elite. I've even sent him drafts of my manuscripts on algorithmic predictions to which I attribute exaggerated importance.

"But you don't want to be a Directorate Scribe only, do you?" he teases me. "That's the modern equivalent of a court-room reporter or a wartime propagandist."

"No, I guess not."

"Then what do you really want to be, Naomi?"

"An original."

"What?"

"An original life form in charge of my own mind—not doing the bidding of someone else."

"You mean, an entrepreneur? An artist?" His hands open, enfolding me around my armored waist.

"A warrior," I reply. "A warrior for good—"

I imagine this: Jens and I are walking down a muddy two-lane road beside hilly pastures where cows and sheep graze. There are cowpats everywhere and we have to skip over them. We see splotches and striations of color, double rainbows that spill in great circles from the skies above the granite cliffs to the sea mist below. I'm sure Jens comes to me as a God Source. Hearing *tremulo* and *rubato* in every lap of waves on a lakeshore; spirits speaking in disguises, urging me to move on, to ignore his entreaties, not to be fooled.

But I won't listen because Jens loves me wordlessly, even without a touch. For a few moments I wish for him to choose me because I'm beginning to feel these crazy human feelings again, though I don't have enough experience to trust them.

A holo-mail intrudes on my thoughts. Chairman Sung has summoned me to appear in Lijiang by daybreak. Managing affairs in Yunnan and Southwestern China, Directorate regional headquarters lie in a compound about a kilometer below the surface of Snow Leopard Mountain.

*

These Yunnan provincials always question my credentials. They'll ask me why I've been fooling around in Manchuria. They'll politely request that I get back to work, conjuring a future before their eyes (a test to resolve both the "cryopod problem" and this Beaux II I'm assigned to disgrace. Only if I succeed in both tasks will I be granted—maybe—Elite status, the highest position an RJ can hope to attain.

Already, I'm feeling sorry Dean Cheung Yuen caught me off guard. By the time I blow smoke in the media, Beaux II will have already disappeared. I suspect he won't even merit the consideration of a 10–day cryo–reprieve, the reward he cooked up to make his recycling system palatable to the elders.

Generally, I anticipate the Directorate meetings without trepidation. But my *Logoharp* presses against my throat now. It's not the thought of Harmonious Recycling that bothers me particularly; it's the envy I feel seeing the cryopod gliders pursuing their dreams. True, to be partially cyborg is an advantage in this case, coupled with my gender. In a sense, I've been able to live a hybrid life thanks to the skill of my surgeons and a robotic commitment to obey instructions when I feel completely numb.

My compass tilts north, but per magnetic deviation we are actually flying southwest over Kunming and then north again, bringing up memories of Snow Leopard Mountain, its patches of snow in the crevasses even now, the mid-tone whites and ivories of dirty ice, the inky grays and indigos. It's as though the scene is out of focus slightly, set against an opalescent sky, perhaps the oily remnants of insects flying into my VTOL windshield.

I was nauseous when Marco and I drove one spring break in his rusty *Geery-Sifang* rental car from Lijiang toward Tibet. It was ambitious to head toward freedom; as we navigated the switchbacks, saplings and tiny spruce on the mountainside sprouting like dragon scales, we drove north to Tiger Leaping Gorge, a cataract of froth, rocks and dung-brown torrents some 87 kilometers north of Lijiang City in Yunnan.

When we arrived the waters of the Jinsha River flowed toward us. Hsu Yang embraced me from behind on the observation deck.

"This is where our presidents meet to play cards," he said, pointing to a circular conference hall perched on a stone parapet above us, its black-mirror glass obscuring whatever goes on inside. "There was a summit six months ago when our President Xi, the great-great-grandson of Chairman Xi, met your President Freud."

He pronounced Freud as *fraud*.

"What do you mean, '*Your* president?' He's *our* president."

"In name only. All Ameriguan presidents are frauds."

I sighed; more Marco cynicism.

"What was the meeting about?"

"Regional ministers in Kunming stashing assets in frozen grandparents' names," Marco said.

"Xi's great-great-grandson has been clamping down."

"He's good at that."

I shout above the cataract's pounding din.

"You want to dive into the river, don't you, Naomi? Join the immortals, right? Fly above the waves? Nothing can crush you?"

His challenge to me. Always goading—always wanting me to be more. Or perhaps mirroring my own ambitions. I was ready, mentally, to rev above the waves, just skimming the crests about the boulders, skimming the tops of the water like flying fish.

He kissed me in the spray.

We kissed wet and Coca-Cola sweet, running back to our seedy hotel room soaking wet, drying ourselves on the sheets, lying together in the late afternoon sunset, spinning tales of a tiger and egret escaping to Shangri-La. We had heard of the myth, but that evening I wrote a poem:

As the Tiger leaped
Across the River
Bounding
Stone on stone,
Quick above, the Egret flew

Diving and wafting,

its shadow drew a line across

The Beast's back.

Pounding were the hunters' hearts,

Eyes shielded in awe

as the Tiger leapt upon the rocks

they had never seen before.

Halfway 'cross the river

The water miles wide;

Hunters drowning,

Swallowed by the roar of the Beast on

The river never tamed,

That had no Name,

As the Tiger leapt and got away.

Marco said I was the tiger; he the egret, casting a shadow across my back, perhaps a marker of temporary possession? That evening we turned around without paying for our hotel room (the tub was full of cockroaches), driving for hours back to Lijiang, which seemed clean and safe to me.

"The Tibetan border patrol would have turned us back anyway, since I'm Chinese," Marco reminded me. "We never could have crossed over."

But I protested, checking the satellite maps. "We could have driven on or hiked from Shangri-la (pronounced *Shan-ge-li la*—not at all the fabled place of eternal youth, but a

199

crummy border town filled with Russian signage and lousy food). We could find a monastery deep in the *Hengduan* mountain passes half a day from Lhasa," I said, my voice breezy in the imagining. "We'd wake in a guest cottage to meet monks and penitents leading their pack horses, or groveling on the mountain roads, praying and genuflecting as is Tibetan holy tradition. But we'd be out of China and free."

"Not likely," Marco replied. "Bullshit but a nice idea."

Today I barely remember what he looked like at age 27. He's middle-aged now, his hair cut short and mottled with gray. I can still catch a glimpse of the man/boy as I land in a Lijiang airfield, resting my head in my hands for a moment inside my cockpit before descending for check-in. Marco's acne-pocked cheeks remind me of his imperfections. But the way he bounced at each step, springing from knees and hips, marks him as eternally young.

*

The meeting in Lijiang takes 20 minutes. Official questions consist of my assessment of the relative "stability" of the Harbin Ice Festival operations, its management of family worshipers and their cryopods on ice. Could the Harmonious Recycling system be replicated in Southwestern China in or around the cold, mountainous parts of Lijiang? (Probably yes, I tell them, depending on security procedures.) Cryogenesis in the *Hengduan* passages would save time and transport fees (the officials perk up), allowing worshipping families in the southwest to remain local while giving their elders a proper send off.

Did I see any problems with the Uyghurs interfering in recycling procedures, or staging more terrorist knifings of passengers at Kunming and Lijiang train stations where elders will be collected? ("Probably manageable risk," I reply. "Some of the behavior depends on how the Uyghurs are paid and treated.") But were there any suspicious figures at the Harbin Ice Festival seen prying open the cryopods with crowbars or remotely controlled implements?

"Of course not!" I tell them. "All is serene. And what a gorgeous display of lights!"

I'm given leave for a furlough. The Lijiang officials invite me for tea and moon cakes, making small talk, one of them patting me lightly on the back. Two of them exhibit large gold incisors in their smiles. All seem grateful for my work.

I remind the group that before I return to the East to take up more routine assignments (including a campaign to investigate Beaux II, the algorithmic architect), I plan a brief fact-finding mission to the moon. A leading biophysicist, Dr. Jens Remker, has requested my presence to assess the magnetospheres in volcanic formations at South Pole–Aitken.

I say nothing more.

18

MARCH 2120

JENS OF MONS RÜMKER

月
之
恋
人

"**N**aomi, ah...thah?"

Jens's voice sounds like someone drowning in my headset. South Pole-Aitken is the largest impact crater in the solar system, 2,500 kilometers in diameter, 13 kilometers deep, engulfing roughly a quarter of the moon's circumference. Yet no one can see it from Earth because it falls on the far side.

Apparently an asteroid five times the size of the Big Island of Hawaii slammed into it roughly four billion years ago, depositing planetoid-sized chunks of nickel and iron so dense they dented the basin elevation by more than .8 kilometers. Our scientists have measured the excess mass; it is so huge ($2.18*10^{18}$ kilograms) that it made the moon's bottom much denser than the top. The material lies dispersed hundreds of kilometers deep inside the lunar mantle. Dr. Remker is trying to sample materials from the interior of the basin—its lowest point is eight kilometers deeper than the jagged mountains at the crater top. He'll use radiometric dating to determine when the rocks were last molten, one indicator of the actual age of the major impact, although subsequent impacts mean that radiometric ages must be reset, confusing the picture, apparently skewing an accurate measurement.

*

I'm wearing a garland of red kika blossoms around my neck as our space transport lands first in Aitken. Do I want to look pretty and relaxed, as though bound for Hawaii? My final destination will require another shuttle hop to Mons Rümker, a volcanic bulge in Oceanus Procellarum—Ocean of Storms—in the northwest lunar quadrant, where Jens and I are set to meet first for a four-day vacation.

Not much time to explore. I expect to see him waiting for me on Rümker Command Center gantry since he has top-level privileges. So within 30 seconds of landing on the first Aitken leg, I've unbuckled my belts and bounded down double ramps to the desert platform leading to *Tian Gong* (天宫) Lunar Readiness station. In the next few minutes, white-coated neoprenes will screen me for physical wiring defects and Earth viruses.

I must pass the standard physiology benchmarks. (Am I breathing? Is my pulse too excitable? Are my blood and oil pressures lower than normal?) Once approved, I'm outfitted with the new bubble helmet and scaly lunar gear, the kind that protects against cosmic rays and seems porous and deceptively silky to the touch, but isn't. Under the new regime, my clear-coated respirator at throat level expands and contracts oddly like an overstuffed paper bag.

Believing this lunar trip is nothing extraordinary, I've tried to dampen my own expectations. With 8.8 million pounds of thrust to escape Earth's gravity, the *Long March 12* rocket has proven itself so reliable and sturdy that China's Mission Control operators render every command and mission check in trochaic monotone. "*Zhun bei:* (Get ready!) "*Shi Jiu Ba Qi Liu—*" (10, 9, 8, 7, 6—) The launches are biweekly now; hundreds of trained taikonauts and science staff depart and return from the moon and Mars without media coverage. On launch, I'm told I'll feel crushed in G-force blackness for just about a minute, my view of Earth partially blocked in a tiny capsule window, though I will detect the oceans deforming the known coastlines of the past.

We're off. I'm in radio silence; no human voice can be spoken or heard right now. Jens Remker will meet me within hours. I anticipate our conversations will be stiff and formal as he explains his research on gaseous plasma and magnetic activity around Mons Rümker, a pock-marked ugliness that looks like acne from space—actually 20 lava domes that rise 1,300 meters above a flat basaltic plane.

The *Logoharp* signals me; my time is running out. Jens, my Creator, has arranged a pass and permission, negotiating all the loopholes. I can't imagine what his fascination with me actually is. But he claims he has a mission for me.

The lander has snaked to the surface and Jens's image is crossing into my faceplate. First, I see him in the reflection of the lunar heliotrope lander blossoming purple in the dust. My transport follows the glide slope over the lava dome closest to our landing port. I deplane and wait. His image in my faceplate centers. His helmet is darkened against the blinding sunlight, but he takes my gloved hands, pulling me toward him. His voice sounds underwater but I can hear his laugh.

"You look exactly the same!" he gestures, thumbs up.

"I've grown, and I'm aging nearly twice as fast as any ordinary human!" I feel Jens's strength and yes, the warmth of his body, even in the lunar cold. "Of course, you and those mad robots are completely responsible for my laugh lines and crow's feet."

"You look lovely, no matter what!"

We nod awkwardly.

"Everything working properly?"

"Yes, thank you."

He leads me off the platform. Showing off, he jumps three meters high in the sunlight and beckons to me—should I copy him? But I remain still, watching him, as though I'm an embarrassed child being entertained by a Flying Dutchman.

We reenter his heliotrope and he pilots us a few kilometers above the lava domes. When we land, about to step onto the elevated platform of his temporary base, we lock arms and together leap up to the top deck eight meters above the gangway.

"Show off!" he shouts at me.

A girl bouncing on a pogo stick, weightless, I've entirely forgotten my position and age. He shakes his head, I think first because he's correcting me, but no, he's elated. And it's not long after the conventional reviews and debriefings that he shows me his quarters, his couch, his kitchenette, his bathroom, his bed. Everything is gray and rubberized and has no distinguishing characteristics whatsoever. Then he takes off his helmet, massages his blond and graying hair for a moment with big slender hands, and strips his outer suit. I do the same. We're standing in black and gray leotards, at least the lunar version of them, with an inverted Directorate "V" insignia emblazoned on our chests and arm patches. My standard black Argonaut suit is packed in my case; I still wear a skull cap.

"Would you like some coffee? Are you hungry?"

I look down at his beautifully tight legs and bony knees, high-arched feet. Massaging his knees, stretching and running in place with that self-deprecating frown he gets in a gesture of befuddlement and humility, Jens leads me to the single porthole that looks out on the black sable and sand-colored domes empty now, no longer active. At least this is my impression. He engages in a few desultory comments about the comparative volcanic youth of Rümker and the magnetic basalt plain, which may have been caused by a comet collision two billion years ago.

"Wow! I pop my lips, as though I haven't heard this at least three times before.

"Remote sensing suggests that the Rümker area has high amounts of radioactive thorium, which may have heated up the moon's mantle enough to form basaltic flows."

My arms fold as I nod politely.

"This place is two billion years younger and more magnetic than any other place on the moon," he goes on. But he stops, realizing I've already accessed his notes. Jens moves toward me, flexing his knees as though he's had a long run. He reaches. He pulls back my skull cap to touch a thicket of blond hair streaked with white; it's grown back unexpectedly since we last met in surgery.

"Naomi, are you reverting to human?"

"Maybe?" Blinking, I ask him with my eyes.

"Tell me everything. What's happened to you?" Reaching to the back of my head, he bends me toward him. We touch our foreheads as one.

I sigh. This is standard greeting. My *Logoharp* registers chords of harmony, exhilaration, abuzz with pleasure.

Trying to breathe deeply, as though the gaseous mix in the station seems geared toward ordinary human physiology, not hybrid borgs, I feel giddy. Maybe too much oxygen; maybe his presence?

"All I can tell you is that the rumors are true. The Directorate puts people down, like dogs, as soon as they reach age 55, and sometimes 50, depending on the lottery and an excess of elders in local populations. The same in my birth country. This program's no longer in beta."

"This is news to you?" he asks.

"I guess you know this already."

"I get the internal reports every day."

"Jens, no one seems to object! The sons and daughters and grandchildren actually seem happy about it. I watched them pushing the ice sleighs along on the Songhua. The children love to slide, talking to the dreamers as though they're alive!"

"They are," he says.

"But not for long. And the doxxers don't publicize or comment at all. Why aren't they more upset?"

Jens places his fingers on my temples, as though reading deeper into my memory. He discovers a reflex: Marco Hsu Yang embracing me. This doesn't disturb him apparently; he grins, sparse blond stubble on his chin; his lips appear full of feelings unexpressed.

"It's cramped in here," he says. "But we'll make room, okay?" He kisses me lightly on the lips. I push him away, perhaps six inches, not much. I feel his circulation of energy flowing into mine, a tingling running throughout the length of my arms and legs, chest, pelvis, throat. *The Logoharp* goes silent. My natural hand rests on his silvered chest, the artificial hand poised, ready to slap him down. But he moves closer anyway, pulling me toward him—a completely irresponsible action from a surgeon to a former patient, I might add, and he inserts his fingers in the port of the *harp*, flipping the switch so that he can unlatch the tines and place it on a sterile tray.

"I want to hear your real voice," he murmurs. "No need for Aeolian vibrations. There's no breeze here anyway."

"It's rather stifling—"

"I'll boost the oxygen."

"No need," I murmur. "Nitrogen overtone good."

He whispers, adjusting feeds. "There."

"I haven't used my own voice in a year. Perhaps you just remember me as I was, Jens? You can't make me human again, can you?"

"I wouldn't try."

The rest is uncanny, a throwback to teenage feelings: Marco holding my body and strumming it like a guitar. I can barely accept what's happening, though I enjoy his fingers treading so lightly, spider-like, as though he's playing scales softly on my collar bone, above my breasts I expose. When he arranges his clothes in a hamper of sorts that slides neatly into a wall compartment, he teases my body suit completely away from me. At his beckoning, he invites me to recline in what looks like a dentist chair suddenly expanding and flattening, surprising me since it's extremely comfortable. He joins me, reclining. The chair is a sofa, then a bed. Out the window I see nothing but lava domes and a hint of earthshine.

"It's all right, don't worry," he whispers. "The airlock is secured."

I can't protest. I just can't.

"How secure? Aren't you bothered by my skin? My colors? Your interest in me is completely unethical."

"No, it's entirely ethical in this wasteland far from Earth. There are no rules here. Besides, you're very tall," he assesses. "I like tall. I see a power in you unlike any human female I've encountered on the moon."

"Which females?"

"That Russian lady...rather squat."

"That's not saying much."

"You're right!"

We giggle.

"Hey, I created you. But you would have grown into this marvelous polyglot no matter who did the surgery."

"You remember what I looked like before," I correct him.

"You're too serious, Naomi. I see you from a year ago, and yesterday, today, and hopefully, tomorrow. All the images are fused for me."

He references Plato's *Symposium*. Do I remember it? The original humans were conjoined—four arms, four legs, two heads, two sets of genitals—but not facing each other. They moved swiftly in cartwheels across the Earth, and were powerful. "Wanting to weaken the humans," Aristophanes wrote in his *Symposium* critique, "Zeus, Greek king of gods, decided to cut each in two, and commanded his son Apollo 'to turn its face...towards the wound so that each person would see that he'd been cut and keep better order.'" But severance engendered the desire for each other, to heal the wound by searching for love in our missing half.

Jens is ripe for this argument, but he's not Platonic in any sense. His fingers touch the half- borg face that looks back at him; his arms reach to the triangle of my shoulders. Then his legs wrap around mine turning gold, then teal blue. As though I've never thought about it before, or at least never thought of conjoined sex as repairing an original wound. I touch his chest, waist, loins, so wet, his bony knees and all parts in between. He shudders. Without protest I nod and look down at his suprasternal notch. He senses my softness, humility and affection. Zeus condemned our mortal power, splitting us into two separate parts, or so the myth goes, condemning us to spend our lives searching for the other half. But I believe there's no point in searching, and I'm no longer tending my wounds. I accept them. This is all I can do.

Is he my lover? My soulmate? No answer.

It surprises me that any pain I feel is dulled; perhaps it's human pain, pain for what I've missed. Any desire is human desire. Dryness, wetness, the lavender and witch hazel smells of Jens against me. The desire that I'm not supposed to feel. We're suspended in our reluctance and joy. For a few minutes I create him in my mind, and he does me, physically and mentally, in a higher sphere. We're conjoined in the vacuum of space where Earth rules don't apply. He tries to touch me in my cave and at first my gloved hand slaps him away. But my harp...no, I can't speak through it. My voice is gone. I can't hear any footsteps, either, and I can't see anything besides his face and throat against mine. He moves slowly as I do, but deftly, gracefully, much like a sleepy acrobat with hands and legs springing, gliding. His touch, and the thing I crave is the smell of him, the roughness of his stubble, the square jaw, his open mouth and his insistence on climbing with me as though we're scaling Rümker. Jens smells of lunar heliotrope, a mixture of gardenias and dentist-chair rubber. Maybe I just imagine this. He doesn't hurt me, he'd never hurt me, but I feel we're diving off a cliff.

"Hold me! I can't stop."

He holds a moment and accelerates. I move with him, whispering to my goddess. He fills me with seed. This is the wound that never heals, Zeus be damned.

*

"I thought of you every time I bounced into those Aitken craters," he whispers as we rest.

"What's it like?"

"Dark. So dark you can see nothing. Frigid. The walls are slippery."

"You have lights, don't you?"

"Yeah, but I have to feel the stone to understand what's there.

"The moon is empty," he continues, holding me tighter. "Sometimes I watch the Earth, but I don't long to go back. The time bomb there—perhaps an asteroid first, or the polar melt, or just a final squelch of selfishness that turns us into dinosaurs."

"The orb looks pure from a distance."

"You can't see the Great Wall from here."

"That was a lie someone dreamed up."

"You don't lie, do you?" he asks me.

"Only on social media."

He nods, trying to understand. His playbook of right and wrong seems different from mine.

"Being with you is like slipping down these crevasses. I'm trying to feel the surface inside to draw my topo-maps accurately. This hasn't been done."

"The same with me?"

"I find your topo-maps intriguing."

He pauses, stroking my hair, moving his deft fingers to place behind my earlobe, tapping there, massages there, as though my mastoid process holds a secret.

"When are you coming back?" He reaches for his canteen and offers me a sip.

I turn deep blue in the dark. "There's an inquest when I return. Someone or something is wrong with the timing of the Harmonious Recycling system, as it's called."

"But can't you get an assignment here?"

"No, I can't. Not now."

"What about documenting the potential for colonization on the northeast plain—perhaps near Copernicus? Maybe a research or agricultural colony? Our greenhouses grow food."

Neither of us pursues the idea. For two nights, we escape talk of greenhouses and the injected *Neisseria meningitidis* bacteria that make 10 days of human pre-extinction in the cryopods so pleasurable. By day, we explore the lava domes and even his beloved craters, though I don't feel entirely comfortable rappelling against the slippery dark walls. He calls down to me, then passes me by, tied to cables as thick as the Dyneema high-density polyethylene bindings on lunar bridges. My heart is racing fast. When he disappears into a crevasse hundreds of meters below, even with his head lamps and microphone, whistling and humming as he plunges, his 14-layered Mylar space suit designed to be impervious, I lose my feeling that he'll ever return. But in minutes that seem like days, he rises finally, hoisting himself up as I grab his hand and pull him over the ledge. A few moments later he leads me on our flying walks, and then back to shelter, embracing me again in our pod.

*

Through his window the sun on this lunar outpost seems to shine forever. Yet I can see the sun setting on the Earth's blue ball moments earlier than it's supposed to, the darkness and shadows creeping at dusk as the continents light up, each in turn. Earth is so overworked now, so dry; I can't see the billions crowding the cities like ants from here, or the desert winds sucking up moisture on every continent.

With Jens, though, I climb to the peaks of the lava domes, the sun behind us. Our silhouettes stretch across the lunar plains to the horizon, foreshortening only when we face a vertical rock wall. It's comforting to see us together this way, lengthening and shortening, lengthening again, as though we have all the time in the world to practice both magic and humility. We don't, of course; the Directorate's Life Clock limits our time exploring any planet, moon or lover's soul. Both of us know this. I memorize his eyes and the look of them as I let go. His question, *"Won't you stay?"* is the only one I need to hear.

19

APRIL 2120

NITROUS SCUM INTERROGATION

剧
毒
审
讯

I'm back in Mother Country too soon, returning my focus to Harbin and Chinese Macbeth. The lunar hop from Mons Rümker to Aitken rocket base was uneventful; my push to home no different, except for the ocean currents that seem as blue as my blood, drawing me back home.

I remember Jens kissed me goodbye; I remember kissing him. Lingering in the launch corridor, he grasped my real hand, not letting it go. Savoring the touch of his chapped lips,

I placed my left index finger on his Adam's apple, feeling the vibrations in his throat making feeble attempts at speech. His sing-song "goodbye" suddenly erupted through the inter-com—our foreheads touched again—my helmet held at my side. I turned without words and went striding to the launch elevator.

Am I different now? The void surrounds me, the blue stars. Rigel. Sirius. Pleiades. One glimpse at the stars and I ask myself, perhaps he was just lonely, pinned against the flatlands and mountains of the moon. Am I? Strapped into my seat on *Long March* I caught sight of booster rockets firing like volcanoes, one after the other, scooping me up in the acceleration, then a few moments of weightlessness. Perhaps I'll never go home.

But here I am. In Lijiang, as instructed again, I await my interrogation. In the casino anteroom to the Chinese Direc-torate two drones noiselessly escort me. This antechamber is titled "Casino of Spades." It's dreary and flecked with silver, the holo-displays behind black curtains detailing the history of Japanese atrocities, something like the Holocaust Museum in Washington subdirectorate displaying piles of silvered shoes taken from Jews going to the showers. Here, in Lijiang, the Singing Directorate focuses on the Rape of Nanjing in the 1930s. There are dioramas and interactive displays of unnec-essary surgeries, eviscerations, gassing, bayonets. Screaming women. The gambling tables are available for play but practically no one uses them.

A similar anteroom, Casino of Clubs, comes decorated with medieval armor, swords, scabbards, torture racks and all manner of golf clubs (an attempt by the Directorate at humor). Witnesses and prosecutors use the room to smoke.

There is no Casino of Diamonds. The mode of exchange among the bureaucrats is bitcoin, promotion, life-extension points, gourmet dinner tickets and fancy apartments.

Drones escort me now into the Casino of Hearts, its floors covered wall to wall with plush ruby-red carpet. Komodo dragons and geckos appear to slither along the Corinthian columns and tiled walkways in the courtyard perimeter, just two marble steps above the central slot machines.

A patron's disorientation produces hypnotic attention. Presumably the idea was to allow patrons to calm their nerves by playing Blackjack or Pie Day Gecko Bet.

The latter game amounts to fixing one's eyes on the opalescent silver geckos and dragons in the colonnade until they come alive, their locomotion rendered convincing in the patron's disordered mind. Indeed, as I stare at the patterns, the geckos multiply and dart this way and that, going motionless as I turn away, then alive again, slithering up and down the columns and dutifully catching ladybugs whose orange and black wings spread floridly, a *thrrrrippp* only I can hear.

As I focus more intently, the geckos crawl down onto the casino tables and floor. Then they swarm up the alabaster columns leading to the Chamber of Inquest. As I blink to refocus, they spread to the ceiling and disappear through a vent, apparently snatching the remaining bugs and licking the air clean.

Logoharp signals disturbance. The Inquisitors may try to force me to reveal a personal secret, then transform this "criminal" secret into a date with the prosecution.

*

A drone hovers over an Art Deco-style chair, ordering me to sit. The chair, rosewood in color, has a back shaped like a delicate fan, its separate spools resembling the strings of a harp.

Dean Cheung Yuen, my Hong Kong mentor, arrives at this moment. I'm guessing she's here to orchestrate accusations with Beijing Council Chairman Dakota Sung. The *Logoharp* picks up their whispered conversations. I can't see them yet, since they sit in a separate anteroom which, I'm told, is equipped with a giant roulette wheel. From the vocal timbre, I believe this inquest is Cheung's doing. A third figure, addressed as "Comrade File Cabinet," sounds feminine, with a teasing electronic lilt. I believe she's a Borg-Server, her function to redact and store the final version of my responses to questions delivered with a spin of the roulette wheel.

The drones escort me to the Chamber of Inquest. ("Escort" is a polite expression; actually, their claws lock under my armpits and I'm lifted, then dropped, into a life-sized bell jar.) I open my eyes to a Disneyland of cryogenic organ pipes, dozens of them, all colored in various pastels: pinks and ambers for the highest notes, pale citron and turquoise in the midrange, aquamarines and indigos for the lowest. A judgment is rendered as a song. The defendant responds with a five-to-ten-note motet indicating compliance, active resistance without appeal, or a motion to appeal, in which case the elders confer and decide the next step.

A first hearing isn't definitive. I'm not exactly sure what my petty "crime" is supposed to be, or whether I'm here to testify about someone else's crime. Perhaps it's my trip to the moon, or my association with Miranda Qian Shuai in Harbin. She's considered a passé journalist and troublemaker, certainly not an RJ, as I am. But now that I think of it, perhaps it's the presence of Lang Fei, who promises to teach me how to cheat at Blackjack or throw souls. He tells me he can fix any lottery, upend any algorithm, even crack open a hermetically sealed cryopod to free the human contents inside. Miranda calls him "Chinese Houdini," although she grossly exaggerates. A few of the elders have learned to reopen their cryopods without him. I don't know how, since they're locked tight.

"You're a witness here, not the accused," Dakota Sung trumpets on the large video holo-screen above me. He's lumpy in his gray Mao jacket and frayed pantaloons, sweating profusely in stained armpits.

"In our procedures of trial, one witnesses one's own actions and critiques accordingly," he continues. "We expect to have an unemotional exchange until the final verdict is rendered *a cappella*, at which point the witness is detained for *coda*, when a confession obtains accordingly. Do you understand?"

"What's the charge?" My *Logoharp* speaks my thoughts bluntly, in studied monotone.

The female voice disguised with flutes and triangles comes from Comrade File Cabinet, but I still can't see her on screen. "Our database of holo-delimited files has to be filled in order for the Inquest to proceed. You must provide the data."

I tune my *Logoharp* to make synthetic voice projections stronger, more vital.

"This is not a normal situation where you might resist or appeal. In this particular instance we know you have data we require."

"Is Comrade File Cabinet in charge?" *Logoharp* asks. "Who will survey and protect my data?"

"Your confidentiality is assured."

"Who's in charge?" *Logoharp* repeats itself.

"Your option to ask questions here, even to cross examine, is prohibited."

The drones reach into the bell jar, detaching my neck plate.

"Proceed then."

I've been warned in low radio frequencies to broadcast only through the *Logoharp*, its voice situated in my suprasternal notch, the reconstructed one that leads directly to the jugular vein and, ultimately, my brain. As I twist the tines tightly at the neck port I smile, a somewhat forced and brittle smile. The tines pinch. In fact, the harp has sharply molded silicon and brass tines equipped with rheostats to measure the exact electrical resistance as the harp speaks. However, if the instrument has not sounded for more than a few weeks, the port begins to clog with blood and phlegm. As the drones tighten my fit, I feel a trickle of ooze and mucus dripping onto my collar shield.

"The *Logoharp* is required to translate all responses into every world language," the female voice announces. "For our holo-delimited files."

"We judge you to be a cooperating witness as this inquest finds," a deep basso voice booms in recording.

"Who, may I ask, is speaking?"

The voice hesitates and coughs.

"Who assumes the authority to speak?"

"I do," Chairman Sung announces, his voice unaltered. "But Comrade File Cabinet will conduct much of this inquest in multiple voices and then register your responses as one of two qubit states."

"You mean 'Yes' or 'No.'"

"Do you know why you're here?" File Cabinet's shrill voice rises in crescendo.

"No, not exactly," I reply, pushing and twisting the tines in a counterclockwise direction. My neck is stinging. "May I speak to Dean Cheung?"

"You are not permitted to ask questions, only to populate the database as required."

My harp sings back in tonics. "Cheung? I still can't see you on screen. If you answer, my cooperation is assured!"

No direct reply. I twist the tines further counterclockwise to lower my frequency.

"You were in Heilongjiang for several days."

"Yes. Part of my research assignment."

"We've monitored your activities in the Ice City and find no particular harm."

An A-major chord in citron yellow indicates agreement.

"We believe it is wise for you to see our True North and its worshippers who revere their ancestors while frolicking among the larger-than-life ice sculptures at the same time."

A high-toned B-flat swells to aquamarine.

"Is this about Miranda Qian Shuai? I ask. "Or my affection for puppies?"

"You will enter your data in each holo-delimited field."

"Is this about my meeting with Lang Fei?"

"Negative."

"Doctor Jens Remker?"

A long pause. "Negative."

The holocubes are replicating in rainbow boxes before me in mid-air, each with a photon qubit that flip-flops on an x-y-z-axis—three polarized states. It's clear to me, as I populate each cube, that my answers, delivered in a fine, truthful arpeggio, will be reduced to a binary on-off yes or no, and that certain dual-colored qubit values can stand for more than one reply. A neutral (silence) on the z-axis measures resistance or reluctance to cooperate.

"We believe Miranda Qian Shuai is enjoying her creative story with you," Sung's voice announces, a slow oboe *tremolo*. "She is naturally attracted to foreign things, and even hybrids like you. Maybe she's in love with you?" He snickers, waiting for a reply. I won't register his implication, though I feel it.

"She does no harm even though she loves the idea of doing mischief," my harp replies.

I flash back to Miranda Qian Shuai leading me down a *hutong* in Shanghai to eat freshly made moussaka. The ooze, now trickling down my chest, is wetting my power module.

"So why am I here?"

"We need data about your former husband."

"What?"

"Locating him is a matter of State security."

As Cheung speaks, one of the hot flamingo-pink pipes flares in sequence with amber, then a pale icy blue. The lower registers chime in indigo, reminding me of a twenty-first century Polestar rhapsody by the composer Jennifer Higdon. The *tremolos* are deafening.

"Your dreams are easily detected," Cheung intones. "You seem not at ease, because your mind is like a rowboat paddling upstream to the past, fantasizing a relationship with Marco Hsu Yang, who is no longer yours."

I swallow. "With all due respect, Dean, I don't believe you know what you're talking about."

Unscrewing the tines counter clockwise, my logo voice drops an octave. "May I be excused? The ooze is distracting me. I need to detach and flush my port."

Cheung gives an order. The drones approach the bell jar; a window unlocks, and they begin squirting citron-atomized 5W30 on my port. They reverse the screws clockwise, making the harp tones rise an octave. It hurts!

"I need my own flush," I repeat.

"You're distracted! We need to know his whereabouts."

The pipes wail, sounding a lament.

"I request permission to detach. The *Logoharp* interface is corroded. It loses congruence after a few weeks of disuse."

"Flush it out, then," comes the command.

The drones uncouple my tines as they flush the port with a hypotonic solution followed by a cryoseal, something like *StipTik*. It stings. Robotic fingers reattach the brass tines, which now bite even deeper.

"Please stop! The tines?"

"Denied."

"I'm not responsible for Marco Hsu Yang's whereabouts. I have no idea."

"Don't interrupt!" the feminine tympany retorts. "Fill in the holo-delimited field."

"We must know about your marriage."

"My pre-transplant life is irrelevant."

"Negative. Our inquest is completely relevant. Details will reveal—"

"What? I write your political outcomes; I'm not engaged in them. Now or at any time. *The Laws of Ice* dictate strict separation. I orchestrate events in accordance with—"

"Public perception!" Chairman Sung shouts an octave above his normal pulseless monotone. "Who was Marco Hsu Yang to you? Why did he divorce you? And why is he tampering with the Directorate's Life Clock?"

"I have no idea about Marco's interference. When we were married, he had free will to stay or leave as he saw fit. It seems you're inquiring to resurrect childish feelings of pity and fear, now fully neutralized," my harp retorts. "If you don't stop pursuing this line of questioning, the flesh trolls will chime in to my defense. Some would be eager to strip you bare."

"Why did he divorce you?"

"His family was higher ranked than mine. I had no control."

"You married 'Chinese Macbeth!'" she said. "In a first marriage, especially between an Ameriguan and a higher-ranked Chinese, either party has the right to block divorce."

"I had no 'rights.' He moved to Beijing."

"Because?"

"He wanted to. I mean, his grandma wanted him to meet a nice Chinese girl—"

"Didn't he give you any warning?"

"Not really."

"We don't sanction mixed marriages," Cheung retorts. "When they fail it reflects badly on our Council. If permission is granted, the match is predicted to be beneficial. We believed yours would produce more hybridized intelligence in the downstream pool."

"You mean, we didn't have children. A great infraction."

Silence. Cheung emerges from behind the roulette wheel and levitates serenely to my bell jar. She turns a switch to flush nitrous oxide, the scum color indicating contamination, just enough to make me feel stupid.

"We looked the other way when you married in secret," she whispers, as though extending a confidence to a dear friend.

"But we were miles from the tunnels. We married in Zion—"

"You married 'Chinese Macbeth!'" she said. "He was destined to be a King, a Leader! It was easy to extend our surveillance, especially when it comes to potentially tragic circumstances."

"Why didn't you tell me before? What made you so curious? Was it the difference in our stained-glass colors? His dark purple spot above his tailbone or my blonde hair covering his private parts while I sucked him dry?"

"Naomi!"

Cheung evacuates the bell jar. I switch to gill breathing. Liquid pond scum fills the chamber. My eyes roll backward.

"Why did you let him leave?"

"*Let him?*"

"You won't be able to carry out your assignments if he's still on your mind."

"He's not. The mention of him is like a floater inside my eye. I don't notice it anymore because my brain wipes it away."

"Enter your responses in each holo-delimited field."

"The hemorrhaging—"

"A little bleed won't hurt you. Why did you let him leave?" Sung shouts.

"He wanted to! Every word that came out of his mouth was 'escape.' There's nothing he liked more than card games, cheating colleagues and clinging to his dear *Lao Lao*."

"If you must know, Marco Hsu Yang designed the most advanced Harmonious Recycling algorithm the Directorate has," Cheung cautions. "I mentioned you'd be flushing him out when we spoke last."

"You mentioned a 'Chinese Macbeth.' Not my ex-husband!"

*

Cheung won't say more. Besides, what connection could there possibly be between the New Left Star of a century ago—the historic Beaux, would-be successor to Hu Jintao—and my puerile, cowardly Marco?

"He's gaming his own system," Cheung claims. "Marco introduced some kind of flaw, a trapdoor. He's allowing certain elders to wake up from the Recycling cryopods to escape decommissioning."

Good for him, I think. "I doubt he can play at that level."

"You sure?"

The drones approach me, pumping isoflurane into the bell jar as I drop down, bleeding in spurts. Assuming the pose of a thumb-sucking fetus. The anesthetic smells of pink bubble bath; my *Logoharp* drowns in fluid…

"You're hiding memories."

"Not at all."

"You're sympathetic to him. Perhaps you wanted his seat in medical studies?" Cheung psychologizes. "You wanted him to leave you so you could take his place?"

"He was abusing his medical privileges."

"Correct."

"He said I was too *lihai*, too aggressive. The woman's always at fault."

"Where is this man now?"

I tug at my port.

"Where is he now? You have impeccable location sensing!"

"My pressure is too low—"

"Your mind is with him."

"Negative."

Cheung levitates above me, little gargoyle. She bats her crepe-thin eyelids.

"Perhaps you need more oxygen?"

I've sunk to the bottom of the bell jar. Stuttering, since I can't voice anymore. She knows that if the Directorate needed me to find him, it would show weakness. Never show weak-ness.

Her voice softens. "Perhaps we're being too hard on you, Naomi? With your circuitry, *Logoharp sensing* and tines in full drive, finding him should be no trouble for you."

She boosts the oxygen. My eyes pop. Breath takes hold.

"You mean persuading him to give himself up? He'd never—"

"You know him better than anyone...at least you have the power to decipher his twisted mind."

"Cheung, half my connectome is replaced. You know that, including memories of an original soul. New synaptic tokens produce a stack of memories like playing cards, all two-dimensional, replaceable, easily shuffled. I don't think I could recall enough, much less persuade him if I tried."

"But you will try! Excessive empathy, Comrade? Marco Hsu Yang is responsible for all the algorithms, cryotubes, timing and temperature controls of a system offering hope to us all. He can't tamper with this! He's our number-one algorithmic leader."

"A conniving idiot! Ah, yes, you compared him to corrupt Beaux from Dalian and Chengdu."

"The trapdoor!" Dakota Sung interjects. "You'll find him and discover what the flaw is."

"It's not my business!"

"It is now, Naomi. Do you want cryotherapy again?" Cheung asks.

Shaking my head, slowly, sarcastically. "Oh that will help. An RJ hosed down in sub-zero washes. Broken teeth and jaws against a white porcelain sink."

"Is this sarcasm?" File Cabinet interjects. "Stricken from the record."

The fluids in the jar evaporate.

I humble myself. "Permission to speak directly?"

My harp—bloody, brown, caked in tine-rust and cilia—falls to the floor.

As I try to stand up, drones inject several shots of sodium pentothal to ease memory. Cheung keeps pushing me down.

"I last detected his presence a few months ago in a way station along the ocean tunnels to Sumatra, Ring of Fire."

"Headed where?"

"Banda Aceh."

"Where?"

"Northern Sumatra. A lost province, one hundred and sixty thousand souls perished when three successive tsunamis came in like freight trains in 2004, pushing the ships and the bodies five miles inland. Marco Hsu Yang has an interest in disasters—"

"He's still there?"

"Not likely."

"He's extremely corrupt," Sung adds.

"Hsu Yang is incapable of official corruption," I remind him. "He's just playfully corrupt in another way."

"You're naïve, Naomi. Normally, algorithmic leaders recite the *Laws of Ice* verbatim, along with the *Qu'ran* and the *Analects of Xi*, all measures we use to weed out corruption. Young candidates take merit exams. Our Directorate physicians also evaluate their brain scans, behaviors, over months before admitting them to positions."

"The Directorate chooses top leaders through merit exams?"

"No. Their wisdom distinguishes them absolutely," Sung replies.

"What about Hsu Yang?"

"He never took the merit exam."

"And now he's the cause of your troubles? Marco couldn't pass the merit exam even if you handed him the answer key."

Cheung slaps my cheek.

"Why do you think he's in the tunnels?"

"Just a feeling. I mean, a signal. A plangent chord. The *Logoharp* indicates his presence. When in doubt, run home to Grandma."

"It must be true!" Sung touches both hands to his crown, triumphant, as though he can actually hear my harp. Of course, he can't hear a thing. "It must be true because the harp is never wrong!" Sung shouts. "Even if he's not in the tunnels now, he will be by the time Naomi gets to him."

Cheung signals, nodding, and the drones drag me away. I'm sure this isn't over. The Casino of Spades dissolves into a mirrored corridor growing narrower and narrower. It ends in a tiny Alice-in-Wonderland exit door. Drugged, I can still hear Cheung and Sung arguing about the success of my witness. Their judgment to File Cabinet is "z"—silence on the axis. The holo-delimited files remain incomplete. No one knows if I'm making up stories or telling the truth.

Neither do I.

20

MAY 2120

MIRANDA THE SPY

间
谍

I wake up in a hyperbaric chamber lined with bullet-proof glass. Miranda has returned to me from Harbin, her face glued tight with apprehension. I'm wondering how she got here; she must know more about this inquest than I do. Perhaps Lang Fei informed her, or someone else inside the Directorate?

"I didn't message you. How on Earth did you find me?"

She reaches for me, her long fingers spreading against the outer window. Someone anonymous transported me to Kamchatka's vertical way station a kilometer below the ocean surface. Still trying to rid myself of barotrauma from the deep dive. The pain and stabbing in my chest must be nitrogen overload.

"Miranda?"

"Yes, Naomi."

"You're working for them, aren't you?"

Her face is covered with tiny welts. She purses her lips but looks me in the eye without fear.

"Don't talk."

I feel her warmth as she unlatches the pod door. Discharging the nitrogen-oxygen mix, she switches to pure oxygen so the baro-pressure exceeds three times normal. I'll be suspended for fifteen minutes to re-equalize. My skin feels fresh toward the blue, even burnished, but only after she adjusts the mixture. Miranda manages a smile because she sees me virtually helpless. I'm still supine in the chamber, half frozen, dizzy and unable to move.

"They gave you the third degree, didn't they?"

"Only the second. The third means execution."

In a few more minutes she'll help me to my feet. Her strength is enough to elevate my entire frame, though with all my new polyvinyl resin fibers my body is supple and light.

I whisper to her, smelling gardenias in her hair. Yes, gardenias in a metallic chamber without light.

"Steady a moment," she replies. "It's those bloody old *Logoharp* trowels. They stick into you. Better to speak on your own."

She unclips and pulls out the voicing module. Throwing the tuning fork and attached wires onto the floor, she sees them caked in blood. My voice is strangulated, the result of too many days of paralysis since my time with Jens.

Miranda props me up so I don't fall. She has unexpected strength. She turns me around so I face her, her lips trembling a moment, tightening, as though she's responsible for what has happened.

Is she a spy? Does she love me? Now that I've been with Jens, I feel strange, open to any desire, as though I can no longer obey *Logoharp* instructions.

I lift some strands of hair to my faceplate. "How do you keep your hair like this?" I lift her hair between my fingers, imbibing her beauty. "Scented oils are forbidden."

"I have a source!" she laughs.

She draws me tighter to her body. I'm unaccustomed to anyone holding me up; normally I'm holding others up.

"I'm so sorry. Your armor is light," she says, "yet you feel weighted down."

I embrace her, kiss her left cheek. Her height is unexpected; I'm thrown off balance because she's nearly as tall as I am. Perhaps she's trying to keep just enough distance to preserve her equilibrium. But she's a spy, or an informer, or both. Then I sink down, my face buried into the crook of my elbow, embarrassed as I collapse onto the floor. She's still grabbing my hands, trying to break the fall.

"How much blood have you lost? How many platelets?" she asks.

"Probably a hundred-thousand per microliter. You didn't answer my question. How did you know where I am?"

She shakes her head, crouching, looking down between her knees.

"Miranda, I can't measure my blood loss exactly. My sensors are down. Go to the console."

In a few moments she starts an infusion. I'm flat on the floor; she watches me cautiously, a doe in the woods.

"How did you get back here?"

"I don't remember," she lies.

"You followed me."

"I figured you'd get lost again. I'm here to protect you."

"How did you get in?"

"I have clearance."

"So you work for the State?"

A breath. "Naomi, everyone works for the State. Journalists *are* the State."

"Even you?

"Yes, to a degree."

"Then you know what this is about?"

She hesitates; the welts on her face expand.

"You'll be asked to bring the suspect back to court," she affirms. "This is your assignment. And mine. My boyfriend Gua Gua knows where he is. I'll find out from him."

"How does he know? What is his relation to Marco Hsu Yang?"

Miranda tells me the story without a word. I can feel her lids stirring again, as though she sees the faraway object of my conjecture. Her pulse rises; she's ready with more data. My hand reaches to her temples.

"Don't be embarrassed. It's not my business, but your thoughts suggest he's a relative of—he's Marco Hsu Yang's son?"

Miranda's eyes cloud over.

"Yes." After a pause. "Am I losing face?" she asks. "Did I do something wrong?"

My fingers reach to the corners of her frown. I push the corners up to assure her. "Depends on your perspective, Shuai. In Mother Country, everyone is afraid of losing face," I tell her. "In Ameriguo, no one cares about losing face, because we've already lost it."

"You haven't met this man you're looking for?" she rejoins, slyly. "You really don't know who he is?" Her voice is singsong, sarcastic.

I swallow. "Adjust the flow, please, at least twenty percent." The air revives me; liquid salts and nutrients puff up my entrails. "I have an idea who he is, of course. But no, I can't visualize the whole person. I'm blocked."

"Oh, come on."

"All right. He's a rich corrupt official, handsome and dangerous, like historical Beaux. I've just not identified his face."

My feeble attempt at a joke.

"It's impossible that you should have missed a mugshot on city screens." She pauses. "Naomi?"

"Okay, what are you doing with Marco's Hsu Yang's son? Or is there some other connection? Is it Marco?" Or both? This Gua Gua, the silly name of a winter melon, a 'thin gourd,' the same son's name given by Beaux and Ms. Goo—?"

"I'll explain later," she says, flipping the air switch.

"Explain now."

"Naomi, this isn't your business."

"It is. I'm a public servant under deadline. I have to know what I'm getting into with the three of you."

"Naomi, Hsu Yang is powerful."

"So what?"

"He protects me, but he's reckless. I seem to dilute his risk taking by acting as his conscience. I write about his accomplishments."

"You mean putting people on ice? You think that's okay?"

"I suppose so."

"What about Gua Gua?"

"He's young. Sexbot, I call him. I can control his outbursts. He uses me to get back at his father, and sometimes to negotiate the man's attention. I don't think Hsu Yang ever loved him."

"I could have told you about Marco."

"You don't have to tell me anything," she says. "Marco is selfish, but he keeps me in stories... protection."

"You find him attractive?"

"Yeah. But there's another thing."

"What?"

"When I'm with him, he tells me stories about the way you argued. The strength in you that he didn't quite believe, your desire to be counted—"

"Why did he tell you this?"

"Maybe a resemblance? A warning?"

Miranda plays father against son. I guess her sexual inclinations are too complicated for me to understand. Pulling me toward her, she stares at my eyes searching for what? Approval? I can't give her that; I don't have the right or inclination.

"Perhaps I need to throw my soul into you," I tell her.

*

The airlock behind Miranda is where the Kamchatka tunnel ships wait. She takes my arm and I hobble through the exit, wondering why she is still taking care of me. A reflection in a mirror: I see my dearest friend who knows too much, and the image of an aging RJ argonaut bent over like a crone, the beginnings of neck cords and white wisps of hair sticking out from a skullcap.

"You're vain," Miranda whispers. "But you still look young! You're just not seeing how you appear to me when you stop frowning!"

21

MAY 2120

KURIL-KAMCHATKA

千
岛
战
火

We've stepped into the Kuril-Kamchatka caves, the monu-
ments of trench and fire paying tribute to the fallen dead
in the Sino-Japanese and Russo-Japanese wars. Miranda and I
go quickly to the anteroom of the "Peak," the holding chamber
connecting the Kuril-Kamchat airships whole en route to my
continent. We slip past bulletproof Lexan cases displaying
Japanese soldier diaries, along with the *Ukiyo-e* portraits of the
red and brown-haired Russians falling bloody in battle, hands

thrown up in surrender. In the Japanese images, soldiers of the Rising Sun are dressed in crisp black or navy uniforms and caps that never fall off their heads. Only the pathetic Russians lie maimed and bleeding on the ground. In the Russian paintings, the Japanese resemble timorous toads with puppet heads, huge eyes and buck teeth, groveling before a tall, skinny Russian officer.

Our underground passage opens the door to the Kuril-Kamchatka orogeny, which is subject to major seismic events, now monitored but not entirely predictable. Miranda and I will be in full compression once we enter the tube for a three vertical kilometer drop to the luge station. Tubes are said to withstand shocks as high as 9.1 on the Richter scale. As we descend, we see pleasing tourist photographs of the Klyuchevskoy, Koryaksky and Kronotsky volcanoes of Kamchatka, one of them in early morning showing pitchfork trails of molten lava down the mountainside, hot orange and red spikes against the blue. The narrative in my headset is calming:

> *Kamchatka's volcanoes have never been bloodthirsty:*
> *The natives of Kamchatka can hardly recall eruptions*
> *that carried death there... The silence alongside the*
> *volcanoes fills the soul with an incomprehensible*
> *combination of anxiety and peace...you feel scared*
> *and at the same time happy...*

Miranda leads me into a hallway adjacent to the reception chamber; she opens a janitor's closet door with her fingerprint. Behind it a series of airshafts radiates from a circular hatch, allowing us to crouch down and crawl. She chooses an airlock at three o'clock, heading down the passage about 200 meters. "I've forgotten, exactly," she shrugs, pausing a moment, then leading me back to the hub. We choose the shaft at seven o'clock; she punches a code; and the pipe organs groan a greeting. Immediately I squelch the volume. A single hatch opens. In another bell jar filled with ether and buoyant gases I make out the figure of a naked male floating in fetal position, the room suffocating and hot like a greenhouse.

"He's in suspension, nitrogen and oxygen protecting him in sleep. This is preparation for the express trip to the Aleutia boundary," Miranda tells me, although I can pinpoint his trajectory on a monitor facing his bell jar. "You become lighter in the luge because oxygen is at a premium and the pressures must be equalized to prevent crushing at the deepest part of the trenches." She nods to me; I lift her up to a trapeze ladder and a platform suspended above the tank. She climbs the ladder and adjusts her oxygen feed and mask, then dives head first into the bubble, tumbling beside him, righting herself, finally pushing against his chest, as though to resuscitate him.

"Marco! Yang!" She shakes him. *Qi lai.* My Heavens, Wake up!" (我的天，起来 起来 !) She voices through an internal microphone, repeating the mantra several times. I hear her voice through my earpiece. As he stirs, she leans over and kisses him lightly on the lips. His neck contracts and his arms reach up toward her. I can see only a partial profile: a head of hair black and silver, still thick, a few pockmarks. I cannot see his body. The two hold each other as though buffeted by shock waves. Panicky, like a child, she clings to his neck as he holds her tight to his body.

"*Ni wei shenme lai zhe-er?* (你为什么来这儿)," he asks. "Why are you here?"

"I brought someone you know," she says. "You must speak to her. Urgently." Without moving, she beckons and I come closer, revving high above, even higher than the diving platform. My arms elongate. Reaching inside the bubble, I dive, advancing into a position twenty degrees above him looking down.

"Are you sentient?"

The man stares at me.

"My task is to retrieve you."

He stares without seeing.

Miranda moves out of our circle and plants herself 45 degrees below us. She is treading in the gaseous liquids like an anemone floating along the sea bottom. This leaves a space for me to descend and examine him.

"Marco Hsu Yang? This is your name, correct?"

"What?"

"But this is no longer your name."

"My name is Tian Jinghui… Marco Hsu Yang was my birth name. But he was decommissioned in Beijing many years ago." He studies my visor. "You don't resemble anyone I know."

Should I be offended by these words?

"My circulation is organic, of course, but most of my body was rebuilt from aftermarket titanium, polyvinyls and abalone composite integrated with human tissue."

My visor lifts. Tian studies my irises, entirely clear, no color at all except for whichever contact lenses I wear to give observers the illusion of natural tint. When my eyes are clear, a few can see into my macula and the crisscrossing optical cavity leading to a zone inside the brain where parallel activity reveals itself, charting time other than the present. I blink out the contact lenses so he can look into my eyes and see my younger face.

"Do you remember," I ask, "what I looked like in extreme youth, when the valves in my heart were first replaced? My parents told me I was born with only a partial heart, a naïve heart of a child. I always thought people should love me and I them. However, medicine was sufficiently advanced—"

"You're talking nonsense."

I study his eyes, cloudy, almost blue, like a stone floating in a scummy pond, thick with cataract.

"Are you going blind, Hsu Yang?" I ask.

"Maybe. Go on."

"You told me once you'd studied familial genetic maps. You said it would happen."

He nods.

"About my early condition," I continue. "At first it was just a hole between the ventricles. And when those were sewn, the valves prolapsed. And when they were repaired, I fell off a bookcase I was climbing as a child to get a favorite module on Renaissance painters. I chipped my tailbone and made my kidneys soft. That wasn't terrible because it did nothing but emphasize the under tuck of the hips critical to ladylike posture. My mother told me that—"

"Your mother? You sound like a third grader."

"Do I? Later, after the cliff hanging accident, when the titanium rods were inserted, I met you in college. And I remember, I was so excited to see you in that freshman year when you visited me in a snowstorm that I ran out of our dormitory door into the frigid January air straight at you, as you rang the buzzer. We slipped on the ice and fell down the steps together, Frankenstein and Bride. I sustained a small skull fracture. This eventually resulted in the plates and titanium implants here."

"Naomi?"

He touches my crown, pulls at my Argonaut cap.

"Yes, Hsu Yang."

In a flash I can feel his hand trying to cushion my head as we collide and fall against those sidewalk bricks.

"You landed on top of me, Hsu Yang, although you slipped your hand in a half second behind my head to break the fall. You were kind. I had headaches for a while, bad ones, and your knuckles were bruised. But I never saw a doctor then; we didn't believe in seeing doctors because we were young! My headaches grew worse, especially during my father's illness."

"You were grieving for your father."

"But then the headaches went away, a fine line between grief and obsession. Grief without catharsis produces guilt, hence obsession. I believe I was responsible for making him sick, that if I hadn't chided him so much about his treatment of my mother, he would have been fine."

"One has nothing to do with the other."

"But you left anyway. You left me more than once. Have I changed so much? Am I unrecognizable?"

"No, I'm beginning to see you clearly."

"Over time," I continue, catching my breath, "several repairs were demanded. When I chose the Scriptorium, the RJ's path, the Directorate ordered mnemonic upgrades, second and third surgeries, replacement for my partial heart."

He presses his hand against mine. Oddly, he doesn't withdraw it.

"More recently, a VTOL accident drove a shard of high-tempered glass into my forehead, which produced the crisscross scar. Then a pelvic propulsion system, the *Logoharp* in my throat and brain for translation and alternate voicing. Actually, I didn't need a replacement for my voice, but the sonar beneath the oceans required more upgrades and channels—"

"Why are you telling me all of this?" His eyes narrow. "I have no idea what your medical transplant history has to do with me."

"I didn't choose to come here. I'm assigned."

"You want me to sympathize?"

"I've no such goal."

"What, then, is your goal?"

"To execute the assigned plan. Turn you over for questioning, then orchestrate the public media campaign to anticipate your downfall."

"You're going to throw me over?"

"Yes. When memory is absent in the masses, we must restore it."

He squeezes my hands. "So cold," he says suddenly. "I don't remember them being so cold."

"I can adjust my temperature."

He lifts his hand to touch what's left of my composited cheek skin. His teeth are nicotine stained.

"You aren't a journalist anymore?"

I repeat my instructions.

"I've been directed to locate you and lead you back to the Directorate for questioning. It's within the realm of the 99s that you'll be found guilty."

"Then I have no memory of you. You're just a puppet, a raggedy one, too." He releases my hand, though we are still suspended in the jar, all gestures in slow motion.

I recollect him singing *Mockingbird* in our dormitory room.

"And you?" I ask him.

Silence.

"Are you a puppet? Or a puppeteer?"

No answer.

"May I be plain?" I nod at Miranda a moment, who stares up at me, innocent that she is.

"You are accused, despite your brilliance, of deliberately architecting a flaw in the 'soft demise' recycling system of our elderly population. In effect, you are altering the Singing Directorate's Life Clock. The Directorate believes your algorithms resemble a stacked deck, in which less than a tenth of one percent win freedom. Harmonious Recycling trades the privilege of elites for nothing like decent or productive work or reward among the remaining 98 percent. After age fifty, decommissioning is inevitable since most have nothing to live for—"

"Not true! Most people turned out to pasture like to play cards or drive off the road while everyone is laughing at them."

"You know my birth date, don't you? Do you see me driving off the road, Marco? You've developed a lottery system that offers the thinnest skein of choice—the three-day survival package in True North or a short-term excursion to cryogenic Elysium. Alternately, the deletion ticket. None of these options seems tenable if a certain percentage persists in surviving."

"Naomi, stop it!" Miranda swims to face me, blocking my view. "You must be reciting from a script! Who's written this script?"

"My information is verified." Lips trembling, I'm shocked at her vehemence.

"It's a puppet script from State Media!"

I acknowledge her correction.

Hsu Yang's tone softens. He grows flirtatious. "You aren't really going to turn me in, are you?"

"I've no preference, one way or another."

"Yes, you do. Unless you're so bitter about our childish mistakes! In which case I would think even less of you than I do now."

"Negative. My memory indicates legitima—"

"Our marriage was a sham! Not even my parents were there! When I was young, I had been brainwashed by too many advertisements featuring Swedish blonde models selling mouthwash. You were my favorite blonde." He waves his finger at me, as though testing my ability to focus after a concussion. Then he flicks his forefinger against my cheekbones. "See, does that even hurt? Your cheeks are all nanocarbon-latex composite now, no nerve endings. Your facial covering is soft. You are genderless, probably without a vagina. There's nothing natural left in you!"

"Not true."

"What then?"

"I have a soul."

My index and middle fingers find their way to his throat.

"Do you remember how I jabbed you? I still can. With my natural hand."

The defendant-turned-interrogator breathes unsteadily.

"Don't you both remember our Party directive, Marco? We learned it in childhood. *Fanshen* (翻身)! Turn over the body! It's revolutionary, an idea that goes way back to Chairman Mao. We relinquish the old for the new. I've already relinquished my body sooner than most, but I'm still here. I have a name and identity."

Miranda takes my gloved hand in both of hers. "Naomi," she says. "Naomi has sacrificed her standing with the Directorate, Marco. She's saved me and my reputation more than once."

"Your reputation? What is that? Why did you bring her here? We've got one foot in the luge."

"Don't talk to me like that!"

"You'd surrender me?"

"Of course not! But I understand her position. She's a sentinel. She's protected me and allowed me to pursue my career."

"You're supposed to be protecting me. It's my reputation at stake here, not yours."

I steady their heartbeats. My voice remains calm.

"The plan is to interrogate you and return you for questioning, and then there will be a media campaign, regurgitating your lies (with appropriate hyperbole) for public consumption. That is the plan. Nothing you've done will go unreported. The *Logoharp* will project your disgrace, merited or not, before it actually happens, and the masses will come to believe all we say is true."

"You think that's good?"

"I have no such opinion. My *Logoharp*—"

"You mean those horns and suckers coming out of your head? You're serious?"

I step back, my hands moving to the top of my head instantly to protect my thoughts. Instructions. Why do I feel trepidation?

"Our campaign will help the average citizen make better sense of why we need Harmonious Recycling. I've already made a documentary about the Directorate's 'Proof in Numbers' policy, which will include a No-Child policy designed to balance the current rate of births and deaths. 'Proof in Numbers' will show how infractions in any system, including Harmonious Recycling of souls or supporting illegal births, can't be tolerated."

"No time to waste!" he trills lightly, his lower lips curled into a grace note. "You're going to legalize forced abortions, too?"

I execute and lift both of them as we rise to the top of the tank, then the diving platform above it. I take his pulse, then hers. Oddly, their pulses are one: fast, thrummy, anoxic and weak, as though they're conjoined. But his pulse belies the rhythm of my memory; I can recollect his strong youth heartbeat against my ear.

He fights my grip.

"She doesn't belong here!" he shouts, turning to Miranda. "She shouldn't be involved. Get her out of here!"

"Calm down!"

"What did you say your name was again?"

"I've come for you."

"That's not your name," he says, looking confused.

"Naomi. Naomi Friedlander."

"Perhaps we should consider our choices for a few moments," Miranda says.

"There's nothing additional to consider, Miranda. My assignment is hardwired. No escaping."

My eyes lock onto him in command. I hold him suspended, hanging like a ragdoll in midair.

"Cheung and the Directorate believe the flaw in the system is deliberate. There's no place for gambl—"

"Every algorithm is a gamble. Didn't I ever teach you Blackjack?" Hsu Yang reminds me. "There's always a risk that any system powered by artificial intelligence will devolve, do something unexpected. A trapdoor, if you will. Every system has one, but mine isn't deliberately put there to defeat the main purpose of the system. Chance can be controlled up to a point. But there's also a possibility of failure through luck."

I release him. We climb down the ladder; Miranda throws a towel over him; she speaks without inflection, as though she's adopting my neutrality.

"A trapdoor. Do you have to play a game to find it?"

"Maybe. I'll demonstrate."

Hsu Yang believes he's convinced me; but I'm onto his tricks. We relocate behind an airlock in an adjoining chamber designed as a cafeteria for maintenance people. He dresses, shaves inside the toilet, drinks tea. Miranda locates a matching orange compression suit she wears proudly beside him.

22

MAY 2120

THE HOLO-READER

He deals the cards, snapping them in midair. Guzzling ionized water, he lets it drip down his stubble. Several times in his "tutorial rounds" his hand lifts hers at an oblique angle, showing, by the hesitation or twist of the wrist, up or down, whether to hit, stand or double down. We use a programmed robotic arm as the dealer. Marco bets casually, 35 *yuan* for a single hand. He inserts the card for the cut randomly, somewhere in the middle of the deck, as though he doesn't care. Yet one eye remains glued to the card's position.

I don't understand his fascination with card tricks and winning. Though I rely on probability all the time in my predictive work, it has no other interest for me. For Marco, though, probability is passion, a mathematical exercise of outguessing unique arrangements of fifty-two cards (8.06658×10^{67}), an exponent so vast it preoccupies him, interrupts the boredom of algorithmic work. Though card games challenge him like a human competitor, he doesn't need anyone to oppose him. He plays both sides of the deck, dealing to find whether his skill can outmaneuver luck nine out of 10 times at least.

Is there a trapdoor? Did he design one to make fun of the Directorate's calls for harmony? Or is it simply an accident of artificial intelligence playing tricks on its own? Miranda betrays her thoughts. She can't help urging him on—pursing her lips, giggling without reason, her cheeks florid. I wince. She's sleeping with him, I'm sure.

Marco now explains the value of each ace, each member of royalty. The simple goal: 21. He shows a split, a soft 17. He asks me to play; I decline, telling Miranda she will play on my behalf. The two crouch down in a protoplasmic pod with convenient seats, martinis from a vending machine and a card table. He recovers his breathing with turquoise and navy flavors of oxygen sipped through a straw.

The robo-dealer provides holo-chips—mere coins of light—as the wager. I assist in creating them, flinging them like stardust onto the table. We agree on one condition. By playing he must reveal a clue to his cryosystem's trapdoor—if there is a door. Just like the 1-in-3.2 billion genetic anomaly, the so-called immortality gene that no one seems to possess. Marco's trapdoor could be an unanticipated hiccup in an otherwise flawless soul of the machine. Its brain gets mad, escapes its own programming, then chuckles when some poor bastard goes free.

My impulse is to let him go. I'm not supposed to think this. If Marco Hsu Yang wins his cards, he leaves with Miranda on the next tunnel ship through Kuril-Kamchatka to Vancouver and further North, in which case I return to the Directorate to face consequences. Alternately, I'll tractor him back to the Directorate, win my Elite status and go free. Miranda Qian Shuai will be questioned along with him, perhaps tortured. Yes, tortured—I see it happening. She'll despise me. In either case, I'll lose.

"No matter what happens, you'll do the right thing," she whispers to me. "We'll go on as before, doing our work and pretending to like it."

We'll go on as before?

But what is before? Before she was his? Before I knew she was his? Before he and I were teenagers in love? Before I knew how much I loved her? I've lost my sense of time. Objectivity. Certainly nothing goes on exactly as it was before. If I return with him, Miranda won't go free. Marco will be punished for anticipating the lottery system everyone in the Party dreamed of inventing, though he'll surely find a way to escape himself.

He deals, licking his lips like a cat after a big meal. He cups his fingers as though he's growing tulips in his hands. Marco appears unbeatable. Whether for a card game or for planning mass executions, he employs algorithms, a little wheel of fortune. Casually he hints that the Heilongjiang burial system is based on that get-out-of-jail free chance of a lottery ticket. Every other number is simply a transcription error to be whited out. This means, with rare exception, all human carbon is recycled painlessly after a certain age, depending on one's status and prior achievements within the upper realms of the Party. A few escape, but not forever.

I watch the two of them play. Performing the parallel algorithmic extraction of future possibilities, I realize I'm forbidden to feel affection or pity for either of them. It doesn't occur to me to turn time backwards; this is something I can never do. My sole purpose now is to watch and wait, weighing the outcomes, realizing that whatever outcome there is depends only on chance.

In the dormitory of decades ago I embraced him from behind as he doodled on a scratch pad or pulled out his joker deck, counting cards, calculating statistical probabilities of all royal-flush combinations while he was supposed to be studying anatomy of the neck. Now the holo-chips flash as he hands them back and forth to Miranda. She wins and loses—not quite by chance. He shows her without words the holo-card reader, a dealer's tool to speed the pace of the game, to reveal to him the next card still unseen by the next player. The holo-reader reveals Blackjack, the holy grail of sequences and patterns—royals and aces or mere pairs flushing hot and cold. But Miranda tires after several rounds. "Let's stop now," she says, throwing up her hands.

"We can't," he replies. "You haven't learned how to go through the trapdoor."

"I can't learn when you flash cards by so quickly," she says.

"Just focus!"

"I can't!" she cries exhaustedly.

"Hsu Yang, you're responsible for teaching her." I chide him. "You've created the nightmare, now show her how to exit."

He stops dealing, turning over Miranda Qian Shuai's final "hit." She is 32 years old minus an ace. Her cards yield the number 21.

She squeals while he gloats without surprise.

"Youth and beauty conquer age and experience!"

"So what?" Miranda takes the holo-chips and places them in my hand. "It's your turn to play with him, Naomi," she says. "He still hasn't shown me the trapdoor."

Marco snickers. "Yes, I have. At least I've suggested where or what it might be."

She shakes her head. "Oh yeah?"

"What about the card reader?"

She stares, nonplussed.

"Pure chance! A game of probability. I have no idea where this 'trapdoor' is supposed to be!"

The card reader? Perhaps he's done something to it, I muse, silently. I see dark edges on a few cards in the deck. Perhaps he's duplicated one of the cards. His eyes don't seem right. They're watery, glazed, the whites turning yellow.

His physicality eludes me, fades away. I'm guessing she sleeps with both father and son, keeping the jealous Gua Gua at her side to maintain balance, of sorts. I say nothing of Gua Gua, not wanting to complicate matters.

"If you know where the trapdoor is, instead of speaking in riddles, you can undo all the damage you've done," I lecture, looking straight at him. "When the elders wake and rise from their coffins, and the ice festival lapses into chaos and blood—"

"The lottery system is actually controlled by atomic clocks in a Beehive Fortress," he exclaims, so casually I doubt his truth. "This distributed network of 'and,' 'or' and 'not' gates co-located across the pan-Asian cloud is actually one of Mother Country's tightest security systems. Tracking the lives, beliefs and whereabouts of billions of souls. Programmed with interlaced loops written in 11 dimensions of code deemed unbreakable without dual public keys, it's as perfect as you can get."

"But there's a flaw?" Miranda interrupts. "There must be one because of the fugitive reports. The elders awakening in their cryopods; the few who are rounded up and deleted."

"What about the children?"

"Guards are reasonably careful not to shoot them."

Marco chews his lip. "I'm somewhat unclear about this. It seems there is an anomaly in the genome or someone or something is disrupting the controls. Seems that once in 3.2 billion iterations of the algorithm, roughly the same odds as a single polymorphism out of 3.2 billion DNA base pairs, an elder wakes up in the cryopod and either escapes or is shot in cold blood trying to run."

"So the flaw is real? It's biological, not virtual or software-defined?"

"It's physical, I guess, some kind of mutation that works its way through the genome," he says. "Maybe it's the cryo-timing device inside the Fortress and a very occasional 'hiccup.' A reset, if you will, perhaps caused by a physical anomaly."

"Come on!"

"I'm saying I don't know. The atomic clock ticks inside the Beehive and the armature spins. In the right conditions, if the system detects a certain polymorphism, or even the cessation of normal breathing or pulse, the clock stops a millisecond and the sleeper may wake."

"As simple as a polymorphism?"

"Not quite. The polymorphism is only a baseline condition. Something else triggers the system reset."

I re-enter their pod and take a seat beside him.

"You must know what the trigger is, don't you?"

"No. I've forgotten how a trigger might work. As a precaution, the Directorate wiped my memory of research notes and the keys to decrypt them."

"Hsu Yang?" Miranda queries him, letting her after-silence sink in.

"You're lying, you fuck—" I place my synthetic hand on his, squeezing his fingers so hard he releases the cards. "It's not even a credible lie."

"Naomi?" Miranda interrupts.

"Hsu Yang hasn't forgotten anything, but perhaps he's still confused! Here, play with me!" Supplanting her at the card table. "We'll see whether your high degree of skill, if not your 'amnesia,' can overcome the possibility of failure through luck."

I shuffle the deck and it flies between my blue-bladed digits. The *Logoharp* links to every server in Harbin, Beijing, Shanghai, Guangzhou, Lijiang, Urumqi and Bryce. "We should be able to recover the codes again, if you've really forgotten. I believe the flaw will reveal itself—"

"Are you the dealer? he asks. "Do you call the shots here?"

"I do now."

"Do you know how to play this game?"

"I have instructions here." I tap my head; my antennae swirl in a dance, then retract. "You wrote in the past about how you've managed to cheat undetected."

"Stop arguing!" Miranda reaches for his hand and joins it to mine. He flinches, pulls back, then relaxes under her gaze. She has the eyes of a child who can't conceive of a jealous or cruel emotion in her lover.

Shuffling, he focuses on the holo-reader, searching for a dark predictive edge to his down card. One of his tricks. His temples rain sweat. I make sure he loses by altering the light with my eyes so he can't detect the dark edges. "You're cheating!" he cries. My *Logoharp* is already connected to his thoughts; I foresee every outcome of a hand before it plays out.

After three rounds he throws the cards down in disgust.

"Hsu Yang, I can't let you escape because whatever clues I find in the Fortress would be useless without your guidance.

At the same time, sending you back to the Directorate will achieve nothing except my exoneration."

"Perhaps that's sufficient," a voice suddenly calls out. "Why not save yourself?"

At the end of the airlock the green light shines. A short shadow with Capuchin legs scoots toward us.

"Lang Fei!"

Miranda locks Hsu Yang's hands in mine again. She stares at me with a startled expression, as though she understands I've already made my decision. Our ears follow Fei's voice.

"Will you join us?" she asks. I catch the light in her eyes. I am sure the flaw in the game is the same one I see in that fleck of green, the lower left quadrant of her iris. The number 32, her age, minus an Ace. Her iris is like a bent card, something just a bit off in the code. Beautiful. Perhaps leading me to the right place.

"Lang Fei, how did you find us?"

"You leave breadcrumbs."

"How so?"

"Your *Logoharp*. Very low frequency emissions, like tracking a dolphin in the sea. I believe it's time for you all to return to Harbin, Naomi. Perhaps your witness will allow Comrade Tian to remember what he's forgotten. If not, we go to the frontier to find the elders to jar his memory."

I nod. Miranda's silence disturbs me.

"We'll have to move faster because we're being tracked," Lang Fei says.

Hsu Yang throws his head back, eyes at the ceiling. "The frontier is the wrong direction," he replies. "Better to create a distraction so the drones will be thrown off our scent."

"I don't—"

"We go back," he says. "Cooperate with the inquest. Miranda will accompany me. Lang and Naomi will try to locate the Beehive Fortress. Isolate the flaw. Make it worse. Break the whole system if you can. We'll communicate even if they take my devices away. Your *Logoharp* detects thoughts and signals, right? And Miranda's?"

"Yes."

"You're clever, Naomi. You'll figure it out."

"They won't spare Miranda."

"I'm wagering they'll keep both of us intact," Hsu Yang interrupts.

"I'll wager once you're questioned, the military will dispatch you both to Heilongjiang with concertina wire around your necks," Lang Fei rejoins.

"At least this will buy some time."

We both turn toward Miranda's voice. It's so easy to think of her as a naïve child, and she isn't. What's the catch?

"I've heard decommissioning isn't all that painful," Miranda whispers. The sobriety of her voice tells me she's imagining it. "There isn't much point trying to escape."

"Perhaps we should locate the elders who escape."

"There isn't time for that."

"But there is a point!" Lang Fei protests. "The question is whether we get to the Beehive first. You must remember, Hsu Yang—'*Mr. Tian,*'"—he clucks, "that Naomi, if she wills it, can win in any game or algorithm you've devised. The flaw in your system will be evident to her assuming she can get close to the source."

"There's a benefit to sacrifice," Miranda interpolates.

"Naomi will inform the Directorate that Hsu Yang will be returned to the Inquest to fill in a few blanks," Lang Fei continues, obviously enthralled with his own plan. "And journalist Miranda Qian Shuai will accompany him to fill in other blanks."

My harp speaks to her, in alarm. Commanding. Desperate. "*Don't go with him. Please.*"

Slowly she shakes her head, refusing me.

"Remember!" Lang Fei interjects. "The course about to be followed is neither random, nor scripted, but inevitable. It may not locate your 'flaw' and unlock the system as we want. But you—if we grant you this chance—will help us try, won't you?"

Marco grunts in affirmative; I've no idea why. Miranda will follow, no conditions, no questions asked of him.

Her lips break into a half smile. Lang Fei produces a small banana that he peels and munches whole, his mouth an open portal. He smacks his lips.

"You're disgusting!" Miranda snickers, touching Lang Fei's checkerboard sleeve. The temperature and color of her skin, and Marco Hsu Yang's as well, turn cooler and darker, as though they're at peace.

Miranda takes a breath. She leans over and kisses Hsu Yang full on the lips. Both of them kiss as though it's their last meal.

I turn away, trying not to watch.

23

JUNE 2120

THE GENDER HARP

性
别
竖
琴

We're leaving the tunnels, bypassing the Okhotsk and Kuril Basin luges for a transport back to the mainland. In the marine darkness we accelerate strapped down. I'm wondering about the two of them, why their entanglement produces such collective amnesia.

My instructions are clear. Regardless of guilt or innocence, I must report their condition and whereabouts. Surely the Directorate will seek a scapegoat.

RJ Special Report
Communications Directorate

National Library of China

WBF+66 Haidian District 100089 Contact N.F.,

Dept. 431

+86-10-83107429

Beijing, August 10, 2120 — Tian Jinghui, formerly China's Number One Algorithmic Architect, has been captured and detained for questioning in the Singing Directorate's Beijing headquarters. Mr. Tian is charged with multiple crimes of maladaptive coding and quantum corruption of the Harmonious Recycling system he created. Officials say Tian deliberately embedded a control system trapdoor in Mother Country's most important cybersecurity system which balances birth and death rates. The State's Life Clock directs Harmonious Recycling and how many elders enjoy viral ecstasy and dreaming toward the end of their lives.

However, Mr. Tian, drawing on an extensive knowledge of physics and card games, introduced a bizarre complication to the Recycling supercomputers known as "quantum entanglement." The explanation of entanglement is complex, but the outcome is an exponential growth of qubits (quantum units of misinformation), along with uncontrolled power surges and loss of nanoseconds in the timing system's Cesium atomic clock. As a result, a number of elders enjoying dreams in cryo-torpor wake up and apparently walk away from their cryopods before life completion.

Tian and his mistress, Miranda Qianshuai, a journalist, are both incarcerated, awaiting final judgment and sentencing for their crimes. Officials believe a spin of the Directorate's Wheel of Fortune, a sister of the Life Clock, could favor the death penalty.

*

My broadcast is complete.

The Directorate will award me Elite status, at last satisfying a desire to be at the top of my craft.

Miranda is about to be questioned. The Directorate has a way of taking it out on accessories, mediators and innocents, allowing the true elites who game the system to escape without a mark.

Oddly, I don't care what happens to Marco Hsu Yang anymore. In the event of waterboarding or Tiger Bench torture, it should be he, not she. If I must witness these confessions before leaving for Harbin, I want to protest out loud with my human voice. Because the *Logoharp* is played only with breath—my own breath—and when it's challenged bitterly, it produces no harmonics at all; it simply adds to my burden of expression, of speaking in two discordant voices.

Why is this happening? The whole purpose of my harp is to shape the extant possibilities of history into a plausible, *sine qua non* future for the masses. But why so many exceptions? The Directorate adheres more and more to a strict path toward "truth," always backing it up with quantitative data, real or altered. I keep hearing the old CCP expression: "Return to correct line," which means only one line, one train of thought, which produces nightmares, punishments, hateful brainwashing. Not all that different from the slavery and "cleansing" events of Ameriguans of the Civil War, or the more recent internments and/or attacks on Uyghurs, Tibetans, Jews, Palestinians, Romani, Ukrainians, Rohingyas, Rwandans, Armenians, Serbians, Bhutanese, Yazdi, Navajo. The list goes on and on.

Long ago I believed someone like me could never disobey *Logoharp* instructions. It would be anathema, physiologically impossible. But if suddenly I cut off these longicorn antennae growing into my heart, would it make any difference? Would I still intuit Directorate instructions? Could I frame a better future by reporting only the present tense without projecting an outcome? Once I believed I could never love in a natural way, not along any timeline we'd describe as human or "forever." But now it's different. Jens Remker tried to teach me about the irrelevance of "forever." But more than Jens, why have I let Miranda go?

I remember my first encounter with her in a foreigner's bookstore. Perhaps in deference to all the fools surrounding her, perhaps in deference to my half mechanical, half human nature that made her laugh as I sat trying to neutralize the emotions affecting my skin colors, she walked over and talked to me. At the first Christmas party we attended, she leaned her head on my shoulder for a photograph, nestling there. As we walked to the trains that night, she told me about this Gua Gua, but not Marco Hsu Yang. I realized she was foolishly in love with somebody, but not this boy.

And yes, along the freezing Huangpu River one night we took selfies together, snarking it up for the camera. She tapped my wind visor for a kiss. It was a child's kiss, very light. I returned it readily, brushing her cheek ever so lightly, then urging her silence with one index finger. It was time to go.

Why now, am I cooperating in this inquisition? It must be the *Logoharp*. It's directing me against my deepest misgivings.

24

AUGUST 2120

A BLOODY DOORSTOP AT MY FEET

血
泊
门
挡

Miranda and Marco Hsu Yang have come with me to the Directorate. They're kept in holding cells during the long delay for paperwork and negative media interviews before interrogation begins.

Lang Fei has already left for Harbin. Soon I'll meet him to try locating the gateway to the Beehive Fortress, the central control unit for Harmonious Recycling.

Officially, I'm the People's Guardian, the keeper of these two suspects. But if I can slip away to Heilongjiang and raise the temperature of the ice cocoons, the dreamers might awake—exactly contrary to my orders.

Marco and Miranda disappear into the Directorate's Green Lagoon. The Lagoon is the briefing zone, its cinematic emerald, teal and gold colors like the cathedral entryway to *The Wizard of Oz*. In the cloaking rooms the two strip for induction and wiring. While allowed into the observation gallery, I see very little, only two separate cubicles where the inquiries will take place.

Hsu Yang gets a space-age orange jump suit to which all acoustics and monitors are attached. He is obviously too valuable to damage. His shackles are acoustic rather than physical. Prior to the examination, he can't hear anything except incessant ringing in his ears. His hands are pressed to his ears, but an assistant produces a pair of silicone ear plugs in a baggie, somewhat effective in muffling the high-pitched (F#) squeal.

She, on the other hand, won't be given ear plugs. To be sure, Cheung Yuen has ordered the matrons to apply high-pitched acoustics to break any resistance. Then come the bamboo sticks with sharpened points, to which I've registered loud objections. Cheung Yuen shrugs. Given Miranda's connection to Hsu Yang and his secrets, though, the matrons will be ordered to extract information Cheung fully expects the algorithmic king to lie about.

In our training, the Directorate has taught us that acoustic jamming and extreme cold work effectively together. Cold increases alertness at first, but with jamming the cold becomes immobilizing. Inspectors call the icing from fire hoses in sub-freezing temperatures "cryotherapy." The accused shiver and thirst, lose teeth and then shrink into meat.

About 60 percent of polled spectators find these theatricals entertaining, especially when they're shown on narrowcast channels. The subject may confess or scream, but soon loses orientation and sensitivity to pain, becoming numb, then sleepy, then fibrillated, then heart-stopped, much like a naked baby exposed to an Arctic night.

During Miranda's first interrogation I can see them tightening straps and restraints around her. She answers "yes" or "no" to routine questions about her identity and relationship to Hsu Yang, but says no more.

Shaving demoralizes and exposes the suspect to a close examination of the phrenology of the skull. Only Miranda Qian Shuai's skull is perfect, smooth and circular, without a flaw. The matrons force her to look in a mirror as they shave her. For a second, because I can see them through the observation deck, the matrons register admiration, one of them stroking her naked shoulder and ribcage. "Such a beauty," she says.

Miranda's face registers nothing. A video plays to her memory: her father, a middle-aged, inebriated man screaming, then grabbing the throat of a woman, presumably his wife, as his daughter jumps at him from behind, piggyback, grappling to pull his arms back. Raging, he twists and wrestles the girl to the floor, then pounds her head several times against the concrete. His dazed wife rises, jumps on him, pulls at his hair, pounds his neck, but he twists again and knocks her out. Presumably this is a choreographed re-creation of Miranda's traumatic family life.

Three matrons now appear in checkered aprons stained with blood. They are thick and stocky, like fireplugs. Leading the naked Miranda to the treatment room containing a white porcelain sink and a splintered bench with nails driven in, they tighten a lariat the size of a badminton racket around her neck. Fiberglass straps bind her hands behind her.

The matrons explain what is about to happen, what the treatment will be and how important it is for her to volunteer any information requested. Miranda nods, looks away, her face tilted upward, her mouth curling into a half-smile. She stares up at the ropes and hooks hanging down from the black ceiling, as though she can blow through it. She signals non-compliance with the set of her jaw.

"Cheung!" I speak into a microphone. "Stop this."

She hears me, but doesn't answer.

I flash to an advertorial from the archives, the reported "confessions" of *Falun Gong* acolytes in *The Beijing-New York Times*. The matrons deliver an icy swill, a byproduct of unfiltered Beijing sewers, drop by drop to the victim's scalp, neck, bowed shoulders and spine, hers so terribly prominent, like the spines of a seahorse. These drops, these spines, cry out, the inky exclamation points from calligraphy. But I can't see or hear any particular mark or declamation now. Miranda's face is turned away from me, a smear.

"So Hsu Yang likes to play cards? What is his winning secret?"

The matrons repeat the question. Dot dot dash. No answer.

They clamp Miranda's head inside a large "space helmet." It's a square-shaped vise made of titanium and polymers, equipped with a tiny funnel at the top for dripping water. She's positioned kneeling, her headpiece tilted above the white porcelain sink. In this way her cranium is clasped and pressurized. It's as though she's a free diver. As the ice begins to drip, the spongy tissue inside her brain and lungs contracts so that only a fraction of the normal capacity for breath is left. All blood rushes into her heart and brain. Her pulse drops to 22 beats per minute; I register them, the images in her brain traced and recorded as points of light reassembled on screen in holographic 3D, much like an MRI. These images yield absolutely nothing. A tangle of seaweed and synaptic confusion.

I escape the gallery deck. Down the hallway I hear the conversations of several Party officials watching the scene from their monitors. Only they're observing remotely, as remote from the action as Cheung Yuen. She's watching from her own private monitor in an even more private briefing room the size of a closet.

"What are they doing? She's innocent! What can't you stop this?"

"Instructions from above. Can't reverse," Cheung replies.

I bound back to the observation deck, banging the glass with my fists and shouting at them to stop. I narrowcast with the *Logoharp*: *Stop stop stop!*

The matrons just tighten the helmet vise and then loosen it again, allowing the shit-stained coolant droplets to drain inside the cube, droplets trickling down Miranda's forehead, nose, lips, chin, neck and chest. Then they take a mallet and bang Miranda's helmet against the porcelain sink, part of the shock treatment. Blood streams from her lips down her exposed throat.

"Why are you helping him?" Lead Matron cries out. "No reason to suffer, he's not worth it! Where does he stash his codes?"

Miranda whispers. But the observation glass I'm stuck behind is reinforced as though to withstand a bomb blast. Her voice is so fractured I can't pick it up. The matrons get edgy.

Then they start shrieking, poking and prodding her naked breasts with bamboo sticks. *"Tell us tell us tell us!"* She flinches for a second, yet her Rubix cube of a helmet doesn't alter or move; her body beneath lies folded, deathly inert, skinny and white, unmoved.

Now I'm hearing the cracking of river ice; I don't recognize the origin, but the seam is growing wider and louder every second. Thudding at first, then repeated bangs and shouts, loud, obnoxious screams, more groaning like a glacier calving into the sea. The sounds seem distant at first, I realize—how do I realize?—I'm pummeling the gallery glass 16.6667 times a second.

My rotor, diamond studded and reinforced, emerges from my synthetic right wrist and detaches. The rotary blades spin at maximum speed, a P-factor so strong that the human side of my brain can't register the separate movements. My left hand, reinforced with diamond studs as well, joins with the right to strike the observation deck glass like a jackhammer in triple strokes registering non-stop.

I'm not programmed to interfere with state-directed torture. But this is Miranda. My fists come reinforced with capacity to kill. The entire glass pane yawns and breaks, crashing in shards two floors below. I leap; my jets fire. Miranda's body, still folded in prayer position, is silent, helmeted beneath a white porcelain sink. No sound at all. The matrons have scattered and run, but the lead matron lies bleeding, screaming, her hand severed, her bloody face a doorstop beneath my feet.

"Qian Shuai? Miranda? I'm here... Can you hear me?"

In two seconds, I peel away the titanium fasteners around her temples and face. She has no features, a Noh mask coated in frost. My rotor reattaches and I lift her up—dead weight, no weight, her contracture so extreme.

Pulling a thermal blanket from my pack, I wrap her tightly. Alarms are screaming, as though I've started a fire. My Perseus switch activates and I push through the atrium panels where the glass used to be, out the corridor and up the stairs to an emergency door, punching out more glass and metal, then the rooftop. Her eyelashes capture remnants of ice. In a moment—I can't tell whether it's smog or dense fog—we're flying upward among the dark canyons of the city.

A landing zone at Jade Dragon Trauma Unit is reserved for Volokopters. But I choose it, tripping fast on the tarmac as I carry her, bending down and listening for breath, shouting for help. The trauma bots, all dressed up in Green Cross surgical get-ups, whisk her away. I've monitored her vitals, placed my left ear against her chest. Crushed ribs, fractured cheeks and chin, mastoid process behind the left ear bleeding, temporal bone bleeds. She's pregnant—a strong fluttering of a second heartbeat. She's about two months gone.

Pregnant.

Cheung's drones have followed us. I've jammed their signals mid-air and they wavered, but regained pursuit.

*

In the waiting room adjoining the ER I question the doctors on call. Is she on life support? What about the hemorrhaging? Pregnancy? Dean Cheung arrives with her escorts in a private Sifang air taxi. She pushes through the doors along with two bot auxiliaries. I get up from my chair, clutching Miranda's bloody sheets, dropping them at Cheung's feet.

"What in the Party's name are you doing?"

Her expression suggests a studied, pitiless distance from it all. She tries to smile, then frowns, her cigarette dripping ash, inhaling in deep addicted puffs. Her bots intervene, pushing me away from her, but two elbow strikes and I've knocked out their sensors, hurling them across the room.

Dean Cheung has never seen me violent, never seen me break glass before. Since I'm 28 centimeters taller than she, we're an odd match in the ward's two-way mirror. I step aside so she can look squarely at the operating theatre where med drones apply oxygen, clamps, IVs and an AED to restabilize Miranda's heartbeats.

"Did you know she's pregnant?"

"No, and that hardly matters." Cheung grasps my arm. "Anyone associated with Hsu Yang is suspect. Especially a journalist who happens to be his girlfriend. You sound crazy!"

I can't restrain myself, no—this isn't my training. I grab her jaw, push her against the wall.

"You're a sadist and insult to the Party—a bunch of sadists with the brains of cats—"

"Sadists, like cats, have nine lives," Cheung says slowly. "Let go! You've got some grip, Naomi! Let go!"

Her lieutenant bots get up, try to slam me against the wall. Like cockroaches, they bounce off my body armor.

"What is your plan?" she says.

"I have no plan. I'm staying right here."

"No! You're a Directorate employee. You follow instructions."

"I'm instructed to preserve life."

"Don't interrupt me!"

Cheung puffs on her fag, blows out. Thinks. Speaks.

"If she dies, well, that's too bad. A valuable resource, gone. Besides, we still have Hsu Yang to question."

"You don't need me for that."

"Naomi?

"What?"

"You'll stay here?"

I nod.

"You'll pay for the glass."

"Happy to—No, I won't."

Four shimmery anodized police bots push through the doors and, with Cheung's nod, take my arms in a vise grip. I haven't known tears of pain since childhood.

Chairman Dakota Sung shows up. Cheung turns to him and his rubber tire gut. He emits a raw rotten smell of seafood and smokes. I'm sure he hasn't showered in weeks. Cheung squeezes her nose, gagging a little.

"We need Naomi back in the Directorate," Dakota says. "The national elections are coming up in Taiwan."

"We'll get somebody else."

"She'll report now."

"The elections are three months away. Plenty of time," Cheung placates.

He pulls out a cigarette. Automatically, I light it with my third digit.

"Calm yourself."

"Calm," I reply.

The drones let go. Sung's order. He knows I'll break free.

"Naomi can be more useful here once the National Committee convenes," she tells Sung. "We can use her media to synergize Taiwan's chaos while we expose Marco Hsu Yang's quantum entanglements, especially with Falun Gong."

"I didn't know—"

"There is a connection," Cheung affirms.

Sung eyes me warily, a bit like a disgruntled father who can't quite express himself.

"Naomi, you're reverti—"

"Maybe—"

"Understandable," Sung exclaims. "Perhaps you need some time to yourself? I think you should stay here as long as necessary to see that your friend, or whatever she is, recovers."

"Thank you."

Cheung smacks her dried-out lips. "You seem not to be yourself, Naomi!"

"And if you're not yourself, who are you?" Dakota Sung leans into my face, a big loud guffaw.

"I'm not programmed to tolerate torture. So you know, I have a complete recording of Miranda's inquest."

"But you wouldn't dare narrowcast this, Naomi?" Cheung replies. "Your job is to project the future. That's where all hope lies!"

"Remember who you are!" Sung whispers.

I nod, turning away, disgusted. It's true, I'm privileged, an Elite Scribe of the State. A mere nod is my sign of compliance.

25

SEPTEMBER 2120

WHY LEI FENG LOVED THE PEOPLE

人民英雄

Miranda is being wheeled into recovery. Half her body is hidden beneath a canopy containing multiple IVs, tubes and wires. She's taking oxygen. Half her face is purple, pushed in. *Leila Goddess! Where is my voice?*

I'm sitting beside her bed, inert, a witness. At the same time, monitoring Marco's inquest via remote.

Cordoned off in a soundproof holding area decorated as an Edwardian drawing room, he is obviously being treated with kid gloves.

The holo-background consists of mahogany furniture and bric-a-brac, gas lanterns and a fireplace, an antique grandfather clock and delicate Chinese ivory figurines placed on the mantelpiece. Four leather chairs in the staging area are real. Two will be occupied by the interrogators, Cheung and Dakota Sung. I've told both of them that any techniques of putting Hsu Yang at ease won't work. They disagree.

"The subject is accessible. So are his women," Sung observes.

"I guess this applies to mistresses and ex-wives?"

"Not all of them. But they seem to be softening up."

He sits back, floppy and shapeless in his embroidered Mao jacket. Scratching his chin, Sung swivels his ass a few times seeking the most comfortable spot on the seat pillow.

Not sure who else is listening. My intonation seems lifeless now, coming from my own voice and devoid of feeling. I gather that, instead of breaking Miranda's bones, and then taking her life, Cheung or Sung directed the matrons to adopt a "middle course." Neither of them acknowledges what that "middle course" was, exactly. But I gather now they realize their mistake, since no data came through in Miranda's scans, especially with the disruptions I created.

Marco—aka Tian Jinghui—plops down in his seat.

"Ah, Leader Tian, you're a trusted official and welcome here. Have some tea and sweets."

They call Hsu Yang by his official name. He sits in a plush off-white leather wing chair, smudged with nicotine stains on the armrests and surrounded by his Inquisitors. Other holo-witnesses are seated in semicircle behind the three principals. These witnesses are overweight half-borgs, basically a throwback to Party apparatchiks of the Second Cultural Revolution. Yang's chair has Chinese lace that hangs over the seat back with a little illustration of Chairman Mao positioned right above his head. The room contains a convincing hologram of a three-meter aquarium hosting colorful Japanese koi and a moray eel.

A *maître d'* knocks on the door, followed by two waiters in white waistcoats presenting Hsu Yang and guests with a bristly deep-fried slug set on a Ming-style porcelain dinner plate. "Bu yao,"(不要) Marco replies. "Just snacks, please." The waiters whisk away the slug and return with moon cakes and oranges.

"We've recorded several eyewitness reports of elders waking in their pods and actually escaping with the help of their families," Sung begins.

He rises, hanging over seated Marco Hsu Yang, his voice rising in the manner of a Grand Inquisitor.

"You, Mr. Tian! Hsu Yang! Why would you, the head of the algorithmic leadership, design such a Trojan horse in a human recycling system? To disrupt the workings of our State's Life Clock? Your DNA must be flawed!"

Hsu Yang pushes a whole moon cake into his mouth. Sung backs away, stunned at his mastication.

"You have no manners."

"I love snacks!" Hsu Yang replies. "These oranges and red bean desserts are very tasty." Chewing like a puppy with his mouth wide open, he continues the show, displaying all the crumbs and paste swirling and flattening under his tongue.

"You know I'm innocent of these charges," Marco exclaims. "Not because I didn't design a flaw—I might have—but because the Leadership wiped my memory of the program and all its heuristics. Right now, I know no more than a five-year old child reading a little red book. What is the point of interrogating me?"

"We can't find the security codes. We can't locate the base pair or the dual keys. We know you designed a private key; you've admitted that much, but even in our searches, we see nothing wrong with the system, and we've combed the Beehive Fortress and ten terabytes of worker data."

"Perhaps the key isn't in the data or the access protocols," Hsu Yang replies. "Perhaps you can't find it because it isn't there."

Cheung coughs. She now seats herself in another chair that instantly appears, pondering in silence. "Do you know what has happened to Miranda Qian Shuai? It's called *cryo-harmonization*. If you want your mistress to return to your life, perhaps you'll try harder to remember."

"Try harder? I've told you. It's an aberration very likely outside the system parameters that we control. In a sense, the external factors influencing the system have a mind of their own."

"Which external factors?" Sung rejoins. "How do we access these 'factors?'"

"You don't. I have no say whatsoever in their appearance," Marco replies.

"Oh, you mean it's an unanticipated, natural flaw."

"Yes, in a way."

"In what way?"

"I can't tell you because I don't know. I only know the manifestation, which is a bunch of old people waking up."

"But very few actually do!"

"Yes, it's rare, and shouldn't cause you worry."

"Any awakening is worrisome if it is unintentional. We'll be the judge of worry," Cheung snaps.

"It's almost as though you're speaking in tongues," Dakota Sung psychologizes, picking up a toothpick and biting on it, then jabbing it between his front teeth to extract the remains of his lunch. "Are you religious?"

"No."

"You don't give a damn about your country, do you?" Sung rejoins. "I mean Chairman Mao's homespun dialectics on materialism have no consequence to you?"

"They're interesting, anyway." He sniffs, eyes Sung. "Isn't there a bad smell around here? Like shit?"

"You're Teflon!" Sung declares. "Everything slides off you! You take no responsibility because you believe everything in the universe happens randomly or comes from an external source outside of your control."

"I'm responsible for showering daily, and using my toilet articles."

"The quantity and quality of things, or even events, change, and who cares? You don't! Change has no reality for you because everything is illusion to you. Nothing is permanent or real."

"This inquest is real," Marco protests. "It's real, but it doesn't feel real, because it has no point."

"You've ignored Mao's teachings, even the most fundamental ones; namely, that the causes of social development aren't external to society, not even external to history or geography or climate. They're internal to us, the actors in our society; and, therefore, we can and will be changed thanks to competing elements of thought and inclination in our hearts!"

"This sounds memorized."

"Your thinking is barren," Dakota Sung continues. "It's stripped down, bare bones, exposed to any force or event outside the thing itself that accounts for the cause of its development—or so you imagine. Why then, are our state-run enterprises and anti-corruption campaigns so successful despite frequent economic crises and criticisms from the West? The reason is that we look to ourselves. The Chairman has told us that every pendulum swing between extremes of position comes from the contradictions inherent in a thing! Which means, unnecessarily or not, you've designed a contradiction within your system, a trapdoor, and you won't even acknowledge it."

Hsu Yang lights his cigarette. Takes a drag. "I don't see a trapdoor anywhere. I wish I had," he says, blowing smoke rings into Sung's face.

Yang takes out a deck of cards with Chairman Mao's image emblazoned, illegally, on the Joker's Face.

"What's real to you?" Cheung asks.

"My winnings."

"What about Qian Shuai?"

He thinks a moment.

"I'd say she's real, a real woman according to your definition. Not like that piece of cyber junk you used to collect me."

He knows I'm within earshot.

Cheung scoffs.

"You're an anarchist," she says. "Stuck in a belief that nothing changes under heaven except your Blackjack odds. I'm surmising the flaw introduced in any algorithm you've designed is for your own pleasure, whether to preserve human capital or to dispose of it after its sell-by date. Derived from yet another 'outside force' you can't control—"

"Do you think you're blameless for everything?" Sung accuses.

"Not everything."

"What then?"

"Involving my girlfriend in your bullshit inquest." Marco's voice hardens. "Is she all right?"

Silence.

"Is she all right?"

"She revealed nothing about you. A stubborn, foolish girl."

Hsu Yang rises from his seat. He turns to the committee of virtual witnesses with his eyes wide, focused, as though boring through their heads with a high-speed drill.

"Why were you created? What purpose do you have on Earth?"

No one answers.

"I mean, really? What purpose do you have in wasting a single molecule of oxygen if you have no free will?"

Staring back at him, cat-eyes shifting, then blank, the witnesses say nothing. It's as though no one has ever asked them this question.

"Sit down!" Sung retorts. "I don't know whether to call you an anarchist or just a traitor. Either way, your ideas are antithetical to the materialism or conscience on which our State and Party depend."

"What about my girlfriend?"

Sung perks up.

"Is she alive?"

"Well, yes. In recovery. She did sustain injuries."

"What does that mean?" Hsu Yang shouts. "Miranda doesn't have a clue about your dialectical struggle! Does our State actually thrive on dialectical struggle? I'd say no—"

Cheung catches her breath.

"After the first Tian An Men massacre of 1989, and then the Second, and so on down the line," Marco goes on, "it became quite clear that anyone representing dissonant interests or pendular swings outside the Party credo had to be dismissed. None of the 'errant ideas' were absorbed or acknowledged gratefully for contributions to a healthy debate. Anyone known as a maverick, adventurist, critic, sex publisher, even a creator of quality TV programs in Hong Kong would be rounded up, censured, imprisoned or simply denied a free-to-air license. In other words, dialectical struggle has pretty much tanked. Do I have this right? In order for the society to stabilize and pursue its correct path?"

"Certain incorrect lines of thought only. Others may compete," Cheung replies.

"What, like underage gymnasts? Cheung, I do believe in internal contradiction, and even in competing thoughts. This makes me a very fine example of a modern materialist, which is why sometimes, even in our well-ordered society, certain contradictory elements get out of hand."

"Yes, including the maverick spies representing Laurentia, Baltica and Ameriguo before the collapse," Sung rejoins.

"Ameriguo?"

"Yes, the old Ameriguan democracy, which lost itself to Towers of Babble—consumer excess, celebrity worship, bickering, conspirators, rigged elections—"

"No law was ever absolute. The elections were doomed. The people were ignorant, the Constitution treated like putty," Marco replies, seemingly in agreement with Sung.

Cheung chews a stick of Trident Victory, as though she's disinterested. "Can we get back on topic?" she asks.

"The Harbin Recycling Program appears to have a life of its own," Marco reaffirms.

"It was your implementation," Cheung rejoins. "And your idea."

"Not one of my best. Mostly it works very well. But on rare occasions, something about the program, perhaps an external trigger, affects the system and goes haywire, allowing certain elders to wake up and, to everyone's astonishment, escape to Truth North. None but three or four who escaped have actually been captured."

"We can't study outliers if they disappear."

"So what do you do with them? Shoot them?"

Cheung skips over the question. "Your algorithms should predict, or at least detect who these escapees are. Do they have any genetic aberration? Are they exceptional, like those who win the lottery?"

"Maybe not. Remember, a generative AI system is creative even when it has a defined mission. It has a progenitive force, in other words, something like making a baby, only it takes much more to make the baby, not just sex. For example, you need robust code to ensure the body is self-replicating, that it has a properly ordered internal structure responding to instructions and to stimuli in the environment. It should know how to secure itself against threats, and to convert energy and the raw materials into functioning activity. So, as we know, babies are full of internal contradictions, aren't they? The biggest contradiction is a display of attitude and resistance toward authority—parents first, usually. A baby learns a moral code, or lack of one, and it manifests both a daylight and dark side. Inevitably, it tries to break away. The baby listens and becomes aware of its own dreams. And what then? The person who was once a baby becomes unpredictable, an unruly preteen, and then a teenager. Quite often the teen appears psychotic and breaks away from parents, pursuing its own will."

"Like your system?" Cheung scoffs.

"You're saying the system is a baby," Chairman Sung rejoins. "It learns and has an independent life of its own."

"Yeah."

"But even children can be directed. That's why parenting is so important."

"Why *you* are so important," Cheung rejoins.

Marco acknowledges her flattery.

"You must be like a wise father, guiding the baby," Sung continues. "With your guidance, helping it resolve its own internal contradictions. Meanwhile—"

Hsu Yang smacks his lips. "You have any more Mandarin oranges? They're delicious."

"No," Dakota Sung remarks. "Let's pursue our conversation. For example, what's the system doing when it breaks down?"

"Acting normally. Creating exceptions. Role models. Little beacons of hope, like Lei Feng."

"Lei Feng?"

"Precisely. Lei Feng, the model Communist soldier, accidentally killed when a truck he was directing for the good of the People hit a telephone pole that fell on top of him. Poor Lei Feng!" Marco clucks. "What a way to become a hero! A telephone pole hammering you into the ground!"

Guffawing, he sips a little tea. No one else laughs. "Can I have another moon cake?"

Cheung snaps her fingers.

"Remember the Party's directive: 'Be of service, love the people, love the Party, love the Chairman, like Lei Feng.' In my way of thinking, the heroic exception escapes from the Harbin ice box and humbly lives out a dream. The one in 3.2 billion exception, man or woman, who just wants to live life and be happy. Loyalty and service, loved by the Party and the People! Maybe the outliers should be left alone."

Cheung sighs, signaling a conclusion.

She and Sung leave Marco Hsu Yang in his chair. The witnesses stand over him. I can see he's agitated. Dakota and Cheung Yuen smoke another cigarette in the anteroom followed by more chewing gum. Speaking softly, *sostenuto*, as though under water, they are deliberately allowing me to hear all their babbling.

"He's elliptical," I hear Cheung say, shrugging as though the matter is of little importance. "Perhaps he needs more tea and delicious cakes laced with sodium thiopental? Eventually we'll break him down."

"Don't be sure. If ordinary persuasion doesn't work, we may need a deeper dive into his 'Fortress,' at least the 11-dimensional gates he's devised. Perhaps our analysis is too superficial. Or something hides in plain sight."

"What about Miranda Qian Shuai?"

"Unclear. The inquest was pointless—and dangerous for us."

"Come on!" Cheung retorts. "We followed protocol. Besides, Hsu Yang won't get to see her now. He's being whisked off to detention. Naomi will stay here until her furlough ends. We should reassign her to Taiwan. Better suited to leveraging electoral ignorance than remaining glued to her victim. Besides, Naomi excels at exposing ordinary flesh trolls. She'll carry out her own 'skin the flesh' parties (*ba pi* 扒皮) while orchestrating Hsu Yang's outing."

"Wait a minute. She grows closer to him every day. Their past history—"

"She will cooperate, given the right incentives."

"How do you even know she's still loyal? She isn't behaving that way. But, as an incentive, we'll locate her father if he's still alive, the one who escaped to Hokkaido or Aleutia or whatever he is. Stage a reunion of sorts, perhaps a virtual meeting. In the meantime, give Hsu Yang a carceral vacation in Yellow Mountain. Allow the doctors to fuss over Miranda Qian Shuai."

Sung shrugs. "Not much hope there."

"Perhaps when he sees the old Party guys, he can relax, play some cards, and spill a few beans along with his expensive whiskey."

"Cragganmore? I drink it all the time."

*

My *Logoharp* reviews Miranda's status. She's in a medically induced coma to prevent further brain swelling. Her skull is obscured in bandages, but I can see from her MRIs that the gashes to the parietal and temporal bones are severe, that she's had numerous brain bleeds, that the swelling is barely under control.

I've gotten up, left her bedside. Wringing my hands. No one here. Nothing.

Returning to the observation window, I persuade the drones to let me pass. I've pushed back her door, leaned over her bed, careful not to disrupt a tangle of IV drips, oximeters and bandages.

"Miranda?"

Look, listen, feel—the instructions of basic emergency medical technicians assessing an accident victim. I take her fingers in mine, her wrist for pulse (thready), touching her temples. Her body, mummified with casts and bandages, shows bruising wherever gauze doesn't cover them. She's intubated, stuck with infusion needles, her wounds smelling of dirty iodine and dried blood. I hold her fingers again, as though she's a toddler, her tiny nails bluish-gray, no doubt from poor circulation. She must have squeezed them hard into her palms during torture to keep silent.

Marco Hsu Yang won't come. Perhaps that's better. He would only complicate things with whatever emotions he has left.

A bot nursing assistant whizzes by me, all huffy on Roller Blades. I detain her with my synthetic hand, speaking in sign language: *Need ointments, tape, fresh gauze, a bin, a tube for siphoning, washcloth, clean sheets...*

She ignores me, scurrying around, whispering among her fellow bots who busily dispense medication. I leave the room, locate a supply cabinet down the hall and cobble together washing trays, scissors, clean spray bottles, bandages.

I wash her skin wherever she isn't covered in casts, wiping away the iodine stains, coagulated blood and pus, hoping the water and soapy wash will refresh her. Perhaps this makes me feel better. She shows no signs of awareness either of the water or my hands stroking her skin with the washcloth.

"Shuai!" Expecting her to wake. A laser light from my eyes. "Shuai!"

No response, not even a twitch of her fingers.

Five days...then a week. I've slept suspended in mid-air above a couch next to Miranda's window, which looks out on the violet-green neon tinge of Beijing's skyline. I messaged Jens to return from South Pole Aitken as soon as he can to examine her with instruments and medicines no doctor here seems to have.

"We played the game," I hear Marco whispering to me, though it's an old tape. "This time we lost. Chance can be controlled up to a point. But there's also a possibility of failure through luck. No guarantees for loyal lovers or friends, either, so get out of here, Naomi. Fly to Harbin. Do what you're supposed to do."

26

OCTOBER 2120

GRAVITATIONAL PINCHES

重力之扭

Lang Fei and I are searching for the Beehive, a treasury of supercomputing servers controlling Mother Country's entire system of cryogenic torpor, aka Harmonious Recycling.

Periodically, my *Logoharp* issues obligatory bulletins about the Harmonious Recycling System, that it's ubiquitous world-wide (it isn't), the most perfect, Edenic solution to global breeding excess (no).

This fortress we seek, named after the House of Atreus's *tholoi*— beehive tombs in Mycenaean Greece— is rumored to be built deep underground, a burial structure created by corbelling of rock or brick. Capped with a false dome, a long passage to a central chamber and a doorway *stomion* of post and lintel construction, the Beehive was once thought to be the evolution of Bronze-Age tumulus designs. But today, the Fortress is a quantum supercomputer whose units of information (qubits) grow exponentially, each qubit capable of supporting multiple spin states, 0s, 1s or some proportions of 0s and 1s, producing incredible power and calculations at unthinkable speeds.

Qubits demonstrate "entangled" properties as well; that is, subtle and mysterious interactions, such that whatever operation happens to the spin state of one qubit alters the spin state in a partner or "correlating" qubit no matter how distant the partner happens to be. Entangled qubits may exist across vast distances, operating in redundant Beehive installations located in Mother Country thousands of kilometers apart. No one really understands the physics of entanglement. Marco Hsu Yang has reminded me the Directorate ensures redundancy in all critical computing systems. He's also claimed repeatedly that his memory and coding access to the duplicate Beehive Fortresses, wherever they are, have been wiped clean.

*

Lang Fei meets me at the Black Dragon sky-luge station in West Harbin, but he's weirdly changed. No facial expression at all. I stroll with him past a scarcely illuminated St. Sophia Cathedral at 12:30 a.m. Only a light dusting of rime covers us now. In the moonlight I see white ice collecting on the copper-green onion domes of the church.

St. Sophia was built during Harbin's Russian-inspired heyday in 1907. The archives claim that the church was supposed to inspire memories of Red Square in Moscow and help restore the people's spiritual confidence in the Russian Army after its humiliating defeat by Japan. Though thousands have visited St. Sophia before, its signature painting, *The Last Supper*, hasn't been restored. Red Guards scratched out the eyes of both Christ and Judas Iscariot during the first Cultural Revolution. At one point all of St. Sophia's stained-glass windows were bricked up. Saplings grew from the roof. Concrete apartment buildings and a pen factory blocked views of the cathedral from the streets, and an auto body shop came within a meter or two of its walls. Chinese officials claim they still plan to restore St. Sophia to its original glory, celebrating kinship with Mother Russia. Last I looked, the icons' eyes were still gouged out.

Lang Fei seems hypnotized. He's forgotten why we're searching for the Beehive. Excusing himself as an insomniac, he shows me around the darkened city as though in a trance. I see nothing in his eyes but the reflections of pink festival lights snaking around Stalin Park's Corinthian columns. Lang Fei stares too long at the green lanterns hanging from the filigreed iron gates of the main street, *Zhongyang dajie* (中央大街), a cobblestone thoroughfare crowded with shops, sleepless tourists and food trucks selling dumplings and sausages steaming in the cold.

"What's wrong with you?" I'm guessing that Lang Fei's memory archives have been hacked, one way to disable strategic thinking. "Which virus has stolen your mind? Why are you wandering around with pink stars in your eyes? We have work to do!"

"I'm okay, Naomi." His voice is flat. "I just love touring this city."

At dawn, the sky is a gray stratus ceiling. We stop for coffee, the cobblestoned streets slick with muddy slush. Scanning the Jewish synagogues painted in daisy yellow, the winged-victory statutes perched atop the pediments of banks you'd expect to see far to the west—in Moscow or Paris, for example—Lang Fei recites the history of twentieth century Euro-Chinese Harbin, once the terminus of the Chinese Eastern Railway. He has tourist brochures stuffed into his tubular vest pockets. "With the October 1917 revolution," he reads aloud, "100,000 White Guards and 20,000 Jews escaped to Harbin in the Far East, recreating their lives in a city that reminded them of home."

But that influx ended in the 1930s with the rise of the Russian Black Shirts and their collusion with invading Japanese armies. Most of the Jews and Russian immigrants fled south to Shanghai. A Japanese medic, Shiro Ishii, received Imperial authorization to establish a biowarfare research laboratory in the Pingfang district of Harbin in 1935. Known internally as Unit 731, the 150-room torture complex housed Japanese physicians who performed live vivisection experiments on captured prisoners—Koreans, Chinese and Russians, men and pregnant women. Rats and fleas infested underground chambers. Medics injected plague, anthrax, typhoid and horse blood into young men to see what would happen. Some victims were brought out to local fields, tied to posts in attitudes of crucifixion as the Japanese experimented with germ bombs and flamethrowers. An estimated 12,000 died in the laboratory. Half a million Chinese died from widely disseminated biological and chemical weapons developed by Unit 731 during the 1930s and World War II.

*

Lang Fei and I tour the commemorative Museum of Human Atrocities adjacent to the Pingfang laboratories. Positioned on Xinjiang Street about 15 kilometers from Harbin's urban center, the museum consists of black marble rhomboid structures resting heavily on subterranean glass, an exhibition space covering more than 3,000 square meters. On display

are thousands of artifacts: gas masks, rising suns, Japanese uniforms, dioramas of straw-stuffed germ bomb victims with heads wrapped in bags, their arms and legs tied to crosses. The museum's halls are clean and antiseptic, but they reveal dozens of photographs of rats, fleas and anthrax spores magnified a hundred times, the latter displaying purple and pink filaments or lenticular shapes, like magic beans sprouting yellow hairs.

I read all the narrative inscriptions on the plaques detailing Unit 731's history.

"Why are we here?" I ask him.

"I have a feeling," he says. "The network of tunnels here is a backdoor to the Beehive's central facilities—if not the supercomputer, at least a node and a storage area for cryopods and recently collected bodies."

"What's your evidence?"

"The cold here. The network of tunnels. The history. I mean the overlay of atrocities. It's logical. This place is remote, out of town; no one comes here. I suspect most locals, thanks to our cleaned-up textbooks, don't even recall what the Japanese invasion was about."

I can't argue. Following him, I notice he walks robotically, legs too straight, not his normal "monkey" scoot at all. I wonder if someone is controlling his movements, even his voice, from the outside.

We're descending a ramp into a sub-basement and I run my hands across the tiled walls to find a latch, a door, an access panel, an opening somewhere, but nothing.

My eyes ask him again. "There must be a way down into the lower tunnels, assuming they exist."

Fei looks up, but doesn't answer. Assiduously he scribbles with his light pen and takes photographs of hairy fleas.

"But we're not finished here," he says finally, leading me to a life-sized specimen jar containing a six-foot long male body cut lengthwise in two. The plaque affixed to the glass says he was a Russian POW, Allied loyalist and avowed enemy of Unit 731, bisected vertically so that Ishii and his staff could expose his brain, heart, lungs, liver, intestines and penis for further study and display.

"Look, his hair has traces of red. Formaldehyde red. Definitely a Russian," Lang Fei says. "The guy is so pickled he looks like a giant fetus."

"Wake up!" I yank him toward me. "Fei, there's no trapdoor here, no dark energy, nothing. My sensors are jammed."

He stares at me, then the Russian specimen.

"Why are you so impatient?"

"We're running out of time." Jostling him back toward the exit. "If I didn't know you better, I'd say you actually enjoy this."

"It's interesting, even if the history doesn't bear repeating. I believe the tunnels still lead somewhere."

"You've been hacked, haven't you? Your judgment is off. Or maybe someone just bored a hole in your brain. We'll see."

*

He leads me to the river. We're standing on a roughly triangular-shaped ice floe as we drift down the Songhua. The sunlight is blinding, even for me. Lang Fei hardly notices. I shut my visor and the display turns night-vision green.

"It's mesmerizing, the shoreline moving past us," he says.

The river ice is breaking up in spots, a breeze from the warmer Korean coasts to the south. I feel it. But Lang Fei still hasn't seen or done anything toward our mission.

"What's wrong?" I ask him.

"Nothing," he says. "I'm happy."

"You're captive."

"I'm happy. Give it a rest, at least for a day."

Lang Fei relates a strange story. He was strolling along the river the other evening and ran into an old couple, crinkly and dressed in rags like poor Matryoshka dolls. He thought it was a tourist joke, but the old lady invited him back for supper in their hut somewhere up river, just beyond a deep thicket of mulberry and birch and down a ravine, though he's not sure exactly where they took him.

"They were tiny people," he relates, "probably Russian Jews who migrated to Harbin after the Second Cultural Revolution. The two live in a forest and she made *kreplach* for me, little dumplings with ground meat and mashed potatoes boiled in chicken soup. Delicious." He breathes deeply, as though he can still smell the kreplach.

"Their little shack has a rough circular door, like a hobbit hole. The couple are so far away from the Orange Guard that the two seem immortal, shielded from any danger.

"To get there, you walk forever," he tells me. "It was cold, and the snowflakes fell on my cheeks, my nose, my hair, but their fire warmed me."

We drift by a stand of Korean pines lining the shore, their slate-blue cones laced with strings of glowing gold. Fei grasps one, so delicate, like Russian-crafted Faberge eggs. Some of the large pines appear in distant forest slopes like hairy monsters, all of them about to move in phalanx up the mountain. Fei starts spouting the Three Witches' prophesy from *Macbeth* "*...when Birnam wood come to Dunsinane...beware!*" He's a madman, his eyes darting with the swaying pines in the wind.

"Remember the Beehive Fortress?" I prod him. "We're here to find the control unit and the trapdoor if there is one."

"Hey. The river will change direction past that bend, and then we'll be heading upstream," he tells me.

"But we have no oars. We can't go upstream."

Lang Fei laughs; already the river is changing direction. We take a bend around a boulder, floating inexplicably up-stream without oars in water that seems incredibly calm. We're heading past a tiny whirlpool to the shaggy pine forest and a ravine far beyond where he believes the old couple resides.

"Come this way." He beckons. We step off the floe and Fei hesitates a moment, not fully sure this was the clearing he found a few days back. But there is one monster Korean pine dressed in gold filigree cones and he nods. We begin walking the thicket past the hairy pines. Near sunset we come upon a thatched cottage low and squat, but sturdily built. A tiny wooden door opens for us, so small we have to crawl on hands and knees to go through it.

Paulina, the crone, moves slowly toward us. A fire burns brightly in a stone hearth. We smell roasting meats, spices, maize, peppers, soups, pie.

"You must be hungry. Delighted you came," she says.

Lang Fei's eyes widen and he flashes a smile.

"I'm Naomi, Lang Fei's friend. Pleased to meet you both. But I don't eat normally," I tell them. "Thank you for inviting us, anyway."

The woman ladles stew for Fei and her husband.

"Both of you look too old to be alive," Fei interjects.

"Not at all."

"What's your secret?"

"No secrets. We woke up while floating inside our warm ice sleighs on the Songhua. It was last winter. Just two oldies assigned to these floating coffins, but when we woke, we pushed them open and started walking north. The pods were so cozy and climate controlled! We hated to leave! And we could dream of an expanding universe, our favorite topic! And now we don't sleep."

"How's that possible? Everyone sleeps."

"No, no, sleeping makes you tired. It makes you old! Just the way eating makes you hungry! Besides, we love to stay awake. Every waking minute we cook and sweep, plant and harvest and hide away our food. When the weather is cold, we solve equations!"

"Maths!" the old man says.

He calls himself Ely.

"Yes, 'maths,' the way it's said in Baltica and Harbin schools, since our ideas are always plural," Ely explains.

"How did you escape?" I ask. "Cryo-torpor is required for any ordinary soul age 50 or above unless you happen to be a Directorate elite. But now we've heard about people waking up—some elders, disabled people, and a few with end-stage disease. The system has a timing flaw no one understands. Perhaps an escape mechanism, an intermittent flaw allowing a few to get up and face their future in other ways."

"We've heard that too," Paulina says. "But we're not insomniacs. We just don't sleep. We don't need to. Our minds are very active. Ely, can you explain this to our guests?"

He shrugs, slurping his soup. Then he gets up. "Let me show you something!" He heads toward another room.

"Not a good idea—" Pauline interrupts him. "How do we know these people will keep a secret?"

"Well, we don't. But hey, they seem nice! Am I being too hasty?"

"Always," Paulina says.

"Not to worry," I interject. "Let's just relax and have some cheer together!"

We sit down to at the table. Paulina serves us tea and biscuits.

"My husband solves differential equations related to the saddle shape of our heavens and the unexpected donut holes of the fourth dimension in the night sky," she says. "Personally, I prefer Euclidean geometry. But there is a world of non-Euclidean axioms applying only to warped geometric shapes sagging like old pillows. The shapes are realistic and refer to the world we know, weighted by gravity, but we use formulas and axioms to describe the next."

"The next?"

"Yes."

Inside an adjoining library, with their backs humped and their heads craned forward to show us the way, the couple open parchment scrolls written in Gothic formulary. The scrolls stack two meters high.

"You seem to be describing the gravitational pinches of space formed by small and large masses," I muse, picking up a scroll to read it carefully. "Why reinvent what's already known?"

"If you look carefully, you will see that the universe is warped only marginally, nowhere near as much as Einstein's formulas predict." Ely grins and points to a large loom in the corner by an upright cherrywood piano, its keys yellow and sagging. "My wife is a weaver. She weaves our mathematical formulas into the woolen coats and blankets we give to local children. In winter, we host them by our fire days and nights, giving them cider and snacks."

"How very nice."

"Where do these children come from? Lang Fei says. "Why weave formulas into woolens?"

Ely speaks up. "We believe our knowledge of warp and woof in the universe prepares us for anything that happens next. Same with children, same with the fabric of time. Children who carry our knowledge in their coats transmit it to their parents during free discussion."

"But how? Where? Where do these children and parents live?" Lang Fei interrupts again.

He sounds anxious. I tap his foot under the table to warn him. "There's no one around here at all," he whispers.

Paulina shuffles to the soup pot hanging over the fire.

"They live behind a wall defined by alternate dimensions, the escaped ones," she mumbles. "You can't see them, but they're safe. The children come visit when they want."

"Why are you here?" Ely interrupts, his voice grinding slowly, suspiciously.

I try to explain my task: Searching for a Beehive Fortress, a high-security computer installation probably near here, underground, controlling the Harmonious Recycling of tens of thousands. Trying to find a technical flaw, the source of the flaw, so that the system can return to normal operation.

"Do you know anything about this?"

"Why do you want to know?" Ely queries.

"My instructions are to find the system flaw and fix it. My assignment is to work in accordance with Directorate policy and the inviolability of its timing devices. Also, to honor those elders disturbed in cryosleep so they can live out their 10 days of dreams—"

I hear gasps, then deep, disturbed breathing.

"It's better to live out your dreams while you're alive, in motion," Ely interjects loudly.

"Uummm," Paulina agrees.

"But actually," I go on, "there may be considerable opposition among the masses to the whole idea of cryo-torpor because the parting of family members induces grief, especially when elders leave before their natural time. In this case, my contrary instinct as a Reverse Journalist is to foresee and report a better solution, a happier one reframing the future timeline."

"One that doesn't rob people of useful life," Lang Fei says.

"Maybe," Ely remarks.

"Do you know where this system is located?"

"No, I don't, exactly," he muses. "But I can tell you, Naomi, there is a *tholoi*, a Beehive of sorts, composed of the pure energy of living things."

"Living things," I repeat stupidly. "Which ones?"

"The Escaped ones. We check in every once in a while; you can see their bodies behind a firewall turning into light, as though they're escaping gravity. Their energy consists of thoughts and wishes, the emanations left after their bodies fall away. The pure ones shine just like the klieg lights in a movie premiere! When they gather, they shed their mass!"

"That's impossible!"

"No, it's not. What's left of us but our emanations captured in the memory of loved ones? We only have a certain amount of time. The elders getting close to the end in these cryopods, assuming they can break free, still only have a decade, a few years, a few months or weeks of useful life. But behind this wall—let's call it a firewall—we can see the photonic traces of ancestors. Parents, grandparents, great grandparents, even children gone but still loving each other. Paulina and I see them still as bobbing, vibrating imprints of light. We register these photonic traces as photographs with my special camera (he points). Photos capture the light of our ancestors on film.

"And in the next world, no one sleeps," Ely continues. "Everyone is thinking, doing, asking questions, exploring, laughing, imparting memories and stories, without discernible mass and all its problems. Everyone is in motion all the time—"

"But Newton describes bodies that must come to rest," Lang Fei, a believer, interjects.

"That's in our classical universe. In the next—and these escapees portend the next iteration of our universe—there will be no bodies, no masses. Only pure energy and communities of spirits pinging around, both light and dark."

"Which means no murder. No hunger. No clock!" Fei exclaims, starry-eyed.

"Where can I see these souls? Which photonic detector do I need to use?" I ask Ely.

Mother Paulina takes my natural hand, leading me to her fireplace. "It's somewhere behind this wall of fire," she says.

"You may only see your shadow now. I think you can only sense the pure ones until you escape yourself."

Ely turns away, studying his scrolls at the table. He puts on his glasses.

"Are you sure you won't eat something, Naomi?" Paulina prods me. "Here, sit at this table, please. Restore your energy by eating a piece of my delicious carob cake."

I nod, studying the veins in her oversized hands. Her arms are like tree stumps. For the first time in as many years as I can remember, I pick up a fork, tasting the delicious cake. I let the sweet flour, butter, egg yolks and carob swirl against my tongue. The taste is so lovely that my mouth tingles. I ask for coffee and a second piece of cake, not caring about gaining an extra pound or two. Mother Paulina is pleased! (I think of Miranda now, trying to get me to eat moussaka.)

Later in the evening we lie on pillows chatting by the fire, drinking coffee and mulberry wine and nibbling on pimento cheese. I feel the strangest emotion—happiness, an infectious mirth, without bitterness or tension. Lang Fei, too, seems relaxed, restored to his original condition, almost, but without his customary intensity. Paulina and Ely tell us stories about their children, all mathematicians and physicists located— where? Their names are Viola, Isadora, Philly, Roman, and Alexandra. All of them reside somewhere else, perhaps choosing a different time to live, but the couple is vague about that.

"This world is just a try-out," Ely grins, referencing a love of the theatre. "Hardly perfect! But while everyone is sleeping, we're fashioning our next lives. Comets, meteors and asteroids hurl by, mostly missing us, but coming close! The next world should be fascinating. We hope you'll join us for the new galactic adventure."

"Mother Paulina—" I frown, recollecting my own mother. "I can't now. I can't, I'm bound to a mission. But soon, I trust, we'll be able to."

"On that day we'll meet again," Paulina promises, waving her hand, as though she's a magician conjuring spirits. She touches my argonaut cap, my exposed forehead, blessing me, injecting insight. "All of us will gather with our sweetest friends, oldies like us, and a few young ones like you, for an all-night solstice party. We'll sit on our blankets in the woods watching the meteor showers. We'll be drinking to earthshine and never sleep while the feasting and watching go on and on."

She lifts her feet, mincing a little, swaying her old hips, grabbing Lang Fei's hand to complete a little twirl. He's awkward, tries to lift her arm to spin her, not successfully. We hug the two of them as we take our leave at sunrise.

I still have no idea why Lang Fei brought me here, unless these two are part of a future I can't foresee. I'm reasonably assured Fei is returning to his natural condition, and that I can trust him. As I say goodbye, entering the pine and spruce thickets once again, I crane my head around, hoping to catch a glimpse of the couple as they disappear behind their tiny door. I wave once more; the door closes slowly.

27

NOVEMBER 2120

UPSIDE DOWN IN ALEUTIA

阿
留
申
历
险

'm saying farewell to Lang Fei. Miranda's condition is unchanged, her doctors report to me. Do I reject her prognosis because I'm already certain of it?

Fei has promised to return to the medical center to watch over her. Our search throughout Harbin has yielded nothing more or less than our encounter with wise Ely and Paulina. What wonderful futures they promise!

But I have to get away, reconstitute. China was never my home. At this moment, I feel drawn to caves of ice, but not in Harbin. I want the Aleutian hinterlands. Perhaps because I believe I can locate my parents in the walls of ice. I'm beginning to think my father never went to Hokkaido. The LIDAR drones have searched everywhere in the surrounding region and have found no trace of him.

For Dean Cheung, I produce daily reports on Marco Hsu Yang's many infractions. He's alleged to have ordered the murders of fellow gamblers and assassins he doesn't like (I doubt it); he's had multiple wives (true), including the most recent, a "Lady Macbeth" type who grieves publicly over the death of Duncan, a celebrated Harbin party boss. She secretly believes the guy was holding her Beaux back. Feeling guilty—perhaps because she instigated Duncan's murder? Lady Macbeth is given to sleepwalking and, eventually, trips to a psychiatric ward. I've uncovered her correspondence: She badgers Marco, complaining bitterly that the Singing Directorate abuses his talents without providing luxurious perks. Apparently, she knows nothing about Miranda.

*

Aleutia is interconnected to Manchuria through sky and ocean tunnels and there are numerous small airports along the island chain. But I don't need any of these to know where I'm going. Closing my eyes, I'm 20 again, taking an old-fashioned ferry for tourists from Vancouver through the Queen Charlotte Islands to Aleutia, where the great roiling sea kicks up at dinner time, sending the guests staggering to the ship's side rails to puke. We're being knocked around like bathtub toys in a whirlpool, great walls of water towering above mid-mast. It's easy to get sucked into the maelstrom. From the latrines below I fight my way back on the deck to let the icy waves soak through my human skin. On this trip I recall my mother bracing against the wind on deck—I was a teen then—her black and white rain gear and piles of strawberry blond hair shedding water like duck feathers. She never got seasick, her constitution indomitable.

On today's ship my freedom means not thinking, not do-ing. Disguising myself in PVC dusters and well-worn boots, I'm an old fisherman's wife. I watch the slate-stained waves lapping against the Cloud Ferry. Passage is cheap, less than half a month's extension points for my passage. It plies the seas at times, but then elevates like the Hindenburg to avoid icebergs; the ship's bellows and helium rockets burn on com-mand, enabling low-level flight.

In Vancouver, I catch a ship to the remaining glaciers above Skagway. These include the teal-colored Mendenhall ice sheets of Juneau (hardly anything left of them) and the Margerie Bergs still calving into Glacier Bay. All of these have retreated since 1940. The Mendenhall is a wet remnant, just rubble and moraine left at the shoreline, an untended highway. But while the eastern side of Glacier Bay has gone to bog and tundra, mountain goats and moose still dot the higher snowy peaks. To the west, snow falls on the Fairweather glacier in late December and January, even into the first week of February, leaving Fairweather intact, advancing. I plan to scale Fairweather, and possibly Matanuska Glacier with its sapphire-colored ice. But why have I come?

Not sure. Though I've watched ice climbers descend into the crevasses with their crampons and pulleys hoisted tight, all of them appear to me like ants strung out on one-dimensional wires. But here, 10 kilometers deeper into Matanuska, it's silence. Stepping into a glacial sub-stream and a tributary cave to my left—nicknamed Athabaskan, after the Copper River people who first inhabited this area—I feel calm. The portal is a sapphire whorl. My crampons are biting sideways; slowly I ascend the eggshell walls, eventually finding my spot as I hang upside down like a bat. In this way my blood flow inverts without much feeling of lightheadedness. After a few minutes, I hang my hammock so that my stakes bite into the ice ceiling above me, and from there I lie back, looking up at a hole in the cave that opens into a night sky glowing with Venus and Mars. Drip by drip, the ice melts onto my brow, refreshing me.

"Naomi," a voice calls out. It's an excited, deep voice, as though someone is happy to see me.

A young man appears. He's the image of my young father. He has frameless glasses and a shock of hazel-black hair standing upright and wavy on the scalp. He's lean and tall, perhaps 30 years of age, his chin cleft and dimpled. His jawline shows a hint of five o'clock shadow; he has mild hazel eyes looking up at me—a hint of fire there.

"What's in our bag?"

"Laundry," he says.

"What are you doing around here?"

"I could ask you the same question."

"I meant to talk to you decades ago in Seattle. I saw you, or what I thought was you, shortly after your disappearance. At the Freemont Express Laundromat, someone there who looked just like you: a grad student, perhaps, youngish, wearing rimless glasses, intent on a newspaper. He could have been your twin."

"What were you doing there?"

"Reading a newspaper and waiting for my clothes to dry. What about you?"

"Washing and waiting for my rags to dry," he says. "Nice to see you're still in the northwest. Why didn't you talk to me then, or was it my twin?"

"I wanted to. But the twin or ghost or whatever he was, was too handsome and I was scared to speak. He looked just like you did in an early photograph. Besides, he was reading intently. I noticed he read every line of the newspaper, not skipping pages; nothing could spoil his concentration. Just the way you did when you were reading in a salmon-colored bathtub right next to a Formica sink decorated with gray and pink paisley boomerangs—the fashion back then. You didn't mind me interrupting you because I was little. You wore a gray washcloth covering your private parts, tossing the wet paperbacks onto the floor as soon as you finished them. Dozens of books, one after the other."

"That was a sloppy way to read."

"It's how you read. You used to walk into the house after gardening with your black Keds sneakers caked with fertilizer after Mom had just mopped the floors. She'd shriek, 'My floors!' You shouted, 'I don't give a damn about the floors!' I was never sure whether you were being callous or just speed dating through life with a few girlfriends on the side."

"Both."

"What's your origin?"

"Brooklyn via Ukraine, Harbin, Dublin, and White Horse, Canada. Does it matter?"

"Not at all. Are you alive? Are you still in Hokkaido? Am I just remembering you?

"I could ask you the same question."

"I'm synthetically transplanted, transfused, not dead yet. Half cyborg. Reverse Journalist. I'm waiting for a sign. Something to happen."

"It already has. You say you're searching for a sign but it's right at the tip of your nose."

"What do you mean? Why can't I see it? I'm trying to find a key to the Beehive Fortress and I don't know what to do or where to look."

He puts down his knapsack. "Think of *Harold and the Purple Crayon*," he laughs, harkening back to my favorite child's book. "Harold doesn't remember where home is. He can't find the moon...he can't find the path... He doesn't know how to get out of his own house, or to find his way back to it. He starts to draw porcupines and apple trees and delicious pie with his crayons. The porcupines eat all the pie. He draws apartment buildings and cities...and then...a bedroom, where suddenly he remembers how to frame the moon in the window right above his bed. Where's your window? How do you exit this life? How do you get people to wake up and quit washing their dirty linen over and over?"

"I guess you stop caring. You leave."

"That's one answer. You could also set an example."

"Like yours? Come on, Dad. You left."

"I tried in the little time I had. I wrote plays. Do you remember *The Day the Russians Invaded Long Island?* We were afraid of the Russians then. They were our monsters. And I argued with local police abusing Blacks."

"There's no laundromat here," I tell him. "Perhaps you could melt some ice and wash your dirty clothes with seal fat."

"I prefer that you help me do that."

"I'm through washing people's dirty linen."

"But these clothes are clean. I brought a sweater for you."

The young man resembling my father but not necessarily my father opens the rucksack in front of me. I stay glued in my hammock, not fearful, but unexpectedly frozen, unable to move. He pulls out a winter sweater and puts it on. The sweater is just as I had remembered it, still smelling of mothballs. The bottom third, a dark wintergreen, is flecked with bark-brown and tree trunks. Korean pine needles overlay an ivory background in the middle, while the upper third is dotted with gold ornaments and bright holly berries.

He hands it to me and I bury my face in it, breathing in all of him.

"Where did you get this?" I rub my wrist against the rough fibers. Long ago, I remember burying my head against this sweater and his chest after I crashed in a toboggan run. I was five years old, not hurt at all, but his chest was a comfort.

"Someone gave this to me as a Christmas gift," he says, finally.

"My mother?"

"You."

He touches my throat. "I suppose you always wanted to save everyone, but you're messed up, Naomi. You can't even figure out if you should save anyone, even your friends, the elders or yourself."

"Given how bad things have gotten—"

"That's an excuse, Naomi. Are you seeing the situation for all it is? Do you understand what keeps everyone up at night? I know your thoughts are divided. What's the point of channeling the harp if it leads you in stupid directions? We're supposed to act, to make every moment count before —"

"Before what?"

"You know what."

My voice catches, as though I've felt specks of sand blowing toward me in a desert wind.

"All kinds of survivors are around, Naomi, even very old survivors, and young ones. They'll help you."

"But they've disappeared. I can't find them. Teacher Bai, for example."

"Look harder, but not with your eyes. Not even with your visor. Try your gut. Guts are underrated."

"I can't feel my gut. I can't feel my heart. Half of me is synthetic."

"You will. Give it time."

Tears well up in my eyes, my extant human trait. I turn away from him, wipe them with one natural hand.

"You weren't supposed to leave so young." My voice is raspy now.

"Well, sorry. I wanted to stay with you longer. Believe me, I did—for you and your mother, but I couldn't. I just wanted to finish my newspapers. And then the wind got me and blew me away. You know I wanted to be an actor?"

His voice is gentle.

"I was trouble for you."

"Not too much. More for your mother."

He steps back now and I try to reach him but can't. I want to touch his stubbly chin to assure myself that he's real. But now he hurls a grappling hook at the ice ceiling above, wiping the moisture from his forehead. He toes one foot, then the other, into the ice wall with his crampons, stepping slowly and heavily up the wall. Hanging upside down like a bat, just like me, his arms elongate, sweeping the ground.

"You look weird!"

"So do you, Naomi! Upside down, all things seem right with the world!"

"What do you see?"

"I see a beanpole smart kid with a hole in her heart! And the way you became...a smart beanpole of a robotic self-doubter with passion for turning things around."

"A half-baked borg! Made of chewing gum and spit."

He drops down, walks toward me, taking my synthetic left hand, then the real one, stroking my skin. "You've got a sense of humor. Don't lose it."

I can feel his skin against mine.

"Go deeper into the cave and stay tonight," he instructs me.

"I'm running out of time. The clock is faster for me than most humans.

"All the more reason to stay young! Go forth, my love... Leila Pallas awaits!"

He presses his lips to my hand. They're soft...the touch and wetness are entirely real. Leaving the rucksack behind, settling it on the ground like a limp animal, he pulls off his jacket and trails it behind him, finally dropping it onto the cave floor. The air still breathes his hair tonic, the witch hazel aroma, the cave swallowing him up—first a whole man, then a silhouette and the back of his head, then his torso without a head, then his boots, shuffling with no legs or feet inside them.

Won't you stay? I voice, but no sound comes out.

He can't. He won't, I know. But I capture each of his footsteps and store them inside my brain, my third eye. Meeting
him gives me joy.

*

Dark subglacial streams flow to my left and right, but no other
signs of movement except for the waterfall a hundred meters
high, frothing and foaming down a shaft straight ahead. I
alter my retinal scans to ultraviolet wavelength, thinking
fluorescent life lurks in the streams, but everything is hard
rock. Glimmering phosphates and amethyst-colored fluorap-
atites, neon green calcites, stunning corundum, opals, yellow
sodalites embedded in the upper rocks. Thundering sounds,
but more than that, a grinding and undulation of air, as though
turbines are supplying hydroelectric power inside this space
to a distant village. I can hear the whirr, smell the burning
ozone. I switch to rainbow light, white light, and the cavern
glows rosy.

"There's no need for you to climb to the very top," a
woman's voice calls out, most likely recognizing I'll ignore
her commands.

Shadows flit across the cavern walls. Tiny fruit bats hanging upside down from a ledge 10 meters above me swoop down
now, swarming around my visor. I reach up to touch them,
but they swerve to avoid me. My crampons bite into the walls
of mica while the bat shadows lengthen and climb with me

until they tower above my head. Crowned with halos that sparkle, the bat wings hum an octave higher than the music of a turbine.

"Danger above. No need for you to climb to the very top," the voice says again, appearing at my side.

It's a feminine voice.

I turn to her. "I'd like to climb up."

She shakes her head.

My gloves, as though possessed, reach for her hood.

"All I see is silhouette."

"Your visor. Lift it up," she commands. "See with your own eyes."

"Listen to her!" the bats sing to me:

> She's the voice you hear inside the hall.
> The turbines' whirl, the fan blades' brawl—
> Long ago she nudged and judged you,
> Wisdom that seemed right --
> Will you listen now? A pebble in your throat.

"Pull up the visor, and you'll see. Then again, if you don't want to—"

I hesitate. Her voice commands me, a sinuous, growly, actress's lilt. She's midnight blue all over, a theatrical monk's cape covering head and body. She has no face, though. Perhaps she's tried this command on dozens of cave visitors without effect and her face went dark.

"When you act, your doubts will disappear."

Her voice flows through me; she's fluorescing in rosy colors. I have no watch. My digital clock is in my visor; I lift it up. Her face comes clear now, a Brâncuși original except for her prominent, high-arched nose. The way she looks at me with acorn-brown eyes reflecting my emerald eyes inside her. She seems tall, but always wears heels, or are they boots, or no shoes at all? Wrapped in rich robes, dark as a queen.

Now she removes the hood, I see that shock of upswept strawberry blonde hair, perfectly pinned.

"You look young," I murmur. "How do you keep your lipstick so fresh?"

"A woman should carry a mirror."

"I keep losing mine."

"Have you had flying dreams?"

"Yes, I fly over wires and rooftops. There's no censorship in my dreams."

Her lips part, as though she understands. "That must be a relief."

"I don't like looking in the mirror. My whole life has been looking in a mirror to see how others judge me."

She places her fingers on my crown, what used to be a full head of hair.

"The others 'seeing you in a mirror' was probably my fault."

I nod. "Are you my mother?"

"In a manner of speaking," she says.

"Wish you, or someone else like you, had freed me to see myself when it mattered."

No words come forth now.

Her face goes dark again. "Perhaps I always wanted you to be better—not perfect—but better. I had no idea you'd replace half your body with mechanical parts. And your mind—"

She reaches for me. Her hand on my cheek comforts and feels warm.

"The secret of all life is relationships, connections," she continues. "But only one or two that really count." Her words repeat themselves. I try to explain that my connections are a thicket of unfinished sentences. Lies. Comrades who go away or die.

"I script the future and then it happens. But nothing changes at all."

"That's too bad. Perhaps something is broken, or needs to be."

I nod; she listens. "You mustn't give up easily."

"I don't know where to look—"

"What are you made of? Your ancestors stole horses and hunted with spears. You have algorithms, atomic clocks, holo-maps. Hold the maps tighter to your chest! Keep checking your clock. Be a little devious; once you win the bosses' trust, find a broken wall, a tunnel, a cave, and go through it."

She waves her hand over my head, as though removing some curse of confusion and hopelessness infecting my being. Her bats swoop around me again and emanate a blinding glory arc. Without my visor, all I can see are their wings flitting close to my shoulders and arms. Another illusion? The touch of these creatures, oddly, gives me strength. Now I see my parents' bodies rising from their coffins at the center of this shimmering cavern. Their faces aren't drooping, or pasty and gray as death. They're living sculpture, as though they've become one with the rosy quartz of this cave.

28

DECEMBER 2120

THE BALLAD OF BLUE APPLE

蓝
果
之
歌

I'm taking an overnight dirigible from Aleutia to Beijing. I've already announced Architect Tian's murderous trapdoor scheme to the masses.

This old-style zeppelin is given to dreams and reflection. It's a low velocity, non-rigid airship affording a perfectly smooth ride. I love this feeling, as if I'm back in the Hindenburg. Seating is roomy and comfortable, beverages served, and the ship has breathtaking wrap-around views of the roiling, slate-stained Bering Sea.

My harp strikes a low chord. "Hi Ms. *Jinleng,* Golden Dragon. I miss your touch." Dr. Jens Remker has sent a text. He's furloughing from lunar station South Pole-Aitken next week. "I miss gravity and Chinese food, too!" Possibly he misses my snake-skin self, the anodized joints, the hard muscle and softer parts beneath. "The tallness and strength of you is what I miss," Jens corrects me, realizing he's reluctant to voice emotion. "Aitken earthshine is lovely," he writes. "Reminds me of our time together."

I amend my impression. No one has ever texted words like this to me.

"I want to see you, even though you have your missions in Harbin."

He doesn't understand what's about to happen. I ask him about Miranda.

Reverting to a dry professional inflection, he texts: "I'll examine her. Her surgeons don't understand why she remains unconscious. At least the baby seems healthy."

I relay that the nurses lowered her body temperature to reduce the swelling. Her electroencephalograph registers normal wave forms.

"But she won't wake up—"

"Perhaps a little more time, more stimulation. Where shall I meet you when I come back?"

I mention the upcoming trial of the algorithmic imposter. My job is coordinating crowd-sourcing and critique in social media along with reporting the outcome before it happens.

"I'll be tied up in video production, camera work, staging, Jens. There will be thousands of volunteer actors."

"Where and when can I meet you?" he repeats.

I pause, a little strangulated. Weighing my RJ responsibilities against the tingling in my chest and throat, I manage: "When do you land? I'll come for you. I'll manage some time with you."

"Most likely in Gobi."

"Oceans of sand!"

On the moon I remember him striding the dunes, wide legged, climbing the escarpments in a sunset that cast long shadows. He's naked—at least I imagine him to be. But as he approaches, I see he's wearing body tights—a gold and black flame-retardant space suit. His leonine mane stands on end, glistens in the desert sun as though he's Apollo, freshly washed.

"I'll send a transport for you if I'm in court."

"No need."

"Yes, I'll be sure to."

I sense his disappointment. His voice has dropped an octave, reverting to short bursts of text and passive voice, as though we're only colleagues.

"Just give me your dates and times. I'm glad—"

"Okay, soon," he grunts. Signs off.

I should have called him. I'm too distracted, watching a documentary about the Gang of Four on a holo-screen attached to a flip-up dining tray. The video features Jiang Qing, Chairman Mao's last wife, the notorious leader of the Gang, a group intent on purging political enemies. Starting in 1966, the first Cultural Revolution, the docudrama features newspaper cartoons showing Jiang Qing cowering before Western bosses who hold up a treaty compromising China's sovereignty. In another cartoon, she wears a crown of bloody skulls, representing 750,000 allegedly jailed, whipped, beaten and humiliated in street trials, most of them conducted by teenage Red Guards. Court documents claim that 34,800 officials, reactionaries and capitalist roaders, were tortured or killed during a decade of chaos.

What most Westerners don't know is that Jiang Qing was a young stage and film actress. One of her signature roles was Nora, in Ibsen's *A Doll's House*. The Nickelodeon film I'm watching contains photographs of her 1935 performance in the play. The video is grainy, maybe deep-fake.

Yet I've always been interested in Jiang Qing because of her notoriety as China's nastiest witch. After her husband's death in 1976, she ascended briefly to national leadership as a ruling member in the Gang of Four (Mao's appellation). While Mao was still alive, Jiang Qing was in charge of Cultural Affairs, Chief of Propaganda as well. Her primary accomplishment, according to my archives, was making rival artists miserable by demoting or torturing them. One notorious case was that of Cao Yu, China's leading playwright, inventor of *huaju* ("word drama") and the masterpiece play, *Peking Man*. Cao Yu was appointed Director of the Bejing People's Art Theatre in the early 1950s. Fifteen years later, Red Guards beat and crippled him, making him a doorman at the same theatre.

During her reign, Jiang Qing famously banned classical Chinese opera and ballet. Instead, she championed eight "model" proletarian operas. These were soapy, cartoonish productions, elaborately staged and choreographed, but simple-minded nonetheless. She used them to teach the masses about exploitative landlords, capitalist roaders and the Japanese, though I was never sure what anyone learned.

I do know that in 1937 Jiang Qing left Shanghai and her various theatrical roles to cross enemy lines into Chong Qing (Chungking), the last Nationalist stronghold. She was fiercely patriotic and had been deathly poor and abused as a child. For a while she worked in a government-controlled movie studio, but eventually dedicated herself to Communist theatre in Yan'an, where she met and fell in love with Mao. Their relationship was scandalous. Mao divorced his third wife, a revered veteran of the Long March, while she was hospitalized in Moscow. Communist Party leaders were so embarrassed by Mao's affair that they approved his marriage to Jiang Qing only on the condition that the actress not participate in politics for twenty years.

Jiang Qing's stage name was *Lan Ping*—Blue Apple. Playing Nora, she informs her husband Torvald that she is leaving him, announcing she must abandon childhood innocence and discover her own life. Torvald has been a patronizing boor, but she doesn't call him that. Instead, the camera captures Nora full frontal, her expression trance-like, misty eyes downcast a moment, as one might expect from a subservient wife. But then, in a glint, Nora wakes up, confronting Torvald, her eyes burning, her posture taller than before, regal, a hint of grown-up fury in her voice: "I'm a human being, as much as you are; at least before anything else I must try to become one."

I wish Jiang Qing had remembered these lines in her real life, taking them to heart when she and Mao launched their Cultural Revolution in full fury.

29

DECEMBER 2120

MISTER TIAN'S 'TRAPDOOR'

老板暗门

"Two minutes to airtime…positions please. Chyron, drones, B-roll, actors, all ready?"

I'm tapping a microphone in the CCTV holographic studio in Beijing, testing algorithms and holo-tracks, ready to divulge the secrets of the systems architect Tian Jinghui—Marco Hsu Yang, my ex-husband—and his conspiracy to derail the Harmonious Recycling of elders.

My harp announces this broadcast of a courtroom drama to all the avid holo-TV watchers in Mother Country and its subsidiary, Ameriguo. In effect, I use artistry to *stage* his guilt through ambience, innuendo, body doubles and phony testimony. Among RJs, we call this "true fakery" if we want to joke about it. The guilty verdict is already a *fait accompli*; publics will have no other option than to accept what has not yet (technically) happened.

It's true that in this time and place, the accused in Beijing's courts are almost always assumed guilty. Statistically speaking, 99.9 percent of all court cases in Mother Country end in conviction; a criminal trial is merely a confirmation of Party line despite protests claiming that judges remain more loyal to their superiors than objective legal standards.

A short documentary broadcast will prepare the public for Tian's official confessions and punishment. The fact that Mister Tian hasn't revealed a single tidbit about the recycling system hiccups doesn't affect my programming guidelines in the least.

As the Chief RJ for this campaign, I master marionettes, including the living ones. It's easy with my headset, laser pointers, spotlights and a music box filled with phasic fugues. I can swipe my hand through the vaporous 3D holo-creatures standing before me, including the court's two theatrically trained attorneys, ready to act their parts courtesy of live transmission and holo-illusions.

*

In this trial, my human stand-in for Hsu Yang is a fine actor, Mr. Zhang Yunfa, who resembles the original man/boy of 25 years ago. We've even re-created his acne-marks in make-up.

I cue the archived 3D video of a youthful Mr. Tian shaking the hand of our current Party Chairman, Guo Taifeng. When Hsu Yang grasps Guo's superannuated hand, the holo-TV chyron flashes a strip of text on Tian's back: "The Accused: Algorithmic Gangster, Cheats at Blackjack." Adding a touch of menace—Bach's *Toccata and Fugue in D Minor*—I synchronize the audio as it descends hellishly to a growling key of D *sostenuto*, followed by creepy *arpeggios* as Mister Tian is seen in archival footage pledging allegiance to the Party, his fingers positioned over his starched heart.

The announcer describes the fallen star, a computer analyst who first devised a foolproof human recycling solution, only to sell out by devising a timing flaw allowing certain elders to wake up, losing their opportunity for an Edenic cryo-dream.

ANNOUNCER V/O

In his youth, Mr. Tian Jinghui was a brilliant algorithmic architect. Here, in archival footage, we see the premiere of his successful Harmonious Recycling system.

CHYRON FLASH:

Songhua Celebration of elders enjoying family fun, rest and recycling!

Creator of the Harmonious Recycling algorithm visits Harbin to see handiwork!

Elder's dreams realized in bonus 10 days of cryo- life!

ACTION:

Elders on their journey lying asleep inside their cryo-pods. Close-ups of happy sleepers and families surrounding the pods and waving patriotic flags.

CLOSE UP:

A shot of the youthful Hsu Yang/Mr. Tian manipulating a test subject's arms as she lies quietly inside a styrene-molded cryopod. The woman, named Gigi, tenderly voices a *xie xie* (谢谢) thanks to Hsu Yang for his important work.

ANNOUNCER V/O

Right now, what you are watching—live—is a new group of volunteers...a dedicated group of elders ready to make their final journey to dreams in suspended cryo-animation, part of the Harmonious Recycling solution. What you see is absolutely real.

PANORAMIC:

An airplane hangar filled with 3000 elders dressed in orange jumpsuits. The elders are looking fit and spry, grinning for the camera as they clasp hands together and hold them high. A long queue of happy faces.

ACTION:

The entire hangar of people sway back and forth in synchrony, singing the beloved Chinese national anthem, *The March of the Volunteers:*

Arise, ye who refuse to be slaves! With our very flesh and blood

Let us build our new Great Wall...

Everybody must roar his defiance.

Arise! Arise! Arise!

ACTION:

Nurses dispense injections of the vaccine *Neisseria meningitidis* to the Elders in their jumpsuits. Everyone accepts the capped syringes, but two younger women draw back in panic. A few of the grandmas congregate around the stricken women, patting their hands, offering them stuffed animals (cat and rabbit) to calm their nerves. Then the groups gather in small circles, popping the syringe caps and injecting each other. A few wince; most smile, gritting their teeth.

As the song finishes, each volunteer mounts a little stool and settles into a cryopod. The fit is snug, especially for the taller men and women who flex their knees. We see close-ups of middle-aged men raising a thumbs up.

CUT TO:

Chairman Guo applauding from a podium. Guo quotes Chairman Mao's words, which are projected on the chyron in Chinese, English, Russian and Japanese. "If you are in charge, I am at ease."

ACTION:

Now the elders don their goggles, lie back and adjust pillows comfortably inside their pods, quickly settling into a breathless slumber.

CAMERA PAN:

We see elders' faces in their pods: individual grins, then Cheshire-cat group grins, then thousands of Cheshire cats grinning prone in the gleaming airplane hangar.

ANNOUNCER V/O:

What are these volunteers dreaming? Do they return to the past? Or a future better than any they can expect?

CUE MARTIAL MUSIC:

Queues of aircraft mechanics spray liquid nitrogen over thousands of pods, each caked in glittery rime. White-coated attendants wheel the ice sleighs out of the hangar onto a ramp that leads to the icy Songhua. Relatives gathered on the shoreline grin and wave their handkerchiefs tearfully as they bid goodbye.

INSERT:

Menacing still image of Architect Tian Jinghui, his mouth twisted into a snarl.

Fade to silhouettes of elders standing beside their broken cryopods on the ice. A few figures lumber north in a zombie-like phalanx. We see them from the back only.

ANNOUNCER V/O:

Despite the seeming perfection of this Recycling solution, Architect Tian is accused of designing a "trapdoor" that causes some dreamers to wake up in advance of their 10-day dream. Breaking their cryopod lids, they wander aimlessly, like zombies, north of the Songhua River. The Directorate is working non-stop to correct the system and ensure it functions flawlessly.

"Cut!"

Actor Zhang stands over my shoulder as I coordinate all the audio and video threads. He whispers: "Every bit of this video is bullcrap right? It works beautifully, but no one believes it."

"Yes, they do."

I try to explain: "The masses can't wrap their heads around the fact that we're knocking off thousands of healthy volunteers in one shot, many of them in their prime. Everyone seems glad to volunteer, a far classier send-off than hospital-bed euthanasia, the technique we used before Harmonious Recycling became widespread."

"But these actors...they'll wake up, right?"

"No. We promised the volunteers generous scholarships and life-extension points for their kin. The vast majority won't wake up. The benefits of complying with the script are enough to ensure cooperation."

"And the others?"

"We deal with them off camera."

"Look at the kids!!"

The children are fanning out on the ice, our cameramen racing to keep up with them as they push the ice sleighs on the glassy Songhua River toward Sun Island Park.

"It's a go-cart race! Look at them go!"

I sigh, my shoulders slumping because I've seen it all before.

"Wait a minute!" Zhang says.

"What?" My eyes snap to my monitor.

The racing stops. One by one, crowds of family members are joining their kids on the ice. A father starts to shout at his son, *"Bie zai tuile!* (别再推了). *Fangguo lao lao ba!* (放过姥姥吧!) *Stop pushing! Leave grandma alone! Stop pushing!"* The boy freezes, withdrawing his hands from grandma's pod, looking up, confused, embarrassed, in front of his father, who grasps and hugs him.

Then another boy, then another freezing in place. Then whole families, stopping, gathering by their ancestors' cryopods.

The father's voice carries across the river and spreads to others. Our audio picks up shouts, conversation, questions, whispers, cries. The camera rolls. Dozens of grieving family members step gingerly on the Songhua ice, then hundreds come out from the shoreline, some slipping and sliding, their arms shooting out to break a fall. The 3,000 cryopods remain still as the living crowd around them.

How could this be?

My *Logoharp* predicted patient acceptance, not protest.

Zhang and I stare, incredulous. Children and parents form giant semicircles, crowding around the sleepers, shouting in unison, blocking the pods from further movement.

Leave our grandparents alone! They're alive!

Fangguo women de yeye nai nai ba! Zhe bu gong ping!

Tamen hai huozhe!

(放过我们的爷爷奶奶吧！ 这不公平！ 他们还活着)

Logoharp screeches—the ear-splitting sound of revulsion. I cover my ears. Actor Zhang does too, shouting: "Cut the feed!" Without thinking, I obey, switching screens to "Live Transmission Temporarily Lost. Please Stand by."

We keep watching. A full-fleshed woman dressed in a turquoise parka and pink gloves and hat approaches one pod with her little daughter. Suddenly she throws her arms around the glass window, facing whoever is inside. She weeps, her daughter starts to cry. Both bang on the window. Crowbars in hand, two young men come up from behind and furiously hammer the glass, trying to break it. Several of the demonstrators rip the family flag-escutcheons from the pods and hold up remnants for the camera.

"Oh shit!"

"Stream next program!"

This can't be. My harp gave me explicit instructions as per the original script. No danger was suggested in live camera feeds from the Songhua showing deep family devotion, necessary sacrifice, pleasurable goodbyes. We scripted these scenes in advance, intent on showing the masses a shared holiday of recycling and jubilation, children gleefully pushing their sleigh-bound grandmas and grandpas on the river ice as they race toward Sun Island Park.

Everyone was supposed to be happy.

What happened?

The *Logoharp* was *wrong*.

*

Dakota Sung is shouting into my earbuds.

"What the *fuck*?"

"I don't know."

"Shut down the transmission!"

I've already cued a popular ethnic comedy featuring a heavy-set Aunt Jemima type who looks like that Afro-American Negro lady from the pancake box (actually a Chinese actress made up as Aunt Jemima in a fat suit). In the show she's supposed to jump out of a pancake box, saying she's serving pancakes from the plantation in Charleston, South Carolina. She's entertaining two Chinese lovers who listen intently to her indescribably garbled Mandarin. The romantic couple dance around Aunt Jemima, spinning her around a few times and expressing profuse gratitude for her pancakes, which they gobble down. There's a lot of piped-in laughter.

*

We can't fathom how our viewers are reacting to the protests on ice.

Social media influencers by now will have chimed in, arguing about whether this "darkly seditious" video of grieving families at the crypods was real or deep fake. Chances are most viewers won't care, since the majority appear to accept the surreal quality of our media, which attempts, above all else, to protect our social skin.

The protests were real this time.

Though I feel for families sending off these elders in the pods, perhaps there is a tad of selfishness inside them. We are a crowded state at the limits of sustainability. Our Life Clock designates age limits to preserve human resources. Why my *Logoharp* failed to anticipate the crowd's weird behavior remains unclear.

30

JANUARY 2121

FIVE MINUTES TO SHOWTIME

开
演
时
间

Marco enters our studio space; he's been released to my recognizance for make-up and costume preparation. Actor Zhang will be called into the courtroom as a body double only when cross-examination requires strict adherence to a pre-written script. The Directorate, incidentally, allows body doubles to appear in court when a celebrity's health is in jeopardy. The object is to avoid delays or embarrassment during cross-examination.

Marco flings open my dressing room door. "Some tea?" I ask, *pro forma.* I notice he has dark circles under his eyes, unshaven stubble, a limp (sciatica). Actor Zhang, in full makeup, stares back at him.

"You don't look like me at all," Marco says. "Much too pretty."

"Naomi will fix that." Zhang tries to smile, then shrugs and departs.

Marco reaches into his pack, showing me a notebook of reflections on his original euthanizing plan. Perhaps he wants me to vindicate him in some way. Nothing in his notes suggests a flaw or trapdoor. Instead, a plea regarding cryo-dreams.

What better way than to enter a state of bliss and satisfaction with a moment in one's past life revisited? Permission to dream not what others would dream for you, but only what you might wish for yourself, a private adventure taking place in infinite locations and in all the colors and verisimilitudes of real life. Heartbreaks and longings resolved, a chance to fix everything!

"Have you ever experienced cryo-sleep, Marco?"

"No. Some of my lab assistants have."

"Do you think dreamers get the chance to fix 'everything?'"

"Of course not, but the drugs provide quite a trip at the end."

Logoharp pipes up instead of my natural voice; at the moment, I'm a little shaky. Hsu Yang focuses on the monitor showing an empty courtroom.

"As I understand your reasoning, Hsu Yang, our citizens will slowly, unconsciously come to accept that cryosleep and torpor need not be experienced as the agonizing, rude or forgone conclusion of life, but as a climax—a state of hypnagogic bliss induced by virus and cold. Why, all these moments of rejuvenation without pain begin to seem plausible and even attractive—do I have you right?"

"You do."

"Perhaps," I say, knowing the Directorate is recording every word we exchange, "you were prescient in inventing the recycling system. But you must help us now to fix the flaw so that no one wakes up."

He exhales, gazing into space. "Can I have a cigarette? Naomi, I told you before, I don't know what's wrong. The recycling system was intended to be irreversible."

"I see. Dreams and no pain." He flinches as I approach him, touching his arm, leading him to a make-up chair.

"Actor Zhang Yunfa is a favorite of mine," I begin.

"He's a chameleon, all right. A little unpredictable."

Marco glances at me. This is where I must work magic to make him look younger but also theatrically devious—at least for the few minutes he appears on camera.

"You seem uncomfortable, Hsu Yang. Remember, too much scrutiny of your body double could produce a backlash."

The voice is soft, almost conciliatory. It's mine, again. I've shut down the *harp* temporarily. I don't even recognize myself talking to him, wondering when he might acknowledge my identity.

Now his eyes return to me.

"Pull up a chair, Naomi," he says, finally.

I locate a black barstool opposite him next to the mirror. But it's not comfortable. I feel like a schoolteacher monitoring a boy for detention.

"I don't need a stool," I say, hovering in a lotus position above Hsu Yang.

"No. Sit here, next to me."

He moves over, reaches for a bowl of walnuts, but doesn't crack them. It's the first time he's willingly spoken my name.

"It took me a while to remember your name," he says.

I smile, remembering how much I used to love his teasing. "You need to get dressed and made up. Quickly."

"I'm fine as is." He turns and bats his lashes. A child's face, with acne scars, turned sheepish and wrinkled. "You'll make me look better, won't you?"

"A little polish and pancake will fix you beyond immediate recognition."

"I'm going blind. The doctors are treating the glaucoma but everything is out of focus."

"Even with contact lenses?"

"Yes."

There's a commercial break. He sighs and moves to the actor's swivel chair facing the mirror. I tie a bib around his chest. His chest and shoulders still seem as taut and tendril-light as I remember them.

Intercom announcement: "Comrade Tian, be ready for camera at break five."

As though with a movement all its own, the eyebrow pencil darkens and accentuates his eyes, one with a double fold, one single. As I apply the matte and daubs of rouge—I try to avoid the pasties—he begins to look like an opera star. I use my latex digits to stretch his skin.

"That's good, very good," he says.

"A little rouge. We don't want you to look like a waxed doll."

He evaluates.

"Too Caucasian," he says, pursing his lips. I mix in a bit of brown, a bit of lavender into the foundation to tone, then fill in the creases, followed by ivory around the eyes to soften the bags.

"You look like a clown, *xiaochou*...小丑," I tell him.

He isn't satisfied. Grabbing a lipstick, as though he's about to make an abstract, he smears color all over, his hands trembling. I notice the hairline scar on his upper lip.

"What are you doing?" My hands clasp his shoulder, feeling his tremor rooted to muscle and bone. Marco watches me in the mirror straight on. Watching his pursed lips, those dark almond-brown eyes imploring my sympathy, as though he needs it—he doesn't—I realize we've become strangers.

He swallows, settles back in his chair, then turns toward me, leaving our reflections behind.

"I didn't mean to humiliate you back there in the tunnels, I mean, with Miranda. When she looks up to me, I can't lose face."

"Oh, that. Everyone here worries about 'face.'"

I remind him about Miranda. "You'll be lucky if she ever looks up to you again, much less at you."

"What do you mean?"

"You know what I mean."

I smear cold cream all over his face and neck. His skin still feels supple to me, smooth and flawless.

"Give me the lipstick; I'll redo it," he commands.

"No, your hand shakes."

"What's going to happen to her?"

"I don't know. She's in a coma."

"You can help her, can't you? Get her out of that trauma unit? Find a better doctor?"

"She has to wake up first. We underestimated the matrons in the torture chamber—I mean, their capacity for cruelty. You got off easy compared to her."

"I didn't know! I had no idea!"

"Stop shouting at me. You know their techniques. A head in the vice? Frozen droplet torture! Tiger benches? Why did you let her come? Why did we—"

He slides his jawbone side to side, gritting his teeth.

"She's pregnant, Marco."

Silence. He pulls his cheeks, as though they'll come off.

"Did you hear me?"

"Yeah, I did. Is it mine?"

"No idea, but you're a real shit," I whisper, too loudly, in his ear. "Faced with a decision to stand up for your woman and your friends, you pull the joker card? Unless you lead the authorities to a trapdoor, or whatever it is, you'll end up in a frozen fort in *Mo He* at minus 40C°, January average.

"What if I say nothing?"

"You'll never see her again."

I'm filling out his lips with a liner, then a dab, then a scarlet, dried blood color across his cheeks.

"I need to go to her."

"You're in custody."

"What about you?"

"Stay still."

"Can't you go to her?"

"I'm not authorized, at least right now."

"Naomi, what's happened to you?"

"Nothing."

He contemplates. "I mean...your feelings? Hybrid borgs like you? Did you eventually marry?"

"I'm not authorized—"

"Was it worth it? I mean, to give up a personal life? Hey I've had a helluva good time here, met a few beautiful girls and married three times. My last wife wanted to kill off a foreign money handler who was threatening our son."

"Get up." Swiveling the chair out from under him.

Hsu Yang's tremor grows visible.

"At least now you look like a *Jing*. Red warrior. Stand tall, please. Act like you have a spine."

He genuflects, which surprises me. I return a likeness of prayer, only it's my hand waving over him, a cascade of beta waves to induce calm. I brace his shoulders, pulling them back.

"Stand tall, Hsu Yang!"

"I've got to speak to you again," he whispers, clutching my sleeve. "You've got to help Miranda."

"I can't anymore—"

"Comrade Tian Jinghui, two minutes!" the page shouts. Marco's spine snaps to attention. "When your name is called, walk behind me to the podium and remain standing."

Placing what looks like a badminton net around his head (actually a yoke, with fiber-optic netting emanating neon green light), the page tugs him forward. A military officer marches behind.

"Be brave, Hsu Yang!"

He blinks, swallows. My visor comes down, official frequencies restored. I watch him shuffling toward the lights.

31

JANUARY 2121

SUPREME PEOPLE'S COURT

最
高
法
院

Hsu Yang appears briefly.

"He looks like a clown," Dean Cheung Yuen tsk-tsks, her nicotine-stained fingers clasping a joint. She's joining me in the holo-studio and I'm supposed to be glad for her support.

I feed a news bulletin into the chyron as we await the start of Mr. Tian's trial. A robo-voice whispers:

We've learned that Comrade Tian Jinghui will be remanded to Fifth District Superior Court to face

Cheung chews gum to calm her nerves. Her yellow un-brushed teeth show the evidence of dried mooncakes, orange snails, nicotine and *baotzu* or whatever else she's eaten recent-ly. Tempted to send her a message, I do subliminally: *Clean up those stains on your teeth and hands in case you're called to testify. Otherwise, you'll look disgusting in TV close ups.*

Her ears twitch, picking up my vibes. "I don't think I'm on camera as a witness, am I?" Her voice rises like a confused teen; her little hands grope at her face and she fingers goop off her mouth.

"Seems you're not on the docket today. But you will be. Soon."

"Tian's guilt is given," she says, placing her hands softly on my tunic sleeve, as though to make nice again. "Tian's body double, Actor Zhang, will confess."

But he doesn't. Something happens.

The real Marco Hsu Yang, aka Tian Jinghui faces the tungsten lights in his Accused Box, stoic and in the part of him no one else sees or hears, hysterical. The judge reads the 22 charges out loud before the camera; most are infractions listed in *The Laws of Ice.* The camera flashes on Tian's scowling face as a "reaction." My make-up works well despite Cheung's comments; he looks operatic, but glossy, decades younger.

As scheduled, replacement Actor Zhang appears for the remainder of the televised trial.

"To allow elders to wake prematurely because of timing flaws is just as bad as designing the weak ceiling trusses of Bird's Nest Stadium!" the prosecutor Li Chin exclaims. "Without system repair, Harmonious Recycling is just like Bird's Nest. Both will surely collapse with the slightest shift in the Earth's magnetic field!"

Zhang leaps out of his seat. "Pot calling kettle black! Nothing wrong with Bird's Nest!" Defense Counsel Gang Qian pushes Zhang back into his seat, mounting an objection.

"Prosecution is proclaiming Architect Tian's guilt by specious analogy to Bird's Nest! Our stadium has lasted more than a hundred years and is indomitable symbol of China's modern power!"

"Sustained." The judge, surprisingly youthful, combs back wisps of purple hair.

"Why is Zhang deviating from the script?" Cheung whispers.

"He's an actor, after all."

Zhang reiterates the Harmonious Recycling control systems were implemented with Singing Directorate's careful review and approval.

"I never willfully designed a trapdoor, though the system's artificial-intelligence module may have created one," Zhang admits. "The AI component might be making executive decisions based on cryogenic inputs or aberrations in elders' physical responses. Alternatively," Zhang explains, "the system is resetting itself because something external is disrupting it."

"What?" Prosecutor Chin asks.

"No idea. An external force, something electro-magnetic. Terrorists, maybe.

"Who?"

"No idea. Uyghurs? Taiwanese? *Falun Gong*?"

Chin sighs. The jury, mostly faceless borgs sitting in the dark and entirely silent up until now, breaks into chatter.

Defense attorney Gang rises slowly. He presents an expert witness. It's Jens, the Aryan doctor sporting wavy hair and European bones, so obviously hailing from a different gene pool.

Dr. Remker. My love. Not expecting this.

Jens is standing ready, his arms folded around a sheaf of documents. I'm guessing he found his way to the trial without telling me. He ambles forward. Dressed in a worsted black and gray tunic emblazoned with a yellow star on his arm against a red triangle, the fashion of guest physicians. The courtroom erupts in buzz, even without my signal.

"Jens Remker, an esteemed biophysicist and physician, has taken the trouble to appear here to testify on Harmonious Recycling."

Cheung frowns. "Naomi, what's this about?"

I ignore her, beaming at him, though I doubt he can see me since I'm stationed with the camera crew in the courtroom galley above. Still, I step aside, craning my neck above the cameras, my skin turning a deep gold, burnished and proud of my friend.

"I've examined the DNA records of the last batch of elders put into cryo-torpor," he explains to Gang and the judge.

"How many?"

"Approximately 1,000 in this batch."

"And?"

"There is one autosomal dominant abnormality among approximately 3.1 percent of the elders in cryo-sleep, at least in this cohort, but I've not been able to meet anyone who has actually woken."

"What is this abnormality?"

"The sleepwalking gene," Jens said. "The gene produces ADA, adenosine deaminase, the most likely candidate associated with slow-wave sleep when sleepwalking occurs."

"Sleepwalking?"

"Possibly. But depending on which research study you cite, there may be as many as 202 areas of the genome linked to insomnia, and 956 genes implicated in any number of sleep disorders, with strong correlations to coronary artery disease, depression, anxiety, schizophrenia, Type 2 diabetes and restless leg syndrome. Which means the possible causations of waking during cryo-torpor are complicated; no single gene may be responsible for those who escape."

"How would you go about determining the exact cause of wakening?"

Jens contemplated first, a pregnant silence. "I suppose if you could catch a few of the wakers; test them for these associated gene abnormalities. Find a pattern, in other words, if there is one. At very least, harvest all the DNA records of thousands and compare them against the ones who escape."

"Are these DNA records available?"

"I believe Directorate Public Health officials keeps them locked up. As you know, Mother Country maintains genetic profiles of every in-country inhabitant and billions of citizens in other countries."

"But the identities of wakers haven't been released. Are they sleepwalking?"

"At least they're getting out of the pods, walking away, suggesting wakeful cognition. A few have been shot—"

"Is someone planning their escape, Doctor Remker?"

"That I don't know."

Prosecutor Li Chin steps up to Remker, bending over the witness stand to study his face. A pause, an air of doubt, then:

"Do you believe that Mr. Tian's Harmonious Recycling system is at fault? Have the timing devices for cryo-sleep been tampered with?"

"Your experts would have to look closely at the controls in the system. There are so many factors that muddy and confuse—"

"You mean you're confused?"

"Well, the situation is confusing, isn't it? If you don't have elderly wakers to study, and the State doesn't allow access to their genetic profiles, much less a deep analysis of the alleged system flaw as it's failing, how can you make a judgment?" Jens looked squarely at the prosecutor, then the judge, who manages a smirk, then up a moment at the gallery, as though he's speaking directly to me.

Prosecutor Li Chin shakes his head. "You're saying you don't have a clue?"

"I'm saying you're on thin ice inferring someone's guilt when you lack evidence to prove it."

More chatter. The judge raps her gavel. The Prosecution cites the numbers of elders reported missing from their pods: 780. Within 25 minutes, the jury returns from conference and renders a guilty verdict. Hsu Yang disappears and Zhang returns to my dressing room. We make small talk. He applies cold cream to remove his make-up, and I compliment him on his theatrical performance.

32

JANUARY 2121

BENEATH THE SEARCHLIGHTS

探
照
灯
下

This night at Kuai Ma hotel in Beijing. We're a few blocks from the courtroom. Jens and I stay in a cramped third-floor studio next to a fire escape. The bathroom has badly seamed marble tile, but plenty of hot water and plush towels, so I don't care.

Jens manages everything, even bringing hot-spiced noodles and green tea for our meal. We stretch out to sleep. With my natural left hand, I knead the sore muscles of his shoulders and back, so sore from cramping during the long lunar flight back to Earth. He holds me, touches my breasts, throat, the caves below, removing all armor. Then unfurling like flags with the scent of each other, we move slowly, trying not to spoil anything. Cushioning me, palm beneath my head, Jens massages every part of my body until nothing feels compressed, nothing hurts. I do the same, but feel only the anticipation of pleasure, not climax. Whatever climax he experiences, if at all, is muted. In the dead of night I spy searchlights outside our window crisscrossing the empty warehouse and fire escapes above us and across the street. Jens is out cold. I cradle him, kiss his forehead. I don't sleep at all.

"I didn't help," Jens reaches out, touching my sleeve.

"You cast doubt on the State's case. At least that's fodder for an appeal."

I recollect that just after the trial was done I had dropped my cloak in an equipment closet. He found me and hugged me tightly, pushing me against a wall, impaling me against a camera. Jens kissed my lips and cheeks again, my neck, my suprasternal notch. I tried to break away; I had to restrain him.

"It's Miranda," I whispered, hissing. "You have to go to her. She's in lockdown; no one gets in, but maybe you can find a way. Please, we have to figure out what to do."

"Doubt she can be moved."

"Are you tired?"

"A little," he said. "Stay with me a little longer. I'll find a place for us."

For a moment I touched my forehead to his, my natural hand resting on his chest, then his throat, feeling his Adam's Apple and the striations of his windpipe as he spoke so af-firmingly to me, so alien from this courtroom mumbo jumbo. We felt the cold stiff air of Beijing and the clouds that drop to fog in the streets, a gray-violet color, depressing all feeling. Where, Jens, is this place for us?

*

It's 5 a.m. now. I have to leave in a few hours after the edited video version of the trial is approved and released.

I tell myself, or at least the *Logoharp* speaks for me, that my lover exists only in hidden spaces, interregnums, no extended period of time. The tracks of our lives run in parallel. I'm altered, biomechanically armored, a State-sanctioned propa-gandist. He seems to think I'm human and worth pursuing, perhaps because I trade in unknowns, projections, so much so that I contemplate the possibility that he's a spy intent on extracting my secrets. But no. "Naomi," he whispers to me, lying next to me in our cot. "You must become someone or something true to your mission."

"What's that?" I don't know what he means.

"Seeking—?" He stumbles. "Perhaps making sure fairness happens for as many as possible, not what you're told to do."

I think he means escape. Perhaps reversing my role, shutting down my *Logoharp* channels permanently. Find the unspoiled left-over places, perhaps the Kalahari Desert in Botswana, its rust-red dunes dotted with black camel thorn trees guiding my vision. Or lunar South Pole-Aitken, where he'll remain.

"Listen to conversations around you," Jens whispers. "Discover life without censorship. Fight for your own life and protect others. But be clever. Don't get caught."

"You sound like my mother."

"Your mother must have loved you."

He reaches out to me. Jens talks like a poet, blissfully naïve, imagining the lights of the sun and moon shimmering on shared virgin forests, celebrating communities of primitives singing arias of praise to Nature, then diving off cliffs into fresh lagoons. But he can't remain with me. There is no permissible relationship between hybrids and human species.

When he's dozing again, I cover his chilled body with a quilt. Memorizing every contour, the sound of his breathing, the ease with which he snuggles and keeps warm. Then I head to the shower for washing, drying off, dressing. I close the door. A quick walk to the elevator without saying goodbye.

33

FEBRUARY 2121

ANVILS OF GOD

天
罚
铁
砧

Overall, your Honor, cryo-torpor is a great achieve-ment. End of life is transformed into dream states deeply satisfying to individuals and their families. Elders sleep comfortably in plush conditions, hon-ored by their families and the State. In the new beta version, elders are free to leave a generous bequest... including the preservation of their last 10 days of dreaming—images in moving dimensions capturing

When I return to the courthouse there is no trace of Hsu Yang. I pass the Accused Box where he was held, but he leaves no breadcrumbs. I suspect the guardian drones have strapped him into a transport headed directly toward the granite peaks of Yellow Mountain, dropping him inside a re-sort-style prison. As long as he stays on the skywalks headed toward the spectacular overlook on the Sea of Clouds, he can indulge his gambling vice and/or random enjoyment of moon cakes and girls brought in daily for entertainment.

Once the helical codes disabling the putative trapdoor are found, the "Zombie Elders" incident in Harbin will be blocked from public media. Human Recycling will resume as normal. That's what Cheung and Dakota expect me to report. But I can't.

In routine procedure, a security bot will appear before me at the outer courthouse gateway to conduct an exit interview. His metallic arms will hold out a recording device allowing me to vocalize my preferences for both furloughs and decom-missioning. I'll say "Aleutia." There I might find my father or mother again, perhaps a cipher, another ghost in a cave trying to share empathy and human news. Aleutia is a better option than being stripped for parts in Mother Country, which will happen soon enough.

Cheung and Sung have returned briefly to my dressing room as I prepare to leave. Neither seems aware that their personal value to the Directorate will also come under scrutiny.

"What's going to happen now, Naomi? Are you leaving for Harbin to help us make sense of the cryogenic systems, the atomic clock?" Cheung muses.

I make some small talk, then excuse myself to the toilet. But before I do, I try to answer her question.

"My harp has evaluated all possible scenarios at this point. And as a Reverse Journalist I can tell you that Harmonious Recycling is likely to fail again. The system has been programmed in eleven helical dimensions of code, a neural fortress modeled after the zipping and unzipping of genetic spirals. With billions of nodes—mathematical functions—and edges—layers of inputs and outputs weighted as parameters, the AI component is just too complex for us to fathom. Humans may have set up the structure, but we have little insight into how the 'thinking' component actually works. The system makes its own rules. It has its own mind. Nothing in my knowledge base can stop it now, though it may be self-repairing."

"Maybe?" Cheung reprises.

"I'll check it." I excuse myself, shrugging.

In the toilet before a smoke-stained mirror, I apply pan-cake to my blue latex cheeks. Dabbing rouge in tight circles on my lips and cheeks for accent, I add lavender-tinted contact lenses and eye shadow to feign Elizabeth Taylor eyes (which I've admired closely in her photographs). Then I leave the building as almost human; it tickles my fancy to abandon Cheung and Master Sung to their nicotine stains as I atomize through double doors without passing through Security.

*

Rising with the cloud anvils, I'm free again. I can even relish a few moments flying above Beijing's 4th and 2nd Ring Roads.

Though I can go invisible to protect myself from most guardians and drones, it's no longer easy to fly. All the storms from sector warming have produced wind shear so powerful that my vertical takeoff and landing instruments can easily be smashed to pieces. More crashes on the news each day, more frozen pitots and static ports measuring air flow velocity leading to erroneous readings of altitude and air speed.

I look up. Blue anvils heavenward. Thunderheads rising into space, winds bellowing. Cyclones and monsoons these days last year-round on the subcontinent, yet there are more dry days. As the rain and hail increase, they come in cloudbursts, microbursts, some of them so extreme that even I couldn't survive a direct flooding hit. This morning in lighter rainfall I take the route of least resistance, mounting my own VTOL that lifts me just high enough to move above the city's Volokopter ports yielding to clouds, and then to alleys and blue space. Flying horizontally, my engine automatically decelerates to glide speed if the rain or winds exceed limits of safety.

I adjust my GPS—a blonde-haired angel appearing in my heads-up display, indicating with an outstretched hand which direction to go.

I've routed to Miranda's Qian Shuai's unit at Beijing Trauma Hospital on Jiangtai Road. The facility is now suspended 15 stories high above the passenger tunnels below. I'm barely skimming the tops of trees, then the free space between stadiums and bodegas. Yet I'm surprised—the air channel is empty. I wonder whether the drones have cordoned off traffic and laid some kind of trap.

Silence.

Only the sound of street vendors hawking their wares.

It's a 15-minute ride and I rev down to the hospital Medivac pad in a drizzle. No one shows up. The security guards allow me through each checkpoint undisturbed. I'm not sure why. There is a guard parked outside Miranda's door, but a few rose-scented nitrous oxide inhalants laced with fentanyl will do the trick. The guard starts to giggle; I laugh back, tapping his Velcroed shoulder as though we share an in-joke. He falls to the ground.

In her bed Miranda Qian Shuai resembles Snow White, her hair unwashed and tangled across her pillow. She stirs a moment, raises her hand, as though she recognizes me, then falls back, half conscious, eyes fluttering, long lashes bending like harps to the top of her lids. Tears I see. She seems to drift between non-REM sleep and semi-awareness. "It's me," I say aloud.

"Naomi," she whispers.

I bend down closer to her ear.

"Naomi?"

I take her question as a clue—and whisper that I'm here to pick her up, get her out of here, find better treatment.

"This is all my fault."

"No, don't," she says.

One side of her face, the left, a polyglot of bluish-black and poorly sewn stitches, reminds me of a childhood monster doll. I feel her skull, a dent in her occipital bone. The other side of her facial skin is sloughing off to a lesser degree. Her left orbit is smashed, an eyelid swollen shut. Her face is yellowish-gray; I'm sure her liver is failing.

I lift her gently; my eyes glaze over. Having lost kilos during her torture and confinement, she has virtually no weight at all. She lifts invisibly as I cover her with a sheet, but I put her back into her bed; there are too many tubes. I place my fingers on her belly but feel nothing; her breathing is shallow, her heartbeat thready. Yet her facial skin seems just a shade rosier than before; she knows I'm here, clamping on oxygen from my own supplies, detaching the other tubes.

Lang Fei scratches on the glass of her door. He's a cockroach, always coming out of the woodwork. But I signal him that it's no use.

"What are you doing here?" I speak with my eyes. The harp is shut down so no one, theoretically, can trace us.

"We're going to have to make a switch," he says.

"It's too late."

Again, I hold her limp against me. All I can think of is to scold him.

"You had better leave her to me," Fei says. "I'll get her to that foreign trauma unit in Yan Qing. You always thought Western doctors are better."

"I'm sorry but she won't make it. She's too sick, and pregnant—"

"What?"

Pulling a scope from my pack, I hand it to him. He listens to two heartbeats; hers and a tiny one.

"Miranda," I whisper to her. "Lang Fei and I are going to put you into a different hyperbaric unit. My friend, Dr. Jens will examine you. It's the only way to stop the pain and swelling—"

No answer.

"Your baby. The baby should be able to grow normally while we figure something else out."

A whisper, a nod. "Love you," I tell her.

Lang Fei is ready to arrange the rest. "If Dr. Remker can see her, perhaps he can help?" Fei asks.

He reaches his arms around me.

"Naomi!"

I push him away, folding back her sheets, scanning the heartbeats one more time. Fei places a finger on her lips, turning blue, as though cooled beyond torpor. Her eyelids turn gray, a red line along the lashes. Her arm twitches.

"*Qing qing de zou,*"(轻轻地走) she whispers. "Qing" means "light." Perhaps she means go lightly in what you do.

I lean over, touching her forehead against mine, lingering for just a moment.

"Get out of here, Naomi!" Lang Fei commands. "Fix whatever is up in Harbin before they catch you!"

34

FEBRUARY 2121

INSPECTOR GUA GUA

薄瓜警督

At Beijing Railway Station, that old CCP Russian-style monstrosity, I change into peasant clothes—the drabbest navy blouse and quilted Mao jacket available for old-fashioned, *incognito* travel. Before the skytrain arrives, I find a snack shop, buy a satchel of moon cakes, oranges and popcorn, as though there's been no change in our diet over two centuries.

A ski mask pulled over my head, enabling my eyes to scan for spies and drones without being noticed. The Directorate is supposed to allow me to go to Harbin and "fix" whatever is wrong with Harmonious Recycling. But there will be "track-ers," spies, surveillance, no matter what.

I see China through blue-green eyes, sometimes transparent eyes, or violet eyes, depending on the light. Hardly anyone among hundreds of passengers waiting in long queues notices me; I'm just another full-blooded (and very tall) Northern Chinese. But now, I see the weakness in my own perception. I see the flaws in our system and in my birth country, Ameriguo, its selfishness and, weirdly, its willingness to give in.

A second-class hydrail for Manchuria shows up, a trip that will take six hours if nothing blocks our passage. I have time to sleep and read, though I have no idea how I'll locate the Beehive Fortress, having failed before. Marco Hsu Yang says his system has no physical flaw, much less a tangible entryway. Nothing is clear; my head is stuffed up. I shut down and simply settle into my seat for a nap, but I can't sleep, not really. The countryside toward Shenyang and Jilin slips by as it always has, a series of flats and rail-slip tracks stacked up above ground like plastic legos without trees. The apartment buildings seem to contract with every degree drop in temperature. All have security gates, front yard ice rinks for the children, and statues of polar bears, now extinct, some of them stuffed in open-air museums.

My ear buds are ringing. Off I go to the squat toilet whose hole rumbles open on the tracks, a perfect excuse for discarding evidence. There I remove the neoprene pinna surrounding what remains of my right ear; I turn up the volume to hear a whiny voice trying to sound like a man, someone squawking in old-style clown Mandarin, a language from Peking Opera I barely recollect.

"Senior Inspector Gua of Harbin White Tigers here. Where is Miranda Qian Shuai?" (恐怕 她 已经死掉了)

"Identify with your ID, please."

I hear a siren and loud, boozy voices in the background, a few arguments and slapping around.

"Inspector Gua...Harbin White Tigers," the voice stumbles a little.

"I want positive identification," I reply. "What's your agency number? Your individual ID?"

I have a recollection of a pre-teen boy, an acne-pitted boy who once looked just like Gua Gua. He sat next to me in a Laurentian University lecture hall where the guest lecturer tried to explain why China's population would shrink rapidly in the late twenty-first and twenty-second centuries, a prediction that seems outdated since China is still loaded with souls. The boy's father, who looked like Marco, sat in the upper gallery—not with us—playing with his smart phone. We didn't speak; I only caught a glimpse of him from a distance.

This Gua Gua is among yet another generation of prince-lings and princesses who grew up without siblings. Three generations of only children are treated as a rare and prized species. Having one child only became a matter of law, then convenience, even when the restrictions loosened up. Young women in business favored a single child, especially those excelling in real estate, maritime law and social media censorship.

Gua Gua fell into the lucky top 1 percent. He was the son of an elite, Marco Hsu Yang's only son, a *hua qiao* (华侨), mixed blood overseas Chinese with dual passports, although I have no idea which wife or girlfriend was his mother. Gua dropped his father's surname, repackaging himself as a "Gua Gua" meaning "Thin Gourd" (薄瓜瓜), a reference to his lack of academic interests. Like the first Gua Gua, Beaux Xilai's son by Attorney Goo, Hsu Yang's son briefly enrolled at Oxford but was "sent down" as they say there—meaning he flunked out—and lived a playboy's life style in the UK. Once he bought back expensive jerky *biltong* from a Namibia hunting trip, a present for his father, but Hsu Yang was displeased when Gua insisted on steaming the meat rather than eating it raw.

"I know where you are, Naomi," the teenage kazoo voice whines. "You arrive on the hydrail to the West Harbin station at 20:07 hours tonight. We'll meet you and take you to your hotel."

He declines to give me his I.D, but I access it in the voice-print archives.

"Inspector Gua Gua? Yes, of course. Thin Melon! Your voiceprint matches my records."

"You'll arrive in seventeen minutes. Tomorrow you'll be interrogated in Volga Manor, which is not too far from the Japanese Unit 731. We have a warrant."

Actually, I muse, the idea is to avoid Volga Manor entirely, a nerve center for Harbin White Tiger apparatchiks like Gua Gua who feast on conspiracy theories. Unit 731 contains plague kept in petri dishes in unclean laboratories where bats fly to nearby hog markets. Besides, Volga Manor is by now a broken remnant of Russian Harbin, where B-list Kazakhstani entertainers dance and sing in frayed costumes to pay tribute to Chairman Mao, Lenin and all the half-forgotten heroes of Revolution.

"Gua, how about an alternate plan? Let's meet tonight at the Noodle Delight shop on Zhongshan Street," I lilt seductively. "It's open all night, has delicious steamy aromatic noodles. Much more conducive to conversation."

"Can't."

"Gua, listen," I tell him in English, in my human voice. "I can't screw around. I'm here for one thing, and I can't help you, your agency, Miranda Qian Shuai or anyone else if you waste my time."

He grunts, hearing but not able to dismiss his programming. He probably knows I want to discover what I can before
escaping 250 kilometers north to Khabarovsk, crossing the
Black Dragon Amur on cargo vessel. But the sky train is slow,
starting up, halting again; it seems as though it's slowing
and lurching for miles. Decelerating without a complete stop
makes me hesitant, dizzy.

"Stay where you are!"

Gua shrieks into my headset. Manchurian guards are comb-
ing the aisles, frisking passengers and checking passports. I've
disappeared into the toilet with my satchel and bags, filling the
hold with vile fecal-smelling inhalants that penetrate outward
to the passenger car, keeping the guards away.

Nobody bangs on the door. I pry a back utility closet open;
there's a window and escape latch. Finally, the train grinds to
a halt as though it has no brakes; I slip through the window,
moisture sublimating like dry ice in frosty air. At -35 degrees
C, the temp isn't as cold as, say, Verkhoyansk or Mo He (-68.7
C), where a truck's axle grease stiffens each night into solid
blocks. But here the temperature is cold enough to punch the
air out of me. I leap, run, but resist the urge to levitate. A
stairwell ahead. Climbing flights up to the engine switching
booths, seeing red and green flashing lights; no human op-
erator; the shadows of the train pursuing me.

"Stay where you are!"

My neck snaps back; a piano wire strung across the stairs for garroting. Gua's thugs pull me off the stairs and pile on top of me.

*

As much as they might desire it, my neck won't sever because of the titanium and steel nanotiles interlaced throughout. I can neutralize them all, but I play along. The boys slam me to the ground, face down, then face up. Gua's thugs wear black ski masks and turtlenecks that remind me of the ancient bubblegum cartoons of Joe Palooka.

"Get off her!"

Nobody moves. A few seconds go by. There must be at least six of them. Gua calls out but nobody listens. Unjamming, I activate stingers in every joint, flipping three of them onto the tracks below. Three more stagger to the ledge, swatting themselves and yowling.

"Fucking hornets!"

"You should have stayed in Beijing!"

"I'm wanted here!"

One of the thugs lunges again, trying to pin my throat against a signaling kiosk. My wrist rotors activate, slicing down on his ulnar bone, rebounding to the windpipe. He falls, clutching his throat.

"Shall I choke him now?"

Gua pushes the others away, gesturing for me to move with him to another platform; more stairs and trams arriving by the minute. Dry ice steams everywhere. Both of us shuddering, lips blue and chapped cold.

"What do you know about the Beehive?"

My *Logoharp* antennae produces the data he requires. I can tell he's shaken. Perhaps not knowing what female RJ borgs can do.

"Gua, I know only that the Recycling Fortress is called 'Beehive' because it's named, weirdly, after the *tholoi* burial grounds in classical Greece. The modern Beehive is surrounded by heavily protected structures underground, but its interior is digital; Q-waves looped together."

"You know more than I do." He brushes the dirt off my cloak.

"Historically, the *tholoi* once held the tombs of King Agamemnon and his wife Clytemnestra, who ordered his murder as part of a chain of revenge. Today the modern Beehive supports a Cesium clock that calibrates, or is said to calibrate, the timing of tens of thousands of lives in torpor—their sleep, end of life dreams, confessions and life termination. Is that correct?"

He pouts.

I repeat: "Is my understanding correct?"

Gua shrugs. "Actually, the drug *Citronella* starts the process. And Clytemnestra murdered her husband because Agamemnon sacrificed their daughter for a favorable wind—just to get his ships to Troy."

"That's legend. Not an answer."

"Orestes killed Clytemnestra and her lover Aegisthus in revenge for his father's murder. You think I'm stupid, don't you?"

"No. Actually I have no idea what you know or how you were educated. I'm here to inspect the system."

He pushes me forward, up the escalator, down through heated tunnels that stink of urine from all the homeless Harbinites who sleep there at night.

A police limo waits in the pickup zone. He shoves me into a back seat, screws up his face like a child about to scream.

"Where is Miranda?" He sticks two fingers into my jammer, the shield over my windpipe. It's protected by armor, but my voice is shut down.

"What's going on with her?"

"*Logoharp* can't speak," I throat.

He jams me again.

My voice drops two octaves.

"You won't find out by jabbing my throat," I sign. "She's hospitalized and out of reach."

Gua blinks. He can't stand my direct stare, skin coloring a deep teal blue now, my armor fully deployed. Our limousine skids on black ice. There's a moment of understanding, helplessness. Lurching, Gua's Charlie Chan goon kicks me out of the car. My backpack follows, crashing into the gutter in front of the Ibis hotel.

"Tomorrow at 0700 hours!" teen kazoo chastises me.

"I won't be ready."

"Too bad!" he screams back.

Slowly I get up and stumble into the hotel. The bottoms of the revolving doors are caked in dirty ice, but nothing ever drips because the lobby is as frigid as the streets. I slap down my Directorate ID; the receptionists stare at their computers and never look up. Lugging my backpack to the elevator, then to a rental compartment, I find a shower inside a tiny plastic stall. Dropping onto the hard bed and elevating a few centimeters above it, I try to sleep for a few hours under a sheepskin cloak.

35

FEBRUARY 2121

EMERALD-EYED EGG LAYER

宝
石
雌
王

At Volga Manor two drones hover above me as I walk a snowy path through cathedrals of pine and spruce. Volga is modeled after the Yaroslav-style churches of eighteenth-century Saint Petersburg. The ski slopes surrounding it are thickly covered in snow and ice. In the shadow of another giant building that sits on top a ski slope before me—this may be a resort or mental institution—the snow appears cyan in morning shadows. There are no skiers. Instead, every single patron is flying down the hills in metallic saucers. The manor itself is separated on a distant hill. We climb to the entrance. Salon Pushkin, whose empty mirrored ballrooms celebrate the elegance of bygone costume parties, is located not far from St. Nicholas, presumably an abandoned church with its copper-colored onion dome. Another building, nicknamed "Vodka Chateau," serves *Stolichnaya* to guests at the bar.

As drones follow me, I'm surrounded by narrow culverts which remind me of Zion Refuge in early days. For a moment, I un-glove, raking my natural left hand through the needles of white pine soft as babies' skin.

Gua awaits me in the Pushkin anteroom. He's flipping through a Russian Constructivist magazine circa WWII, one depicting KV-8S flame throwers superimposed on the cheek of a heroic soldier.

"You're a history buff?" I ask.

"Don't have much time for reading. You want some tea?" He holds up his mug in a friendly manner.

"You're calm this morning," I oblige, assuming he's toked a joint or two. A cherry-haired female assistant enters the room, revving a holo-projector. Particles in a cloud chamber surround us. Buzzing like bees, flying past each other in the cloud, the particles make corkscrew swirls.

"Gua, why are you showing me this?"

"The 'Harmonious Recycling' architecture you seek is impregnable," he says.

"But my *Logoharp* senses these drones—your leptons—are hapless, undirected, searching for a central controller, a Queen, in other words."

"A Queen bee," he rejoins. "Emerald-eyed."

"There doesn't seem to be one."

He reflects.

"The whole thing seems abstract to me. We've been trained to believe the entire Beehive is protected with nuclear-strong force. Its relative strength to gravity is a hundred times more powerful than electromagnetism. Nothing gets in there."

"But where's your Queen?"

"No idea."

"Wherever 'she' is, the Fortress seems to have the power to modify cryogenic timing, to reset, especially if it detects a threat."

I ask him if 'She' (or something else?) directly regulates the thermostats, dreams, timing—beginnings and ends—of all the sleeping ones? Is the system control distributed across multiple nodes? How does the Recycling clock reset itself when it detects an error?

Gua stares at me, shaking his head.

"You have emerald-colored eyes, don't you, Naomi?"

"My irises are clear. I once had blue eyes with a few flecks of green. These days I wear contact lenses to look more human."

"Your eyes look emerald to me," he clucks. "You the Queen? But all this other stuff you're asking, I can't say. May I call you by your first name?"

"Of course!" His sweetness feels odd, bewitching to me, especially now.

"Gua, do you know the Beehive location exactly?"

"Yes, *dang ran shih* (当然是). We can visit the outer gateway. Otherwise, I can outfit you with a VTOL and skis."

"No need. I can get there on my own."

The thick-leaved black oolong tea steams in our cups, and I clasp my hands around the warming celadon. "The tea is delicious."

"Yes."

"Have you studied *The Laws of Ice* lately? Considering its framework, vast amounts of human talent and experience go down the toilet."

Gua brightens. "True, but there isn't enough room for everyone now, even the brilliant ones."

"Perhaps a different colony somewhere else? Maybe dispatch Elders to our lunar colonies? Or Mars?"

"The Directorate is exploring all possibilities. Besides, I heard you took a furlough at Aitken Crater. What were you doing up there?"

"Visiting. Exploring crevasses and lava domes."

"What else?"

"Experiencing love and sex. Briefly."

"What?"

"You heard me."

"How was that? Your face—"

I relay that my lover is a biophysicist investigating the composition of impact craters. In the recent past he's monitored the rate of cell death—*apoptosis*—in humans subjected to cosmic radiation with only minimal shielding. But cyborgs appear to hold up better on the moon because they need less shielding from radiation. In my case, though, human cell death is accelerated thanks to a compromised immune system. As a result, preparation for end-of-life suspension or decommissioning appears justified.

"That's straight out of *The Laws of Ice*," he says.

"There's something odd, though," I rejoin. "Cryo-torpor without a timer to end life actually can *prolong* survival by reducing metabolic rate. In some cases, we've seen cell death begin to reverse, especially among argonauts in cryo during the nine-month trip to Mars."

"Meaning?"

"Individuals grow *younger* as they suspend in sleep. Ten days in some females can turn back the clock two years. After 30 days—"

We imagine this.

Gua replies. "The system is designed so that no elder in Harbin is kept in torpor more than ten days, of course. But is metabolic reversal a contributing flaw in the system? Is that the reason some people just wake up?"

"I doubt it. There must be a triggering event."

"What's the trigger? Something's missing—"

He puts the mug on his desk and lights a cigar.

"See here?" Walking to the projection table. The assistant flashes a slide showing giant trawling bulldozers lifting cryopods out of the marshes.

"In some cases, the containment pods aren't harvested for three weeks or longer. Some drift into the marshes downriver, in which case the bodies may revert to a state months or years younger. A few apparently wake up, though we don't have the numbers."

Gua covers himself by lecturing me.

"Naomi, we're well into the Sixth Extinction. There's no room for anyone on Earth getting *younger*. I'm betting that ten days of cryopods skidding on the ice will be shortened to ten minutes once the Confucian farts die out."

"Still, you haven't explained the triggering event, if there really is one. Come closer to me, Gua."

He reaches to my temples so we can share thoughts. My gloved digits clasp around his. Our thoughts meld for a few moments, as though two heads will create discovery that neither can accomplish alone. One example: Anyone in decent health suspended long enough in torpor, much like the Deep-Space Argonauts approaching light speed, won't age at all. Theoretically at least, time and physical deterioration slow down. Cognitive and language faculties renew in a matter of weeks, along with bone density, skin collagen, heart, muscle tone. Argonauts grow years younger in cryo-sleep; their renewed youth shows in their faces when they return to Earth. And what of elders? Without the timing device terminating their lives within 10 days as specified, the system may be achieving exactly the opposite result.

"Perhaps this *is* the trapdoor, or at least a portal? The system is creating renewed life, at least for a few?"

"Yes, I think so." He breaks away. A jamming signal. "Shit!" He howls, massaging his temples.

"We're being monitored. Every wall has a microphone and camera."

"So." I drop my hands. "Get back to business."

He nods. But my eyes go transparent, my visor lifts, and I ask him in my human voice, not really understanding why he seems to like me. Perhaps because we share some grief about his father. "Do the authorities trust you?" I lift my hands toward his cheeks, not touching, but feeling his contours, studying him. Instinctively he pushes my hands away again since he's embarrassed by the acne scars.

"Gua, why didn't your parents take care of you?"

Instinctively he touches the uneven scars, even rubbing the tiny black hairs rising out of the pits of his cheekbones.

"Too busy, I guess. Most of the time my frog-faced aunty raised me in Beijing. Every kid gets acne in Beijing from the sewer air."

I pull his hands down again, studying him. No pustules, only bird tracks and moon pits.

"You can still be treated."

"Who cares? Where's my father?"

"In Anhui, I guess. I don't know, exactly."

"Where is Miranda?"

"Not sure."

"You're lying."

"She's in coma—in and out of coma. We're trying to get her transferred to a hyberbaric chamber."

"Naomi, you love her, don't you?" His words spill out.

"Was she your lover?" he asks.

"No. Not in a literal sense. We're not permitted."

"Hsu Yang loves her, too," Gua replies, bitterly. "He takes everything of mine."

"Yours? She's not yours. She was never yours."

"You're a hybrid. Are you even capable of normal love?"

"Sorry? What's normal? There doesn't seem to be such a thing in this world. Do you miss your father?"

"No!"

"Now you're lying."

"Okay," he shrugs. "If you must know I'd like to put a bullet in his head!"

"Miranda—"

"What about her?"

"She went to headquarters for the inquest. The matrons—she's pregnant—"

"No!"

"Gua, she wants me to solve this puzzle. She wants me to disobey my embedded instructions, but how can I? I'm confused. But I can fly now, my wings—"

"You've got jets and rotors, Naomi, not wings."

"It's a metaphorical way of speaking."

"Is the baby mine?"

"I have no way of knowing without the tests."

"Can't you retrieve her? Can't we do something?"

"No, not now."

He turns away a moment, shoulders sagging. He blinks several times, raises his hand to wipe his eyes. I offer him my sleeve.

"Gua, if you want everything to return to normal, then help me. We have to enter the quantum fields in the Beehive."

"No one can enter the core."

"There must be a code."

"No!"

"If the system clock or the control unit times out, it's not unbreakable."

"You don't need my help."

"Oh I do, Gua. My signal processing is breaking down every day. I feel it. I'm no longer capable of auto-navs in the manner of dead reckoning, like wasps and bees. There are times I confuse my dreams with reality. It's difficult to detect higher order frequencies—"

"You don't need my help, Naomi."

"But I do!"

He smirks.

"I won't help you!" he repeats loudly for the microphones.

Gua says no more. Easing open a door to a back alley, he nods, grabbing his leather jacket as I follow him.

36

FEBRUARY 2121

COLONY COLLAPSE

蜂
群
没
落

We're flying low over the Songhua and coming fast on discovery. Disturbing me, reminding me of my mission, *Logoharp* competes with my human thoughts.

Which do I obey? What should I do? How can I save the system? How do I find this flaw? Should I just let it go?

We're skimming the river in his rickety troika, surveying the landscape for possible entryways, tunnels and drop elevators going deep underground. Gua isn't really on my side. I'm not sure whose side he's on. He wants me to restore everything to new normal, loudly pronouncing for the airborne detectors that I must restore the Beehive's central control unit so that cryo-sleepers won't wake.

This awakening—what is it, really? Just an implacable desire to regain sentience among a few metabolic miscreants? I've already reviewed the theory of aberrant DNA base pairs without pinpointing a single pattern; yet those who wake appear to be revitalized. I suspect the Directorate never anticipated the pods' rejuvenating qualities.

The trapdoor, too, is just a theory about an undetected escape route. Perhaps there is an interdimensional bubble in Beehive space, where ordinary laws of physics don't apply, or maybe a tiny black hole in the fabric of space-time, allowing just a few to fall into it, wake into it. But that's speculation at this point.

I've told Gua that any upset or momentary stopping of the atomic clock could lead to Beehive collapse and the end of Harmonious Recycling. All the elders could wake up. For the record, the natural collapse of beehives became common in the early twenty-first century as our climate grew foul. Beekeepers would wake in the middle of the night to find their thriving hives abandoned by workers and drones. The term, "Colony Collapse Disorder" was invented to explain this, but today, government officials adopt the term "colony collapse" to describe the undoing of top-secret, securitized electronic systems.

"Naomi?" A voice crackles in my ear piece. I can barely hear with the VTOL noise. Gathering clouds and sleet obscure visibility. It's Jens. His voice cuts in and out, as though under deepening ice. "Naomi, I'm here with Lang Fei."

His tone is stiff and formal.

"What? Speak louder, Jens."

"I—I'm sorry. Miranda has—"

"What? I can't hear you!"

"Miranda. She's gone. Brain hemorrhage, no activity. We tried everything, including surgery, CPR. It happened just as I was arriving."

A whiteout. Sleet like daggers. The engine sputters.

Gua turns to me, his facing tightening. An empty river—

The troika strains, thuds.

"We're being forced down, a storm, Jens. The wind—"

"Naomi, are you there?"

"What did you say? Did I hear you correctly?"

Jens' signal cuts in and out.

"What?" I catch my breath. Silence.

"Was there any pain?"

"No, I'm sure of that."

"The baby?"

"So far, okay. Miranda is on full somatic support to try to save the baby. We have to keep her systems functioning at least 90 days. If the baby is viable then and can survive outside her body—"

Gua hears this. Abruptly he turns away from me, covers his eyes.

"Don't do that!" I shout at him. "You're the pilot, damnit!"

I switch to text. "Jens. An inspector is with me. We're flying low over the Songhua. There's a storm."

"I have to go back, Naomi. Tonight. There's a launch in Hainan at 3 a.m.; I have to take it. The crew's waiting for me back in Aitken. There's a strike."

"I have something to tell you—"

"What?"

I can't form the words. He can't really hear me anyway.

"What exactly is this mission you're on?"

I switch on my harp, detecting his thoughts, the lingering question.

"You know what I'm doing, Jens. What I'm trying to do—"

"Ok, whatever it is."

"I'm sorry. I'm grateful you came here to help. Where will Miranda—"

"She'll stay in this unit."

"I can't come back this moment."

"Secondary purpose, Naomi—"

"Jens?"

"Just finish your mission, whatever it is."

"All right."

"I won't be available for a few weeks at least. The unions up here. A mess."

"Jens, did you hear what I wanted to say?"

"I can't hear you!"

"I—love you." Whispered. "Goodbye, safe journey!"

A pause. He signs off.

I wave, though no one is there. Gua's tears congeal on his cheeks. He's wiping his eyes with my sleeve. I'm shouting, "Where are your goggles?" The sky is spinning wildly like a top.

As a child I punched my chest in grief to see if my heart would die. It didn't, obviously, though the pounding left bruises on my chest. I pumped tiny fingers up and down in goodbyes when my father left for work, weeks or more at a time. I didn't know how to wave in the conventional adult way. Yet now, with my real hand, I pump my fingers as I did as a five-year-old.

Gua idles power, pushes his yoke forward, applies opposite rudder. "Is your hand numb?" Gua asks.

"Not at all."

I grasp his hand. He pushes me off.

*

A cavity under the Earth leads to the Harmonious Recycling nerve core. Cavities, at least, are obvious to me due to their conspicuous absence along the Songhua banks. Gua has recovered somewhat; we're flying toward Sun Island Park. The core must be subterranean. There's nothing on the surface remotely detectable.

Equus Bots appear and fly beside us, dutiful escorts. The bots resemble mechanical sea horses, propelled in mid-air, providing aerial stasis in case the troika falters. Our engines strain now, allowing us to fly just a few meters above the river. But I'm sure the engine is icing; even with carburetor heat, it's like a wrench thrown into a crankshaft. At any moment we'll crash.

Ahead is a bank of gigantic convex mirrors, at least three stories high, forming a perimeter around the Songbei Rocket Launch. I'm not sure if the mirrors are actually transmitters or protection for the gamma ray containment stations. Gua tells me that Siberian tigers are released periodically in the area to clear curious crowds away.

My sensors *feel* an opening. Gua puts the troika down on a riverfront landing site about a kilometer west of the Rocket Launch. The *Logoharp* in the mist clears an image of Xanadu, that old-fashioned Atlantic City penny arcade replete with posters of circus clowns, tigers and acrobats. Partially collapsed, the roof has a copper onion dome sinking toward the arcade center. I'm guessing this place no longer entertains anyone, part of the Directorate's crackdown on summer dances and children's merry-go-rounds.

We run for shelter.

Gua pries open flimsy two-by-fours nailed to some plywood across the arcade's back entryway. He leads me down a white basement ramp; an elevator door squeals open, but it's odd. There are benches inside the elevator bolted to the floor. He straps a seatbelt on me, then on himself. Button pressed, descending rapidly.

My stomach flip-flops, a sensation of floating upward, weightless, then sideways. We're being pulled underground laterally at faster and faster speeds. My harp shuts down. Oxygen masks pop out from the ceiling. Gua puts his hand on my shoulder. (Strange, in his official position he detests me, I think, so why would he try to reassure me?) The G-force is so strong in acceleration that our jaws slacken.

Then the elevator or tram or whatever it is assumes constant velocity. We're traveling through tunnels at hypersonic speed, but there's no feeling of acceleration.

"Don't worry, you can't get lost down here even if your GPS won't work!" Gua's teeth chatter; he snorts the words in his most guttural Beijing accent. "These passages have already been mapped. I've struggled to keep up with the spelunkers and engineers."

"We're being pulled extreme west."

He replies slowly: "True."

He looks away, goes silent, as though all words are stolen now.

"So where?"

"My team calls it K2 of the underworld. No one knows where the caves begin or end, much less the exact location of the atomic clock."

I feel a sputter inside my heart, as though it's skipping beats, then stopping, then starting again, perhaps in synch with the clock. Swift passage through the tunnels makes me feel exceptional, alive, exhilarated. How can an elevator be accelerating laterally westward at four times the speed of sound?

Gua offers me a memory chip. Images flash before me: the cerulean Boysuntov sky above the slate-stained Uzbek peaks. A voice reads aloud: "Harbin's Unit 731 is a false door, a security cover only for the westward corridor. In fact, one of the Beehive Fortresses is mounted permanently inside *Heixing* (Black Star), Uzbekistan's most remote cavern located nine-hundred meters beneath the Boysuntov mountain range."

"Why Boysuntov?" I ask him. Gua reminds me, his voice sputtering with exuberance, that China's close relationship with Uzbekistan, a Silk Road epicenter, has been active since ancient times.

"So China claims Black Star as its own?"

"A deal with the Uzbeks, I'm sure. Leasing the caverns from Tashkent for a decent price and security guarantees. Natural gas and chemicals. Uzbeks sell a lot of that to Mother Country. The Central Asia-China Pipeline connects Turkmenistan's gas supply in the West through Uzbekistan to our grid in the western regions of Xinjiang and Tibet. The cliffs here are virtually impregnable!"

"But we're here."

"Nobody else knows," he claims.

*

Quickly decelerating, the elevator lurches, grinding to a halt. Gua tells me only the most daring explorers have been able to scale the outer caves 2500 meters above sea level, but now the Uzbek guards keep everyone out.

"So why put the timing devices here?"

"It's redundancy, most likely the State has multiple timers throughout Asia. But these caves are ideal: impregnable, hard to get to, resistant to phishing, encrusted in crudely magnetized rock. Think of it as Mother Country's precious lodestone. The Directorate has chosen a cavern so deep that no explorer has made it to the end. When we get to the Outer Rim, you'll be standing on top of cliffs dropping forty-five-hundred meters to the valley below."

"Really?"

The *Logoharp's* antennae rotate, trying to stabilize my sudden vertigo. "Don't get too close to the edge," Gua warns me.

He leads me along a narrow passage. We enter the cavity of Half Moon Hall—it's the size of a Moscow train station—one of the largest antechambers abutting a smaller passageway. Shaking in the cold, Gua pulls two parkas and heat packs from a survival kit embedded in the flowstone.

"Stay warm in this. The mild hypothermia is just enough to assure the best conditions for cryo-suspension."

Now he leads me up a stairwell carved in the rock, at least a hundred steps straight up. Inside, the cave's ice formations are robin's egg blue, then deep aquamarine and green celadon stippled with tiny cracks, just like Chinese pottery. Some adjoining tunnels are too narrow for a child to crawl through. I hear the rush of a bellows, or is it jet engine? Perhaps it's a shaft inhaling and exhaling air to equalize the barometric pressures outside.

"Where are we exactly?"

"Izhevskaya. The entryway."

"I thought the fortress was impregnable."

"It is. We're in the outer shell."

As we proceed the cavern grows darker, dustier. I have no markers here, no navigation, just foreboding. The *Logoharp* forecasts nothing.

Several meters below the rock shelf in Half Moon Hall, my eyes adjust. A coterie of male figures sitting in a rocking-chair circle half a story below us. It's bizarre. Each figure resembles a life-size wax doll floating in a sinuous bubble of rainbow-colored gel.

"Boysuntov is the rebirthing place of Mother Country's future!" Gua exclaims, reminding me of his teenage zealotry. "The Beehive is actually a quantum computer archiving the codons of all our leaders living and dead—plus, of course, tens of thousands of elders in their pods. The central computer performs calculations and factoring at incredible speeds, enablIng RJs like you to extrude the future much more accurately than you can now using classical means.

"Ah! This is the Beehive! A quantum tomb! There was a physicist named Ely who told me about it. The fortress contains the pure energy of living things, he said. And some dead ones, too. But you can't really see behind these walls of fire until you join the dead yourself."

Gua asks me to elaborate. I don't.

So he picks up a remote and clicks; a monitor emerges from a meter-long slit carved into the rock shelf. A Chinese announcer explains the workings of the tumulus timing devices:

> *The accuracy of our CPU depends on the Cesium 133*
> *atomic clock, which measures the hyperfine tran-*
> *sition frequencies of electrons driving an electronic*

I query the archives, but the data on Beehive's internal operations are locked. Apparently, the system keeps track of the timing, down to the nanosecond, of every individual's entry and exit from Earth.

"The clock keeps all our systems running—our records, DNA imprints, the mapping of viruses, the activities of the masses, births and deaths. Our purpose is sustainability, preserving an orderly future, to keep track of everyone eligible for life and its transitions," she intones.

"I thought this was my job," I reply, eyeing the rocking chairs.

Gua understands my ability to script the future is somewhat limited—limited mostly by the questions my mind can no longer escape.

"The figures you see are reproductions, clones. We've preserved their DNA, the writings, the memory of our most esteemed leaders, from Chairman Mao and Deng to Great Great

Grandfather Xi. When the timing is right, we can resurrect them, or at very least, extract the secrets of their leadership in genetic maps."

"Why repeat the mistakes of the past? Most of these men were responsible for the displacement, deaths and misery of millions," I interject. "The Life Clock, in other words. Where are the women?"

"No woman leader has yet been tapped for this group," Gua replies. "Madame Jiang Qing, the notorious leader of The Gang of Four, for example, is excluded. Lesser officials outside this group get their ten days' cryo-dream like everyone else. They wake long enough to see the drones descend on them. Everyone makes a confession wordlessly inside their pods. As their stories complete, so do their lives."

"You approve?"

"I have no opinion."

Turning abruptly, I leap down, heading toward the extruded pods—dozens of them—sitting atop individual stalagmites positioned in a semicircle behind the rocking chairs. I touch a few of the coffins with my natural hand. Apparently, these pods contain minor officials still in torpor.

But in the rocking-chair center Chairman Mao's avatar is clear enough, his big drooping jaw slack, his mole fleshy.

"I'm sure you'll agree with Comrade Deng that Chairman Mao was right 70 percent of the time,'" Gua Gua announces, conscious of the surveillance equipment surrounding us. "He had to make sacrifices for the good of our people. But back then we had no way to capture every citizen's heroic story—say, the peasant shouldering sacks of grain to satisfy rent collectors, the daughters sold as concubines. But here, we have a flawless recording of recent history. Billions of stories recorded in digital archives. It's as though human lives continue in this cavern, but no physical evidence remains. A special compaction vehicle recycles all the carbon of these bodies," Gua continues.

"Clean and sustainable."

"Absolutely."

Gua watches me closely. I remove my visor. I have a human urge, suddenly, to tear out my harp so that my voice is entirely my own. The ticking atomic clock—wherever it is—really irritates me. My heart beats to its ticking, the armature coils rotating, winding, the dials flipping, counting nanoseconds. Above us, the jet engine noise—perhaps the security network, the air shafts or the strong force drones grow persistently louder, rising to a high-pitched squeal, as though an engine is trying to rise, but can't achieve lift.

My sensors dart around, natural eyes wider than I've ever known them to be. I'm struck by the oddness of it, the undulating waves of silence, then noise, as though workers of the Beehive are straining to find the missing Queen.

Can I stop it? Can I stop all of this?

An irresistible urge to break things—atoms, pieces of glass, cryo-coffins, Miranda's suffering—these feelings grow intolerable. I can only surmise out of my own failure to see the truth; no can write a script of the future, not accurately, not even with a universal harp, so why bother? Why not opt for uncertainty?

"Gua, where is the atomic clock? Where exactly?"

Lights flickering, then flicker out. We're in absolute darkness.

"You caaaaan't ack-cess the clock," Gua drones in sing song, flicking on a flashlight. "I told you, no one gets near it."

There's groaning, then silence.

"Listen."

"I hear nothing," he says.

"Exactly. I believe the clock just reset itself. I'm sure of it. Apparently, the mechanism resets itself when an external force disrupts it."

"*You* of the emerald eyes, Naomi?"

"Not me! Something else—"

37

FEBRUARY 2121

LOST SECONDS

光
阴
失
措

"Your hands—" I look down. Gua points to my synthetic hand and the real one, both growing red, molten as though superheated. I feel the flames, cracks in my skin, but nothing hurts. The same cracks you'd see in the cavern's limestone, growing visibly larger. I watch with curiosity, as though my hands and arms don't belong to me.

Surely a human body can abandon the heart when thoughts are completely unaligned. I know it. I've lied to myself too many times, even to Hsu Yang, Miranda and the Directorate. The fact is I'm guilty, at least partially guilty of disrupting the Life Clock and causing all the trouble Marco is in. For years I've wanted to break the clock, the one speeding its second hand toward duty calls, obedience, life-numbing routine. The hand that robs us of choice.

The *Logoharp* detects quantum blips in the Life Clock. It also directs me to listen carefully to the heartbeats of others, how they speed up, falter, regain strength, especially those who wish to live out their lives more fully than I will ever do.

Remember physics: Qubits replicating inside our supercomputers demonstrate "entangled" properties. These interactions are a fact; what happens to the spin state of one qubit somehow (and no one knows how) alters the spin state in a partner or "correlating" qubit no matter how distant that partner bit happens to be. In "superposition," a quantum state can be seen as a linear combination of other distinct spin states, like overlapping waves in a pond that form a more complex wavelet pattern.

I've used this knowledge secretly. In fact, I've exploited it in addition to whatever Marco designed to trip up the mechanisms of life timing.

To be clear, the *Logoharp* explicitly instructs me to follow Directorate orders. But now I can respond in full duplex to my precious instrument of wisdom, reversing the flow of command. This time—indeed, many times—the *Logoharp* listens and converses with *me.* But how?

Able to execute my commands, even without conscious volition on my part, the harp increases the speed and scaling of quantum calculations. When I detect dissonance, unfairness, a protest among those wanting to live just a bit longer, for example, quantum entanglement increases and qubits scale exponentially, causing power surges and blackouts. The electronics of the *tholoi*, even the Cesium clock, may shut down for nanoseconds and even longer.

Entanglement, in other words, causes unchecked birthing of qubits in opposite spin states, disrupting the Beehive timing device; in other words, it causes the atomic clock to skip beats. I *feel* the skipping in my heartbeat, but also in the heartbeats of cryo-sleepers. Those few whose hearts defy fate suddenly open their eyes and wake up when the Cesium clock briefly shuts down.

I should have been the one on trial. Whatever Hsu Yang did, whatever Miranda paid for, it was my *Logoharp* obeying my deepest wishes to betray—and save—these sleepers.

*

In the cavern, the harp makes an announcement, her voice deadpan. "The Cesium clock is resetting." I hear a child's cry. The cave floor begins to shift; we hear rumbling, then the walls around us vibrate, begin to shake back and forth.

"What's that? What's happening?" Gua cranes his neck, seeing nothing, voice rising in hysteria. He heads toward me, tripping over the rocks that begin to break off and slide down the cavern walls. The clones in their rocking chairs shift just a bit, side to side, up and down, a rolling sine wave beneath their seats.

"Quake!" Gua shouts. The cavern floor lifts and drops, knocking him off his feet. I lift into the air, wings fully deployed (or are they rotors?) dangling in the ether and darting this way and that as my eyes search for an opening.

The child's screams grow louder.

Now a vacuum sucks out the cavern air. There's an aperture, a small tunnel in the ceiling above me. I follow it, nitro switches in my ankles ignite. Both hands on fire. Without a conscious thought, my wrist rotors detach, corkscrewing three meters through solid rock until they reach a surface. I follow, spitting dust.

Above me, a wall of electronics and glass tubing in cabinets attaches to a knurled rock face. A clock, but no discernable sound. Just flipping electronic readouts. My rotors reattach and retract inside my arms. Hands in flames, my fingers turn to blades, cutting into the bank of super-cooled tubes, coils and armatures. *Logoharp* commands it. My ears capture the *thrum* of the Cesium lattice inside a containment chamber of glass. Viscous, frosty, packed inside a vacuum tube at 2 degrees Kelvin, the timer is just beyond my reach.

"Break it!" I pull back a moment, uncertain, unwilling to take responsibility.

"Break it!" I hear a child's cry again. The readouts, the hum of the lattice grows louder as I reach up, my hands like blow torches.

An alarm sounds. *Warning. Do not disrupt the clock. Do not—*

It's too late.

The outer glass and the armature cabinet inside it break apart. I have no more control; my entire body is igniting in flames—molten titanium, carbon, flesh—all in flames, yet no heat or discomfort. The vacuum tube feels frigid to the touch; my rotors reattach. I hold the tube like the treasure of a curious child.

"Break it!" The voice—my voice—shouts. The urge is too strong. I rip out the Cesium atomic oven, the magnets, then the resonators. The polyflex glass of the tube explodes into pieces.

Am I still alive? My ticker stops, decouples, resets.

Lang Fei appears before me, but I'm sure it's a holo-projection.

"Fei, you're not really here, are you? Who is this child? Why so upset?"

Before me a boy, not more than five or six, weeps and coughs, sucking breath between spasms of upset. He clutches Lang Fei's twisted thigh.

"Fei? Is this your son?"

"No time to explain, Naomi. Get out of here!"

Gua is shouting at me from Half Moon Hall. The cave groans. More rumbling, the ceiling—my floor—starts to collapse. The clones in their rocking chairs fall face down.

"We've just lost the clock. Gua, come with me!" I grab and hoist him up. He dangles in my arms, pure dead weight, as we fly toward the elevators.

"Did you start this?" he shouts at me. "What kind of robot are you?"

"I'm not!" No more to say. "But at least your jelly boys down there won't survive."

38

MARCH 2121

SYNAPTIC ARMIES INVADE

突
触
进
攻

Mother Country's Seismic Monitoring Administration recorded the quake at 9.1 on the Richter scale. Fortunately, there were few casualties thanks to *Logoharp's* forecast of a geomagnetic pole reversal before the quake actually occurred. Evacuations in Tashkent, Samarkand and Urumqi led by Red Army soldiers saved tens of thousands of lives. Gua and I didn't have time to watch Black Star implode.

I'm sure the loss of the Cesium clock and all its data were deep losses for the Directorate. In those split seconds, roping Gua like a screaming toddler in my arms, I had no time to reflect. We escaped just as Black Star and the outskirts of Tashkent and Samarkand swayed wildly and turned to rubble.

My RJ colleagues made no reference in text or broadcast media to the loss of 22 seconds of Coordinated Universal Time (CUT) when the atomics failed. Scientists claimed that the Earth had experienced "magnetic reversal" or "geomagnetic excursion"—that is, the magnetic poles reversing South to North, North to South, disabling all clocks worldwide. No media outlet reported the true nature of the Beehive or its contents. I saw to that.

Yet secretly I rejoiced, losing all objectivity. Seeing those jelly-clones falling on their faces gave me hideous satisfaction. No one in the Party had given us access to any information about them. For me, the earthquake, expected or not, was just icing on the cake.

But now my time grows short. I still can't understand the sounds of the wailing child. Or Lang Fei's appearance with him. Perhaps the Directorate was sending Synaptic Armies to distract me from what I needed to do. Perhaps it's my wish that Lang Fei should be united with his son in real life, to finally act like a father.

I'm sure that the Singing Directorates in both China and Ameriguo will repair their Beehive CPU units. For the time being, both countries have suspended the lottery until alternate systems come online.

In Harbin, the Songhua River grows slushy. Eye witnesses have reported scores of elder sleepers suddenly rising from their cryopods and walking away, their steps halting and measured. Children and grandchildren help the elders steady themselves on the ice. Their families continue heading to True North, the unknown.

*

Unfortunately for me (though I expected it), I'm in custody for interrogation.

As expected, I've documented the lost seconds and my errant behavior, though I'd never tell interrogators Cheung or Chairman Sung the whole story.

What I do recall is that as I reached the Cesium clock above Half Moon Hall, those "impenetrable" strong-force particles suddenly dispersed. I don't fully understand why. The distraction of seeing Lang Fei and his wailing son impeded my concentration; otherwise I could have torpedoed the entire CPU and possibly ruined Harmonious Recycling for an extended period of time.

In those lost 22 seconds Miranda came to me. At least I envisioned her. She seemed to be suspended vertically in a golden sepulcher high above the Cesium chamber. Her half face—the good half—tilted obliquely toward me, as though trying to avoid other spectators.

Miranda? My mind called to her; she responded, inviting me to share her memories. The intact half of her face looked younger than I recalled, her lips parted slightly, that goofy malocclusion of unfixed ivory teeth.

"Are you dead or dreaming?" I asked pleadingly, embarrassed by my uncertainty. I reached for her hand; she took mine. She was all done up with peacock combs and feathers in her hair, wearing an elegant, blood red and gold *Hanfu*, like a Beijing opera singer.

What did she dream?

Sleigh bells. I hear them. Children are singing and shouting "Three Tigers Running Fast." A high-stepping black and white pony pulls a troika filled with children. The troika goes fast on the frozen Songhua, heading toward a forest of gnarly Siberian crabapple and hawthorn. Winter swimmers mount the diving board. A quick dive and they make it to the pool coping, hopping out as orderlies wrap towels around them. No one notices that the kids and the troika are pulling away fast.

The merry driver disappears. Now the pony gallops by itself, moving the troika faster and faster down an icy river track heading west. The swimmers begin shouting after the children, running in their bathing suits and bare feet trying to catch up to the troika, but it's too late. Miranda flies above the ice in a tank suit and black cape, tumbles like a weed from one tree to the next, but she can't quite reach the children in time.

"What does this mean?" I ask her.

She can't tell me because she's mute. And I can only intuit her thoughts about children she will never have, though I hope her one baby will be saved.

Then Chairman Mao's wife, Jiang Qing, shows up with a crown of bloody skulls hanging crookedly on her head. "Naomi," she instructs me, "this young woman all done up as Beijing Opera star is frivolous! Forget her!" Jiang Qing shouts at me. She is standing beside me, gesturing with a diamond-studded Rolex watch hanging loosely from her wrist.

"I doubt she has any awareness of history, or why any criticism of our Party and its leaders must be considered suspect," Jiang Qing says. "Miranda never had a proper Communist education. It's obvious no one corrected her foolish ideals. Certainly not you."

Jiang Qing continues to berate me. I still can't determine whether she's part of Miranda's forbidden dream, or mine.

"It's your mistake," Jiang Qing says, "to have unleashed all these passive crowds from their deserved sleep, their dreams of redemption. Thousands, then tens of thousands of them. You've woken the outliers, the ones perpetually dissatisfied, who dream of waking up."

"You wanted people to wake up," I reply.

For a moment her lips curl.

"I *did* want the masses to wake up," she said. "They needed to follow the correct line."

"Which line is that?"

Jiang Qing replies, "The line that leads to the future! To progress! Your birth country disintegrated because of greed and partisan bickering. No one could agree, much less compromise on a 'correct line.' The masses supported leaders who did nothing for them. The media guided this ignorance, leading peasants to the wrong conclusions. Besides, Naomi, with your 'Write the Future' propaganda, you've got nothing to gloat about."

"I scripted the future," I reply, dispassionately. "Per instructions. But I'm glad some sleepers are awake."

39

APRIL 2121

SWEPT AWAY

浪
潮
吞
噬

’ve been garroted. Nearly. Under Directorate orders, the goons are dragging me out of my Translator's pod with piano wire around my neck.

Inside a surgical theatre, my higher order circuits for mobility and machine learning are being cut, my rotors deactivated. I can't feel my cheeks as I try to mouth words. However, preemptively, I've issued a set of encrypted instructions that will decode and transmit across the public network after my decommissioning is complete.

No longer can I atomize or deconstruct. Except for the hoped-for survival of her baby, Miranda's dreams of love and glory remain unrealized; they have no particular meaning for the future as far as I can see. Yet I'm glad, at least in her dreams, that she pursued the children speeding away in that troika.

Inside a control room at Directorate Headquarters, I watch a bank of video monitors in dim light. Several technicians work at displays exhibiting aggregate data from heartbeats, frigid temperatures, blood pressure readings dropped to sub-normal, and urinary functions of the lesser political leaders in cryo-torpor. All may be primed for reawakening, if that's the plan. Most likely, they're being monitored from a redundant Beehive fortress in an even more remote location.

Jens is reported to be missing. This news pains me the most. The Directorate Science Team claims he came untethered and fell thousands of feet during a spelunking episode in the iron-rich lunar Aitken crevasse. The technicians cited evidence of his disappearance, showing me a grainy video of an anonymous spacewalker, about Jens's height and weight, bouncing up and down merrily on the foothills of the Leibnitz Mountains, part of the moon's southern tier. But the astronaut's face isn't shown. His sun visor is down so I can't identify him. The video also depicts a team of two assistants lowering an astronaut into one of Aitken's deepest crevasses, just like the ones we explored together. They call out to him and feed cable from a winch as he descends.

"A little more. Keep feeding the line!" It's Jens's voice, but I hardly believe it. I don't believe anything they say.

"The shaft is slippery and crusted with ice," the voice continues. An image of white and gray-gloved spacesuit hands hammering into the rock. "There's a tunnel about a hundred meters below. I'll go lower." The film clip continues briefly, showing feeds from his headlamp, heavy breathing and more rock as he descends down a narrowing shaft of ice. I hear shouting, screaming. The video goes blank. "Where are you, Dr. Remker? Do you copy? Are you injured? Where are you? Oh my God—"

There won't be time for me to investigate his disappearance. It's a trick—or a murder. I trust, somehow, perhaps beyond the firewall, we'll meet again.

The orderlies have asked me to watch another video replay of my trip to Black Star. They claim the tape is what actually happened; not what I recall. I have no direct memory of this, but the tape shows Lang Fei entering Half Moon Hall and making his way down the catwalk to my side. No explanation as to how he got there. (If he did, he's betrayed my whereabouts; perhaps he's been working for The Directorate all along?) We both comment on the rocking-chair circle of clones below. Gua gives his standard speech, and then: "Well! Dakota Sung and Professor Cheung!" Gua exclaims, extending his pudgy hands to welcome them both as they emerge from the Izhevskaya portal elevator.

"We have a really nice cafe down here," Sung exclaims. "Let's go have coffee. Naomi, we've had a hard time locating you. You're such a slippery creature."

Very soon the four of us are having black coffee in the cave cafe two flights below the rocking-chair circle. Dakota takes out a pack of *Chunghwa* cigarette and offers one to me. I pick one up, lighting it with my index finger, smoking without inhaling, which in this case allows the nicotine to anesthetize my throat. The military guard maintains a respectful distance. They are smoking too, sitting in a corner with their assault rifles slung on knobs nailed into the cavern walls.

"What do you want?" I say finally.

"We thought you might show up here," Cheung says.

"I'm assisting your boy here, Gua Gua, who wants to understand why the Cesium clock resets itself; hence an apparent liberation—I should say—waking up of common elders inside their frozen dream state," I reply. "Gua, I'm guessing, also wants his father Marco Hsu Yang restored to his presence so he can assuage his feelings of abandonment. And what of that Madame Tussaud's exhibit above us? Are you charging admission?"

"All part of the black-collar class," Sung replies gaily. "The emperors, idealogues, terrorists and military geniuses of the top regimes, each cloned from original tissue. Like Dolly, the sheep."

"Prepared to be reawakened," Cheung laughs.

"If necessary, when the time is right. We can't release all of them at once," Sung continues. "That would be chaos, of course! Depending on the circumstance you create, it's our assurance of a smooth succession."

"What about the Mandarin princess?" Cheung asks, dragging heavily on her Chunghwa.

"Where is she?" Gua gulps.

I don't understand their reference.

Sung shakes his head. "Miranda's carefully preserved."

"Really?" Gua bursts into tears.

"What about her baby?" I ask.

"We don't know about a baby."

"Where is she? Where is her body?"

"Naomi, she's bait, alive or cryo-preserved, to attract the errant Marco Hsu Yang," Cheung replies. "We're sure your algorithmic whiz kid will try to find her, being the true romantic that he is. Gua, we're sorry for your loss, even your father's loss. Hey, why aren't you drinking your coffee?"

"You don't know where Marco is, do you?" I ask. "He's so clever that way, slipping away from your grip no matter what you do."

"I assure you he's quite near," Cheung reminds me.

Rising from the seat I hear the beep of a cell phone. I want to answer it, but the ringing stops.

"Did you lose your signal?" Cheung teases. "I can hear it loud and clear. You're not answering me."

"Naomi, sit down!" Dakota Sung barks, grabbing my arm and pushing me back to my seat. "Make your report! Stop mulling over the past. Your relationships with Miranda and Marco are as useless as spilled soy."

"You write the *future*," Cheung continues. "The future is what we determine, what we allow you to know. And maybe a few things you don't know. Remember that. We have work to do. From all the probable scenarios you've calculated, taking the Directorate's guidance as you report it, the future (as we want it) happens."

"I've written the outcomes already," I say plainly. "All archived and ready for broadcast. The masses will doubt the announcements at first. They will resist, argue, then, tacitly, slowly come to agree, or at least acknowledge a twist of fate. Then the denouement."

"Go ahead," Sung says.

"First, the Taiwan election will be overturned and the rebel political party defeated when officials discover that hackers and terrorists, most likely *Fa Lun Gong*, are cooperating to flip the voting tallies. China will attack and retake Taiwan, as it did, *defacto*, earlier in this century. Only this time it will forcibly weed out any political opposition."

"Good," Sung appraises me.

"Second, the flaw in the Harbin Harmonious Recycling system will be corrected thanks to our team of Blue Army cyber-detectives and Reverse Journalists working cooperatively to keep the masses informed. As a consequence, the outlying sleepers who wake from their cryopods inexplicably will be rounded up. Security will pick them off as they try to escape with their families to true North, possibly to the forest settlements inhabited by other escapees."

"Which ones?"

"Reportedly, a family living hundreds of kilometers north of Songhua, though they're impossible to find; they may not be real. But we should circulate the story that if they are real, they may be giving sanctuary to the wakers and should be apprehended."

"Go on!"

"Marco Hsu Yang will be executed and anyone who cooperates with him. Under torture, he'll reveal the secret trapdoor that lets some elders with aberrant DNA escape. Then there's the threat of insurgents launching germ warfare!"

"How? How are the three related?"

I revert to my *Logoharp*, but no sound comes out.

In plain human voice I say this: "There are those who would use anything to disrupt our Mother Country's peace." I recite this, sipping a little coffee with sugar to regain strength. "Besides, the connection between corrupt and inept is very strong. You've trained your people to exploit any gap in knowledge among the masses, leveraging their ignorance through media, whipping up distortions and fear to mask the incompetence and corruption of officials all around you, including those monitoring the Harmonious Recycling nodes.

"I suggest you apprehend the hackers working in Taiwan to see if they can explain—or at least shoulder the blame—for time outs on the Cesium clock. Consider that the wakers are being assisted by the insurgents who are holed up in the Ping Fang district in Harbin where the Japanese once raised rats and fleas infected with plague—"

"That's brilliant," Cheung says.

"I assume," continuing in my own voice, "you haven't caught any wakers yet."

"We haven't, Cheung says. "But we shall."

"In any event, you know what to do," I tell them both.

The video transmission suddenly stops, goes blank with static. I'm reasonably sure I had this conversation with Cheung and Sung in a cave, though it may not have been *this* cave. All scenarios can be restaged on the holo-platform. But I do know my last wish is surely to lead them astray.

*

The Directorate has suspended me in a nitrous oxide pod. Unlike the chosen elders, I won't be able to have my 10 days of dreaming, nor can I return, even briefly, to my memories of Jens, Miranda or Marco Hsu Yang or any lost cause in my life's journey, as so many other dreamers have.

I envy them. Instead, I see the icy flatness of the Songhua River in my tiny window display, and all the children pushing the ice sleighs of their grandparents. The river is thawing; it's April 15; the cryofans have been turned off, and soon the pods will float down the river on the icy floes, leaving the children behind.

But I'm sure that my predictions about Harbin and Taiwan won't work out exactly as the Directorate hopes. The messages I've left on the network for public consumption are exactly the opposite of what I predicted so confidently to Sung and Cheung. It's within my purview to alter messages to set future events in a different direction, and given the encryption algorithms at my disposal and the speed with which messages are decoded in social media outlets once released, I anticipate they will be read and heard even as the Blue Army hackers race to delete them. As follows:

1. The independent opposition will win the Taiwan election despite the Directorate's claim of voting machine fraud perpetrated by hackers. Independents will garner more than 60 percent of the vote. Millions of Taiwanese will rally to support the Green Party victory. Further, election monitors will demonstrate that no amount of tampering could have changed the result. China's Directorate will abandon war plans, at least for now, attempting to negotiate a favorable treaty in the near term.

2. A flaw in a timing device controlling Heilongjiang's Beehive Fortress was secretly housed in an Uzbekistan cavern known as Black Star. When the atomic clock skipped a second, then disintegrated, it caused hundreds, then thousands of elder sleepers to wake inexplicably. They'll escape in groups, then in phalanxes, so many that Directorate soldiers will be forced to stand aside, unable to pick them off without causing mass tele-

vised carnage and a huge embarrassment to the Directorate before the cameras.

3. Marco Hsu Yang, the notorious architect of the Harmonious Recycling system, has eluded authorities by escaping from an Anhui prison. He has left coded messages on the network that he will no longer cooperate with the Directorate because the recycling system is irrevocably flawed.

4. Escaped elders who hold secrets to the universe actually exist. But they're invisible, and won't make an appearance until Harmonious Recycling systems are terminated. At this point, all sleepers will awake, and some, the most stubborn and determined, will have a chance to live out their lives.

In my cryopod, the nitrous oxide is having its effect. Given in modest doses, the gas is only a mild depressant, just enough to make me a bit giddy, incautious and willing to let go a bit. But I'm starving for breath. The surgeon generals have placed a cathode shunt in my brain to deliver a higher steady concentration of isoflurane, an end-tidal concentration of 1.9 (SD.2%), without sufficient oxygen. Hypoxia makes it difficult to concentrate. My EEG burst suppressions have decreased from 53.5 to 34 percent because of the nitrous overload. My brain state is characterized by high voltage electric activity, followed by null activity or flatlining, as though I am being anesthetized into coma.

Coma. Where is Jens? I don't believe he's dead; I can still feel him repelling down that shaft, calling out to me, reassuring me. He's touching my cheeks and natural hand again, tucking my blowsy hair into a surgical cap, asking me if I really want this change.

"Yes." In the end my *Logoharp* reverts to deeper instincts, the future-speak of love.

My confession begins and ends. None of it makes sense. I try to follow the script using my own voice. But all I can see before me are Hsu Yang and Miranda Qian Shuai walking hand in hand along the riverbanks, walking gingerly, without fear, in the muddy streams of ice melt from the Songhua. She's carrying a baby girl in a papoose. He kisses her hand; there's a breeze and the ice is melting. The Directorate has decided to film me live, removing my shackles so I can stand with a microphone on top of a diving board suspended over the swimming pool carved into the icy river. I'm describing for the masses the spring cleanup operations that accompany annual recycling as the children let go of their cryo-sleighs, pushing them off with great energy. A few cry salty tears; their parents crowd behind them and wave handkerchiefs.

"There are no wakers today," I manage for the camera. "Everyone is peacefully asleep, in torpor, and the annual cleanup operations are proceeding as they should."

Marco and Miranda approach me. As they come near, their faces begin to block out all other things in my field of vision. They climb up to the diving board; I can see his pockmarks and her crooked smile close up. She's leading him because his eyes are shut; he's blind. I can see her long jet black hair; his jagged cheeks and cords of gray hair. They both stand beside me, each to one side, their hands extended, clutching my bony shoulders as I try to remain upright.

"Naomi," Marco whispers, as he once did when I was young. "You're the missing flaw, my trapdoor, the hand that breaks the clock."

He laughs.

"Is that a good thing? Why are the wakers still alive?" I ask expectantly, like a child waiting to hear a fairy story at bedtime. For now, though, a warming wind blows, and I sense that many will continue to live on.

"You don't trust clocks, remember?" Miranda teases. "The wakers are like you, not ready to die. Too mouthy, too *lihai!* Some unfinished business, I guess."

Gua runs up to the diving board from behind. He has a Glock Gen17 pistol in his hands. He aims to fire it at his father's throat, for all the times he felt gagged as a child. But he can't pull the trigger; he can't get the bullet out. When the Glock unjams and he fires, the bullet misses Hsu Yang and hits Miranda, but it barely grazes her throat.

At least that's what I see now, feeling such a burst of happiness, of feeling loved once more. I know the nitrous oxide is working; I'm giddy. I've stopped breathing, but my *Logoharp* lives and speaks for me.

Though I've been packaged and dragged back to Harbin, I'm traveling again. I feel the lateral elevator scooping me up and hurtling me at hypersonic speeds through the ocean tunnels, my cheeks fluttering and puffing out in the acceleration.

Tunnels again. I can live happily in tunnels. I love subterranean life.

// THE END //

ACKNOWLEDGEMENTS

I started *The Logoharp* as a handwritten outline in spring 2012, having just returned to my home after a year teaching journalism, film and technical writing at the International College Beijing. A subsequent stint at the University of Hong Kong teaching journalism while covering mass citizen-democracy protests gave me a clearer picture of the future journalists will face. From these beginnings *The Logoharp* sprang. The book took umpteen rewrites that morphed a fact-filled story into a science fiction novel with a mix of historical and imaginary characters based on personal experiences in Asia, Europe and Africa.

Special thanks to my readers—editor Mary Green; visual artist Alan Soffer; Jing Guo, an extraordinary scholar; Jenny Lu, expert translator; Neil Dietsch, my husband; astronomer Steven Lord and Kelly Falconer of the Asia Literary Agency. My former teachers—Charles Johnson, winner of the National Book Award, and Gene Roberts, Pulitzer Prize winner and former Executive Editor of *The Philadelphia Inquirer*—offered needed encouragement. Jonathan Oliver, a UK-based science fiction editor, provided important critique and questions regarding apparent gaps in the narrative. Expert proofreaders Richard Boudreaux, Candice Hughes and Dr. John Howell Brown offered invaluable corrections. In addition, my editors at *Smithsonian Air & Space* magazine—Linda Shiner, Tony Reichardt and Chris Klimek—gave me an extraordinary opportunity to explore the dimensions of aerospace and moon flight. Most importantly, I discovered the contributions in interplanetary science that multiple countries—China included—have made.

My late mother, Nathalie Donnet, once wrote a short story about the fate of elders who were terminated before their time in glass coffins. My sister Rowena Emmett offered both inspiration and belief that this novel will one day become a movie. And for the people who believed in me and my work, and to all the readers willing to explore the world of *The Logoharp*, my deepest gratitude and best wishes.

– Arielle Emmett

ABOUT THE AUTHOR

Arielle Emmett, Ph.D., is a writer, visual journalist and traveling scholar specialising in East Asia, science writing and human interest. She has been a Contributing Editor to *Smithsonian Air & Space* magazine and a Fulbright Scholar and Specialist in Kenya (2018-2019) and Indonesia (2015). Her work has appeared in *Technological Leapfrogging and Innovation in Africa* (Edward Elgar, pub., 2023), *Mother Jones, Smithsonian.com, The Scientist, OMNI, Ms., Parents, Saturday Review, American Journalism Review, Boston Globe, Visual Communications Quarterly, Washington Times, Philadelphia Inquirer, Detroit Free Press, Caixin* (Beijing), *Los Angeles Times Book Review* and *Globe & Mail* (Canada), among others. A Mandarin and French speaker, Emmett has won first prize in magazine and journal competitions staged by the American Society of Journalists & Authors (ASJA), and the International Communications Association (ICA). She has taught at the International College Beijing, University of Hong Kong Media Studies Centre, and Strathmore University Law School (Nairobi). Her first science fiction novel, *The Logoharp*, about China and America a century from now, is part of a planned series on dystopian paths to utopian justice.